HORSEMEN'S
WAR

ALSO BY STEVE McHUGH

The Hellequin Chronicles

Crimes Against Magic

Born of Hatred

With Silent Screams

Prison of Hope

Lies Ripped Open

Promise of Wrath

Scorched Shadows

Infamous Reign

Frozen Rage

The Avalon Chronicles

A Glimmer of Hope

A Flicker of Steel

A Thunder of War

Hunted

The Rebellion Chronicles

Sorcery Reborn

Death Unleashed

HORSEMEN'S WAR

THE REBELLION CHRONICLES

STEVE McHUGH

Text copyright © 2020 by Steve McHugh
All rights reserved.

Published by 47North, Seattle

www.apub.com

Amazon, the Amazon logo, and 47North are trademarks of Amazon.com, Inc., or its affiliates.

ISBN-13: 9781542017312
ISBN-10: 1542017319

Cover design by @blacksheep-uk.com

Cover illustration by Larry Rostant

Printed in the United States of America

*After eight years and thirteen books, if you're back
for more, this is for you.*

LIST OF CHARACTERS

Nate's Story

Nate Garrett: Sorcerer and necromancer. Created to be the Horseman Death. In a relationship with Selene.

Selene: Dragon-kin. In a relationship with Nate.

Eos: Sister to Selene. Dusk walker.

Tommy Carpenter: Werewolf. Best friend of Nate Garrett. Married to Olivia. Father of Kasey.

Olivia Carpenter: Water elemental. One head of Avalon's law enforcement. Wife to Tommy. Mother to Kasey.

Kasey (Kase) Carpenter: Half-werewolf, half–ice elemental. Daughter of Tommy and Olivia.

Remy Roax: Fox-man hybrid. Likes to swear. A lot.

Sky (Mapiya): Necromancer. Adopted daughter of Hades and Persephone.

Zamek Merla: Royal prince. Norse dwarf. Alchemist. Searching for the rest of his people.

Lucifer: Sorcerer. One of the original devils. Thousands of years old. Doctor.

Osiris: Spirit in the land of the Duat. Husband to Isis.

Isis: Sorcerer. Wife to Osiris.

Sobek: Gatekeeper of a realm gate. Likes crocodiles.

Katia Lopez: Vice president of the United States.

Mordred's Story

Mordred: Sorcerer. Created to be the Horseman Conquest. Video game enthusiast. In a relationship with Hel.

Hel: Necromancer. Leader of Helheim. In a relationship with Mordred.

Athena: Sorcerer. Sister to Judgement.

Diana: Half-werebear. Dating Medusa.

Medusa: Gorgon. Dating Diana.

Judgement: Sister of Athena. Created to be the Horseman Judgement. Has social issues.

Layla's Story

Layla: Umbra. Able to manipulate metal.

Chloe Range-Taylor: Umbra. Able to absorb and discharge kinetic energy. Married to Piper.

Piper Range-Taylor: Umbra. Able to harden her skin to near-unbreakable levels. Married to Chloe.

Tego: Saber-tooth panther. Layla's companion.

Nanshe: Sorcerer. Leader of the realm of Olympus.

Jinayca Konal: Norse dwarf. Alchemist.

The Rebellion

Hades: Necromancer. One of the leaders of the resistance. Married to Persephone.

Persephone: Earth elemental. One of the leaders of the resistance. Married to Hades.

Loki: Hodgepodge of different species. Father of Hel.

Brynhildr: Valkyrie. Mother of Nate. Leader of the rebellion in Valhalla against Rela and her forces.

Orfeda: Dwarven queen.

Viv: Elemental. Lady of the Lake.

Irkalla: Necromancer.

Tarron: Shadow elf. One of the last of his kind. Searching for the rest of his people.

Avalon

Arthur: Sorcerer. Leader of Avalon. Not a nice guy.

Gawain: Sorcerer. Brother to Mordred. Partially responsible for Arthur's rise to power.

Merlin: Sorcerer. Father of Mordred. Brainwashed by Gawain to help Arthur but now doing so of his own free will.

Demeter: Earth elemental. Hates a lot more people than she likes.

Sir Lamorak: Knight of the paladins.

Lamashtu: Assassin who can shape-shift into other people.

Estaliar: Shadow elf imprisoned for murder.

Alecto: Fury. Psychopath.

Megaera: Fury. Psychopath.

Prologue

NATE GARRETT

Virginia, United States, Earth Realm
1798

The interior of the barn was covered in blood. None of it was mine.

The two dozen inhabitants had arrived here believing they were meeting with me as an envoy from Avalon. I was meant to discuss future business deals, bring them more prosperity, and they, in return, would keep Avalon's influence alive in the newly free country of America. Things had changed.

There was a gargle in one of the four empty stalls. The horses that had been kept there were long gone.

I walked over, stepping around the top half of a torso and a severed head, and found the still-living man inside the stall. The smell of blood and shit was overpowering, but I pushed it aside. I didn't plan on staying long.

His tunic was bathed in blood, and more blood covered his face. There was a deep cut along his chest, and it continued to bleed heavily.

"Why?" he asked, a look of betrayal in his eyes.

I followed his gaze to the body of his nearest companion.

"You are murderers, thieves, slavers. Scum who relish and traffic in human misery," I said, my voice completely calm. "Why should so many innocent people die while people like you continue to make wealth off their pain?"

"But we work for Avalon," he said, his face waxy. He did not have long. "*You* work for Avalon."

I nodded. "I was sent here by Merlin to ensure that Avalon's reach continued into this new world. But I decided that it was also an excellent time to remove the rotten parts of the system."

"We work for Avalon," he said again.

I didn't remember his name. It didn't really matter. He was one of hundreds I'd killed since arriving in America in 1784. All of them had deserved it. Their deaths had made the world a better place.

"I don't care," I told him.

"Merlin will find you," he said with a gasp. "He *will* punish you."

I smiled at him. "And you'll still be dead." I drove a blade of fire into his chest, ending him properly.

I stood and removed the long black coat I'd been wearing. It was covered in blood, as were my dark trousers and black boots. I tossed the coat onto the floor. There was a second one on my horse, outside the barn.

I pushed open the partially stuck wooden door and stepped outside into the cold. I ignited my fire magic, keeping myself warm as I stared at the familiar face of the man who stood fifteen feet away. He was taller than me, with long dark hair tied back with a blue bow. He was clean shaven, and his hurt expression was clear. He wore a long black coat, similar to the one I'd dropped in the barn, and like me, he carried no weapons. He didn't really need them. I'd once seen him tear a man in half with his bare hands.

2

"Tommy," I said, feeling like the word would get stuck in my throat.

"Nate," he replied, taking a step toward me. His voice was calm, almost sad.

"They *deserved* to die," I said, my tone harder now as I let my anger fuel my voice.

"Probably," Tommy said with a slight shrug. "Not for us to say."

"Why?" I shouted. "Why not for us to say? We have the power."

"Because that's not what we do," he countered immediately. "We're not here as judge, jury, and executioner to people we deem to be bad. Humanity is meant to police its own."

"Why should innocent people die and bastards like this continue to live?" I snapped, marching toward Tommy until I was only a foot away.

"Because we're *better* than them," Tommy said. "Because we can't rule humanity—especially through fear. That's not our place. They are ignorant of our existence for a reason. Their safety—and ours! Your actions are putting us *all* in danger."

"They. Are. Monsters." Each word was said louder, the last a bellow.

"You killed bad people," Tommy said, his voice never rising. "But what about all the innocents who also died because of that? We don't just blindly kill people we disagree with. We can't. We're not conquerors. They've literally just had a war here to destroy oppression. You were not sent here to decimate the population of people who *you* deem to be unworthy. Mary Jane would never want that."

I punched him in the mouth, my hand wrapped in dense air magic. Tommy flew back ten meters and collided with an old wooden shed, which imploded from the impact.

The silence that followed felt like a lifetime. I wasn't sure how to take back what I'd just done. I wasn't sure how to stop the anger and hate inside of me, how to burn away the pain that had all but consumed me.

"Did that make you feel better?" Tommy asked as he hurled a large piece of wood a hundred meters into the fields beyond.

"Don't you *ever* say her name," I snapped, feeling the warmth of the hate return to push aside the pain.

"Mary Jane was your wife," Tommy said as he strode back toward me, shrugging off his coat and dropping it onto the snowy ground. "I know her death hurt you, but it's been sixteen years. Everyone involved in her murder is dead. You killed them."

"I said, don't mention her name," I seethed.

"We found the soldier," Tommy continued. "We found him without his tongue, his eyes, his fingers, his toes, lips, and several other parts you'd removed. He didn't even look human. You think Mary Jane would approve of that? You think she would be standing beside you, telling you this is a job well done?"

I threw another punch, and Tommy caught it in midair as if he were catching a child's toy.

"Mary Jane was a *good* woman," he said, pushing my arm away. "You disgrace her memory with every life you needlessly take."

I threw another punch, this one wrapped in fire, but Tommy growled, low and mean, and struck me in the chest with the palm of his hand.

I smashed through the barn doors and crashed into one of the beams inside before dropping to the floor. I charged out, leaping over the blood, directly into Tommy, who had turned into his werewolf beast form. He caught me one handed and threw me aside into the fence that surrounded the barn. I wrapped myself in air magic as I bounced along the frozen ground into the field beyond.

Dirt and snow rained down around me as I got to my feet, ready for Tommy, who was methodically walking toward me.

"I don't want to do this," I shouted at him.

"Then stop," he said sadly.

I created a blade of fire in one hand and extinguished it. Tommy was my best friend. I wasn't going to fight him. I just needed to get away; I needed to finish what I'd started.

"Mary Jane would be *disgusted* at what you've become," he said.

Blind rage took over, and I charged Tommy, trying to drive a short blade of fire into his chest, but he punched me in the jaw with enough strength to spin me in the air but not break every bone in my face, which he certainly could have done.

"You're not doing this for Mary Jane," Tommy said as I spat blood onto the snow and took another swipe at him, cutting him across the chest.

"Stop saying her name," I screamed at him.

Tommy backhanded me across the face, and I felt my entire head ring from the impact as I hit the ground once again.

"You're meant to be my friend," I snapped at him.

"Yes," Tommy said. "And that's why I'm here. You need saving from yourself."

"Liar," I said, spitting blood onto the ground once more. "You're here to stop me from what I have to do. What *needs* doing."

"You're delusional," he said softly, even through his werewolf mouth. "You've lost yourself to pain, anger, hate, and hurt. You think that if you somehow drench yourself in enough blood, you'll either make up for your wife's death, or you'll just become numb to it all. But it'll never be enough, Nate. Not ever. You *know* this."

"You think beating me senseless will do the trick?" I shouted.

"I'd *hoped* to talk," Tommy said with a sigh.

"Why do *they* get to live, and Mary dies at the hands of some piece-of-shit English soldier while I'm not there? Why, Tommy?"

"I don't know," Tommy said softly. "I wish I did. It's not fair. It's not right. But neither is how you're dealing with it. You can't stop the hurt inside you by hurting everyone else."

I threw another punch at my best friend, but he caught my hand again, dragging me toward him, where he enveloped me in a hug, taking us both to our knees.

"No, Nate," he whispered softly. "No more."

"Why is she gone, Tommy?" I screamed to the heavens. "I miss her so much," I whispered, my voice breaking.

"I know," he said, his own voice cracking and tears running down his face. "I'm *so* sorry."

I cried then, for the first time since Mary Jane's murder. I cried for her, for me, for the horrors I'd inflicted. I cried in a snowy, blood-speckled field in Virginia as my best friend held me and brought me back from the darkness that had enveloped me. And right then and there, I knew there was nothing I wouldn't do to repay him for that kindness.

Chapter One

MORDRED

Somewhere over the Atlantic Ocean
Now

Mordred stood at the rear of the open cargo door on the heavily modified Airbus A400M Atlas. Hades had made some calls to a few friends who still had access to military equipment and found two identical planes that he'd been able to borrow.

The Atlas's twin had already made its pass and was on its way back to its base in England. Hopefully without difficulty.

"Don't tell me you're afraid," Hel said from beside Mordred, using her earpiece and mic to communicate over the sounds of the engine.

"No," Mordred said as the plane continued along above the clouds. "Just hoping this works out as planned." He touched his cheek, just under where his eye had been ripped out almost a year earlier. The eye itself had grown back, but he still couldn't see out of it, and occasionally the constant healing itched.

"We have a good team here," Hel assured him.

Mordred looked behind her at the team. Each of them had joined knowing they were going to do a military free fall, or HALO jump. Few of them had done one previously, and certainly never one that culminated in landing on a moving target. Mordred wasn't even sure it would be possible, but his air magic was going to ensure it was as smooth a landing as he could make it.

"We ready, then?" Remy the foxman asked as he pulled down the visor on his specially designed mask. He made sure the two black-bladed swords in the sheaths on his back were in place and did the same for the two custom Colt revolvers in holsters against his hips. "I'm looking forward to this."

"Me too," Diana said, loading her MP5 with hollow-point silver rounds. As a werebear, she was acting as the muscle of the group, muscle that Mordred was fully aware was going to get a workout, but not everything could be killed by brute force or magic, so everyone apart from Remy carried an MP5.

Heading up the team were Zamek the dwarf and Chloe Range-Taylor, an umbra with the power to absorb and redirect kinetic energy, both more than capable of holding their own. Although Zamek had been less than thrilled about having to wear a face mask for the jump. He held his double-bladed battle-ax in one hand, rolling his shoulders as if about to fight the clouds themselves.

"No one tell him what happens if there's lightning," Remy said in a stage whisper.

Zamek gave him a scowl and placed the blade of the ax in a sheath before attaching it to his back.

"We know what we're here for," Mordred said to his team.

"Yes, but maybe next time we could pick something to land on that isn't moving on an ocean," Zamek said. "Like *not* a passenger ship."

"I like his suggestion," Diana said.

"You all complain a lot more than you did before I was king," Mordred said as the red lights beside him flashed green.

"We'll complain more later, if we survive," Chloe said with a grin. She was the first to jump out of the plane, followed by everyone else, with Mordred last.

He wrapped himself in a shield of air as he fell through the clouds. He spotted his teammates below him and pushed the air out in front of them to ensure that they moved smoothly.

The target was thousands of feet below, a small patch in an ocean of blue. If this went wrong, they'd be hitting the water or the cruise ship fast enough to, if not kill them outright, certainly do a lot of damage. None of them were human, but that didn't mean that they were invulnerable to being killed or seriously injured.

Mordred had not made his council very happy with his announcement that he'd be joining the mission. They'd wanted him to stay back in Shadow Falls, to help organize the resistance, but as he'd pointed out, the resistance didn't need him to organize anything. His friends did need his help. Mordred was a target, and landing on this cruise ship was going to make him bait. The mission needed the enemy to be focused on him and his team.

The *Harmony of Oceans* moved ever closer. The ship was one of the largest in the world. According to the reports, it could hold more than five thousand passengers. Mordred hoped that there would be considerably fewer people aboard to deal with than five thousand.

"If we're wrong about this . . . ," Hel said over the comms.

"Then we'll grab some cocktails, sit on a sun lounger for a bit," Mordred said. "Nothing wrong with a lovely day out with friends."

He heard Remy snort through the comms.

Mordred started to hum the theme tune to *Final Fantasy IX*'s battles as he checked the reading on the altimeter. He had several thousand feet to go before he needed to pull the cord for his parachute, so he continued to watch his friends beneath him, each of their lives in his hands.

The closer they got to the gigantic ship, it seemed to Mordred, the faster they moved. Another check on the altimeter told him he was only a short distance from needing to pull his chute.

Mordred built up a massive amount of magical air around him, pouring more and more power into it, then used the magic to reach out in front of him like a huge invisible hand. He tapped the comm button on his helmet. "Now," he said.

Everyone pulled their rip cords at once, but there was not enough distance between them and the ship to ensure a safe landing. Not without Mordred's magic, anyway. He used the air that he'd pushed out in front of his team like a huge brake, slowing them all down as they descended toward the ship and touched down softly on the deck, close to a huge swimming pool.

Mordred was still a thousand feet above them when the sirens climbed out of the portholes just below where everyone had landed. They clawed their way up and over the railings, moving toward the team, who were themselves heading toward the nearest door to take them into the ship. It looked as though they were unaware of the danger of the approaching enemies, but Mordred knew that wasn't the case.

Encased in a shield of dense air, Mordred disconnected his own parachute and plummeted to the ship at high speed. He hit the swimming pool with an explosion of air and water, using his water magic to freeze the contents of the pool as it exploded up around him. Thousands of shards of ice drove into the dozen creatures who were all in front of him, waiting to move into the ship. None of them had time to escape the frozen projectiles. Most of the water dropped back harmlessly into the pool, and Mordred walked out completely dry, deactivating his magic.

The door to the ship opened, and Hel stepped out. She looked down at the bodies of the sirens. "Nice work," she said. "We could have taken them."

"Not quietly," Mordred said. "At least one of them would have made a noise or jumped overboard. Couldn't risk it. Besides, there are plenty more inside you can deal with."

"Where to first?" Zamek asked, poking one of the sirens with his foot. It had a three-foot spike of ice embedded in its eye and emerging from the back of its skull. Sirens looked human, right up until they were hunting. Then features became almost serpentlike, with long, thin gray-skinned bodies covered in hardened armor across their chests and necks. They were made for killing. Their razor-sharp claws on long bony fingers and their sharklike teeth were more than capable of tearing a human adult to shreds in seconds. "I always thought sirens were female."

"No one really knows," Diana said. "They can change their appearance at will. Lots of sailors were men, and these things like humans. To eat. Turns out when attractive women make suggestive comments to large numbers of sailors who have been at sea for months, they become easy prey."

Mordred and his team unslung their weapons and reentered the ship, moving from the bow through to the main living areas of the guests, who would normally be out and about. It was eerily quiet.

"Nothing good happened here," Diana said. "It reeks of death."

"A lot of death," Remy said.

There were chandeliers in the middle of the main foyer, as well as a stunning staircase that Mordred assumed would normally have a mirror shine but right now was, like everything else in the foyer, drenched in blood.

"This was a massacre," Hel said. "How many people were on board this ship?"

11

"Just over four thousand," Remy said. "The distress call was sent out for exactly twelve seconds, before someone cut it off and said that it was a false alarm."

"And no one came to check?" Mordred asked.

"USS *Burton*," Hel said. "A destroyer-class ship was the closest one to the emergency signal."

"What happened to the destroyer?" Mordred asked as he looked around the foyer for signs of anyone who might still be alive.

"Two hundred men died," Hel said. "Those sirens out there tore the inhabitants of the destroyer apart. It was found floating a hundred miles off the coast of Nova Scotia with all hands lost."

These creatures were not pushovers; they had murdered thousands of people in their insatiable need for blood and flesh.

"Why, though?" Remy asked. "Sirens are a pain in the arse, but so long as you're not a horny, drunk sailor, you're pretty safe. And for them to attack a cruise ship is unheard of."

"Did you read the mission briefing?" Diana asked Remy.

"I skimmed it," Remy said. "Sirens, missing ship, bad guys, possibly some kind of mobile prison. The ship has been missing for three months, the tracking removed. All attempts to get out here have been met with hostility. It's all very interesting, but nowhere does it explain why they attacked and took control of a cruise ship. Nor does it explain why they didn't just blow it up."

"There are innocent people on this ship," Diana said. "Not sure how happy the public would be to hear that a government blew up several thousand people because they were scared of sirens."

"Besides, someone is leading them," Mordred said. "We find out who and stop them, and hopefully nothing gets blown up."

"Do we know who's behind this?" Zamek asked.

Mordred shrugged. "I have no idea. That's why we're here—to find out."

"The intel said something about prisoners," Remy said. "We know how many might still be alive?"

Mordred shook his head. "Honestly, I'm not sure what to expect. This ship has docked in three separate ports in South America. Each time it docked, we have intel telling us that prisoners were brought on board. We don't know why. We just know that they were Avalon prisoners, so we can assume they're high-value targets."

"A rescue mission where we don't know who we're rescuing," Diana said. "Sounds about right."

"So we don't even know if they're still alive," Chloe said. "A lot of people have died in here already. There were a lot of passengers on this ship too. I wonder how many of them became food after the initial attack."

Diana picked up a piece of blood-drenched uniform. "Marines died here," she said. "The sirens waited until this ship was boarded before they attacked."

"So if you're in charge of this ship, I assume you'd want to stay somewhere nice," Zamek said.

"We'll try first class later and go from there," Mordred said. "Bridge first."

They slowly walked up the staircase, Mordred wishing the floor wasn't so sticky.

Diana led the group up a second flight of stairs, these thankfully clean, to the floor above, which was devoid of blood-splattered surfaces.

"Someone cleaned up," Remy said as the group stopped just outside the door of the hallway where the first-class cabins were. "I smell lemon disinfectant."

Mordred looked out of the massive windows beside him. The uninterrupted view of nothing but ocean stretched as far as he could see.

"How long do you think before the rest of the sirens go looking for us?" Chloe asked.

"I imagine they'll be with us soon enough," Mordred said. "Whoever is in charge probably knows we're here. Maybe they want to meet us themselves first."

They moved around the top floor of the foyer toward a sign that said EMPLOYEES ONLY. There was a bloody handprint on the white door, next to the card reader.

"So, key cards," Remy said. "Anyone have one of those?"

Chloe placed a hand on the card reader and used her power to burn a hole in the door, completely destroying the lock.

Chloe took a step to the side, frowning as everyone else filed through the door, leaving Mordred last. "You okay?" he asked.

Chloe nodded. "Missing Piper is all. I read the manifest for the people aboard. Most were couples just wanting a romantic getaway. Wrong place, wrong time."

"We'll make sure to get justice for them," Mordred said, walking through the door after Chloe and up the short flight of stairs. "How is Piper, anyway?"

"We've spent the last year grieving for everyone we lost in Asgard and then trying to find Arthur," Chloe said. "I'm not sure we've done either properly. Piper has been helping the search party for him, but everyone involved is exhausted and frustrated. The monster is still out there, God knows where, doing God knows what."

"More blood," Diana said from the top of the stairs, which, according to the blueprints, would lead them to a horseshoe-shaped hallway with the bridge at the front, overlooking the bow of the ship.

There were several doors along the pristine white corridor, but after Diana stopped at the first and a low growl left her throat, no one really wanted to open it.

Hel sighed and pushed open the door, revealing the mass of blood and gore from what had once been people inside.

"Holy fuck," Remy whispered.

"The sirens' storage area," Chloe said. "It's why it's so damn cold in here."

Mordred hadn't noticed the temperature, but she was right: it was at least twenty degrees colder inside the room than in the corridor. He had no idea what the room used to be for; any remnants of its old purpose were lost in a sea of horror.

"The sirens are killing these people and then just storing the bodies for when they're hungry," Zamek said. "Parts of them, anyway."

Diana closed the door as everyone left. No one wanted to check the other three rooms before the bridge, but they did anyway. They contained piles of body parts similar to the first. No one spoke until they reached the door to the bridge, which was already open.

The dozen people inside almost screamed in terror as Chloe and Zamek burst through the door, demanding everyone get down on the floor. The seven men and five women did as they were told. All wore grimy white shirts and black trousers and were clearly members of the crew.

"Captain?" Mordred asked.

A middle-aged man with a bald head raised his hand.

"Okay, everyone back on their feet," Mordred said, helping the captain up.

"Everything is fucked," Chloe said, pointing to the radio.

"The navigation is still working," Zamek said, checking various instruments and panels. "But it's not in use. The engines aren't propelling this ship. They've been switched off, except to create power for the ship itself. It's an interesting piece of technology. The ship uses partial solar energy to—"

"Later," Mordred said.

Zamek nodded solemnly. "Apologies."

"Not needed," Mordred said, looking out the window down onto the bow. "The sirens' bodies have gone."

Hel joined him. "Shit. Do we know what sirens do with their dead?"

"Eat them," Remy said. "That's my best guess, anyway."

"He's actually right," the captain said.

"I'm smarter than I look," Remy said.

"You'd have to be," Zamek said with a smile.

"I'm pretty sure this is now bullying," Remy said with mock indignation.

"What happened here?" Mordred asked the captain.

Several of the humans shared concerned glances.

"My name is Mordred," he said. "We're here to stop whatever is happening and hopefully get you all home safely. But I need to know a few things."

"They came at night," the first officer said as she helped one of her colleagues up and put him in a chair.

"Let me take a look at that," Chloe said, moving over to help with what looked like a nasty wound on his leg.

"The passengers in the ballroom were attacked," the captain said. "Hundreds of them died. The survivors were separated, the crew kept alive to maintain the ship and feed the bastard. The lifeboats have been mostly destroyed—a few tried to take one of those remaining, but they were killed the second the boat touched the ocean."

"The sirens?" Diana asked.

The captain nodded. "We didn't have a name for them."

"Who's the bastard?" Remy asked.

"The man in charge. He's in a suite in the first-class cabins. They keep us in here and the adjoining rooms. There are twenty of us in total. Two shifts a day. The sirens bring their kills to the corridor outside so we know our place."

"Any idea of how many are alive?"

The captain shook his head. "The marines boarded us and were all killed. Anyone who fought back was killed. I think a lot of the passengers and crew are still alive, belowdecks. That's what *he* told us. We've stopped three times to refuel. Venezuela, Brazil, Morocco. Each time we picked up supplies and people."

"Prisoners," Mordred said. "Any idea where they are?"

The crew shook their heads. "The chef and his team will. They're in the kitchens; all of them are still alive, so they tell us. They have to prepare food for two thousand people."

"The *bastard* likes his good food," the first officer said with barely contained anger.

"Okay, so we have a lot of crew alive," Diana said. "Sounds like a lot of passengers too. Why keep them alive, though?"

"Food," Zamek said. "I'm beginning to think there are a lot more sirens down there than we'd anticipated. Also, it sounds like the marines filled them up for some time, so there are more passengers alive. Sirens eat once a month at most."

"How do you know all of this?" Remy asked.

"I read," Zamek said. "I watch videos online."

"I bet your search history is all kinds of messed up," Remy said.

Mordred ignored the others and looked out of the huge wraparound windows. The water moved unnaturally, as if disrupted by something beneath the waves. He continued to stare for several seconds, until a siren launched from the sea toward the ship. A second later dozens more did the same.

"I think we have company," Mordred said. "Any chance we can get those doors on first class unlocked?"

"I have a key. The one leading them is in room 102," one of the people on the bridge said, fishing it out of her pocket and passing it to Chloe as the sirens reached the deck and screamed as one up toward Mordred and his team.

"I think they spotted us," Zamek said.

"All of you, get somewhere safe," Mordred said to the crew. He touched his fingertip to the comm unit in his ear. "Room 102. First class. We'll give these creatures something to think about."

"See you soon," the male voice on the other side said.

None of the crew needed to be told twice, and all of them on the bridge left through a door that took them outside onto a balcony, around to where the rest of the bridge crew had been kept.

"Good thing these assholes didn't lock the door," Remy said, drawing his swords.

"No one needs locks when there's nowhere to escape to," Diana said.

"We need to make some noise," Mordred said. He placed a hand on the window of the bridge and used his air magic to shatter it before capturing the huge amount of glass from the massive windows and flinging it at the sirens like a thousand daggers as they swarmed up the walls, scurrying like insects in their haste to get to Mordred and his team.

Mordred leaped out of the window, blasting half a dozen sirens away. Remy and Zamek leaped out behind him.

Remy landed next to Mordred and began shooting anything that moved, as Zamek unsheathed his ax and removed the heads of two sirens before they could get close enough to be a problem. Diana landed in her werebear beast form, larger and more terrifying than any normal bear that Mordred had ever seen. She tore into the sirens as if they were made of paper.

Hel used the necromancy power inside of her as pure force, blasting sirens over the side of the ship before they'd even managed to touch down on the bow.

Mordred hit an incoming siren that had leaped toward him—deceptively strong arms stretched out to plunge its claws into his body—with a blast of light hot enough to rend flesh from bone. The creature dropped to the deck and screamed in pain, only silenced when Mordred put a round from his MP5 into its head. He fired at the attackers, taking out a dozen sirens in less than a minute as they continued to scramble over the deck of the ship.

When the gun ran dry, instead of reloading, he created a sword of light in one hand and cut through the sirens that continued to attack, until they were almost overwhelmed by numbers.

A siren sliced across Mordred's cheek, and another barreled into him, knocking him off his feet and into the swimming pool. The siren opened its mouth, showing the dangerous teeth, and screamed, the blast hitting Mordred in the face just as he raised a shield of air in defense.

The water around them boiled as Mordred's hands turned bright white before he detonated his light magic, causing the siren to cry out, even underwater. It swam for the surface, with Mordred on its heels.

He reached the siren just as it was leaving the swimming pool, only to watch the creature fall back in, a huge chunk of its chest missing. Chloe reached out and offered Mordred a bloody hand. She noticed and offered the other hand instead, giving Mordred a sheepish look of apology as he climbed out of the pool.

Mordred created a sphere of light in one hand and threw it into the air. "Eyes covered," he shouted and waited for the count of two before detonating the sphere.

The blast rushed out across the bow of the ship, followed quickly by the screams of every single siren that hadn't been shielding its eyes. The screams continued for several seconds, becoming more and more distant as the sirens dived into the water.

"Well, they know we're here," Diana said.

"Good," Mordred said. "That's sort of the idea."

The team made their way to the entrance to the first-class compartment, where Chloe used the key card to open the door. They walked down the hallway beyond before stopping outside room 102 and using the key card again. With the door unlocked, the team stepped inside the lavish suite. Everything was tastefully decorated, and the windows were open, leading to a private balcony.

A man sat in the middle of a large leather sofa. He had bare feet, white three-quarter-length trousers, and an open blue-and-yellow shirt, revealing his hairy chest and six-pack. His dirty-blond hair was long and tied back with ribbons of varying colors.

"Mordred," he said with a sigh. "I've been watching you play with my sirens." The man pointed to the large monitor on the wall, which showed camera feeds from around the ship.

"Poseidon?" Diana asked. "You *little* fucker."

Poseidon's hand turned into water. "I wouldn't, Diana," he said. "Let's not make this any worse for you."

"You notice you're outnumbered, yes?" Remy asked. "There is only one of him, right?"

"I am a *god*," Poseidon said.

Remy shrugged.

"You had thousands of people murdered," Chloe snapped.

"Actually, the sirens did that; I just didn't stop them. Workers need to feed, you know." Poseidon got to his feet and paused. "Why are you smiling?" he asked Mordred, walking behind the sofa, putting it between himself and Mordred's people.

"I wasn't sure it was you," Mordred said. "We knew about the cameras, though. We found someone who worked on the ship; they told us that there had been a special request for it. I'm guessing you were in part the financier of this ship."

"I have lived aboard this ship for some time," Poseidon said. "Always moving, always near my beautiful oceans. And I like people watching. I paid a lot for the privilege. It's why I didn't have the crew killed. I need them to make the ship work, but also to keep me in the manner I'm accustomed to living in. Can't very well murder the people who change my sheets and cook my food."

"Well, we also knew that you'd be watching us when we landed," Mordred continued, ignoring the man who climbed up over the railing from the ocean. He wore all black and had a balaclava on, hiding his face. He crept slowly across the carpet until he was behind Poseidon.

"You're going to answer some questions," Mordred said.

"And if I tell you to go fuck yourselves?" Poseidon asked with a smirk.

"You know, I think I'm powerful enough to kill you myself," Mordred said. "Almost certainly, but someone else wanted to say hi, and I told him if he got here before the questions started, he could take part."

A blade of lightning punctured out the front of Poseidon's chest. He convulsed and dropped to the floor, whereupon the masked man removed the balaclava to reveal Nate Garrett.

"Hey, Poseidon," Nate said, looking down at the man, whose eyes filled with sudden terror.

Mordred walked over and stood beside Nate, looking down at Poseidon. "I think we'll find a way to get the answers we want. I just don't think you're going to enjoy them very much."

Chapter Two

NATE GARRETT

The Atlantic Ocean

We tied Poseidon up and placed him in a bedroom, and Zamek drew runes on its walls, limiting his power in case he broke the sorcerer's band I'd put on his wrist. Poseidon was one of the most powerful beings in any realm, and taking chances would get us all killed. The sorcerer's band ensured he couldn't use his elemental powers, and if he tried to remove it, the runes on the wooden beads would explode, turning him to steam. I hated the things, but when needs must . . .

"Sorry I almost missed the party," I said to Mordred. "There are a lot of prisoners belowdecks. A few thousand people. Mostly passengers, but a fair few crew. Lots of sirens patrolling the ocean around us too. Thanks for taking a few of them off our hands."

"The plan was that I would make a show of it, and they were happy to oblige," Mordred said. "We found a few crew members too. While you were in there with Poseidon, I sent Chloe to go retrieve them, bring them here. I think it would be best if we got off this ship sooner rather than later."

Everyone apart from Chloe and Diana sat in the living room of the suite, taking a breather. Diana was on the balcony, scanning for possible siren attacks. She'd smell them well before they got to us.

"Tarron is busy making a large elven realm gate," I said. "Fortunately we found a lot of sirens so used their blood to make it more powerful."

Tarron was, to anyone's knowledge, the last remaining shadow elf. His entire people had been turned into monsters who called themselves blood elves.

"How'd you get on board with so many sirens there?" Zamek asked.

"Viv," I said. "We dropped into the ocean, and she masked us from their view. Turns out Poseidon's friends aren't quite as good at being guards as he'd like to believe." Viv was the daughter of the Lady of the Lake, who had been murdered by Merlin centuries earlier. She'd helped Mordred retrieve his sword, Excalibur, although I noticed he wasn't wearing it.

"Excalibur?" I asked, pointing to Mordred.

"It wasn't exactly the kind of thing I wanted to bring with me," Mordred said. "If Poseidon had seen it and contacted Arthur to tell him, we might be sailing into a shitstorm."

"Also, you still don't like it," I said.

"And there's that," he agreed.

"So is there a second part of this plan?" Remy asked. "Just curious, because I don't remember the plan involving Nate stabbing the guy with a blade of lightning."

"How is Poseidon even alive after that?" Hel asked.

"He's a water elemental," I said. "A powerful one. Lightning and water don't mix all that well, but I was pretty sure it wouldn't kill him."

"So you didn't know for certain?" Hel asked. "I like how so many of our plans revolve around just seeing what happens."

"Sometimes we just have to wing it," Mordred said cheerfully. "Zamek, this bit is all you, my friend."

Everyone turned to Zamek, who smiled. Things were about to get geeky.

"So, summoning circles," Zamek started.

I tuned out. We all knew what they were, we all knew how they worked, but Zamek was someone who found realm gates, summoning circles, and basically anything that the ancient dwarves had been responsible for fascinating. He tended to allow his enthusiasm to bubble over to everyone in the vicinity, and while what he was saying was important, I'd already heard it three times. Once was enough.

The long and short of it was that summoning circles allowed two people to talk in different realms. They were both set up to only work for the people using them, and both parties had to agree for the link to be made. They were dangerous and easy to disrupt. Feedback would kill both involved, and that was only if they were lucky. They'd fallen out of favor, as they took a lot of power to use, and frankly people hated them, but we'd discovered Merlin and his people had begun to use them again.

"How did you know there was a summoning circle here?" Diana asked from the balcony, drawing me back into the advanced lecture on runes and their uses.

"Oh, that was easy," Zamek said. "We knew that whoever was here was in contact with people somehow, and a lot of Avalon people don't like technology all that much. Odds were good it was a summoning circle."

"So you didn't *know* for certain?" Hel asked.

"No," Zamek said. "Not until I just saw the summoning circle in the room next to where we put Poseidon. I can't hack it, before anyone says anything. It's literally coded to Poseidon. No one can use it but him, and if they try, they only do it once."

"So we came here to hopefully figure out what is going on?" Remy asked.

"We came here to stop the sirens and rescue anyone here," Mordred said. "Discovering that this is all Poseidon is a bit of a bonus. Now we just need to get him to tell us what we need to know and get off this ship."

"And sink the ship," Remy said with far too much glee. "Never sunk something this big before. Not even sure how."

"Is that a good idea?" Diana asked.

"Not much choice," I said. "The sirens here are in numbers I've never seen before, and this ship has been made into a floating sirens' nest. I'd rather that nest was sat on the bottom of the ocean. If this lands somewhere and people are sent to check it out, a lot will die. We could scrub this whole place clean of them, but that would take days, at best. They're not exactly the easiest things to hunt, and we don't have time. This is the best lead we've had at figuring out where Arthur is."

"And if he's in Avalon?" Chloe asked as she returned.

"Then we need to figure out how to get into Avalon without it becoming a bloodbath," Mordred said.

"Any ideas?" Hel asked.

"No," Mordred admitted. "You?"

"Not one," Hel said.

"Well, this is all going swimmingly," Remy said, clapping his hands together. "Let's go talk to the twatnozzle in the other room and see what happens."

"Nate," Diana said. "There are sirens at the stern of the ship. They're keeping their distance for now, but they know we're here. Are Viv and Tarron safe?"

I nodded and passed Diana a small radio. "Any problems and we'll hear about it. Besides, we brought backup."

Diana raised an eyebrow in question. "And who might that be?"

"Irkalla, Kase, and Isis are down there too," I said. "Between the three of them, I almost pity anyone who tries to pick a fight."

"I'm pretty sure anyone trying to pick a fight with those three deserves what happens to them," Remy said. "I thought it was just you, Viv, and Tarron."

"Well, it was decided that you all might screw up and blow the ship sky-high before we were meant to," I said mockingly.

Everyone looked at Remy.

"As I mentioned earlier, I've never even blown a ship up," Remy said before pausing for a second. "Okay, there was one time, but that was a boat, so shut up."

"You okay with Poseidon being in there?" I asked Diana.

"Apart from wanting to tear his face off," she said without any hint of exaggeration.

I left everyone to continue talking and entered the expansive bedroom, where Poseidon lay on the bed, his hate-filled eyes staring at me as I grabbed a chair from the side of the room and sat on it.

"Nathaniel Garrett," Poseidon said, the words dripping venom.

"Nathaniel Garrett Woden to you," I said.

His eyes opened wide in surprise. "You found out who your father was. I heard Odin is dead; that must have been awful. *Good.*"

I leaned back in the chair. "My father died fighting Avalon. I killed War for what he did. He did not die a good death. If you know who my father is, then I'm going to guess that you know what I really am."

"A cross-blood mutt," he snapped.

"If you want to think of me like that," I said with a shrug as Mordred opened the door and stepped into the room, followed by Hel, who closed the door and leaned up against it.

"You're *both* monsters," Poseidon said. "Created from blood magic to be weapons. You're unnatural. Hera told me about you centuries ago."

"I assumed as much," I said.

"That lightning hurt," Poseidon whined.

"Good," Mordred said. "You murdered a lot of people."

"As I said before, the sirens did that."

"And who called the sirens?" I asked.

"Well, me, obviously," Poseidon said. "You going to unfasten my bonds, or do I have to lie here and stare at you?"

"You don't really get to make requests," Hel said.

"I should have killed you when I had the chance," Poseidon said to her. "But I wasn't sure whether I was going to get to fuck you or not, and it would have been a shame to remove such a piece of ass from the world before I got a ride."

I looked back at Hel, who burst out laughing. "You really are a pathetic little ant, aren't you? You think that being misogynistic is going to cause me to burst into some sudden fit of rage? I've been dealing with men like you my whole life. You think you're stronger because you happen to have a penis, no matter how tiny or limp it is. You're not. You're not brave. You're not strong. You're just a child in a man's body who never learned the word *no* and thinks everyone owes him something."

Poseidon looked over at Mordred.

"You expecting me to do something because you insulted my girlfriend?" Mordred asked. "She could pull your lungs out through your asshole. I think she's good without my input."

"And let's all thank Mordred for that lovely image," I said, turning back to a considerably paler-looking Poseidon.

"What do you want?" Poseidon asked.

"You're communicating with Merlin," I said. "Using a summoning circle. We know about it. We know you were using this place as a sort of stop-off point to pass information along. We'd found a few of the command centers in Europe, and they led us to you. Where is Arthur?"

"No idea," Poseidon said. "Only spoke to Merlin. And occasionally Gawain. No one else."

"Where is Thomas Carpenter?" I asked.

Poseidon laughed. "Your pet werewolf?"

I reached out with my air magic and wrapped tendrils of it around his chest, squeezing tighter as Poseidon's laughter turned to wheezing and his face grew panicked.

"I don't think this will kill you," I said. "But I think if I explode your heart, it's going to hurt like hell. You want to rethink your attitude?"

Poseidon nodded quickly, and I released the air. He took in deep gulps for a few seconds. "I don't know where he is," Poseidon said eventually. "No one has brought him up in conversation."

"You're going to tell us what the last orders you got were," Mordred said.

"I write them down in a book inside the room next door."

"You don't use a code?" Hel asked.

"It's in ancient Atlantan," he said. "You know anyone who can speak it?"

"Yes," Mordred said. "A few, actually."

The look of surprise on Poseidon's face was worth the journey alone.

"Is Arthur in Atlantis?" I asked.

"I told you, I *don't* know," Poseidon snapped. "It's a dead realm. No way in or out. There's literally nothing left of it; the Titans turned the entire realm to ash. I don't see why anyone would want to go there."

"You wouldn't be lying to us, now, would you?" Mordred asked.

"About Atlantis?" Poseidon said with a chuckle. "I was there when it happened. I only just got out alive before the realm gate was turned to slag. There's *nothing* there."

"I think the fish boy doth protest too much," Hel said.

"Wow—can you talk to fish?" Mordred asked. "Like Aquaman?"

The look of rage on Poseidon's face suggested he was done being mocked.

"I bet *Jaws* is in your computer's porn folder," Mordred continued. "Or are you more of a *Free Willy* kind of guy?"

"You won't keep me here forever," Poseidon said, enraged. "And you won't kill me. You need me."

"To talk to fish?" Mordred asked. "I don't really think that's important right now."

"Fuck you," Poseidon snapped.

A smirk spread across Mordred's face. "We do need you, yes. You're going to contact my father, and you're going to find out where Arthur is."

"No, I'm not," Poseidon said.

"Can you both give me a second?" I asked Hel and Mordred, who nodded and left the room.

"You going to torture me?" Poseidon asked.

I shook my head. "It's going to take us a while to decode your diary, so you're going to tell me where the next Knights of Avalon attack is going to be directed."

"And if I don't?"

"I let Diana in here," I said. "You might know who Diana's girlfriend is."

"Another bear?" he asked with a laugh.

"Medusa," I said.

Genuine fear spread across his face.

"You and she have history, yes?"

Poseidon nodded.

"You want to find out what Diana will do to you?" I looked back at the door. "You're in a room that stops your power but not anyone else's. And you have a sorcerer's band on. I think you would die in here. Eventually. I think it would take a long time."

"Merlin will have me killed," Poseidon said, seemingly scared now.

"Probably," I said. "But I let you go, and you have a chance. A chance to run and hide. You stay here, and I guarantee you nothing except pain and death."

I got to my feet. "You have ten seconds to decide."

"Please don't," Poseidon said. "This isn't how a god dies."

"You're *not* a god, Poseidon," I said. "You just played one, thousands of years ago."

"How do you even know there are more orders?" Poseidon asked. "You worked for Merlin for centuries—was he all that chatty with *your* orders?"

"Do you know what I've been doing this last year?" I asked. "I've been fighting Avalon bastards. The Knights of Avalon, the Blade of Avalon—same bunch of arseholes, different names and uniforms. Human governments are slowly returning to being controlled by humans. There are large pockets of resistance fighting in every country against you, more than I can think of. More than once Avalon forces got hold of nuclear material and threatened to detonate a bomb. More than once, I've been forced to kill people who believe in nothing but their own superiority, simply because they had the fortune to be born with or be given powers.

"You are like them, Poseidon. So convinced of your own self-importance. You will tell me, because I stopped playing games with you people years ago. Who is the next set of orders for?"

Poseidon stared at me for several seconds before sighing. "Secretary of state, in DC."

"He's one of yours?"

Poseidon nodded. "He relays information to those senators, congresspeople, and pretty much everyone on the president's Secret Service detail who work for us."

"Not the president?" I asked.

"He does as he's told if he knows what's good for him."

"Why is this important?"

"DC is about to enter a very difficult phase. There's going to be a civil war in a country with enough firepower to burn the entire planet to ash." Poseidon smiled. "If Arthur can't have Earth, if you people are so intent on stopping him, he'll turn it into a wasteland and see how you like it then."

"Where is Arthur?" I asked.

"Go fuck yourself, Nathaniel Garrett," Poseidon said. "I hope your pet wolf got skinned."

I leaped forward, grabbing Poseidon by the throat and dragging him off the bed, across the floor, and to the window, where I smashed him through the glass to the balcony beyond. He fell to the floor, bleeding badly from several cuts, before I lifted him off the floor again and smashed his forehead into the steel railing. The sky above darkened, and thunder rolled across above us.

"Where is Arthur?" I asked again, turning Poseidon over so he could see the heavens as lightning streaked down and slammed into the balcony a foot away from his head.

"Want me to repeat myself?" I asked, moving his head to the singed metal, letting him feel the heat of what the lightning had caused.

"Killing me won't bring back your friend," he screamed.

"No, but it will kill you," I whispered. "I think that'll be enough."

Poseidon looked up at me, genuinely terrified. "Atlantis. He's in Atlantis."

"And what's the real plan in DC?" I asked. "Arthur would never burn this entire realm. He's spent too long wanting to rule over it and crush the resistance. He can't rule over a wasteland."

"The last person I received orders from was Gawain," Poseidon said. "President Reed is going to sign a declaration stating that

Avalon is now in control of both the military and policing inside the country. There are people inside every organization inside the country ready to take control. We're going to turn the United States of America into a police state.

"The resistance might have taken back the UK, and you might take back some of Europe, but you'll never take back all of America. We've worked too long to set this up. The blood of those who oppose Arthur will run in the streets. Once the USA is ours, we'll finish with Canada and South America. Russia is already falling into line, most of eastern Europe too. Those countries who resisted will be small fry compared to those who are loyal."

Arthur would cause the deaths of millions of people. "What's he waiting for?"

"What?"

"Well, why not just sign the damn law?" I asked. "What's he waiting for?"

Poseidon shook his head. "I don't know."

The sky rumbled.

"Honestly, no idea," he said hurriedly. "All I know is it has to wait until midnight. Gawain is doing something and needs time to prepare. I swear, I don't know what."

"How do you contact President Reed?"

"I don't," he said. "I contacted Gawain and the head of the Senate. The latter by encrypted phone."

I dragged Poseidon back into the room and dropped him on the floor before opening the bedroom door. "Anyone found a phone?"

Chloe had one in her hands and tossed it to me, which I caught one handed. "It was in the room with the summoning circle. The circle and its runes are drawn in blood, by the way. Because of course they were."

I looked back at Poseidon. I placed a foot on his chest and pushed down. "Make the call," I said.

"I need assurances," he said.

"I can assure you I'll rip your face off if you don't," Remy said from the doorway. "I bet none of the fishes will want to fuck you after that."

"I do not have sex with fish!" Poseidon screamed.

"Oh, I'm sorry," said Remy, looking contrite. "I meant make love . . ."

"Nate, I think you're going to want to see this," Zamek shouted from the doorway of the room he'd been investigating.

"Keep an eye on Poseidon," I said to Remy and went next door to find a glowing purple summoning circle on the wall and a second one on the bare wooden floor.

"What'd you do?" I asked. "They're not meant to activate unless someone uses them. Did you use it?"

Zamek shook his head. "I tried to figure out exactly where it goes to. And it goes to Avalon."

"Like we expected," I said. "But?"

"But it doesn't end there," Zamek said, pointing to several runes drawn on the floor and mirrored on the wall. "This pings the signal. You can't use a summoning circle and bounce around the same realm, but if you figured out a way to send it to one realm, you could ping it back to this realm and a third circle."

"So that's what this is doing?"

Zamek nodded.

"Do you know *where* it's being pinged to?"

"No," Zamek said. "But if we activated it and got Poseidon to talk to whoever is on the end, I could, yes."

I went next door and found Poseidon still on the floor, while Remy sat on the bed beside him, using the remote control to scroll through the films on the internal entertainment system.

"You okay?" I asked Remy.

"Just trying to find Poseidon *Dolphin Tale* to watch," Remy said with a snigger.

I pulled Poseidon to his feet. "You're going to talk to whoever is on the end of that summoning circle."

"They will kill me," Poseidon said.

"Maybe, but I will for certain if you don't," I said. "And I'm here right now."

Poseidon walked with me into the other room, where I untied his hands, although I kept the band in place. He knelt in the circle on the floor and placed his hands on the runes. A second later the circle on the wall shimmered.

"Say what you like," I told him.

"What?" Gawain asked a second later.

I could see Gawain from where I stood, all long blond hair and handsome features. He was a monster the likes of which I'd rarely met before. I wondered how many people had lost their lives because of his charm and looks and the way he used them to make himself appear approachable. Until it was too late.

"Nate is here," Poseidon said.

I walked around until Gawain could see me. "Hey, Gawain. How's being a mass-murdering dickhead?"

Gawain smiled. "My brother is with you, I assume."

"Fuck you, Gawain," Mordred called out from the doorway. "I look forward to cutting your head off."

"I did wonder if you'd eventually be able to track down Poseidon and his sirens," Gawain said. "It took you long enough. I assume he told you about everything."

I glared at him.

"Arthur is in Atlantis, and you're in the Earth realm," I said, looking beyond Gawain at the library of books behind him. "Bit weird how you got here, though, considering there's no realm gate from Avalon to here that we don't know about and aren't keeping tabs on. Oh, wait, I guess there must be." I took a guess with the last part, but the look on his face told me I was right.

"Arthur *will* rule this realm," he said. "We will make an example out of those who stand against him."

"Yeah, I've read the brochure," I said. "Still not buying."

"Poseidon," Gawain said. "You have been of great service to our cause, but now our time has ended." He removed a small device from his pocket. "Goodbye, gentlemen."

There was a massive explosion outside the room.

Zamek, Mordred, and I ran out to find black smoke billowing out of both sides of the ship.

I ran back to Poseidon, who stood in the middle of the room. "Gawain will hunt me down and make me pay for what I told you. There's no way out for me now."

"We'll keep you safe," Mordred said.

"Fuck you," Poseidon said. He tore off the sorcerer's band, and the explosion of magic threw me back out of the doorway. My magic protected me as I smashed into a wooden cabinet, obliterating it.

"Shit," Remy said. "*I* wanted to blow up the ship."

"You okay?" Chloe asked me, offering me her hand, which I was happy to take.

"Let's get the fuck off this ship," I said before thanking Chloe and looking over at the pile of ash that used to be Poseidon. There was a third explosion, which rocked the boat, and it started to tip slightly to one side and then the other, as if we were in an earthquake.

"And fast," Mordred said.

"Women, children, and foxmen first," shouted Remy, heading for the door.

Chapter Three

NATE GARRETT

There were no sirens on the way through the ship. Although the sounds of tearing metal echoed around us, a result of the explosions that had been deeper inside the guts of the vessel.

Mordred's team met up with my original team inside what had once been a dancing hall of some kind, where the wooden floor made it easy for Tarron to make an elven realm gate. Carving the letters into the wood made for a more stable gate than just drawing them. And seeing how quickly the ship was currently being torn apart, stable was good.

Tarron was crouched on the floor, finishing up his realm gate, while Isis, Kase, and Irkalla were trying to keep several hundred passengers, prisoners, and crew calm, which was no mean feat in itself.

"I'm not sure what you did," Tarron said. "But this is bad."

"Poseidon," I said.

"He dead?" Kase asked.

I nodded.

"Good," Isis said as she walked over to me. "We need to leave."

"I second that idea," Remy said.

"Where are the rest of the prisoners?" I asked.

"Too many people to all go at once," Tarron said. "This is a second realm gate. I burned out the first gate down in the engine room. Sent about fifteen hundred people through to Shadow Falls in a little under an hour. Hence this second gate. Elven realm gates were not made to take so many so quickly."

"But it works, yes?" Chloe asked.

Tarron nodded. "We have a lot of dead to use for blood," he said. "But that much power probably didn't help the integrity of the ship."

Somewhere outside was a howl that belonged to something quite inhuman.

"What was that?" Zamek asked.

The windows to the ballroom exploded open and water poured in, causing several of the humans to scream in fear before the water remade itself as a young woman.

"Viv," I said. "Always a pleasure."

"I brought help," she said.

"Are we going to ride dolphins out of here?" Remy asked. "Because I would be okay with that."

"Ichthyocentaurs," she said. "There's a herd of them who have been following this ship for a while now. Apparently, they prey on sirens, and seeing how there are hundreds of those monsters here, the ichthyocentaurs have been having quite the feast. They're going to keep the sirens busy while we get everyone out of here."

There was an almighty creak, as if someone had opened a door that needed oiling, and everyone was silent as the noise reverberated around the room. A second later there was silence, followed immediately by the deafening sound of the ship being ripped apart from the inside.

The entire deck lifted up, and everyone slid along the room to the far end before the ship smashed back into the water.

"Tarron, does that thing work yet?" I shouted.

Tarron slammed his hands onto the wood, and the realm gate came to life.

"Everyone on there—now," Irkalla shouted at the humans, moving them all toward the realm gate as more and more awful sounds echoed through the room.

The ship listed, and several humans fell onto the realm gate, vanishing from view before they could be helped up. Hopefully whoever was in Shadow Falls—the destination for the gate—would be able to help out.

"Mordred, Viv, Isis—with me," I shouted. "We need to stop this ship from going over."

We all left the ballroom and made it outside as the ship began to list again.

"You got a plan?" Viv asked.

"We just need to give them time to get everyone through the gate," I said as we all ran along the side of the deck.

An ichthyocentaur leaped over the railing of the ship, its fish tail turning into the legs of a horse, matching the front legs. His long green hair swept over human shoulders. He clicked his lobsterlike claws.

"There are many sirens down there," he said to Viv. "The damage to the ship is total."

"How total?" Mordred asked.

"There's a hole in both sides of the lower decks, letting in water fast," he began. "Two propellers are all but gone, and there's a deep gash running under the stern of the ship that's about twenty meters long. At some point soon, this ship is going to split in two."

"Can you keep the sirens away from us?" I asked.

A siren leaped up onto the deck behind us and died a second later when I threw a bolt of lightning into its chest.

"Apart from that one, yes," the ichthyocentaur said calmly. "We have lost two of my brethren, but they have lost many more."

"That water looks a lot closer than it did when I last saw it," Mordred said, looking over the rail as the ichthyocentaur jumped over it to the ocean below.

The deck forty feet in front of us groaned and began to crack open, the wooden floor bursting as if something were trying to escape from within. I poured air magic out of my hands, wrapping it down the side of the ship and into the crack, flooding the inside of the ship with it, just as Isis and Mordred did the same. The ichthyocentaur and Viv jumped over the rail, and she turned to water before she hit the ocean.

The half of the ship we were on began to lift, and all three of us dropped to our knees but continued to pour magic into the wounded ship, trying to fill the gap.

"I don't think we're going to be able to do this long," Mordred said as sweat poured down his face.

"We're powerful, but not enough to hold hundreds of tons of ship together," Isis said.

I looked back at the front of the ship as it lifted further and further off the ocean. "You're right; we need a better plan," I said.

"Can you fly everyone off the ship?" Isis asked, clearly nearing exhaustion. Even sixty seconds of trying to keep a ship the size of the *Harmony of Oceans* in one piece was too much for the three of us. "Because I'm not sure we have a *better* plan."

Viv appeared beside us. "The stern is fucked," she said. "It's almost broken away from the bow, but when it fills, it will drag us all under."

"What's stopping it?" Mordred asked.

"The ichthyocentaurs are essentially water elementals," Viv said. "They're keeping it all together, but there's only so much they can do. A third of this ship is going to come apart, and then the rest will go down too. There's nothing any of us can do to stop it."

The ship listed again, and I wrapped myself in a shield of air as I was thrown across the deck into the outside wall of a medical room. The ship almost immediately listed back, and I dropped to my knees.

"How long do the ichthyocentaurs have before they can't do any more?"

"They're fighting the sirens *and* doing this," Viv said. "You have a few minutes at most."

"Mordred, Isis, get back to Tarron. We need to—" I was interrupted by the bow of the ship lifting high into the air.

I wrapped myself in magical air, anchoring me to the metal posts that were nearby as Isis and Mordred did the same. I dared to look back at the stern, the rear of which was now under water. The groaning increased from the pressure it applied on the fractures that had already been caused.

"We need to go," I shouted over the noise of the ship ripping itself apart.

Viv, who had vanished into water the second the bow had lifted, reappeared next to me. "Everyone is gone. Tarron is waiting on you three."

"Tell him to go," Mordred shouted. "We'll figure something out."

"You will die here," Viv said. "The ship will drag you underwater, and there's no escaping that in time. Not with the cold too. You're not elementals; you can't breathe underwater. Even Mordred, with his power to breathe anywhere, can't keep that up forever."

The ship was almost completely vertical when it snapped in two, the bow dropping back to the ocean with a huge crash that I felt through my entire body. Followed quickly by enough water to drench everything, even as high up as we were.

"Run," I shouted as the remains of the ship began to list to the side. It wouldn't be long before we were in the ocean.

No one needed to be told twice, and I saw dozens of ichthyocentaurs in the sea, firing jets of water at the side of the ship, trying to keep it upright for long enough to let us escape.

"Get the ichthyocentaurs out of here," I said to Viv as we reached the ballroom.

"You took long enough," Tarron said, getting back to his feet. He'd used two daggers to drive into the wood just outside the realm gate he'd made, giving himself something to hold on to while the ship destroyed itself.

"You coming?" Isis asked Viv.

"I'll see you all soon enough," she said. "I'm going to help the ichthyocentaurs finish this fight."

"Take care," I said as we all stepped into the realm gate and appeared in the realm of Shadow Falls a moment later.

"I do *not* wish to do that again," Tarron said.

"This realm gate pays for itself," Mordred said, hugging Tarron. "Have I ever told you how awesome you are?"

"I bet you say that to all the people who save your life," Tarron said with a small smile.

Mordred chuckled. "And you know what, my friend? It's always true."

The guards all around the cave that we found ourselves in looked more than a little shaken by what they'd seen. The elven realm gate was usually pretty quiet. They all bowed to Mordred, who sighed. I wasn't sure he was ever going to get used to that part of being king.

"Anyone want to tell us where all those people went?" I asked.

One of the guards pointed down toward the exit with his spear.

"You think Viv is okay?" Isis asked.

"She's one of the most powerful water elementals I've ever met," Mordred said. "She'll be fine."

I left the realm gate cavern with Mordred while Tarron set about deactivating the gate. It was unlikely that anyone was going to use a realm gate that was soon going to be on the bottom of the Atlantic Ocean, but better safe than sorry.

Outside the cavern, high above the city of Solomon in Shadow Falls, Isis, Mordred, and I stood in silence as we waited for one of the lifts to arrive to take us to the bottom of the mountain range that we were on.

"Did we at least learn anything of use?" Mordred asked.

I nodded. "We need to go see your council," I said to Mordred.

The lift arrived with Persephone and my mother, Brynhildr, on it.

"I was worried," Brynhildr said to me as we got onto the large lift and Persephone operated it, making it slowly move back down the mountain.

"It wasn't the most fun ever," I admitted. "We have news, though. Poseidon was there."

Persephone appeared shocked at the news. "Honestly, I thought he'd died centuries ago."

"He's dead now, if that helps," Mordred said.

I told them both what had happened on the ship. I was probably going to have to repeat the information half a dozen times before I was done, but I had a lot of pent-up frustration and wanted to vent.

When I'd finished, Brynhildr and Persephone shared an expression of resignation.

"I don't think the president is going to be a big problem," my mum said.

"Why?" Isis asked.

"Twelve hours ago, we got information that Gawain was on a civilian flight into the United States," Persephone said. "He landed in DC and went straight to the White House."

"We had a chat," I said. "Not sure how he got into this realm, though. Where did he fly from?"

"Egypt," my mum said.

"How the hell did he get to Egypt?" Mordred asked.

"We're looking into it," Persephone said. "But two hours ago, our allies in the American government arrested those senators and congresspeople who were helping Arthur. They went to the White House to arrest everyone there, including Gawain, and were met with resistance. The White House is in lockdown, but we've scrambled all communications entering and leaving."

"You can just go and arrest the president?" I asked. "Because that seems like something that takes a lot of time and effort."

"The president, no," Persephone said. "The people who work for him are somewhat easier. Besides, these are strange times."

"What's their endgame?" Mordred asked. "They said Gawain had to wait until midnight before the law could be signed. Why?"

"We need to go ask him," I said.

"My father would have a plan for such a contingency," Mordred said. "I would assume there's a realm gate inside the White House, but then why would Gawain fly in? No, it can't be that."

"Do they have access to launch codes?" Isis asked.

My mum nodded. "Yes, but we've been slowly taking control of all missile launch sites for the last year. Despite what Poseidon said, we've made sure that the military is clean of Avalon influence."

"Who do they answer to?" I asked.

"The vice president," Persephone said. "As strange as this sounds, she had no involvement with Arthur. She's been feeding us intel on her boss for the last year."

"Arthur needs America," Mordred said. "It's too wealthy to lose. He'll have a plan to make sure he doesn't lose control."

Persephone nodded. "Yes, he needs America, not just for its riches but also because of the amount of military here. He can't risk that falling into the hands of anyone else. Same with Russia. He's lost Germany and the UK already, and western Europe is removing Avalon influence. Canada, Mexico, large chunks of North Africa and South America aren't under Avalon influence either."

"China, Japan, and South Korea aren't far behind," Brynhildr said. "Arthur can't risk losing anyone else with the military clout he needs. If he controls America, Russia, eastern Europe, and big chunks of Africa and Asia still, he'll have enough to spread back out across the world. Just Russia and America under his control would be enough to cause serious problems worldwide."

"We beat him once; we can do it again," I said.

"I get the feeling that's why he's so keen on controlling the Earth realm," Isis said. "He wants the one thing he's been told he can't have. Like some spoiled little child."

"We have to trust that our allies across the globe are still fighting back," Mordred said. "We need to find Arthur and stop him from making things worse."

"So I guess we need to go to DC?" I said as the lift stopped.

"I'll get ready," Mordred said as we left the lift, heading toward the tramlines.

"It's not that simple," my mum said. "Right now we have the White House contained, but we can't have the king running off over there, helping to drag out the president of a country. We'll just be swapping one dictator for another. In fact, none of *our* people can do the dragging."

"So who does?" Isis asked as we entered one of the trams that traveled above the city of Solomon.

"The humans have to," Persephone said as the tram started.

I looked outside the window as the tram moved up the rails until it was at its peak height, a hundred feet above the city. Solomon had grown constantly in the years since I'd come back from the dead, so to speak. There had been a lot of refugees from Asgard and Valhalla and a lot more from the human cities in the Earth realm who had been driven from their homes by Avalon.

"You listening?" Persephone asked me.

I shook my head. "Sorry, the humans have to take President Reed alive and drag him out with all the rest of his cockroach friends in front of the world's cameras, yes?"

Persephone nodded.

"Human law enforcement, backed up by the government, yes?"

Another nod.

"Sounds like a plan," I said. "I'll go to DC and get people inside the building. It'll be up to the humans to sort it out from there."

"You need to see the council first," Persephone said.

"Sure thing," I said with a sigh. I'd been building up to a question I'd asked a hundred times in the last year, and a hundred times I'd heard nothing of any use. "Any idea about Tommy?"

Thomas Carpenter was my best friend, and a year ago he'd been taken by Merlin and Arthur before they'd destroyed Asgard. No one knew where he was or whether he was even alive. There had been neither hide nor hair of him in twelve months, and the only thing I could do was find Arthur and ask him personally.

"No," Persephone said.

"Gawain might know something," Isis said.

"And he's in DC," Mordred continued.

"Mordred, how would you feel about me asking your brother a few questions?" I asked him.

"My brother is a psychopath and mass murderer," Mordred said. "You can cut his fucking head off and use it as a football for all I care."

"There's an image I could have done without," Isis said as the tram stopped and we all got out before making the short journey to the palace.

I was halfway up the steps when I heard Mordred sigh.

"Still find it weird you live here?" I asked him.

"I have people who *cook* for me, Nate," he said. "I am not accustomed to the luxuries of having someone come make my bed for me. I had to stop that one. And also stop them from pouring my wine and opening doors for me. I can open my own damn doors."

"Do they announce your entrance?" Isis asked with a grin.

"Oh gods, what's that about?" Mordred exclaimed, throwing his hands in the air.

"When I was revered as a god, people would do things for me all the time," Isis said. "I once had a man burn my bed and carve me a new one from some wood I'd found. Just to see if he would do it. We were all assholes, drunk on our own power and believing our own mythologies. Don't do that. Don't act like you're above everyone else, or you will start to believe it. I was told from birth that I was better than everyone, and it took me a long time to realize it wasn't true."

"Well, I was pretty much ignored from birth," Mordred said. "It may have had an effect on me; who's to know?"

Isis smiled. "The best rulers are those who have it thrust upon them. People who seek power are usually not people you want having it."

We reached the top of the stairs, and two guards pulled open the doors, bowing to Mordred as we entered.

"I can't get them to stop doing that," Mordred complained. "I've asked nicely several times."

"I think that's one of those things you'll just have to get used to," I told him.

The five of us walked through the busy palace, with everyone bowing toward a frowning Mordred as he passed them, until we eventually reached the main hall, where two more guards opened the door and bellowed an announcement for King Mordred.

King Mordred sighed.

I tried very hard not to smile.

The main hall was full of people, and the sounds of their chatter stopped as Mordred walked into the room. A large wooden oval table sat in the middle of the room, and as Mordred entered, people began to take their seats on the multiple chairs that surrounded it.

"Your Majesty," an elderly woman said, taking his hand in hers. "It's good to see you unharmed."

"I got a bit wet," Mordred said. "But nothing too awful."

"Have you heard about DC?" Loki asked him. Loki was Hel's father, and he sat in the corner eating an apple.

Mordred walked over to Hel and kissed her hello before turning to Loki. "Yes," Mordred said. "Sorry, just happy that everyone got off the ship in one piece."

"We're all fine," Hel said. "We've got a few thousand new refugees to sort out. A lot of political prisoners that Avalon have taken."

"Avalon is responsible for so many deaths," Hades said from his seat. "Sometimes I wonder how we're ever going to heal the realms even when we've won."

Persephone walked over to her husband and kissed him on his bald head.

"Before we even think about winning, I'm going to need a team," I said. "To take to DC."

A few people shared nervous glances.

"Are you really the best person for the job?" a dwarf asked as he rubbed his large ginger beard. "No offense, but trouble appears to follow you."

"Well, trouble is already there, so I'm ahead of the curve," I said with a smile.

"You'll have your team," Olivia Carpenter told me.

She looked tired. Tired from helping to organize a resistance, tired from being a mum to a small bundle of never-ending energy, but mostly tired from spending every waking moment when she wasn't working worrying about Tommy. I knew it ate at her. Knowing he was out there somewhere but not knowing where. It was tough for her daughter, Kase, and Olivia's young son, Daniel, but Olivia was burning both ends of the candle. I understood. I'd been doing something similar, but I'd also had people to punch to let out my frustrations, while Olivia just added them to the ever-growing list.

I walked over and hugged her, feeling her sag against me. "You need rest," I whispered.

"I need my husband," she said. "Go home; be with Selene and Astrid. We'll come find you in a few hours."

"Business first," I said. I told everyone what had happened on the ship, and when they were done listening, they agreed with pretty much everything I wanted.

"Mordred can't go," Jinayca said. She was one of the Norse dwarves and had been a large part of the rebellion since its inception so many years ago. She was also one of the smartest people any of us knew, so when she spoke, everyone listened. "Sorry, you're a king now."

"And a king should lead," Mordred said sternly.

"Yes," Jinayca said. "And we need to stop Gawain, stop Avalon's plans for DC, and we need to find Atlantis. If you go to DC and involve yourself in matters there, we'll have to send a guard with you, and then we're putting everyone in one basket with no clear way forward afterward. We need to be proactive. Arthur and Avalon want us to react to everything they do, to keep us off balance. We can't win this way."

"And your plan is?" Hel asked.

"We need to find out how Gawain got into the Earth realm," she said. "I assume you have some contacts, Mordred."

Mordred nodded. "I have one or two, yes."

"A request from a king would be better than a request from me," Jinayca said.

"You want me to be more statesmanlike," Mordred said. He looked over at Hel.

"I agree with her," Hel told him. "Gawain would only try to get you involved in a fight you don't need to be involved in. We all go to DC, and then Arthur launches something else, and we're all there fighting. Jinayca is right."

Mordred nodded, but I knew how much he wanted to confront Gawain. "Right, let's figure out who is going where," Mordred said, leaning back in his chair. "Nate, go home and rest—that's an actual order. We'll get your team together. You have a few hours. See your wife and daughter."

There was no point in arguing; besides, I wanted to see my family, so I did as I was told and went to my home at the far end of the city. You could see the realm gate temple on top of the hill from where we lived. The four-story building looked like a Roman villa, something Leonardo had been keen on. He'd called it a touch of class for the classless, which Selene had found hysterical, and I'd tried not to tell him to piss off. I'd failed, but at least I'd tried.

There were guards posted outside my home, which didn't exactly make it look welcoming, but Mordred had insisted, so I'd gone along with it. To be fair, we were a few minutes' walk from the nearest neighbor, so it wasn't like they were going to terrify the locals.

One of the guards opened the large black metal gate and nodded to me. I returned the gesture as the door to the villa opened and Selene walked out, followed by a slowly tottering Astrid, who saw me and yelled until I picked her up. I gave Selene a kiss before we walked back inside.

"Whatever mission you're going to go on next, I'm coming," Selene told me as I closed the door.

"We get to go kill Gawain," I said, bopping Astrid on the nose and making her giggle.

"About fu—" She caught herself before she finished. "About fudging time," Selene said.

Chapter Four

NATE GARRETT

City of Solomon, Realm of Shadow Falls

After Astrid had been born and my father had been murdered in Asgard, Selene and I had settled in Shadow Falls, agreeing it was the safest place to live. We took turns going on missions, because neither of us wanted to sit around all day, but that meant not spending much time as a family. It had been a hard year, although the last few months had been easier with the appearance of Eos, Selene's sister.

Eos had moved into our home. Her children had moved to Shadow Falls, too, because it was safer for them. Arthur wasn't above going after the families of people who had helped us. I'd come back from a mission to discover Eos firmly ensconced. We'd discussed it before I'd gone, but I hadn't realized I'd be coming back to a done deal.

If anyone ever told you that having someone who was essentially your sister-in-law living with you full-time was weird, they were right. It was *really* weird, but either way, Eos was wonderful with Astrid. She knew she wasn't a warrior, although she was perfectly capable of taking care of herself, and her days as an assassin were long behind her. Now, she just wanted to protect her family.

Eos walked down the stairs as Selene and I sat on the large comfortable sofa, Astrid in front of us playing with one of the approximately five million toy cars that had seemingly appeared in the house over the course of our living here.

"So how bad was it?" Selene asked me.

I gave a rundown of what had happened, culminating with me being told about the mission in DC.

"We're going to DC?" Selene asked. "I've never been there."

"How?" Eos asked. "You're thousands of years old, and you've never been there?"

"You've never been to Ireland," Selene countered.

"Touché," Eos said, taking a seat nearby. "Have you heard from Father?"

Hyperion was in Helheim helping to resettle the hundreds of thousands of people who had been displaced by Avalon before their eventual defeat. It had turned out he was good at the job, although being one of the most powerful beings ever born probably went some way toward others treating him with respect.

"When this is all over, we'll go to Helheim," Selene said. "I think Hel is missing the place."

"I think Mordred would be happy for the break away from being king," I said. "He's still not exactly used to it."

"I don't think he ever will be," Eos said.

"Speaking of you Horsemen," Selene said, "have you seen Judgement?"

Astrid threw a green car at me and laughed when I picked it out of the air with magic and dropped it back in her lap. There was a time when using magic in Shadow Falls had been unpredictable and wild, but over the years, as I'd increased in power, I'd learned to control it better. "She's in the forest to the north," I said. "She doesn't do well around crowds of people."

"She'll come with us to DC," Selene told me. "You should ask her."

"She does like hitting people," I said thoughtfully. "And I think the higher the rank, the more she enjoys it."

"We really going to drag the president of America out of the White House to be arrested?" Selene asked. "That doesn't sound like something we can do easily."

"Honestly, I'm not sure what's going to happen," I said. "Gawain is there, so I definitely want the chance to have a long, slow conversation with him about the error in being a . . . bad man," I finished after remembering Astrid was in the room. Sometimes being a parent was hard. Harder still when you *really* wanted to swear and couldn't. I didn't want to be known as the parent whose kid ran around telling people to fuck off. Although, thinking about it, I could always blame Remy's influence.

Astrid motioned for me to pick her up. "No, you can walk to me," I told her.

She stared at me for several seconds before getting to her feet and toddling over to me. I picked her up and sat her on my knee. "You're going to be a good girl for Eos?" I asked her.

Astrid looked over at Eos and waved. "Good girl," she said enthusiastically.

"How did you two ever make a kid that cute?" Eos asked.

"She got all of Selene's . . . everything," I said.

"Wait until she's a teenager and she turns into a mini-Daddy," Selene said. "Burning down houses, throwing bolts of lightning at everyone."

"I think by the time she's a teenager, I'll have concocted an elaborate escape plan for me to live underground," I said, giving Selene a kiss.

"Oh, not without me, you don't," Selene said.

"You two sicken me," Eos told us, picking up Astrid. "I'm going to go take this one for a walk, if no one has any objections."

"Thank you," Selene said.

Once Selene and I were alone, we went to bed, predominantly to get some sleep. Eventually, anyway.

I'd had a good extra hour when I woke up to the sound of the front door being rhythmically beaten.

"If that's Mordred, give him a bottle of vodka and tell him to relax," Selene said as I left the bedroom. I went downstairs to find Hel and Mordred at the front door.

"Nate," Mordred said. "You wanna get dressed?"

I looked down, realizing I was wearing only a pair of shorts. "No," I said. "I want to go back to sleep."

"Sorry, but the team is ready for your incursion into Washington," Hel said.

"Well, it was nice while it lasted," Selene said as she walked down the stairs, pulling on a T-shirt.

"The White House has turned into somewhat of a battle-ground," Hel said. "The humans went to arrest several senators who were there, hoping to get distance between them and the president, and it all kicked off. There are a lot of Avalon personnel in that building, and now quite a few dead Secret Service and FBI agents."

"How long ago?" I asked.

"An hour," Mordred said. "We only just got word, as our people there have been trying to stop Avalon insurgents from killing innocent people."

"It gets worse," Hel said.

"Of course it does," I said.

"Looks like the president *isn't* involved with Avalon," Mordred said. "At least not how we thought. Gawain threatened to execute him if anyone tries to get into the White House."

54

"So the president is one of the good guys?" I asked. "That's not the impression we got from Poseidon."

"Yeah, it's all a little confusing," Mordred said. "But right now, the president and his family are in the White House, and they're hostages. Along with several dozen workers and members of Congress."

"Yeah, that's pretty bad," I admitted. I ran upstairs and put on a pair of jeans and a T-shirt before we left the house, and all of us made our way to the temple realm gate, where Leonardo and Antonio were waiting, along with several dozen others. Antonio hugged me and Selene in turn.

"Good to see you both," he said. "I'm pretty sure I now live in this temple, considering the amount of time I've spent here. Leonardo wants to make it even bigger. He thinks there's a way to move whole armies through the gates."

"And you think?"

"I think he's always trying to push the boundaries of what's possible, and sometimes he doesn't stop to think what's safe."

I smiled. "That sounds a lot like Leonardo."

"I love him, but he can be hard work," Antonio said, with a warm smile of his own.

"So we're really going to send a group this big?" I asked Hades.

"The Knights of Avalon have been running skirmishes against a lot of the humans there. The army has been drafted in, but even with guns it's hard to kill people who can throw fireballs at your face before you've even raised the weapon."

"They're going to start a war in the middle of the city," Selene said from beside me.

"Yes," Leonardo said. "Several from here have already gone through the realm gate. Nate, I just want to say that something feels off about this. From what I've been told, these KOA were attacking the human forces not long after the White House went into lockdown. It feels like this was planned."

"Great," I said. "So where does this realm gate go?"

"Ah, we changed the address," Leonardo said. "It goes to a realm gate under the Lincoln Memorial."

"There's no realm gate under the Lincoln Memorial," I said. "I know, because I've been there several times."

"There wasn't until three months ago," Zamek said as he joined us. "Jinayca and the dwarves we met in Valhalla worked together to get one working. They found one under Valhalla—it's what destroyed a big part of it—and while that didn't work properly, this one does. They built six new realm gates; DC was one of them."

"So these gates . . . they're safe?" I asked.

"Completely," Zamek said. "They're dead gates until linked to another gate. And seeing how very few people can change the realm gate destinations, we didn't need to worry too much about them being used for evil purposes. Besides, we made sure there are guards and the like."

"You ready?" Antonio asked.

I nodded. "Keep safe out there," I said. "And Leonardo, check to see if you can find anything about a gate in Atlantis."

"Mordred already told me," Leonardo said. "We're looking into it from here."

"It will be everything he does for however long it takes," Antonio said with one of his usual warm smiles.

"Keep him out of trouble," I whispered to Antonio.

"I'm not bloody *deaf*," Leonardo snapped.

I stepped through the realm gate and found myself in a dimly lit basement the size of a football field. There were dozens of people from the resistance alongside me, with many more making their way up the stairs toward what I presumed was the exit.

Jinayca walked over. She was a dwarf who had seen her people taken almost to the brink of extinction, only to lead those who remained to survive for centuries. A second dwarf stood beside her, a young female whom I'd met a few times. She was Zamek's sister, Queen Orfeda. When Orfeda and her people had learned that Zamek was alive, they'd tried to get him to take the throne. It had not gone as they'd planned. Zamek had no interest in being a king and was happy to let his sister lead the dwarves.

"Your Majesty," I said to Queen Orfeda.

"Just Orfeda will do," she said. "You are not one of my subjects, and considering your friendship with my brother, I think we can dispense with formal speech. Unless you want me to call you Horseman Death all the time?"

"I'd rather you didn't," I said.

"So just how bad is it up there?" Selene asked.

"The White House is completely inaccessible," Jinayca said. "The human law enforcement have set up a camp in Lafayette Square, but the White House has snipers on the roof and enough firepower inside to stop anyone from a full frontal assault. The Secret Service are all human, from the best we've figured out, but Gawain is in there with some of the BOA, Blade of Avalon, and that's bad."

"And the incoming forces?" I asked as we joined the exiting group and made our way up the stairs to the outside, where the darkness of the nighttime would hopefully make our job a little easier.

"Four thousand KOA and roughly an equal number of BOA," Orfeda said. "The first group of Avalon forces are only three thousand strong, coming over the Rochambeau Memorial Bridge and Potomac River by boat. They've already engaged several groups of FBI and Secret Service, and both sides have taken heavy casualties.

There are several Special Forces units being sent to help, but it's not looking great."

"This isn't a spur-of-the-moment reaction," I said. "This was planned."

"Agreed," Orfeda said. "They may have had to move up the timetable of taking the White House—Gawain certainly didn't seem happy about it—but the number of forces heading toward the capital suggest this has been on the cards for a while."

"And the rest of the enemy?" I asked. "Where are they heading in from?"

"The majority of them are coming from the northwest through Rock Creek Park," Orfeda said. "There are maybe five thousand there. The remainder were already in the city; they have been running battles with the local law enforcement, starting fires, causing problems, keeping everyone busy. They're KOA, mostly human supporters of Arthur and Avalon."

"Where have you put the defenses?" Selene asked.

"Everything within a six-block radius of the White House is completely locked down," Jinayca said. "It's where most of the resistance members are."

"Anyone in charge at the park who we can trust?" I asked.

"A few people," Jinayca said. "Loki is there, as are Layla and her team. They've been patrolling the exclusion zone and have managed to stop several incursion attempts by the KOA. Judgement is there too. She's . . . eager to involve herself."

"I'll head off," I said. "You guys keep safe."

"The rest of your team are already heading to the exclusion zone," Orfeda said. "Good luck."

"You too," Selene said as we set off at a run toward the edge of the park.

We continued on toward Lafayette Square, making sure to stay far enough back from the White House, although it was always in our field of vision. No one was out on the street, despite it only being midnight, although there were plenty of lights on in the buildings around us. I wondered if their occupants were going to be moved away from danger or whether the city was going to be put into complete lockdown while we figured out a way to stop the streets from becoming a battleground. It had been a few hundred years since the last time Washington had been home to war, and I would rather it not happen again, considering the number of civilians who lived in the city was exponentially larger than it had been back then.

We reached Lafayette Square, where several large, heavily armed FBI agents barred our way.

"It's okay; they're with us," Loki shouted, and the guards parted before us.

A large wall had been erected across the park between the rebellion forces and the White House, and several armed agents stood behind the metal structure.

"You having a problem with snipers?" I asked Loki.

"We were," he said. "They've stopped now, but occasionally they take a shot at the wall there and see what happens."

There were maybe a hundred personnel in the park. Several tents had been put up, and Loki took us both into the nearest one, where the few dozen people inside wore bulletproof vests with various acronyms on them. The FBI seemed to be in the majority, although there were more than a few Secret Service members there too.

I recognized a man at the end of the map-covered table and smiled. "Roberto Cortez?" I asked. "Is that you?"

Roberto shook my hand. He was a little under six feet tall and appeared to be in his early fifties, although in truth he was hundreds of years older than that. Roberto was a shape-shifter and had been placed in Washington for a long time. Every now and again, he'd modify his appearance slightly and change jobs. He'd been put here to keep an eye on those in charge, although like everyone else, I doubted he'd expected Arthur to return and become a tyrant.

"It's been a while, Nate," Roberto said.

I introduced him to Selene, who looked up from one of the maps at the table and shook his hand. "You worked with Nate when he was at Avalon?" she asked.

"I don't think anyone really worked *with* Nate," Roberto said. "He wasn't exactly someone who toed the company line, so to speak."

"I'm shocked," Selene said, giving me a mocking grin.

"Come with me; we need to talk," Roberto said, suddenly serious.

"Who is everyone in there?" I asked when we left the tent.

"Members of the military, several senators, high-ranking members of the FBI, Secret Service, and the CIA director. The shit has well and truly hit the fan."

"And what is the press doing?" Selene asked.

"Well, the press are divided between trying to give information, keep ratings, and in a few cases kissing Avalon ass because they're hedging their bets. We're keeping the ones we trust informed, and the ones we don't trust will just make shit up no matter what we tell them. We do a citywide broadcast to tell people to stay inside and quiet. We've got people going door to door to make sure that civilians are safe, but it's a hard job."

I looked up at the full moon. The cold was creeping in, and I wondered if it might start to snow soon. That wouldn't help matters at all.

"Nate," Roberto said.

"I'm listening," I said, looking back at him. I followed him into a large tent, where two dozen men and women stood around a large table.

"The president and his family—wife, three kids—are hostages," a stern-looking man in a blue uniform said. "They are our main priority for extraction."

"And everyone else?" I asked.

"The president first," the man said.

"Yeah, we're going to at least try to get everyone out," I told him. "There's no ifs, ands, or buts here. Gawain is in there with highly trained members of Avalon and several of your own people. If we get the president out and leave the others, it'll be a bloodbath. We go in, get everyone, shut this shit down, and leave."

Everyone started yelling—mostly at me—which I ignored as I looked over at Roberto. "You know we can do this," I said.

Roberto nodded as everyone quieted down.

"As good as your people are," I said to the various officials in the tent, "those people in there have powers. You need powers to face them. Guns won't be enough."

My team and I left the tent with Roberto walking beside us.

"There are at least four snipers on the roof," Roberto told us, pointing to where the snipers looked to be situated. "They'd already killed six agents before we put up those shields. At least twenty Secret Service inside are working for Avalon. Maybe a hundred personnel overall."

Roberto went on. "They've executed two senators and a member of Congress since they took control. And that was after killing a dozen police officers who tried to intervene."

"This doesn't bode well for getting all of those hostages out alive," I said.

"No," Roberto said. "No, it doesn't. It might help to know that the security feed inside the White House was shut down by several members of staff as the building was taken. They got word to us; it makes entry a little easier without them having eyes all over the place, but we lost two good people getting it done. Gawain contacted us directly to let us hear them die."

"I'm sorry," I said.

"What's a good guess for the number of hostages to make it out in one piece?" Selene asked.

"A front assault is zero," Roberto said. "A stealth assault, maybe half. There's no good end to this, Nate."

I looked beyond the trees and wall to the White House. "How about an army of one?" I asked.

"You're going to go in alone?" Roberto asked me.

I shrugged. "Thinking about it."

"That's insane," he said. Someone from the tent waved him over, and Roberto left Selene and me alone.

"You're not really thinking about doing that, are you?" Selene asked me with a frown.

I shook my head. "People are going to die here, no matter what we do."

"Yes," Selene said. "It looks unavoidable."

"We need intel as to what's happening in the White House," I said. "Or at least above it. You think you can scout it without anyone shooting at you?"

Selene transformed into her dragon-kin form. Her massive silver wings beat once, and she took high to the skies at a speed I could barely track. Her vision thousands of feet in the sky was better than a hawk's. Only it was Avalon members who were the tiny mice scurrying for safety.

"Nate Garrett," a voice said from behind me.

I turned and saw Layla Cassidy. Her blue-and-green hair was up in a ponytail, and she'd lost one arm just below the elbow in a battle a few years back. Thankfully she was able to manipulate metal, so she'd made herself a new arm. I smiled. It had been a while since I'd first seen her as a new umbra, a woman with no idea of the power she possessed. Now, several years later, Layla was a formidable warrior capable of great power.

She hugged me and stepped back. "So you're here to make things go boom?"

"Well, you all seem to suck at it, so they brought in an expert," I said. "Nice wall, by the way."

"We can't all be sorcerers," Layla said. "Some of us have to work to get our power."

I laughed.

"So I guess my team and I are going to be making sure no one starts a war in the blocks around here," Layla said. "I get the feeling it's going to be a full-time job."

"There's a large force coming from the north, so I hear," I said. "I would imagine they've sent several smaller groups into the city. But you look geared up already."

Layla wore black leather armor that was rune scribed to stop magic, or at least slow it down. A sword sat in the scabbard at her back, and a large saber-tooth panther covered in armor padded over beside her. Tego was the size of a small horse and was inseparable from Layla. She did let me scratch her behind the ear, though.

"She likes you," Layla said.

"She likes being scratched," I told her.

Tego snorted. She was able to understand us, but no one was quite sure just how smart she really was. All anyone needed to know was that human-level intelligence in an animal that could tear apart an adult elephant was probably not something you'd want to piss off.

"You think we can all get through this in one piece?" Layla asked.

I nodded. "I have to; otherwise I'd just curl up in a ball. Astrid needs a better future for when she's older. Arthur needs to be stopped. People need to be able to live their lives without fear of persecution. And Gawain needs to die, because he's a massive asshole."

"Can't dis—" Layla started just as an explosion somewhere in the blocks surrounding us caused everyone to stop and look over.

"Be careful," Layla said.

"You too," I said as she ran off. "Keep her safe, Tego," I told the panther, who licked my hand and chased after Layla.

Selene landed beside me, making me jump a little. "There's fighting further out. It's getting bad. The National Guard are out there, but they're humans fighting against giants and werewolves; it's not going to end well."

I looked over at the White House. "How bad is it?"

"Four snipers, four spotters. One took a shot at me, but I was too high, and it was an easy avoid. There are rockets up there, too, and from my thermal vision, it looks like a lot of people moving around inside. Can't see too deep through; the walls are too thick."

I sighed. "It's going to be a long night."

"Yes, it is," Selene said, taking my hand in hers. "But we'll get through it."

I kissed her. "I'm going to kill Gawain and anyone supporting him, even if I have to tear down the entire building to do it."

Chapter Five

Layla Cassidy

Washington, DC, United States, Earth Realm

Layla had been preparing for a fight from the second she'd landed in Washington with her team. She'd fought Avalon in different realms countless times, but the end result was always the same: innocent casualties on a grand scale. Avalon's forces simply didn't care if civilians were in the way; they considered them fair game.

Layla's team consisted of people she'd known for a long time. Chloe and her wife, Piper, were both umbra. After Tego, there was Tarron, who had been keen to get back to fighting on solid ground after his exploits on the ship.

The final member of her team was the one who was the keenest to fight: Judgement. Since being discovered in Valhalla a year ago, she'd been relentless in her need to find her sister Athena, who'd gone missing on a scouting mission. Usually that involved killing as many Avalon soldiers as she could find.

The team ran through the deserted streets of Washington, DC, toward a raging inferno that used to be a restaurant. They were four blocks away from the White House, and the sounds of sirens could be heard in the distance.

"Judgement," Layla shouted.

"On it," Judgement replied as water magic poured from her hands into the burning building. She was the daughter of Zeus and the Lady of the Lake, Nineve. Both of her parents had been murdered by Avalon, so Judgement had a pretty big reason to want to deliver that pain back tenfold.

A fire truck sped toward them down the street. "Looks like the professionals are here," Piper said.

Then came a sound that Layla couldn't quite make out followed by a rocket streaking down from one of the rooftops. Layla tried to reach out to take control of it, but it moved too fast, and she couldn't stop it from smashing into the fire truck. The truck exploded in a ball of fire.

"I'll help Judgement," Piper shouted, waving everyone else on.

Layla and Chloe sprinted toward the building where the rocket had originated, but Tarron reached the door before them. He pushed through and took the steps two at a time—Layla and Chloe right behind him—as they sprinted up four flights of stairs to the roof, where Chloe simply kicked the door open, ripping it from its hinges and sending it bouncing across the rooftop.

Chloe and Layla moved around Tarron as several people on the roof opened fire. Their bullets slammed into the three-foot brick wall near a giant air-conditioning unit that Layla's team dropped behind.

"Your hat got hit," Chloe said to Tarron as another round of bullets slammed into the wall. He still wore his long black coat and the black cowboy hat he had started to wear.

Tarron removed his hat and looked at the hole just above where his scalp would have been. "Damn," he said softly.

Layla reached out with her power and took hold of the metal in the guns, tearing them apart. She would have thrown the metal back at the attackers, but they really needed one alive, and as she couldn't see them, she couldn't be sure of not killing them all.

Layla stepped out from behind the wall as Chloe sprinted toward the closest of the five. He saw her and raised his hands to defend against the incoming punch, but Chloe absorbed kinetic energy, turning it into blasts of pure power or enhancing a part of her. Namely her strength. The crunch of the man's arm as it shattered from the blow was nothing compared to the scream of pain that left his mouth a second later. She kicked him in the chest, and he flew off the side of the roof.

Chloe had already taken out the second attacker when Layla threw the metal she'd gathered at two more. One tried to escape, but he ran straight into Judgement, who picked him up by his throat and tossed him across the roof as if he were a tennis ball. His head bounced off the ground before he lay still and didn't move.

A few seconds later, the three who remained alive were tied up using the metal from the guns.

Layla peered over the roof ledge and saw Tego and Piper waiting below.

"Tarron, can you take two of these down to the ground, please?" Layla asked.

Tarron picked one up in each hand and walked off the edge of the roof, the prisoners screaming the whole way down. The sound ended with a crunch as Tarron landed on the sidewalk below.

Layla smiled as she looked over the edge of the roof. Tarron had placed multiple elven runes inside his clothes, and while he couldn't keep jumping off roofs forever, they did allow him to absorb such energy and redirect it, presumably into the now-totaled car that he'd landed on.

The final prisoner maintained his resolute glare at Layla and Chloe.

"I guess this one is the tough guy," Chloe said, crouching beside him. "So you murdered a bunch of firefighters; you must feel like a *big* man."

"If you are not with us, you are against us," the man said without turning to look at Chloe.

"You all KOA?" Layla asked.

The man continued to stare ahead.

"Chloe, can you go help Tarron?" Layla said. "Between the two of you, I'm sure you can get someone to talk about any other reinforcements."

When Layla was alone with the final KOA member, she sat down in front of him. "We know that you're coming in from the north," she said. "We know that you've sent small groups into the city to cause problems. We know that you're here to kill and maim and cause terror. You are *not* a hero; you are *not* the good guys. You are thugs and bullies, and I was born in this country, and I will die before I let you take it from the people who get up every single day and fight and struggle and love being here."

"That's the plan," the man said with a smirk.

Layla tore metal from the roof all around her and snaked it around his body. "No," she said softly. "The plan is that I'm going to kill any of you that I find. I'm done playing. I'm done trying to find a way through this mess where we can heal the wounds that you've all caused. You want to know how we heal the wounds? We cut out the cancer." She tightened the metal, turning the edges sharp so that they cut into the KOA soldier's flesh.

"You're insane," he screamed.

Layla put her face right up against him. "No, I'm angry," she whispered and tightened the metal whip further.

"We have incursions by several small teams," he blurted out.

"I know," Layla said, not moving her face. "What are they targeting?"

He yelled out again. "Police stations, hospitals—any infrastructure where people might go for help."

"Hospitals?" Layla asked, releasing the pressure on the whip. "There's an emergency room near here. Is that one of them?"

"The George Washington University Hospital," the man gasped. "The emergency room is a target."

Layla moved the whip away from the KOA member, allowing it to move back and forth like a cobra ready to strike.

"Why?"

"Fear and panic," he said. "The peons of this country need to understand who they owe their allegiance to. Arthur is the true ruler of this planet, and everyone on it is alive because he allows them to be. We are honor bound to ensure Arthur achieves his goals."

"The KOA are a bunch of fascist thugs," Layla said with a sneer. "There's nothing honorable about you. You're just murderers and thieves, people who use their power to hurt others. Well, see how you like it."

The metal snake moved forward at incredible speed, slamming into the eye of the KOA member and punching out the back of his head. Layla stepped off the side of the building, using the metal from the roof to create stairs as she walked.

"Your commander is dead," Layla said to the two surviving members of the KOA kill team. "Your troops are about to attack a civilian hospital emergency department. You have betrayed your own kind for the promise of power."

"Arthur is our salvation," one of them shouted.

"I hope you meet him, then," Chloe said as they heard sirens coming toward them. "I hope whoever comes for you treats you as well as you treated the innocent people you murdered tonight."

One of them tried to run away, but Tarron threw a small dagger at the back of his head, killing him before he'd taken more than a few steps.

"There was a time when that would have been abhorrent," Layla said. "How far over the line I've come. We've all come."

Piper placed a reassuring hand on Layla's shoulder as a police cruiser pulled up, followed by a military APC. Several soldiers left the APC, the commander coming over to speak to Layla, who told him everything they'd discovered. They moved on toward the hospital, and Layla hoped they could overcome the forces there. She would make sure to check soon.

"Warfare in my own city," one of the cops said, shaking Layla's hand.

"It's not been a great night," Layla said. "This one is the only surviving member of the team who murdered the firefighters and presumably started the fire."

One of the policemen dragged him to his feet. "Arthur will rule over all," the man said, elbowing the cop in the face and going for his gun.

Chloe was the closest to him, and she placed a hand on the man's chest and expelled a measure of the kinetic energy inside of her. He bounced off the road ten feet back and impacted with a burned-out car outside the restaurant.

"Thank you," the younger of the two officers said.

"Keep safe," Chloe said, and Layla nodded toward the older officer before the team moved on. "The police aren't going to be much help when those who aren't human turn up."

"No," Layla replied. "But they'll do what they can. With any luck that means some people will be saved. And we'll do what we can and hopefully help."

"You really think they can retake the White House without hostage casualties?" Piper asked.

"No," Chloe said. "I think they'll try, and people will still die, because Gawain and his cronies just simply don't care."

Layla didn't say anything, but she felt the same way. In the last year, she'd been to villages around the globe that Avalon had reached first, and she'd found the total devastation of everyone and everything that had once been there. If they didn't surrender and join Avalon, they were expendable—it was as simple as that. Gawain was a butcher of men, women, and children. A monster.

They walked another block and were passing by an alleyway when they spotted several people huddled inside. They turned and started down it, Tego taking point, with Chloe behind them. It was a good spot for an ambush, but Layla was pretty sure that the people inside the alley weren't there to hurt anyone.

"You shouldn't be here," Chloe said as the six adults inside the alley huddled behind a large dumpster.

"We ain't got nowhere else to go," one of them, an elderly man with a large white beard, said, his eyes fixed nervously on Tego. "We tried to get into a shelter, but they're full."

"If Avalon find you, they will hurt you," Layla said.

"They don't scare me," a middle-aged woman said grimly. "Just bullies. And I've dealt with bullies my whole life."

"These bullies will ensure whatever they do hurts," Tarron said.

Judgement stepped forward. "You are not safe here," she said, her voice calm. It was the most words Layla had heard from her in one sentence for several hours.

"Then where do you suggest we should go?" a younger man asked hopelessly, his knees pulled up to his chest.

Layla looked around the alleyway and saw a metal fire door further along. Approaching, she took control of the lock and forced the door open before stepping inside.

"Anyone home?" she shouted, looking around the abandoned restaurant. Tables had been left untouched; Layla assumed that everyone who had been here at the time of the cordon had been told to evacuate quickly. She found the register, took a piece of paper and pen, and wrote, *People needed shelter. If they used anything, contact Roberto Cortez.* She wrote his phone number below. Roberto would forgive her.

She found everyone still outside and explained about the restaurant.

"What if the people who own it come back?" the lady asked.

"I left them a note," Layla told her. "Also, just stay there for tonight. I'll make sure the police know you're there, and hopefully it will be okay. Basically, don't have some sort of mass party, and it should be fine. It's safer than staying out here."

"You did a good thing," Judgement said when those in the alleyway had moved into the restaurant.

"I try," Layla said. "You okay?"

Judgement smiled fiercely. "I want to rip and tear," she said, flexing her fingers. "I want to find my sister. I am angry. I wish to hurt a great number of our enemy."

"You'll get your chance," Layla said. "We all will."

"I am not used to working in a team," Judgement said. "I was trained to kill alone. It is an odd feeling, but not an unpleasant one."

Chloe exited the restaurant with her finger against her ear, activating her radio. Everyone wore one, but they were mainly used for communication between team members. Unless an outside person contacted one of them personally.

"Persephone wants to know if we can move toward Georgetown," Chloe said. "There's fierce fighting there, and the KOA are trying to gain entry to an apartment block. It'll be a massacre if they get inside."

"Who's protecting it?" Piper asked.

"There's a number of rebellion members on the way, but it looks like this is another KOA splinter group. The people living there are protecting their homes, but they're outmanned and outgunned."

"How do we get there quickly?" Layla asked.

"Persephone is sending an armored personnel carrier to take us," Chloe said.

Thirty seconds later the dark-green APC arrived, and everyone piled in the back. The female driver and male passenger told them they'd heard that the assault on the residential block in Georgetown sounded bad, but then everything Layla had seen had sounded bad, so the definition of awful had swung wildly.

Layla heard the gunfire well before she saw anything of the assault on the three seven-story buildings, which were set in a horseshoe pattern. The actual number of assailants appeared to be small, certainly much lower than Layla had expected, and they were hunkered down behind large SUVs while several people inside shot at them from the windows high above.

The driver stopped the APC and used the attached microphone to demand that all KOA members surrender and relinquish their weapons. The shooting stopped inside the building as three KOA dropped their guns and stood, arms up high, while several more made a run for it down the dark streets.

Layla and her team got out of the APC and apprehended the KOA members before taking them to the apartment complex, where they were greeted by three uniformed police officers—a man and two women. One of the women was bleeding from a head wound, and Piper sat her down inside the foyer to assess the damage.

Layla turned back to the APC. "Park up and get in here," she said.

The two soldiers did, then joined the team, police, and half dozen civilians who had congregated in the foyer. Layla was trying to block them out, as they were all talking at once.

"Right," Chloe said, with more than a little irritation in her voice. "Everyone needs to shut up. You're all talking at once, and we need to get organized."

An elderly woman opened her mouth to say something, and Tego let out a slow growl, so she immediately closed it again.

"Residents, back to wherever you were," Judgement shouted. "We'll come talk to you soon."

The uninjured female police officer took everyone away, while Piper continued to work on the officer with the head wound.

"Got hit with glass," the officer said.

"I need some tweezers," Piper said. "A medical kit. This needs stitches."

"We've got some upstairs," the male officer said.

Everyone went to the next floor, where there was a foyer that was smaller but similarly decorated to the lobby below.

"What happened?" Layla asked.

"KOA," the female officer said as Piper opened a medical kit and started removing the items she needed.

"You can hear the explosions from further north," the male officer said. "A lot of people are scared. We took residents from this entire block into this building, as it's the easiest to defend."

Layla nodded and looked out of the window. It was good to defend, plenty of visibility to the sidewalk, and if they had snipers on high floors in all three buildings, anything below was a kill zone.

"Is there any way for me to get into that adjacent building from here?" Layla asked.

A middle-aged man with a bandage on his arm stepped forward from the rapidly increasing crowd that had gathered at the edge of the foyer. "You can get across from the roof," he said. "I'm the caretaker for these buildings."

"Show me," she said. "Judgement, you want to come?"

Judgement nodded.

Chloe joined them, and along with the uninjured female officer and the driver of the APC, they ran through the building to the maintenance elevator, took it to the top floor, and then used the caretaker's keys to open the door to the roof.

Layla smelled burning the second the door opened. She knew it was in the distance, but it was strong enough to carry through the air.

"Is this locked all the time?" Judgement asked as everyone arrived on the roof.

"All residents have their own key to the roof," the caretaker said, pointing to several separate gardens that adorned the rooftop. "They like to come up here and relax."

"But you need two different keys to get from this building into another?" Layla asked.

The caretaker nodded.

Layla walked to the edge of the roof and looked down at the two-foot gap between buildings. Someone had built a small metal bridge across it.

"The residents wanted to be able to talk to others without having to jump," the caretaker said with a smile.

Layla crossed the span and ran to the edge of the other building, looking down over the sidewalk below. It was still empty, but the fires in the distance were getting closer.

"They're burning it all," the cop said in horror.

Layla nodded.

"It's not the tactic I'd have employed," Judgement said. "The problem with burning everything as you go is that you can't retreat through fire if you encounter resistance. And there's nowhere to hole up and regroup. They clearly don't expect to be forced back."

"They're heading this way," Layla said as there was a ping in her ear. She tapped the communication device.

"Layla," Jinayca said.

"Jinayca," Layla said with a smile. "I'd love to chat, but I think we're about to have company."

"That's why I called," Jinayca said. "I'm working at the base in Lafayette Square; we have satellite images of the bastards heading your way. Layla, this is a big group. Maybe a thousand KOA. All heavily armed. They're dragging people from their homes and executing them in the streets."

"They need to be stopped, then," Layla said.

"We're sending reinforcements your way," Jinayca said. "But the KOA will be on your doorstep before they get there."

"Thanks for the info, Jinayca," Layla said.

"Take care, Layla," she said, and the comms went dead.

"How bad is it?" the APC driver asked.

"How many weapons do you have in that vehicle of yours?" Layla asked.

"A few rifles, pistols, a sniper rifle . . . bits and pieces," the driver said.

"Good, we're going to need *all* of it. We need all of these doors boarded up and that APC positioned down there. I want anyone who knows how to shoot up here targeting these assholes when they come."

"We're going to kill them?" the cop asked.

Layla nodded. "That's the plan, yes."

The cop nodded.

"Good," Layla said. "Let's get this place locked down and make these assholes regret coming here."

Chapter Six

NATE GARRETT

Washington, DC, United States, Earth Realm

There was a lot of running around. Reports were coming in that KOA to the north were executing civilians, and while I desperately wanted to join those fighting against them, I elected to stay and deal with Gawain.

Leaning up against the corner of the metal wall, I looked toward the White House. I'd constructed a shield of dense air a meter in front of me, just in case any of the snipers decided to try their luck.

"I assume that you're trying to piss them off," Roberto said from behind me.

"I'm just trying to figure out the best way to get from here to that building without anyone dying," I said without looking back. "It's not exactly an easy spot. I assume the tunnels are a no go."

"They blew them the second they took the building. Lots of C4 down there too. Even if we could get the tunnels clear, there are too many booby traps to do it safely."

I looked back around the wall. The lights in the garden and around the White House exterior had been turned off, leaving only those inside the structure on.

A bullet smashed into the shield of air I'd placed between the pieces of metal wall, only a few feet in front of Roberto. There was a crack as the sound of the shot registered, and people threw themselves to the ground while I plucked the bullet from where it hovered in midair.

"Good shot," Roberto said.

A second bullet smashed into the shield of air, two feet away from my head.

"Nate," Selene said from beside me. "Stop winding up the sniper."

I took a step behind the wall, and Roberto passed me a map of the interior of the White House, which I studied for a second and then passed back to him.

"Do you have a plan?" Selene asked.

"Sort of," I said. "I need you to get the rest of the team together. No sorcerers."

Selene stared at me for a second before nodding and heading back into the camp.

"What do you need?" Roberto asked.

"You see those big powerful lights that you've got aimed out around the park?"

Roberto nodded. "I think I know where this is going. I'll be back in a minute."

A few minutes later, Selene returned with Zamek, Remy, Sky, Diana, and Kase, the latter of whom was beginning to concern me, as she hadn't given herself a break in a year.

"Good to see you," I said to Sky. "It's been a while."

"Yeah, yeah," she said with a smile. "Let's go be heroes."

"That's the plan," I said.

"I have a question for you," Sky said. "Haven't seen you in a while, but what happened to the blood magic?"

"I've been meaning to ask that myself," Remy said. "I heard it came back after Portland, but you didn't use it on the ship."

"Didn't use it in Asgard either," Diana said.

"It's fading," I told them. "I don't like to use it. Don't like to rely on it. It's too weak to be a serious threat to anyone, and I assume one day it'll be gone completely. I can't even use it to power my magic for more than a few seconds. I'd rather not use it than rely on it. I figured that was what was going to happen seeing as that's what happened the first time my necromancy reared its head, but thank you all for your concern."

"Not concern," Remy said. "Just wanted to know if you were going to go all blood magic crazed if you kept using it."

"Thank you for your concern for yourself," I said to Remy, who gave me a thumbs-up.

Roberto returned. "There will be a lot of light flooding the White House lawn. Can't do it for long, but it should be enough."

"Oh bollocks," Diana whispered. "I don't want to do this."

"What are we doing?" Sky asked.

"The shadow thing?" Remy asked with a sigh. "This sucks monstrous amounts of ass."

"Can't Selene fly us over there?" Diana asked.

"Not all of you, I can't," she said. "And if I take out those on the roof and Gawain radios them with no contact, that's probably some dead hostages. As much as this sucks—and my God, it sucks—it's probably the safest way forward."

"It could be a trap," Remy said. "We go in and get grabbed."

"I do not think they would like to grab me," Kase said softly.

The shadows leaped up from the ground, and my team and I sank through them into the shadow realm.

"I hope none of you have a gun with silver bullets; the wraith doesn't like it," I said.

"I hate this," Diana said.

The realm consisted of darkness everywhere except for circles of light every few dozen feet, until they were only pinpricks of light in the far distance. Each circle corresponded with a shadow that I could use to come back into the realm above. The circles of light were small, though, and none of them were where I needed to be.

"Remind me," Remy said. "You can tell where these beams-of-light things take us back up to, yes?"

I nodded.

There were movements in the darkness. My wraith, who lived in the shadow realm and feasted upon those I sent down here, was prowling just beyond our field of vision.

"And that thing isn't going to kill us?" Remy asked suspiciously.

"Not while I'm here," I said.

The wraith passed through one of the beams of light, which illuminated the dark, shadowlike ropes that covered the skeletal appearance beneath.

"I feel blind down here," Diana said. "There is no smell. No sound, except for the movement of your wraith."

"Would it help if I told you, you get used to it?" I asked.

"No," Diana and Remy said in unison.

All at once the number of light circles quadrupled, and a flood of knowledge entered my head telling me where each light would return us.

"You should know that we have to go out and back in again," I said. My destination was one of the far pinpricks, something I couldn't reach in one jump. The furthest I'd gone in a single jump was about fifty feet; any more than that was impossible, it seemed.

I couldn't just walk from one pinprick to another, so I had to drag the next exit over to us, exit the shadow realm, and go back inside. Over and over.

"How many times?" Zamek asked.

"About six," I said. "Give or take. It's about a hundred meters from where we were to where we need to be."

No one looked particularly thrilled at that news.

I moved one of the circles of light toward us, ensuring that we were never in the darkness. Even I wouldn't be able to stop the wraith attacking people if they left the safety of the light. We popped out of the shadows behind a large tree and immediately sank again. We did this three more times. By the third, it was starting to take its toll on me.

"Damn it," I said, blinking as we all arrived in the shadow realm again.

"Two more?" Selene asked. "You okay?"

I was sweating and a little bit shaky as I took us out of the shadows for a fifth time and dragged us all back down into the shadow realm again immediately after. Several of the team looked unwell as I dropped to my knees. I'd never tried to move so many people so far before.

Selene knelt before me and took my hands in hers. "You can do this," she whispered.

"The last jump will put us all on the roof," I said, pointing to the circle of light. With Selene's and Sky's help, I got back to my feet. I tried to bring the shadows toward me, but I couldn't control them enough and ended up bringing three at once. They crossed over one another as everyone but me vanished.

I had no way of knowing where any of my team were. All I knew was that they were either on the roof or inside the White House. The circles of light sprang away from me, leaving me stranded as they began to fade. I got to my feet, stepped out of the light, and walked through the darkness to the nearest circle.

The wraith appeared beside me, its robes passing over the exposed skin on my arms, making them go cold.

"I am not food," I said, turning to the wraith, who towered above me. "You know this."

The wraith bent down toward me. "You are exhausted."

I nodded. "Still have to leave this place," I said. "I can't very well live here."

"Feed me soon," the wraith said again. Its breath smelled of nothing, but it was as if a fan of warm air were aimed directly at me.

"That's the plan," I told it.

It reached out and tapped me on my chest. "Rage hidden. I see it. I see all. Can't hide forever. I will protect you when the time comes."

I stared at the void where the wraith's eyes should have been. Occasionally there was a flickering of orange-and-red light, as if a fire were being smothered.

I looked down at the ground and back up at the wraith. "You'll get your food," I told it before walking into the light and ending up inside a room in the White House.

I looked out of the window at the lawn beyond. The light that Roberto had supplied was being switched off. There were over 130 rooms in the White House, and I had no idea which this was. I was near the door, and there were books stacked all around the room, like a small, untidy library.

The room was well lit, and there were several uncomfortable-looking chairs that had been placed around a coffee table. I opened the door slightly to a familiar place—the lobby. I'd ended up in the East Wing entrance. I heard two voices at the end of the lobby and stepped out of the room. I threw daggers of air at the lights adorning the walls, which got the attention of the two men, although the shadows that snaked out of the group, encircled them, and dragged them into the shadow realm were a surprise to them.

I sank into the shadow realm, only to hear the screams of one of the men as the wraith attacked. The other stood in the middle of a circle of light, firing wildly all around him. I grabbed his wrist and disarmed him before tossing the gun aside. It vanished from view as it left the shadow realm.

"What's out there?" the man demanded.

"Something hungry," I told him, punching him in the face and knocking him to the ground. I felt the swell of power as the second man was devoured somewhere in the darkness. "It will kill you unless I stop it."

"Stop it!" the man pleaded.

"Not yet," I told him. "First, you're going to tell me everything I need to know about the hostages and those working with Avalon."

"The hostages are kept in three places," he stammered. "State Dining Room, Yellow Oval Room, and the Solarium."

"Nicely spaced out," I said. "How many guarding each?"

"Half a dozen for the first two," he said. "The hostages are all humans, so the Secret Service and military contractors brought in are doing that."

Military contractors? I thought, making a note to come back to it. "And the last set?"

"Avalon personnel," he said. "There are nonhumans in the group up there. They had people draw runes in the Solarium a few years ago. Gawain said he was afraid that people would come for him, and he wanted equal ground."

"I'm sure it was *all* his idea," I said sarcastically. "And these military contractors?"

"They were brought in to work alongside those in the White House," he said. "They were planted as cleaners, cooks, people who worked in admin. They're highly trained, and they've killed already. The president is in the Solarium, his family up there too."

"How many dead?"

"A dozen," he said. "The initial takeover was bloody. That wasn't the plan—it was meant to be cool and calm, but the schedule got moved up."

"Gawain?"

"Yes, him," he said, looking around as the wraith patrolled around the light.

"Where is he?"

"Oval Office."

"How many did you kill?" I asked him.

"What?"

"How. Many."

"None, I swear," he said pleadingly.

He was lying.

"Make it quick," I told the wraith, and I heard the sounds of the agent's cries as I stepped out of the shadow realm. A second later there was another shudder of power. I was beginning to feel normal again. I was pretty sure all the power would be needed to confront Gawain.

After opening the door, I ran down the East Colonnade and stopped at the door to listen for anyone inside the visitors' foyer beyond. None of the hostages were in the East or West Wing, so I didn't have to run all over the premises to find them.

I heard nothing inside the main foyer and opened the door, revealing several dead bodies at the base of the stairs. They all wore the uniforms of Secret Service, suggesting that they had stood against Avalon. They'd paid the ultimate price for doing their jobs.

The door to the library beside me burst open, and Remy, Sky, and Selene exited, ready for battle. They all stopped once they recognized me.

"You okay?" Selene asked.

I nodded. "Tired but good." I explained where the hostages were.

"So we need to split up?" Sky said.

"And find Zamek, Diana, and Kase," Remy said. "I think Kase might be on the edge of becoming murderous and slaughtering everyone who annoys her. Her dad's loss is really affecting her."

"She'll be fine," I said, remembering that Kase hadn't even spoken when we were sorting out the assault on the White House. Tommy being missing was causing us all anguish.

A door further along the corridor opened, and Diana and Zamek exited the room. "We wondered where you'd all gone," Diana said as we walked over to join them. "Map room was very nice."

"No maps, though," Zamek said. "I'm honestly disappointed. On the plus side, the three thugs in there made me feel a bit better."

"Any alive?" I asked.

I got a glimpse of the bodies inside the room.

"Not unless they can live without a head," Zamek said.

"They do look pretty dead," Remy said.

The six of us all took the stairs up to the first floor, where there were no guards at all.

"Anyone else find this odd?" Selene asked.

"We'll leave the hostages until last," I said. "Search these rooms; I don't want to be ambushed."

I set off with Remy to the Green Room, where I pushed open the door to find it covered in blood. Kase stood in the middle of the room, bathed in the stuff from head to toe, her hair matted with it. She was in her human form, and as I looked around the room, I saw dismembered limbs and organs. Ice covered one wall, with at least one person beside it having been frozen before being torn in half.

"Oh fuck," Remy said from behind me.

Kase turned toward us, growling, with nothing but rage in her eyes.

"So I'm guessing this is *not* your definition of fine," Remy said to me.

Chapter Seven

Nate Garrett

"Kase, I know you're struggling right now," I said. "But we don't really have time."

Kase let out a low growl.

I turned to everyone behind me. "I've got this—go secure the hostages. Be aware of more guards."

"Why didn't they shoot?" Diana asked, looking at the dead. "Their guns are still holstered."

"I must have dumped her right in the middle of this lot," I said. "She was probably too fast. And there's nothing in this room for them to use as a weapon. Fists against a werewolf is never going to end well."

"It's all in here," Zamek said, looking through the passage from the Green to the Blue Room. "The exits on the other side into the Red Room are boarded up."

"Diana, go with him; see if you can make sure that no one tries to escape from the dining room."

Kase tracked them both as they exited through the passageway to the room beyond. Then she looked back at me, her eyes showing nothing but a need to fight. To hurt someone.

"Kase," I said softly. "Come on—I don't want to have to fight you."

"You should be looking for my *dad*," she said, her words flooded with rage.

"I don't know where he is," I told her.

"Why aren't you looking for him?" she shouted at me. "Why aren't you tearing this realm apart, tearing all the realms apart, searching for him? You're doing *nothing*."

I knew that this wasn't Kase talking; this was a year of emotion boiling over and letting out the beast inside of her. The beast only wanted to fight, to kill, and I was as good a target for that anger as anyone else. She was close to losing control, and if that happened, we were going to have a *really* big problem.

"That's not fair," Sky said from behind me.

"I don't care," Kase said. "He was meant to be my dad's best friend. And he's done *nothing*. My dad has been kidnapped, and Nate and the rest of you have gone about your day like nothing happened. Arthur has my dad." She screamed the last few words.

"You could have triggered the guards to kill the hostages," Sky said. "People could have died here."

"I landed in here," Kase said. "I lost control. I lost my temper. I didn't care about anything but hurting these people."

"Sky, go help everyone else, please," I said.

Sky looked between Kase and me before nodding and walking away.

"Why aren't you looking for him?" Kase asked.

"What am I meant to do?" I asked calmly. I didn't want to trigger her anger and give the beast more control. I needed her to calm down; I needed her to realize how close she was to losing the fight against the werewolf inside. "I don't know where he is; I don't know where Arthur or Merlin are. There's no way to get into Avalon, and the only person who might know something is Gawain. And you lost control, and now you want to pick a fight with *me*."

Kase looked around at the chaos and death she'd caused. "He's my dad," she whispered, but her voice was still angry.

"I know that, Kase. He's my friend, and I die a little every day that we can't find him. But this is a mission! You're done here," I said. "I can't risk you losing control again."

"No," Kase snapped, punching her hand through the wall.

"Yes, Kase," I said softly. "If you want to be angry at everyone for having done nothing, we'll have this conversation later. I thought that by keeping you busy, you'd keep it together, but honestly, I just think you need time away. The beast is too close to the surface; it's too close to being let loose. I can't risk that. I really hoped that the mission might help you focus, but I didn't realize just how close to the surface the beast is. You need to sit this one out."

"You can't," she said.

"I can," I told her. "I can't send you back to the base—certainly can't do it with you covered in blood. So you're going to have to stay here."

"I want to help."

"No, you want to *hurt* people, and while we are going to do that, I can't risk you running in and tearing Gawain's head off before we've even had the chance to talk to him."

Kase looked at me in a way she never had before. There was nothing but contempt in her almost wolflike eyes. The beast was gaining control.

"So I just stay here?" Kase asked.

I nodded. "Until I say otherwise, yes."

"And if I don't want to?" Kase asked, the growl in her voice rising as she took a step toward me.

"Do not push me, Kase," I said, my voice hardening a little.

The beast only knew a pecking order. The only way to stop the beast from thinking of me as prey was to make sure it damn well knew what would happen when it came out, giving Kase time to take it back under control.

"Push you?" Kase asked, taking another step. "You have left my father in the hands of Avalon. You have condemned him to torture and pain. Push. You. You have no idea what I want to do to you."

"Do not do this, Kase," I said, my voice holding more than a little anger now.

Kase shoved me in the shoulder. "Make me."

Diana appeared in the doorway. "Hostages on this floor secure. Twenty-six in total, all human. No guards out there, so I assume they didn't deem the humans dangerous enough to need more than the dead ones in this room. Thankfully Kase killed them all without a single shot, so we still have the element of stealth on our side. Still more hostages on the floors above, but it's a start. They're going to stay where they are until we're done clearing the place out." She looked between Kase and me. "Kase, I would seriously consider stepping back," Diana said.

"You don't get to tell me what to do," Kase snapped without turning away from me, her eyes now very much those of a wolf.

"Fine, but if you pick a fight with Nate, he's going to bounce your skinny ass across the White House lawn like a fucking tennis ball."

Kase remained where she was for several seconds before turning and walking away, pushing past Diana into the Blue Room.

"She's angry," Diana said.

"Yes, she is," I said. "She's angry, hurt, scared . . . and all of that has let the beast closer to the surface than we'd thought. It's not aimed at anyone in particular, but she needs to get the beast under control, or she's going to hurt a lot of people."

"I know that feeling well," Diana said sadly. "She wants a fight. The beast wants a fight even more so. You were trying to get her to swing at you, hoping you could put her down and calm the beast?"

I nodded. "Didn't work out so well, but hopefully benching her has given her time to think."

Sky entered the room from the door behind me. "Kase will calm down."

"I hope so," I said. "Because if she sees Gawain, I can't trust that she won't kill him. Or try to and have to be stopped."

"I'll stay with her," Diana said. "Send any hostages you find back down this way, and I'll make sure they're all kept in one place and that they stay away from the death room here." I thanked her and left Diana to deal with an angry and scared werewolf.

"I hope we get information about Tommy from Gawain too," Selene said, having returned from her search of the nearby rooms.

I nodded. The alternative didn't bear thinking about.

Zamek walked back into the room. "Found two wards," he said. "Both simple stuff—a child could do them—but they contained a great deal of power. They're disarmed, but let's not be thinking they're the only ones."

"Remy, Selene—with me," I said as everyone gathered outside the Blue Room. "We're going to take these stairs on the left. The rest of you on the right. The remaining hostages are in the Yellow Oval Room, and we have no idea just how bad it's going to be up there. Stay in contact; let us know when you're in position."

We split into two teams and made our way up each staircase to the floor above. Voices could be heard before we'd reached the top of the stairs. I reached out with my air magic, slowly moving it out of the stairwell and across the second-floor hall. The number of rooms up here was larger than the first floor, so there were more places for enemies to hide and wait to ambush us. While Roberto had told us that the internal security systems had been stopped, my main concern was the eight guards between us and the hostages. We had no way of knowing exactly *what* those eight guards were.

"We're in position," Sky said through my earpiece. "Any chance we know what we're up against?"

"Not a clue," I said. "We've been lucky so far, but I doubt that we're going to be able to take out those above us quietly. The ones here were guarding people they didn't deem a threat; they were stupid. Let's not assume all of them are."

"I have a suggestion," Remy said. "Nate goes up to the third floor; we deal with these assholes on the second floor."

"As I just said, there's a good chance Gawain has put some more wards up there," Zamek said. "A very good chance."

I looked over at Remy. "And you want me to go up there alone?"

"You can make as much noise as you like up there, Nate," Remy whispered. "We'll be dealing with these guys. You only have to keep them busy—or kill them all, depending on what you think is best."

"I'm hesitant to say that Remy has a good idea, but apparently that's the world we now live in," Zamek said.

"Something about dogs and cats living together and mass hysteria," Selene said.

I smiled. "You going all film geek on me?"

"You know you love that film," she said. "Besides, it felt apt. Anyway, we don't have all day. Pick a plan."

I sighed. "I'll see you guys back down here. I'll keep going."

Selene looked over at me and winked. "Just be you, and it'll be fine," she said with a smile.

I moved around the top of the stairs and continued on up. It wasn't that I was worried about what I'd face—I'd been up against superior numbers before—it was more about trying very hard not to do anything that might jeopardize the hostages. If a stray bolt of lightning hit a ward, it could explode and take half the floor with it. Trying not to get innocent people killed always made things harder, I'd found.

I reached the top of the stairs and pushed out air once again to sense my surroundings. Four people in the hallway beyond. I was going to have to be quick. One of them had a dagger of ice in his hand and was spinning it up into the air and catching it again. A sorcerer. At least that confirmed these were the bad guys.

I tapped my earpiece. "Ready when you are," I said.

"Go," Selene said.

I rushed out of the stairwell, straight into a man dressed in combat fatigues. The shock on his face lasted only a second before I drove a blade of lightning into his chest and detonated the magic inside him, turning his internal organs into paste. I removed his head as he fell forward, just in case. Not everything could be killed by magic, but pretty much everything died when decapitated.

I continued on, toward the sorcerer with the daggers of ice. He threw one at me, and I raised a shield of fire, pushing it out toward him, forcing him to move aside. Then a blast of air magic hit him in the chest, sending him back through the wall behind him.

Two more came at me, one turning into her werewolf form and the second sending a plume of fire at me that I had to wrap myself in a shield of air to avoid.

After throwing a ball of lightning at the werewolf, I detonated it with a snap of my fingers, causing her to dive into a nearby room to evade the blast. It hit the flame elemental in the ribs, taking him off his feet and dumping him in the room beyond the broken wall where his friend had been thrown.

The sounds of gunshots below distracted me for a split second, just as the werewolf let out a roar and charged, her razor-sharp claws dragging through my shield of air like it was paper. She was clearly much more powerful than a regular werewolf, and that meant that decapitating her might not actually kill her. Powerful werewolves were weird like that.

She swiped at me with a claw; I moved aside, smashing a lightning-wrapped elbow into her ribs, then hitting her in the jaw with an uppercut. I detonated the lightning magic wrapped around my fist, and it tore up through her face, destroying part of the ceiling above. A blast of air sent the werewolf flying back, and I turned the air into a whip and snapped it shut around her legs. I heard bone snap before she screamed.

Ice and flame poured out of the hole in the wall where I'd thrown the sorcerer and elemental. I covered myself in a shield of air and sank into my shadow realm, found the correct shadow to leave from, and ended up behind them. The shadows leaped up from the ground around the elemental, who screamed, throwing balls of fire at the darkness, which caused me pain as it retreated.

The sorcerer saw his opening and darted forward, but tendrils of shadow leaped out of the ground, wrapping around his arms and throat. I stabbed him in the head with one of my soul weapons—manifestations of my necromancy power. In this case a jian, a weapon that had meant a lot to me when I'd first been given it centuries ago.

The sorcerer died with a blade of fire to his temple.

The elemental hurled fire at me, and I wrapped myself in a shield of flame, walked through it, and created a sphere of air that I drove into his chest and detonated, throwing him to the floor. The shadows leaped out of the ground and pulled the semiconscious elemental into the shadow realm as I walked toward the werewolf, who was struggling back to her feet. I removed her head with a blade of fire, feeling the wraith feeding on the elemental, and sent her down to join him. I walked down the corridor toward the Solarium and stood to one side of the door before using my air magic to tear it apart. I threw the head into the room, and gunfire filled my ears as bullets tore into it.

I waited for the shower of bullets to finish and glanced inside the room, igniting my matter magic. Matter magic allowed me to be stronger and faster, neither of which were very helpful if I stepped inside the room and my magic cut off. In this case, I just wanted to be able to see all the runes, and my matter magic let me see where they were and which ones were weaker than others.

There were two men with AK-47s in the middle of the room, and a woman was guarding the seven hostages.

"We're good down here," Hel said in my ear. "Just dealing with the hostages."

"All clear apart from three assholes in the Solarium and seven hostages," I said. "Multiple runes; they all have guns."

"You need a hand?" Selene asked.

"I'll be okay," I said. "You guys head up here; it'll be over by the time you're here."

"See you shortly," Selene said.

"You three want to put your guns down and head out peacefully?" I shouted.

"You come in here and these fuckers are dead," one of the men shouted. "You hear me?"

I heard him. I sank into the shadows and came out in one of the bedrooms, which had a wall joining to the Solarium and a glass door that would let me out onto the promenade. Something I'd noticed when scouting the room was that the curtains were closed, presumably so that no enemy sniper could take a shot.

Moving out of the bedroom doorway, I tapped my ear. "Jinayca, you got eyes on any guards on the promenade outside the third floor?"

"Two shooters," Jinayca said a second later. "One at each corner. You want them taken out?"

"No, it's okay," I said. "I'm already on it."

Once past the offices, I exited the building through a door to the promenade and spotted the first sniper at the corner, looking over the front of the White House. I moved slowly toward my target and used my air magic to snatch him away from his post before driving a blade of air into his temple.

I removed the sniper rifle from the floor and picked up a Sig Sauer P320 that he'd had in a holster on his hip. I checked the load and found it had silver bullets inside. *Perfect.*

Taking the weapons, I moved back inside the White House, stopped at the end of the corridor leading to the hostages, and crouched down. My magic wouldn't work inside the Solarium because of the wards, but it sure as hell did outside it. I ignited my matter magic, increasing my speed, and moved around the corner, raising the M24 rifle as I did and firing twice. I hit the female hostage guard twice in the head before dropping the magic and firing twice more, once at each remaining hostage taker. I hit the first one in the shoulder and the second just above the eye. I dropped the rifle and drew the Sig, firing as I did, hitting the hostage taker who was still alive twice in the knee and once in the head as he fell forward. All three down in under ten seconds.

I motioned for the screaming hostages to get down and stepped inside the room, feeling my magic vanish. I knelt down and aimed at the rear door to the room as it opened slightly. I fired twice into the rune next to the door, which exploded outward, blowing the door apart and throwing the sniper who had opened it over the balcony to the ground three stories below.

My magic flooded back into me, and I dropped the gun on the nearby table. "Ladies and gentlemen, I'm here to rescue you," I said as my team came running along the corridor behind me.

"We've got a hostage taker over the balcony," I said, passing the rifle to Sky, who took it to go look.

"Senators," Selene said. "Glad you're unharmed."

"We were too important to hurt," a male senator said. "They killed people, though—took them into the other rooms, and we heard them executed. No one wanted to fight after that."

"How many?" I asked.

"A dozen, maybe more," a female senator said grimly. "The president isn't here; he joined them, walked off with them. He threatened to have us executed too."

Well, that was unexpected. "How's his family?" I asked.

"Shaken," she told me. "I thought I knew him. I've known him for thirty years, and I know he's been acting odd recently, but I just put that down to stress. For him to turn like this . . . it just wasn't like him."

"Where is he?" I asked, wondering exactly how entrenched the president was with Arthur.

"He's in the Oval Office," a male senator told us. "Lots of guards. And there's an Englishman with him. I've never met him before, but he's the one in charge."

"Gawain," Remy said. "He's a dick. We'll kill him too."

The male senator stared at Remy, obviously bemused by the talking foxman, before Remy winked and blew him a kiss. The senator turned away, and I caught a smile on Remy's face.

"I need you all to move down to the dining room," Zamek said as a shot sounded out from the promenade. Sky returned to the room.

"He's done," she said.

I placed a finger to my ear. "Roberto, the hostage takers are dealt with."

"Casualties?" he asked.

"A lot," I said. "Sounds like it, anyway. They were taken to other rooms and executed, according to the senators. A dozen at least. Gawain is in the Oval Office. So that's where we're going next. All the hostages will be in the dining room, where Diana and Kase are. I would advise your people to stay as far away from Kase as possible. She may not be in the mood to play nice."

"Anything I need to be concerned about?" he asked.

"The president might be a traitor," I told him.

"What?" he shouted.

"Not sure yet," I said cheerfully. "We'll figure it out."

"And the snipers on the roof?" he asked, clearly exasperated.

"Ah, bollocks," I said. "I forgot about them. I'll get Kase and Diana to deal with them."

"We'll wait for your signal, then," Roberto said.

Chapter Eight

Nate Garrett

The senators had been right, and on the way through the White House to the West Wing, we found multiple rooms with bodies in them. Most had been shot at point-blank range, but more than a few had been attacked by things that were definitely not human. The rage I felt at such needless slaughter made my desire to find Gawain and hold him accountable even stronger.

"They're going to know we're coming," Sky said.

"I hope so," Zamek said fiercely. "I prefer beating the shit out of people who are prepared for it."

"They executed so many people," Selene said angrily.

"I'm guessing guards and Secret Service who weren't on board with Avalon's vision," Sky said.

"And anyone who looked at Gawain funny," I added bitterly.

"He always was a twat," Selene said. "So what do we do with him when we've got him?"

"We'll take him to Mordred," I said. "He has Excalibur; he can use the sword to get the answers we need without having to tear him to pieces."

"Can we tear him to pieces just a little?" Remy asked. "Asking for a friend."

I shook my head as we reached the first floor, where Diana was waiting for us. "Kase is sat in the Green Room calming down," she said. "She's angry, Nate, but she hasn't tried to kill anyone. I took her to the pantry and had her wash herself down. None of these hostages need to see a blood-drenched Kase and wonder if the cure was worse than the disease."

"Fair point," I agreed.

"I moved the hostages to the East Room too," Diana said. "It's away from the West Wing entrance, and I didn't want any snipers taking shots at them."

"You're on a roll," I said with a smile. "Roberto and his people will be here soon, but there are snipers on the roof. You think you can deal with them?"

Diana nodded. "I'm sure I can manage."

I chased after the rest of the team as they continued down the stairs to the ground floor of the residence building and along to the Palm Room, which looked out over the Rose Garden and entrance to the Oval Office. I saw no one out there, but that didn't mean they weren't waiting.

Remy drew his revolvers, and I placed a hand on the Sig that I'd kept from the third floor. Sky and Selene were unarmed only in the sense that they didn't have guns or swords, and Zamek kept his bloodstained battle-ax in his hand.

I looked over at the wall that separated where we stood from the press offices. "Any chance you can make a big hole in there?" I asked.

Selene followed my stare, turned into her dragon-kin form, and spat a jet of ice to cover a huge piece of the wall, which Sky punched, her fist wrapped in her necromancy power. It took a few blows to get through, and eventually Sky got fed up with punching it and just blasted it with the same power, tearing the wall to bits and leaving us with a makeshift archway.

The press offices were empty, as was the briefing room beside them. I'd considered just using the West Colonnade to get around to the Oval Office quickly but was certain that Gawain would have people watching it. And I didn't want to have to deal with whatever traps and unpleasantness he'd have prepared for anyone trying that tactic.

We stopped at the stairwell and stepped out into the corridor. "We'll split into two teams," I said.

"I'm coming with you this time," Selene said, leaving absolutely no room for argument.

"Fine," I said. "The rest of you, go through the press secretary room, around the maze of corridors, to get to the Oval Office past the study. We'll go the more direct route and generally piss everyone off enough that their attention will be on us."

"Do *not* kill the president, even if he is a traitor," Sky said. "We kind of need him."

"Well, that's my afternoon ruined," I told her sarcastically.

"I'm just reiterating for the sake of those who are here who might forget."

Everyone turned to look at Remy.

"Yeah, that's fair," Remy said unrepentantly.

When everyone left, Selene turned to me. "Right, just how exhausted are you?"

I shrugged.

"It took you longer to deal with those people on the third floor than I'd expected," she said.

I nodded. "Yeah, well, I didn't want to go all out because who knows what we're going to face with Gawain."

"There's something else too," she said.

"Yeah . . . I'm worried about losing my temper," I admitted.

"Why?"

"Honestly? Because once that anger is let loose, it might not stop. If I'd lost my temper up there, my magic would have destroyed that entire floor. There would be pictures all over the world of a sorcerer who had just ripped the White House apart. I don't want the people who feared Arthur and Avalon to fear us too. We're better than them. I figured restraint on my part would be for the best."

Selene kissed me on the cheek. "Just try not to get hurt. I doubt that Gawain and those in the Oval Office with him are going to be as easily dispatched as everyone we've faced so far."

"I've been saving myself," I told her with a grin.

There was an explosion somewhere within the West Wing, powerful enough to shake the walls.

"Remy?" we both said in unison.

"I guess we're doing this, then," Selene said.

We walked down the corridor past the Cabinet Room until the hall turned right toward where the president's secretary normally sat. The position was currently occupied by two large men. They spotted Selene and me and charged to meet us.

One turned into a werewolf midstride and collided with Selene, who threw him over her shoulder into and through the wall behind her. She tore through the remains of the wall into the Cabinet Room as the man before me paused, looking a bit more cagey about what his chances were.

He created a sphere of air in his hand and threw it at me, but it was half-arsed, and I deflected it, sending it into the now-ruined wall of the Cabinet Room as I continued to move toward him.

"How many are in there?" I asked.

The man was sweating. His tattered suit suggested he had once been Secret Service. But now he was nothing better than a traitor to his own people.

"Five paladins, the president, and Gawain," he said, the second sphere of air in his hand dissipating to nothing. "They were meant to take the place bloodlessly."

The shadows around me crept across the carpet and under the man's feet.

"I can't lie," I told him as the shadows leaped up, dragging the man down into them as he screamed. "You deserve worse."

Selene stepped through the hole in the wall, covered in blood that I was certain wasn't hers. Her face was halfway between her human and dragon-kin forms, and I doubted the werewolf had fared well.

A tinge of power ran through my body as the wraith finished his meal.

"Nate, Selene, we have a problem," Sky said through the earpiece. "There are mines in the walls."

I stopped moving and looked around the short corridor we were in.

"Say again?" Selene asked.

"Mines in the fucking walls," Remy repeated. "Not magical ones but modified to contain silver pieces. One of them detonated while Sky was fighting a sorcerer. The sorcerer took the brunt."

"It killed them?" I asked.

"No, I did," Sky said. "But I doubt getting a face full of silver shrapnel felt too good."

"Found two more," Zamek said. "They appear to be attached to motion sensors."

I searched the room.

"Bollocks," Selene said behind me.

I turned and followed her finger to the large device that was inside the remains of the wall. How it hadn't detonated when the wall had been partially destroyed, I'd never know.

"Okay," I said. "We're going to get to the Oval Office. You hear that, Jinayca?"

"I did, as did Roberto," Jinayca said. "He's getting a team ready to search this whole place when we get inside."

"There will be some mines inside the rooms either side of the Oval Office," I said.

"Seeing how this is Gawain, I would certainly assume so, yes," Jinayca said.

"Have I told you lately that Mordred's brother is a dick?" I asked.

"It's come up once or twice," Jinayca said dryly.

"Everyone hear what Jinayca said about the team?" Selene asked.

Everyone confirmed that they had.

"What are the chances that they've put up runes to stop any magic being used?" Selene asked me.

"No idea," I said. "Let's assume they have."

We stood on either side of the door to the Oval Office. Selene grabbed the door handle and wrenched it free, tearing the door off in the process. I created a dense shield of air and stepped into the office to find four paladins kneeling on the floor with their hands on their heads and Gawain sitting behind the president's desk. A large glyph on the far wall had been cut through. The president, his chief of staff, and three senators were all sitting on comfortable-looking sofas. The president had a smug look on his face, which told me pretty much everything I needed to know about what was going to happen next. Nothing good.

The opposite door was ripped apart, and Zamek, Remy, and Sky stormed inside.

"What the . . . fuck?" Remy said, a sword in one hand and a gun in the other, ready to raise hell on anyone who moved.

"We surrender," Gawain said.

"Not going to lie," Zamek said. "I didn't expect that."

"Snipers are clear," Diana said in my ear. "We're heading down to you."

"What does that do?" I asked, pointing at the damaged glyph on the wall.

"We felt that if we were going to be arrested, we should remove the glyphs stopping your power," Gawain said. "As a show of *good faith*."

"Good faith?" Selene asked.

"You want me to talk, I will, but right now, I imagine you must have your hands full with a large contingency of my allies coming from the north."

Remy laughed. "Hey, butt plug, I don't think you should be considering backup to be your best way forward at this time. I think they've got their own problems."

"Butt plug? Remy, that wasn't great," I heard Zamek whisper.

"Yeah, I can do better," Remy admitted.

Zamek stood by one of the senators and put his arm around the seated man. The senator, normally a man of power, looked like he was going to pass out from fear. "And your own problems are much more *immediate*." He hissed the last word into the senator's ear, and the man visibly paled.

"You have absolutely no proof I've done anything wrong," the president said, still looking relaxed and smug, while the senators beside him looked a lot more terrified.

"We have lots of proof," Sky said, looking up from the third paladin she was disarming. "Like, all of it."

The president frowned. "Well, that's that plan gone to shit." He looked at Gawain with raised eyebrows. "What am I supposed to do now?"

"What you were paid for," Gawain said with a pointed look. "Improvise."

Everyone turned to look at the president, who gave them a snide smile. "Is he going to juggle or something?" Remy asked.

"Sky, can you please remove the president from my sight and make sure he makes it outside in one piece?" I asked her.

"I feel like that was directed at me," Remy said. "I could guard the president. I've *never* stabbed a president before; I see no reason why I'd start now."

The president stared at Remy with pure hatred.

Remy blew him a kiss.

"Why surrender?" I asked Gawain when everyone else had gone.

"Because you won't kill me. You need me," he said.

"I'm not sure I'd use the word *need*," I said. "This feels like a trap."

"It might be," Gawain said, sitting back in the chair and putting his feet up on the desk. "I could be sitting here lulling you all into a false sense of security."

"You're not smart enough," Selene said.

"She needs to keep quiet," Gawain snapped, pointing at Selene.

"Does he need all of his fingers to talk?" Selene asked, her eyes narrowing in anger.

Gawain wisely stopped pointing. "You see, there's a lot I could be telling you," Gawain said. "I know where Arthur is, I know how to get to him, and I know you want that information. I might talk; I might not. I'll see how I feel and how nice you are to me."

"Arthur is in Atlantis," Zamek said. "We know."

Gawain's expression was quite frankly worth the trip to Washington. Although he soon had his mask of smugness back in place. Gawain smiled as he stared at me. "You still missing Tommy?"

Selene placed a hand on my shoulder as my anger bubbled inside of me.

"Fuck you, Gawain," I snapped.

"I know the things that have been done to him. The torments he's endured." Gawain laughed. "But more importantly, I know *where* he is. But sadly, he'll be dead before you ever get there." Gawain laughed again.

I blasted him in the chest with a torrent of lightning and air, which tore the entire back of the Oval Office apart, flinging Gawain into the garden a floor below.

I walked over the ruined desk and stepped out into the darkness. It had started to rain heavily, and Gawain had hit a patch of grass, ripping it apart and quickly turning it to mud as he scrambled to get away. I used my air magic to slowly float to the ground, remaining just above it as I moved toward Gawain.

"I cut him," Gawain shouted at me. "Your pet wolf. I cut him good, and I watched as he knitted himself back together. Over and over and over. It was fun."

I continued toward him without a word, lost in my rage and desire to hurt him.

Gawain got to his feet; a whip of fire grew from his hand.

Shadows sprang out of the ground to hold Gawain's wrists before he got close enough to be an issue. Gawain was an old sorcerer and, given time, a dangerous one, but his level of power was never going to be anything I needed to worry about. And he knew it. Even so, he swiped at the shadows with the whip of fire, and they shrank away. But it gave me the opening I needed to slam a sphere of lightning into his chest and detonate it.

Gawain was picked up and thrown back fifty feet toward the front entrance of the White House. He'd covered himself in a shield of earth, which took the brunt of the explosion, but it must have hurt.

I caught up to Gawain and punched him in the face before kicking him back toward the White House. He threw a ball of fire at me that I swiped out of the way, smashing an elbow into his ribs before twisting and catching him with an uppercut to the jaw when he staggered forward. He managed to stabilize himself and kicked out at my knee, forcing me to hold back and giving him the opportunity to dive toward me with a dagger of fire.

I hit him in the chest with a gale of air that threw him across the front of the White House steps, where he collided with a column.

Gawain scrambled up the steps and threw a ball of fire at me that I deflected up toward the first floor of the White House. The magic exploded, tearing out a large part of the balcony above us and raining rocks down over the ground.

Tendrils of air wrapped around Gawain, and I dragged him back from the White House door, using my matter magic to enhance my strength. I flung him back across the tarmac, and he skidded onto the lawn as his earth magic kept him from more injury.

Thunder boomed.

"Where is Tommy?" I asked Gawain, using my air magic to ensure he heard every word.

"I can't say," Gawain said. "I *won't* say. Not even Excalibur can force me to talk. I have runes on my body; I will not give away anything."

"Then what use are you to us, you coward?" I asked him as the gates to the White House burst open and Roberto, Jinayca, and several dozen others ran toward me. The sounds of people shouting my name were drowned out by the roar of thunder above.

"You won't kill me," Gawain said, spitting at me. "I'm not afraid of you. None of us are. You can't defeat Arthur; he's too powerful. He will kill you all and drink from your skulls."

I raised my hand, and lightning streaked down from the skies and hit my outstretched palm. It flooded through me, mixing with my own magic. Lightning poured out of my eyes, my mouth, every part of me trying to contain the power inside.

"Tommy is in Atlantis," Gawain screamed.

I spotted the tiny red light as it touched Gawain's face, and I turned, unleashing the power directly into the third floor of the White House, where the sniper was. As the magic hit, it vaporized a large portion of the front of the floor, leaving a massive hole where the Solarium and its balcony had once been. The remains of the sniper toppled out of the building.

I turned back to Jinayca as she arrived with a flustered-looking Roberto. "Apparently, we missed one," she said.

Roberto continued to stare at the hole in the White House.

"Gawain's all yours," I told them. "The president is untouched. As are his senators. There are a few paladins in the West Wing. They all surrendered. Gawain was bounced along the lawn because he decided to open his mouth."

"Nate," Jinayca said softly.

"Tommy is in Atlantis," I said, ignoring her. "We already know that's where Arthur is, so now we just need Gawain to tell us how to get there. Or if Mordred has already figured it out, we don't need him at all, and you can just execute the little weasel."

I set off back toward the Oval Office and spotted Kase and Diana standing where Gawain had landed, Kase's mouth open in shock. "You asked me why I'm not full of rage at the thought of your father being Avalon's prisoner. That's what happens when I let it go for just an instant. Tommy is in Atlantis, and when I find those who have kept him, that rage is going to be aimed directly at them."

Kase continued to watch me as I walked over to the broken West Wing. If Gawain and his allies hadn't feared me before, they clearly hadn't been paying attention.

Chapter Nine

MORDRED

City of Solomon, Realm of Shadow Falls

Mordred had paced up and down inside the realm gate temple for the better part of an hour. He'd wanted to go to Washington with Nate and everyone else; he'd wanted to confront his brother and see him brought down a few dozen pegs. Unfortunately, as he'd been told more times than he cared to remember, he was a king now and had to do king-like things. He'd assumed being king meant he could have other people do those things. He'd been wrong.

"We're trying to work," Leonardo said to Mordred.

"I know," Mordred said with a smile as he made another lap of the temple. "I'm working too."

"At pissing me off," Leonardo said with a sigh.

"See, we all have jobs," Mordred told him.

"Can you do something with him?" Leonardo asked Hel.

"Mordred," Hel said. "Leonardo thinks you're being a pain in the ass."

"Leonardo is correct," Mordred said. "But I'm thinking."

"About what?" Hel asked, stepping in front of Mordred to stop him from completing another lap of the temple.

"We need to go to Olympus to persuade them to join our fight; they've been sitting on the fence for too long. We need their help," Mordred said. "And we know that Arthur is in Atlantis, but no one knows how to get to Atlantis because it was destroyed."

"Correct," Leonardo shouted.

"I thought you were working," Mordred replied and caught the smile on the face of Antonio as Leonardo turned back to the realm gate, muttering.

"Anyway," Mordred continued as Loki and Irkalla entered the temple. "There's no point in my trying to get the Olympians on our side if I can't give them an enemy to fight. So how do we find a way into Atlantis?"

"Hopefully Gawain gives us that information," Loki said.

"Yes, because Gawain is well known for being forthcoming," Hel replied.

"Nanshe," Irkalla said. "She's in Olympus. I think she might be able to help."

Mordred grimaced. "The last time I saw her, I remember trying to kill her," he said. "You know, old evil me, not *me* me."

"Yeah, we got it," Irkalla said. "Nanshe's not exactly a grudge holder, but she is unbelievably smart."

"Can't we use Yggdrasil?" Mordred asked. "No one has mentioned it."

"It's still repairing itself from when we kicked Avalon out of Helheim," Hel said. "We can't get it to fix on a location. It might decide to dump us anywhere in a hundred thousand different realms."

"Yeah, let's not do that," Mordred said.

"Done," Leonardo declared, standing back and clapping his hands together. "This will take you to Olympus."

"Why'd it take so long?" Loki asked.

"Because Olympus shut off all external entrances to their gate," Antonio said. "We had to work around their security. A bit like what the dwarves did in Nidavellir. It should be fine now."

"How happy are they going to be that we broke their security?" Hel asked.

"Not very," Irkalla said.

"You sound a lot more cheerful about that than you should," Mordred pointed out.

"We done yet?" Medusa asked as she entered the realm gate temple. Like everyone else, she wore black leather armor with runes inscribed across it. Medusa's snakes slithered over her shoulders.

"They excited?" Mordred asked, pointing to them.

"They don't like realm gates," Medusa said.

"Is this it?" Loki asked.

"Small team—we're in and out," Mordred said. "No matter what everyone else says, I don't need a bunch of guards to go everywhere with me."

"Good luck," Antonio said and operated the realm gate. Everyone stepped through a moment later.

"Well, this is nice," Mordred said as they entered the realm gate temple in Olympus. It was, in Mordred's mind, exactly how a realm gate in a place where Zeus lived would look. The temple had marble columns that stretched from floor to ceiling, fifty feet above. The ceiling had a mural on it depicting the fall of the Titans by Zeus and his allies. All the Olympians were semiclothed and looked like they spent more time in the gym than Mordred felt was probably healthy.

"That looks like an advert for a porn site," Loki said.

Medusa, Hel, and Irkalla all turned to look at him.

"What?" Loki asked. "It does."

"He's got a point," Mordred said. "It's quite exceptionally porny."

"I don't think that's a word," Medusa said.

"I don't think it matters too much," Irkalla replied. "'Porny' is actually pretty accurate. I'm a little surprised it doesn't depict Zeus holding a foot-long penis and waving it around like a sword."

"Hers was way worse than mine," Loki said, mostly to himself.

"If Zeus commissioned this, it would be three feet long and shooting lightning bolts," Medusa said with the expression of someone who had met Zeus and had found him much less entertaining in person.

Mordred noticed that Hel ignored the playful conversation and was looking around. "This place is much neater than I expected," she said. "There's no dust. No evidence of wear on the mural or those marble columns. It's like a time capsule."

"How's that possible?" Irkalla asked.

Hel shrugged. "Someone is taking care of this place."

Mordred placed a hand on Excalibur and drew it from the sheath on his back. "Let's see what's happening here." He activated the power within the sword, and the rear of the temple shimmered and changed, revealing a doorway, which opened.

There were thirty guards, all dressed in red-and-silver armor that reminded Mordred of the legionnaires of Rome, and all of them pointed spears at the team. The squad of soldiers parted slightly, allowing a woman through. She was just over five feet tall, with olive skin and dark hair that was extravagantly plaited. She wore a light-blue toga and sandals, which Mordred admitted to himself were probably more beneficial than his dark leather armor, considering how hot it was.

"Nanshe," Irkalla said, running over to her old friend and hugging her.

"Sorry we broke your security," Mordred said.

"Mordred," Nanshe said, walking over and taking his hands in hers. "It has been a long time. I hear you're a new man."

"Same man, just not evil," Mordred said with a smile. "Can your soldiers stop pointing spears at us?"

Nanshe smiled, waving a hand without looking back. The soldiers lowered their weapons and turned to march away toward a nearby guard post.

"Why are you here?" Nanshe asked.

Mordred sighed. "It's a really long story," he said. "But basically, I'm now the king of the rebellion and rightful king of Avalon, and we need your help to get into Atlantis and stop Arthur from murdering everyone."

"You're a king?" Nanshe asked, looking around at everyone.

"He has Excalibur and everything," Medusa said.

Nanshe's eyes widened in surprise. "Well, Your Majesty, welcome to Olympus."

"Please don't call me that," Mordred pleaded.

Nanshe took the team up a winding road that led to the top of a large hill. The closer they got, the more noise could be heard, and as they reached the summit, they could see the sprawling city before them. To the right was the temple of the Olympians, the gleaming white stone building towering over everything around it.

"You've seen the temple before, yes?" Nanshe asked.

Everyone nodded. "Not for a long time," Mordred whispered. "A *really* long time."

"That's the palace," Nanshe said, pointing to the equally large building at the far end of the city. "The council chambers are beside it."

The red-and-white stone buildings littered the city, and Mordred wondered how no one on the team had been able to hear so many people on their way toward the city. He looked around as they walked down the steps into the city and saw more and more runes carved into the stone.

"You stop the sound from traveling," he said, more to himself.

"Yes, we wanted this to be a place of safety," Nanshe said. "You've shown how easy it is to break our security."

"Good," Loki said. "Get better security."

Nanshe chuckled. "I will tell those in charge."

"I thought you were in charge," Irkalla said.

"I am the head of the council," Nanshe said. "But everything must be voted on. Even helping you."

"This is going to take a while, isn't it?" Hel asked with a sigh.

Nanshe stopped walking and turned to the group. "What do you actually want, Mordred? Troops? People to die for your cause?"

"Aid," Mordred said quickly.

"And that means?" Nanshe asked.

"We need two things," Mordred said. "We need to find out how to get into Atlantis, and we need the help of anyone who will stand beside us. I cannot say that those who do will live, but I'd rather die with a sword in my hand, doing the right thing, than hiding away to wait and be conquered."

No one said anything for several seconds.

"That passion in your voice," Nanshe said. "Use it. You will be talking to a hundred senators. You need only sway fifty of them."

"Not fifty-one?" Medusa asked.

"You have my vote already," Nanshe told them with a shrug. "Olympus is neutral, something I'm pretty sure you'll all agree that Zeus would have hated, but here we are. I do not want war, I do not want to send people to die, but war is coming. We either help when we can, or we die when Avalon and Arthur decide we're too dangerous to leave alive. Not much of an option in my mind."

"Thank you," Mordred said.

"Don't," Nanshe said, continuing on. "I remember the old Mordred, the one who terrorized, who terrified. I remember the darkness in your eyes. A lot of the senators will remember him too. They will not see a difference. They will see a killer with a sword of power. Excalibur. A weapon used to make you more dangerous. This will not be an easy sell."

"I'm the king," Mordred said with a sigh. "If I wanted an easy life, I'd have run away the first time someone told me to find Excalibur."

Nanshe placed a hand on Mordred's shoulder. "I always knew you were capable of greatness. I'm glad to see you in a better place. I'm sorry I couldn't help you get there."

"No one could have," Mordred told her.

As they continued on, Hel took Mordred's hand in hers and squeezed slightly. "That went better than you thought."

Mordred nodded. "Let's not celebrate just yet," he said softly.

The palace was awash with guards, who watched the newcomers suspiciously, and as they traveled through to the council chambers that were attached to the side, Mordred wondered whether bringing war to even more people was ever going to be enough to stop Arthur. He mentally told himself to shut up—he had to be prepared for whatever came next, and second-guessing himself wasn't going to get the job done.

While the palace was all marble and white brick, the council chamber was considerably humbler. It was made of white-and-red brick—much like most of the city buildings—but there were no large marble statues of various gods, nor ornate murals depicting battles. It was just plain and functional.

The council building was a giant circle, with various rooms for the workers around a central circular room. There was a large white stone dais with ten rows of benches encircling it, tiered to look down on the dais.

"We have a few minutes before the senate resumes for the day," Nanshe said. "You came at a good time. An hour later, and you would have walked in on a session already in progress. I will go and send word that this afternoon is mandatory attendance. You will have a full house, Mordred."

Nanshe left the team alone in the curia, and Mordred spotted the guards standing at the entrance to the palace. Nanshe might trust them, but that didn't mean the guards wouldn't be cautious.

"Do you know what you're going to say?" Loki asked.

"I have a good idea," Mordred said.

"Do you, really?" Hel asked.

"Mostly, yeah," Mordred said.

Senators started to come into the curia and took their seats on the benches as Hel kissed Mordred for luck, and the rest of his team went to sit. Nanshe entered and stood beside Mordred as the shocked whispers of the senate flooded the room, echoing. Mordred looked around. Among the shocked and curious faces were a lot of angry ones.

"Ladies and gentlemen of the senate," Nanshe said, her voice turning the din of whispers into silence. "This is King Mordred. He has come from Shadow Falls to suggest an alliance. He *will* be heard. He *will* be afforded the respect that we would give anyone who comes to us for help. As leader of this senate, I suggest that anyone who takes umbrage with this leave now, and their vote on the matter will not be counted."

No one moved.

"Excellent," Nanshe said. "Mordred, state your case."

Mordred took a deep breath. "Judging from the expressions in the room, all of you know who I was. Not am. *Was.* I was a murderer, a thief, a monster. I admit this. For a century I was imprisoned by my own father, Merlin, in a blood elf dungeon. My mind was torn asunder every day for a hundred years. Avalon tried to use me as a weapon, until I finally escaped. I can offer no excuses for what I did during that time. I can only assure you that I am *not* that creature anymore. My mind and spirit were healed, and it took a long time to be able to look at myself in the mirror and not see the monster I once was."

Mordred let out a slight sigh before he continued. "I do not expect those of you I hurt to forgive or forget. But I beg that you do the right thing. Not for me but for *all* of us. Arthur and Avalon are coming. They will destroy everyone Arthur considers a threat, and if you are not allied or a slave state to him, then you *are* a threat."

Mordred looked around the room. Most were listening intently, but more than a few radiated hate and anger. Mordred placed a hand on the hilt of Excalibur and drew it from the scabbard on his back. "This is Excalibur," he said. "The sword can only be claimed by the rightful king of Avalon. That is me. The sword makes me stronger; this is true. When activated, it removes the magic of those in proximity to me—also true. But it ensures that no lies can be uttered when someone activates the sword's power." Mordred turned to Nanshe. "Can you hold this for me?"

Nanshe took Excalibur. "How do I activate it?" she asked.

"Just think about it," Mordred said. "The sword will do the rest."

A wave of power swept over Mordred, and he knew that his magic was gone, but he also saw Nanshe's shock as her own power vanished.

"Ask me what you will," Mordred shouted. "I will tell the truth."

"How do we know it really works?" a man asked.

"It works," Nanshe said. "Do you doubt me?"

The man shook his head.

"Why are you *really* here?" a woman shouted out almost immediately after.

119

"I seek your help," Mordred said. "I seek a way to find Atlantis, and I need people who will stand beside me and fight Arthur. That is all."

The woman nodded, the answer apparently satisfactory.

"And what will you do once the war is over?" a man asked, getting to his feet. "What will you do with Olympus?"

"Nothing," Mordred said. "I have no wish to conquer. I have no wish to become your king. Anyone who wants to live under my rule is welcome, but I will not force people. I am not a tyrant."

"Do you remember those you murdered?" a woman shouted.

"The innocence you took?" a man shouted after her. Both got to their feet, expressions of hate on their faces.

"I remember them *all*," Mordred whispered. "I remember every single horrific thing I've ever done; I remember it and I live with it. I use that to ensure that no one else *ever* goes through what I went through. I was forced to murder people I loved, forced to hurt those who cared for me. My father, my brother—they turned me into a creature of pure darkness."

"You killed my son," the woman shouted with tears in her eyes. "His name was Christopher. He died by your hand in 1211. He tried to stop you from murdering an Avalon soldier in a small town outside Rome. You'd already killed twelve that day."

"Red hair," Mordred said, feeling the lump in his throat at the pain he'd caused. "He had long red hair."

The woman nodded.

"He was brave," Mordred said quietly. "He fought bravely. And I wish that it had been me that died instead of him. I am sorry. I am trying to make amends every day. Help me make sure Arthur doesn't do this to hundreds of thousands of other innocent people. Help me stop it. *Please.*"

The woman wiped away a tear and sat down without another word.

"Are you going to do that to each of us who lost something because of the monster you became?" the man shouted.

"If I need to," Mordred said. "Without a combined effort, we will not win. Whatever I need to do to show that Arthur must be stopped, that our alliance is the only hope, I will do it. If that means begging forgiveness from every person who I caused pain to, then I'll do it."

"That won't be necessary," Nanshe said. "We don't really have time for it, anyway, but the thought is appreciated."

Nanshe gave Excalibur back to Mordred and stepped back off the dais.

"People tell me that I need to be statesmanlike," Mordred said. "But I'm not a statesman. I'm a warrior, someone who is trying to live up to the ideals that this sword is meant to represent. Some days I think I do a good job, and some days I think I'll never reach that ideal. But I try. And I'm here because I want to make sure we all have a chance to stand up as one and say to Arthur, *no*. To tell him that we will not become his minions; we will not be subjugated; we will not be afraid. We will do what's right, and we will make sure that future generations look back on these moments and see something good happen in a sea of darkness. I hope you help us; I really do. Thank you for your time."

Mordred stepped off the dais as Hel and the rest of his team moved over to him, and with Nanshe, they left the amphitheater.

"That was good," Nanshe said. "I think you swayed a few."

"Let's just hope it's enough," Mordred said. "I'm pretty sure the others in Washington are already having a less-than-ideal time; I'd quite like to give them some good news."

Chapter Ten

Layla Cassidy

Washington, DC, United States, Earth Realm

"That is a lot of very angry psychopaths," Judgement said from the roof of the apartment building as more and more people could be seen heading their way.

The horde of pro-Avalon forces was two blocks away. Layla could hear their shouts and the screams of war that accompanied them, see the flames leaping from the buildings they torched. There were a few thousand of them, and more and more people had fled their homes and taken temporary residence inside the three residential buildings that Layla and her team had sworn to protect.

"How long before reinforcements arrive?" Layla asked Jinayca in her ear comm.

"Not long," she said, sounding rattled.

"Not long isn't *quick* enough," Layla said.

She looked over the edge of the roof. The APC had been moved to sit at the far edge of the walkway between two of the buildings. As the three buildings formed a horseshoe, it was imperative that they funneled everyone down between them. The APC's positioning was designed to help do just that, putting the incoming horde into a kill zone they couldn't escape from.

At least, that was the plan.

Chloe lay on the rooftop beside Judgement with a scoped rifle, aiming at the group heading their way. It was their only rifle— while the APC was chock full of weaponry, no one had seen the need to be sniping people from hundreds of meters away.

"How are things your end?" Layla asked Piper.

"We're keeping the residents as calm as possible," Piper said. "Tarron is doing most of it. He has a way with people. The driver and passenger of the APC have helped arm anyone who has shooting experience and a few who just wanted to help. Tego has growled at anyone who steps out of line. Turns out people don't like that."

"You used Tego as a way to keep people in line?" Chloe asked, and Layla knew she was smirking.

"I am shocked and appalled," Layla said with a slight smile. She looked over the edge again at the members of her team who were on the other roofs. Piper waved.

"Where'd you put the residents who can't help?" Layla asked.

"They're in their homes," she said. "There were a few off-duty cops who live here, so we've let them keep people from doing anything stupid. Also, you know, we told them that Tego would be about."

"Layla, you need to see this," Chloe said.

She looked over at the approaching horde, but they were still a few hundred meters up the road. There was an explosion in the distance as another set of apartments was set aflame. Layla wanted to do something to help, but doing so would leave the now hundreds of people inside the apartment blocks with even less protection.

Chloe passed Layla a pair of binoculars without getting up, and Layla knelt down beside her and used them to watch the rabble as they marched ever closer. They stopped periodically to slaughter anyone in their path, leaving their bodies on the sidewalk before continuing on. They were in the middle of torching cars when someone inside an apartment four floors up crashed through a window and landed on the railings below to the cheers of the horde.

A man poked his head out of the broken window and raised his arm in victory, receiving more cheers.

"Do it," Layla said.

Chloe pulled the trigger, and Layla watched as the bullet smashed into the man's skull. He toppled out of the apartment block onto the same railings as his victim. The group below fell silent.

"First person who steps forward," Layla said.

It took six seconds for the first of them to step forward, a large man with a huge beard and an ax in one hand. He crumpled to the floor a second later, a hole where his forehead used to be.

Layla turned back to Judgement. "War's coming."

Judgement smiled and hit herself on the chest with one fist. She was ready.

"Anyone who moves first, take them out," Layla said.

"I have twelve rounds left," Chloe said. "It'll be like shooting fish in a barrel."

Layla walked away as shot after shot rang out over the night. She ignored it, walking to the far end of the apartment building and stepping over the makeshift ramp to the building beside it, where Piper greeted her.

"How's Chloe?" Piper asked.

"Taking out her frustrations on mass murderers," Layla said.

"She's good at that," Piper said. "We're as ready as we'll ever be."

Layla took a deep breath and let it out slowly. "I'll go make a big wall, then." She ran to the far edge of the building opposite and looked down over the APC in the middle of the road. It wasn't much of a hindrance, if she was honest, even with cars on either side of it. That would soon change, though.

Layla reached out with her power and took control of the metal in the car directly beneath where she stood. She concentrated and twisted her hands, and the car tore apart. It took her a few seconds to do the same to two more cars, by which time the horde had full on charged toward their position. Layla worked quickly and moved all the metal into a sizable structure, wrapping it around lampposts and other cars to make a wall that stretched across the street. It wasn't going to stop anyone who was determined, but it was seven feet high, sharp, and unpleasant and would hopefully ensure that their attackers didn't continue further into the city.

"Jinayca," Layla said, touching her earpiece. "When those reinforcements get here, there's a metal wall just beyond us. They're going to need me to move it."

"I'll let them know," Jinayca said. "Layla, be careful."

"I'm always careful, Jinayca," Layla said. "It's why I'm still alive."

The first part of the horde arrived, with the rest not far behind. They stopped next to the APC and looked at the wall. Several Molotovs were thrown, and they opened fire on everything around them, but the structure held, and to Layla's eyes, they were just making a dangerous climb even more so.

Layla walked away from the edge of the roof, back toward Piper, who dumped four large bags in front of her. "Shrapnel," she said.

"Thank you," Layla said.

Piper placed a hand on Layla's shoulder. "We will be waiting for you."

Layla nodded and opened the bag. Hundreds of screws, nuts, pieces of random metal, and what appeared to be knives and forks. Each bag probably weighed fifty pounds. That was a whole lot of shrapnel. She looked over at Chloe, who had taken up position with an MP5 at the edge of the roof, looking down over the kill zone. On the opposite side were the soldiers from the APC, both with identical weapons. Several windows on the top two floors of the apartment buildings were open, and Layla knew that more of her team were inside, waiting for action.

Layla took control of dozens of the pieces of metal and lifted them out of the bags, content to keep them hovering beside her as more and more of the gang arrived. Several of the group were already pointing at the apartment blocks and shouting obscenities; Layla ignored them.

The mass below—emboldened by numbers—turned toward the three apartment buildings and began lobbing Molotovs at them. The exposed walls caught fire, and a few hit the windows of the lower levels, but Layla had spent time going from room to room of the lowest floor, covering the windows in sheets of metal she'd removed from the hoods of cars at the front of the building. She hoped it would be enough. The last thing they needed was a fire.

When it became apparent that the buildings were not about to burst into uncontrolled flames, the crowd charged between the three buildings toward the front entrance, which, like all three other entrances, was now blocked with furniture. It would take them a while to get through.

It wasn't a smart plan of attack, Layla thought as the screaming mass filled the gap between the buildings. But then a crowd of people baying for blood who had killed countless others without worrying about it was running on bloodlust, not brainpower.

Layla fired the pieces of metal at those charging through, using enough force to make them as deadly as bullets. They struck a half dozen targets as the defenders with weapons opened fire.

It was the bloodbath Layla had known it would be. Bullets and metal tore through the crowd below like it was paper, leaving corpses all across the space between the three buildings. Two dozen were dead in under a minute, nearly double that by the time the horde outside the kill zone decided to stop charging in.

Layla had all but emptied one bag when she spotted several newcomers at the edge of the apartment. One wore chain mail armor that glistened golden and a long black cape. Layla tapped her ear. "We've got problems."

"Oh fuck," Chloe said as one of the newcomers created a ball of air the size of a basketball and flung it at the building, detonating the magic and tearing apart a large chunk of the wall.

"Fifty dead," Judgement said. "Only a few thousand to go. I'm going to go remove the stragglers. The last thing we need for them is cavalry. Be back soon."

There was no point in telling Judgement what to do; she was her own person and wasn't someone who took orders easily.

Layla picked up a screw and began to rotate it in the air, spinning it faster and faster until it was a blur. She flung it at the sorcerer with every bit of power she had at her disposal. The sorcerer wrapped himself in a shield of air before the screw ever hit. And a second later, he flung it back toward Layla with enough magical power that she had to move aside as it smashed into the wall behind her.

"We have a *really* big problem," Layla said. "That's not some two-bit sorcerer."

"Ladies and gentlemen of Washington," the sorcerer said, his arms wide open, his air magic pushing his words far enough that Layla could hear him as if he were standing beside her.

"My name is Sir Lamorak," he said. "I am one of the Knights of the Round Table and a paladin in the employ of Arthur Pendragon, your king and ruler. I was tasked with the destruction of this filthy city, and I am to carry out my king's command. You are in the way

127

of those orders, you have killed the king's men, and I will take time out of my day to show you the error of your ways."

"What a pompous ass," Chloe said in Layla's ear.

Layla sighed. "Shit, wasn't he supposed to be one of the greatest warriors the world had ever known?"

"You have but one chance to ensure you do not taste my wrath," Sir Lamorak continued.

"I can hear him through your comms, and he sounds like a giant dick to me," said Judgement. "I'm a bit busy with these idiots, but I'll come kill him in a minute."

"You will kneel before me and beg forgiveness, and I will allow you a quick and . . . *relatively* painless death. A death with honor. But if you continue to stand against me, I will have your souls torn from your bodies as I rip you to pieces."

"That's vivid," Piper said.

"There is no escape this day," Sir Lamorak said. "There is no tomorrow for you people. There is a good, clean death or agony the likes of which you have never even considered. You have sixty seconds to decide."

"Have we decided?" Tarron asked immediately.

"Does anyone want to take him up on his offer?" Layla asked.

"He's going to butcher everyone," the APC driver said. "Fuck him and his fancy cape."

"I like her," Judgement said.

"Anyone think otherwise?" Layla asked.

"Death or death?" Piper asked. "No one down here is mad keen on those options."

"So I'll give him our answer, okay?" Layla asked.

"Go ahead," Chloe said.

Layla collected enough metal to turn into a baseball-size weapon and threw it at Sir Lamorak. The paladin watched the ball hurtle toward him, his hands aflame, until he caught it out of the air as if it were nothing. He crushed the ball in one hand, the individual pieces of metal dropping over the ground at his feet, and looked up at Layla with hatred in his eyes.

Layla flipped him off with both hands.

"How fucking *dare* you," Sir Lamorak screamed. "I offer you honor, and you spit in my face. I will have your head for this. You have made your bed—die in it."

He flung balls of air at the two closest walls and tore huge chunks of them down as Layla grabbed a handful of metal and sprinted across the roof to the edge closest to the mass of attackers below, opposite where Chloe stood, her rifle aimed at Sir Lamorak.

"Do it," Layla shouted.

Chloe took the shot, and once again Sir Lamorak stopped the attack with a shield of air. He whipped the shield up at the roof of the apartment and smashed it into the brick and concrete just below where Chloe stood, forcing her to throw herself back as part of the roof collapsed.

Layla threw the metal out in front of her, forcing it down with incredible speed onto the exposed horde, causing screams of pain as it found targets, but a moment later she heard a whir and tore metal from the roof to wrap around herself as a missile smashed into the edge closest to her. The shock wave threw her back; she collided with the wall of the entrance to the stairwell and all but obliterated it, leaving a hole in the roof.

"What the fuck was that?" Piper asked.

"They have a rocket launcher," Layla said, coughing and spitting blood onto the floor. "Of course they do. It's turning into one of *those* days." Metal wrapped around her or not, that had hurt.

"Do you understand now?" Sir Lamorak asked. "We have more firepower, more magical power, more determination, and we will not be stopped. Enjoy your deaths."

Layla crawled back over to the edge of the roof in time to watch the multitude below scramble up the brick and concrete that had once been the outer walls of two of the buildings and were now a ramp giving easy access to everyone inside.

Gunfire sounded soon after.

"Get everyone back to the center building," Layla yelled. "Do it now."

She rolled onto her back as Piper appeared beside her. She wordlessly helped Layla to her feet, and together they ran across the building to where Layla had hoped they would never have to defend from.

Layla looked back as gunfire and shouting broke out in the two buildings closest to them.

"The bastards are piling in like wasps to a beehive," one of the police officers said as Piper and Layla reached the top floor of the apartment block.

Layla looked around and saw a lot of frightened faces of civilians as they looked out of doorways before closing and locking them.

"You think that'll help?" Piper asked.

Layla shook her head. "Chloe, Judgement, how's it going?"

"I collapsed a pretty big part of the floor above me," Chloe said. "Should slow them down. They can't get to the hole we made in the wall unless they have a few dwarves with them."

"We could use some dwarves right about now," Judgement said. "There's a big group of assholes coming toward our position. I've killed a few of them and am heading back to the building. I'll kill anything that moves, but I can see several dead police outside. These thugs do not behave like humans."

"How so?" Layla asked, looking out of the window at Sir Lamorak, who hadn't moved. She spotted the man and woman sitting on the street behind him.

"There are empaths in the group. I suspect they're control-ling the emotions of this group," Judgement said, sounding out of breath for the first time. "They're surrounded by guards, so I doubt we can get to them easily. I could kill one, maybe both, but I'd be swarmed pretty soon."

"Get back to the apartment building," Layla told Judgement. "We'll figure out a way."

"Already ahead of you," Judgement said, and a nearby window shattered, Judgement jumping through a moment later. "That was a bitch of a climb up."

"Glad you're okay," Layla told her.

"It's hard to scare people who don't feel anything," Judgement said.

"These humans aren't going to feel fear or pain, guilt or remorse," Piper said. "They're just going to keep coming until either we're dead or they are."

"Well, let's give them what they want," Layla said.

Judgement picked up a rifle from one of several positions manned by the police and civilians, aiming down it and measuring the shot. A few hundred meters. "Chloe, you got a shot on these empaths?"

Chloe arrived on the floor a few seconds later, looking out of breath. She said nothing but winked at Piper and stood beside Layla, peering through her riflescope at the sorcerer and empaths. "I can get them both," she said. "I'll take the man; you take the woman."

Judgement looked down the rifle. "On three."

"One," Piper said. "Two. Three."

Both fired simultaneously, and Judgement fired a second time almost immediately after. Layla watched as the sorcerer stopped the first bullet from hitting the female empath, but he had to adjust his shield in an instant to stop the second from hitting him, leaving him no time to stop the third from striking the male empath in the face, killing him instantly.

Sir Lamorak was incensed and began throwing balls of flame at the residential buildings, igniting the interior of the right building. Black smoke billowed up into the night sky.

"I think we pissed him off," Chloe said.

"Good," Layla said and continued watching as the sorcerer and dozens of his horde sprinted down the middle of the path between the buildings, his shield stopping any bullets that went his way, before he tore apart the entrance below where Layla and her people stood.

"I'm coming for you all," he screamed.

"I think we made a new friend," Piper said.

Layla looked back at the lone empath, now shielded by two dozen humans. "Judgement, how do you feel about going after that last empath? If we have to fight all of these bastards, let's even the odds a little."

Judgement smiled, her eyes almost sparking with intent. "That sounds like a plan to me."

Layla pointed to three civilians and told them to go with Judgement but made it clear who was in charge. "Tarron, Judgement is coming your way. You're going to go kill that empath."

"Good," Tarron said.

"So what are we going to do?" the APC driver asked.

"We're going to kill as many of those bastards as possible," Chloe said.

"And the sorcerer?" the APC passenger asked, and Layla saw the fear in those around her.

"We'll deal with him," Layla said. "I've killed sorcerers before."

"You think we can do it?" Chloe asked as Tego bounded onto the floor, her maw covered in blood.

"Hey," Layla said, stroking Tego behind the ear. "Yes, we can do it. Because if we don't, all of these people die."

Chapter Eleven

LAYLA CASSIDY

The team reached the remains of a makeshift barricade that had been constructed in a small foyer halfway down the corridor of the third floor. Blood saturated the ground, but there were no bodies, no fighters, no enemies—nothing.

Tego walked beyond the remains of the barricade and let out a low growl. Layla flexed the fingers of her metal arm, which changed into a blade as Tego's growl became louder.

The floor beneath them was torn apart by a blast of magical air, collapsing a large part of the structure and sending Layla and her team through to the floor below with a crash. The human gang was on them almost immediately, attacking with clubs and blades, as the sounds of gunfire broke out. Layla reached out, dismantling anything that was even vaguely gun-like as the rest of her team engaged their attackers.

Layla was concentrating on tearing apart a number of firearms and forcing any bullets into the walls around them when a man and woman attacked her with clubs. She deflected one strike, stabbing the second human in the chest with her arm, before spinning back to the first human and cutting across his throat before he had time to readjust to what was happening. Chloe and Piper had been engaged by several attackers, with Chloe using her ability to absorb and redirect kinetic energy to blast one out of a window. Piper had hardened her skin to near-unbreakable levels and was deflecting blows of blades with her bare arms before using her considerable strength to hurt her opponents.

Layla continued on, parrying and dodging attacks from the multitude of humans, taking control of their guns to turn them on their wielders with ruthless efficiency, until bodies littered the floor in her wake.

Sir Lamorak stood at the end of the corridor, the same smug expression on his face that he'd worn outside. Wave after wave of his followers pushed past him, forcing those fighting them to retreat before overcoming them and moving forward again.

"He doesn't care if his supporters die," Chloe said. She had a nasty cut above her eye that had soaked the side of her face in blood.

"He has enough to spare," Piper said, rolling her shoulders.

"I think they've finally figured out that bringing guns to this fight isn't going to work for them," Layla said. She'd been hit several times—once in the ribs, hard enough for them to break. Her power ensured that they were fixing themselves, but they'd be sore for a while, and she would certainly feel it in the morning. If they survived until then.

Layla placed a hand on Tego's head, the feline's fur matted with the blood of their enemies. The four of them had held off the mass of attackers so far, but they had all taken hits, and they couldn't do this all night.

Sir Lamorak took a step forward. "Having fun?" he asked.

"Sure," Chloe said. "You?"

He threw knives of fire at them. Layla blocked several of them with a metal shield, while Piper and Chloe dived into a nearby apartment to escape. Tego let out a whine as one of the blades hit her in the flank, and Layla dropped her shield and threw herself toward her, recreating the shield to cover them both, but not in time to avoid one of the blades cutting her across her hip. Layla stifled a cry of pain and, placing her hand against the shield of metal, caused it to explode, raining thousands of tiny bits of shrapnel down the hallway toward Sir Lamorak and his people.

Layla checked Tego's cut. It was deep, but the fire had cauterized the wound almost immediately.

"All that armor, and he hits you in the joints," Layla said, stroking Tego's face. "Go check on Chloe and Piper; I'll deal with Sir Lamorak."

Tego licked Layla's face and limped away. She would be okay; she healed quickly. But Layla was now beyond furious.

She sprinted down the hallway toward Sir Lamorak, who laughed as he threw more and more blades of fire and air at her. Layla turned her arm into a shield, and while each one that hit hurt, the anger she felt inside spurred her on. Reaching Sir Lamorak, she collided with him, lifted him off the ground, and pounded him back on the floor with a vengeance.

Sir Lamorak grabbed Layla's metal arm and unleashed lightning into it, the current traveling through her body. The pain was all-encompassing as she collapsed to her knees. Sir Lamorak stood up as Layla blinked and tried to remember how to make her body work.

He grabbed her by the throat, lifting her from the ground. "This will hurt," he told her and threw her out of the window.

Layla hit the ground from two floors up, her body still paralyzed from the lightning shock. Thankfully, she hit soft earth, and her body rolled with the impact, but even so, the air was knocked out of her.

Grabbing hold of a wooden bench, she used it to help pull herself back to her feet. Layla looked over at the mass of rioters standing on the sidewalk between her and the empath.

"Judgement," Layla said, tapping her comm unit, only to discover it was dead. "Shit." She took it out and tossed it away.

Another blast of lightning from above hit Layla in the back, and she was thrown forward over the bench. She could do nothing but watch as Sir Lamorak landed on the ground and calmly walked over to her.

Layla tried to take control of Sir Lamorak's armor, but nothing happened.

"I read about you," Sir Lamorak said with a sneer as he banged his fist against his armor. "Layla Cassidy, who killed a dragon, who slaughtered trolls, blood elves, and giants. Who defeated the Valkyries. And now you crawl at my feet like the pathetic, feeble creature you are." He looked down at her. "The runes on my armor stop your power from taking control of it. Your friends will die, you will die, and everything you care about will be wiped from the surface of this puny world."

Layla snarled, kicking her foot into his groin, putting all her anger and hatred of him into it. Sir Lamorak gasped and staggered back, giving Layla time to get to her feet. She tried to shift her metal arm into a blade, but the pain was overwhelming. The lightning magic had done something to disrupt her ability to morph her arm, and until the effects lessened, it was no longer an option available to her.

Sir Lamorak threw more lightning at Layla, but she had already moved. She kicked him in the head, grabbing hold of his wrist as he tried to push her away. She narrowly avoided being hit with more magic as she aimed his hand back toward the crowd of his followers charging toward them, and the magic tore into them like they were made of paper. Bodies hit the ground; others were screaming as they were engulfed by flames.

Layla tried to break Sir Lamorak's arm, but he rolled over, lifting her off the ground with brute strength, and threw her across the pathway.

She reached out with her power to take control of the tiny pieces of metal inside Sir Lamorak, and for a moment he froze in place, before he gave a smug grin. Purple glyphs lit up over Sir Lamorak's arms and hands, and he took a step forward.

Layla's eyes opened wide in shock.

"Surprise . . . ," Sir Lamorak said gleefully. "Matter magic. It's different for every sorcerer, but for me . . . well, it means your power has *no* effect on me."

"It also means you can't use your elemental magic," Layla said.

"There is give-and-take with every power," Sir Lamorak said. "I do not need my elemental power to kill you. I'll be happy to beat you to death."

He raised his fists in a boxer's stance and moved toward Layla, who spat blood onto the ground and raised her own hands, her metal one making a satisfying click as it formed a fist.

Layla noticed Sir Lamorak's continued smug expression. She was pretty sure he had some sort of trick up his sleeve.

Gunfire broke out from the top floor of the building, and Layla forced herself to not look.

"My people are murdering everyone here," he said. "Any survivors will learn to bow to Avalon, as you all will."

"Are we fighting or chatting?" Layla asked.

Sir Lamorak snapped forward with a jab, which Layla easily deflected. She dodged his powerful cross as she stepped around him and smashed her metal fist into his exposed ribs. The fingers of her hand fell to the grass at her feet, and a second later her entire arm was falling apart. She stared at it for a second too long and received a kick to her chest that sent her crashing over a nearby piece of fencing and landing in a small flower bed.

"Were you not listening?" Sir Lamorak asked with a chuckle.

Layla used her good arm to push herself back up to her feet as one of the windows on the top floor of the building behind her exploded, raining glass and pieces of burning paper around the courtyard behind her.

"Your friends are *losing*," Sir Lamorak said.

Layla put herself in a fighting stance and used the fingers of her good hand to motion for Sir Lamorak to come fight. Something he did happily.

Sir Lamorak was powerful, but he wasn't particularly fast or technical. One more kick to her chest, though, and she was sent sprawling once again.

The humans around them were panicking and fell away from the wall they'd made, revealing Judgement standing over the body of the empath, a bloody sword in her hand. She nodded to Layla, dropped the sword on the corpse, and sprinted toward Sir Lamorak as many of the Avalon supporters felt every emotion that had been suppressed by the empath come flooding back at once. They either collapsed sobbing or fled into the city.

The look of fury on Sir Lamorak's face was easy to see, and he ran toward Judgement. That was a mistake.

Judgement dodged a punch and drove a blade of light into his chest, then moved past him, tearing the blade out as she did. The armor he'd been so proud of provided no protection against someone as powerful as Judgement. She drove another dagger into his back, twisted it, and detonated the magic inside him as he spun to face her.

Sir Lamorak was slow now, barely able to keep up with the number of times the twin blades of light pierced his body, each one leaving his shining armor drenched with more and more of his own blood. He dropped down to one knee as Layla pulled herself back to her feet. She wasn't about to get involved; Sir Lamorak had brought this on himself.

"Damn it," Layla said to herself, cursing the thought as it passed into her head. "What if he knows something important?" she shouted to Judgement.

Judgement drove a blade of light into Sir Lamorak's head and detonated the magic inside his skull. "He doesn't," she said casually as Sir Lamorak's body dropped to the ground. "He was always just a thug with delusions of grandeur."

Layla dropped back to the ground, exhausted.

"You did well against him," Judgement said, placing a hand on Layla's shoulder. "Sorry I missed the rest of the fight. He was a tough bastard."

The rest of the fighting inside the building was brief as Judgement led her cavalry inside to exterminate anyone stupid enough to get in her way. Judgement scared a lot of people, but Layla had always found her to be pleasant, if odd. A side effect of living through hundreds and hundreds of years of fighting and killing, she imagined.

"How many did we lose?" Layla asked Piper, who looked singed and was covered in blood.

"Forty-six human civilians," she said as they walked the hallway of the top floor, heading up to the roof, where the rest of Layla's team waited. "The APC driver and six cops too."

Tego lay on the ground, basking as the dawn broke over the sky.

Layla bent down to scratch the large feline and checked her wound at the same time. "You're okay," she said softly as Tego purred.

"Avalon forces have moved further across the city," Piper said. "I think we may actually be able to call this a win. Not a particularly good win, but I'll take what I can get at the moment."

Tarron sat cross-legged, further away from everyone else. His eyes were closed, and he breathed methodically in and out.

Layla walked over and stood behind him. "Thank you," she said.

"I can't have you die," Tarron said with a slight chuckle, although he didn't look back over at her. "We have a lot more fights to win before we're done. A lot more lives to take."

"Hopefully once we're done, we won't need to do that anymore."

Tarron looked back at Layla. "And that would be a world I'd like to live in."

"May I?" Layla asked, motioning to the spot beside Tarron.

Tarron nodded. "Of course."

"Today was a bad day," Layla said. "You helped make it better. You might not like war—and honestly, I'd be *really* concerned about someone who said they did—but we saved lives. A lot of lives."

"I know," Tarron said. "Taking lives to save lives is an odd way to live, but so long as it tallies in the right column, I can deal with it."

Piper stood by Layla, her ear mic in hand. "For you," she said.

Layla took the mic and put it in her ear. "Layla," Jinayca said, her voice excited and concerned all at once.

"I'm okay," Layla said. "We're all okay. Judgement sort of pissed everyone off, killed them all, and I think we sort of won."

"The KOA are folding all over the city. You're needed back here; we got Gawain."

Layla looked up at Piper. "We got Gawain?" she repeated. "Any casualties?"

"Not on our side," she said. "But there are a lot of people yelling about how the White House is no longer in one piece."

Layla paused. "They broke the White House?"

"Sure, let's say broke," Jinayca said. "Just get back here. I think this is just the start, Layla."

"We're on our way," Layla said, passing Piper her mic back. "Get ready, everyone—we're not done yet."

"Who gets to tell Judgement?" Chloe asked.

"Not it," Tarron said, raising his hand.

Tego raised a paw in the air.

"We'll finish up here and head back together," Layla said, shaking her head in amusement. "Sounds like the shit is about to hit the fan. Again."

Chapter Twelve

Nate Garrett

After the end of the White House siege, considering the building was still a little bit on fire, I left everyone else to get on with their jobs and found a quiet park bench in Lafayette Square to sit and gather my thoughts.

Gawain had been frog-marched off to a tent, where he was to be interrogated. I still didn't believe he'd just surrender like he had, and seeing how Merlin and Arthur liked to play the long game, it wasn't out of the realm of possibility that Gawain had a longer-term plan. We just had to figure out what it was.

"How you feeling?" Selene asked as she sat beside me.

"It's been a long few days," I told her as she rested her head on my shoulder. "It's been a long few years, if I'm being honest."

"This was a win," Selene said. "A lot of our people are going back to Shadow Falls, but there will be a contingent left here to help out. Jinayca thinks Gawain knows how to get into Atlantis."

"Getting him to talk is a different matter," I said. "Mordred isn't here with Excalibur, and according to Gawain he's had runes placed on himself to ensure the sword doesn't work. Which I didn't think was possible. We'll take him back to Shadow Falls and find out, I guess."

"His surrendering bothers you," Selene said.

I nodded. "Yeah, it really does."

Roberto ran over to where Selene and I sat. He looked out of breath.

"You okay?" I asked him.

"The president went rogue, and people are freaking out," Roberto said. "So not really, no. The vice president wants to talk to you."

"Go," Selene said. "I'll help out here with our people. I hear Judgement killed a paladin."

"Good for her," I said and walked off with Roberto, who was practically pushing me forward.

"Roberto," I said, looking back at him. "What is wrong?"

"It's all gone to shit," Roberto said. "We thought the president was a hostage."

"Where is he?" I asked.

"That's part of the problem," Roberto said as we reached a tent and stepped inside to see the human commanders, along with the vice president, Queen Orfeda, and Jinayca, the latter of whom was rubbing the back of her hand.

"Who'd you punch?" I asked her.

She pointed to a metal cabinet with a hole in it. "It was that or General Pompous Twat over there."

"How *dare* you?" the general shouted, before seemingly discovering who was in the tent with him and taking a deep breath.

"So this is going well," I said.

"You," the general almost shouted, his finger pointed at me accusingly.

"Hi," I said.

The general stormed over to me and prodded me in the chest with a large finger. "I am four-star General Blake," he said. "And *you* have committed an act of treason against our country. What the *fuck* did you do to the White House?" He prodded me again, and I looked beyond him to Roberto, who looked like he might throw up.

Two of the large men—one had an FBI jacket, and the other I assumed was Secret Service—looked like they'd rather be elsewhere, while Vice President Katia Lopez appeared to be genuinely intrigued by what was going to happen.

"So what do you have to say?" the four-star general shouted, drawing looks from several dozen service personnel outside the still-open tent, who tried very hard not to be interested.

I looked down at the spot where Blake had prodded me. "General," I said softly.

"Yes?" Blake said.

I looked up at the general and met his stare. "If you *ever* poke me in the chest again or shout at me like you're doing right now, we're going to find out how long you can survive without any oxygen."

Blake's face went bright red. "How dare—" he started, before I waved a hand and removed the oxygen from his lungs.

I stepped past the general, barely bothering to pay attention to him as he dropped to his knees. I stopped at the vice president. "Can't you control your attack dog?"

"He's angry," Vice President Lopez said. "And I'd rather he wasn't dead."

I snapped my fingers, to the sound of audible gasps from Blake. "I do not *play* games," I said without turning back to Blake. "I destroyed a portion of your building, a building I believe has been rebuilt before. I did so because there was a sniper up there who may have wanted to kill Gawain. The same Gawain who I'm pretty sure was working with *your* president to kill *your* people. Tonight we saved your capital city, your Senate, your Congress, your innocent civilians. How many died?"

"Sixty-eight thousand at last count," a woman in an FBI jacket said. "That's a rough estimate based on figures we're getting in."

"It would have been two hundred and sixty-eight without us," I said. "And you know it."

Vice President Lopez nodded.

"I do not expect to be liked," I said. "But I do expect your people to show me the respect I deserve. The respect we all deserve. I broke your building; it can be rebuilt." I turned back to the general, who was back on his feet. "I promise you one thing: I am not someone you want to pick a fight with. The enemy is still out there, and your country is still going to need people like you to help it through what happens next. So my advice, General Blake, is to grow the fuck up and act like the goddamn leader you're meant to be."

Blake nodded slightly before looking at the ground.

"Nice speech," Roberto said.

"I've been listening to Mordred," I told him. "Madam President—because I'm pretty sure you're about to be that, if not already—I wish you the best of luck. Once we're done, I'm sure that King Mordred will want to come back, and we'll talk about what happens next. I'd like to come with him, so long as you'll have me." I offered my hand.

President Lopez shook my hand without hesitation. "I'd be honored."

"Thank you," I said. "Roberto, I assume you're staying to help."

"I would like that very much, yes," Roberto said.

"Good," I told him. "So now that the pleasantries are done, why is everyone freaking out and getting angry?"

"The president has been taken captive by your people," President Lopez said. "We want him back. Obviously."

"Actually, I don't think we have taken him anywhere," I said. "Last I heard, he had been taken into the FBI's or Secret Service's custody. He's not our prisoner." I looked at Jinayca and Orfeda, who both nodded.

"Then tell us where he is," General Blake said, although it sounded a lot less like a pompous demand now.

I shrugged. "How do you lose your own president? He has to be here somewhere; it's not like he can just get up and walk off."

"He was seen with several human agents," Orfeda said. "They were taking him back into the White House."

"The house that is still on fire?" I asked. "That seems like a bad idea."

"So no one knows where a possibly traitorous president is," President Lopez said, clearly exasperated.

"Anyone asked his wife?" I asked.

"She's as surprised about it all as anyone else," General Blake said.

"I'll go check the White House," I said. "I'll try not to set fire to your building again."

"Please do," President Lopez said with the tug of a smile at her lips.

"Roberto, you want to join me?" I asked.

"Go with him," President Lopez said. "Nate, if you find the president, please don't hurt him. We'd like him unscathed when we press charges."

"I'm coming too," Jinayca said. "Anyone who argues will get a punch."

No one argued.

Roberto, Jinayca, and I had only just left the tent when a young black woman wearing a charcoal suit that was more than a little singed walked over. "Nate Garrett?" she asked.

"I'll catch you up," I told Jinayca and Roberto before turning back to the agent. "That's me."

"The president's wife wants to talk to you."

"After you," I said and followed the agent to a tent at the far side of the square, where four Secret Service agents stood guard.

I was ushered inside and found the president's wife sitting at a small wooden table, a notebook in front of her and pen in hand. She placed the pen on the book as I walked in.

"You are Nathaniel Garrett, yes?" she asked.

"Nate," I said.

Heather Reed, at only forty-six, was ten years younger than her husband. She was five three at most, petite, with long hair that was partly gray. From what I'd heard over the years, she did not suffer fools gladly and had been the backbone of her husband's campaign to be elected.

"Nate, my husband is being called a traitor," she said.

"Pretty much," I said.

"I don't believe it," she replied. "My husband is not perfect. He's stubborn and impetuous, but he's *not* a traitor."

"He sided with Avalon," I said. "I was there. I saw it. I saw the smugness on his face."

"My husband is not normally a smug man," Heather said firmly. "I've seen a change in him in recent weeks. He's cold, distant, and sharp with people. He's quicker to temper, and he scares me. It may seem strange, but he doesn't feel like the man I married and have supported all this time."

"Heather," I said as softly as possible, "I don't know what to tell you."

"Tell me you'll find Andrew," Heather requested, getting to her feet. "Just find him. The man in the White House today is *not* my husband. Every now and again, I think I see flashes of something else, just behind the face." She looked thoughtful. "Something *wrong*."

"I'll find him," I told her, if only to put her mind at rest.

She reached out and took my hand in hers. "Thank you."

I turned to leave.

"It was his eyes," she said.

I stopped at the tent entrance and turned back to her. "What about his eyes?"

"I caught sight of them the other day," she said with a slight shudder. "He'd lost his temper, throwing things around, hurling abuse at staff. I walked in, and his eyes . . . they weren't his."

"What were they?" I asked.

"Like fire," she said with a frown. "I know that might sound silly."

Oh shit. I sprinted out of the tent without another word, catching up to Jinayca and Roberto, who were just entering the White House grounds. "We have a *big* problem," I said, running past them without stopping.

"What's going on?" Roberto asked after catching me up as I stopped at the front entrance to the White House and pushed open the door slightly.

"The president had eyes of fire," I said. "Heather told me. Her husband had eyes of fire, and she thought she saw something beneath his face."

"Oh shit," Roberto said. "That can't be good."

"What has eyes of fire?" Jinayca asked.

"Goddamn shape-shifter—and there's only one I know working with Avalon," I said, stepping inside the White House to find two dead Secret Service agents on the floor beyond. Their throats had been torn out.

"Damn it," Roberto said, drawing his gun from his holster.

Five Secret Service agents left a nearby room and were soon shouted at to stand down by Roberto.

"Someone is in here," Roberto said. "Someone killed these two agents. Have you seen them?"

All five agents shook their heads.

"Have you all been together long?" Jinayca asked.

"Jerry here just arrived," a young man said, pointing to Jerry, a heavyset individual who looked a lot like one of the dead agents.

Jerry smiled. His hand turned into a claw, and he grabbed the nearest agent and threw him at us. He collided with Jinayca and Roberto as Jerry cut the throat of another agent with fingers that were now long and bony, before he set off up the stairs, taking them three at a time.

I gave chase, and Jerry ran into a room and jumped out of the window, crashing through the glass before falling the thirty feet to the rear of the White House. I followed suit, using air magic to land, as Jerry doubled back into the White House through another window.

"Goddamn it," I shouted, jumping back into the building, where I found two dead Secret Service men, one missing his head. It had been cut off in one smooth motion.

I blasted the door to the room with air magic, and it tore apart, ricocheting around the hallway beyond.

I sprinted out into the hallway to see a shape vanish through an open doorway beyond. I had no idea where I was inside the White House, as I'd been turned around, but I followed the shape into a small office.

At the far end, next to the door of an adjoining room, was a woman. She had bony, clawlike hands and dark skin, and her eyes blazed red and orange, as if there were two tiny furnaces in her skull. She opened her mouth, revealing dozens of piranha-like teeth, and flicked a long red tongue over them.

"We haven't officially met," I said. "I assume you're Lamashtu."

Lamashtu smiled, which was even more terrifying than when she hadn't been. "My reputation precedes me, as does yours, Nathaniel Garrett."

"You've been masquerading as the president," I said.

She nodded. "For a few weeks now."

"Where is he?"

"I was hungry," Lamashtu said softly, her voice like the purr of a cat.

"You didn't need to eat him."

"No, but I wanted to," Lamashtu said. "No evidence of him being missing. Gawain offered to bury him in the basement or incinerate him, but waste not, want not."

"You can't escape," I said.

"Now, that's not true," Lamashtu said with another smile. "Be seeing you soon."

She tossed a hand grenade in my direction, and I wrapped myself in a shield of air as she burst through the door before the explosion.

I ran after her as quickly as possible, but all I found was the decapitated head of the woman she'd killed earlier. I cursed myself for not bringing a comm unit with me and noticed that the drawer to the large wooden desk was open.

I walked over and checked, only to find a small wooden bracelet on the floor. There were runes burned into it that were slowly fading.

Jinayca, Roberto, and a dozen armed men and women burst through the door a few moments later.

"Lamashtu," I said, tossing the bracelet to Jinayca. "She was heading here to find that. A portable realm gate bracelet. I'm going to guess that whoever worked in this office was working for Avalon. Find them; find out where that bracelet led to."

I walked toward the exit and stopped. "President Reed is dead," I said, to several gasps. "Lamashtu has been playing him for a few weeks now. Gawain knows about it."

"Where is his body?" one of the Secret Service agents asked.

"She ate him," I told the young man. "When you tell Heather, I'll leave it up to you whether or not she needs to hear that bit."

"And what are you going to do?" Jinayca asked.

"I'm going to go talk to Gawain," I said. "Possibly kill him. I haven't decided yet." I looked around the room, waiting for an objection, but no one had one.

I walked out of the White House alone, wanting a moment to not think about how we had no idea where an enemy as dangerous as Lamashtu had gone. No wonder Gawain had surrendered; I expected that he'd hoped she'd be able to free him.

One of the Secret Service agents told me where Gawain was, and I set off across the White House lawn to a park bench surrounded by three large tents and at least two dozen human members of the army. They were guarding Gawain, who sat on the bench itself, the runes carved into it appearing to ensure that he behaved himself.

"I've never liked you," Gawain said to me as I was waved past the soldiers guarding him. Gawain's wrists were adorned with sorcerers' bands, but other than that and the rune-graven bench, he was not restrained.

"You know, Gawain," I said, taking a seat on a wooden chair that one of the soldiers brought for me, "you really are a cunt. I know Americans don't like that word, but I'm pretty sure that the soldiers have heard worse, so I'm just going to say it. I've wanted to tell you that for a *really* long time. It felt good."

"Fuck you, Nate," Gawain snapped.

"Arthur is going to die," I said, my voice completely calm. "Your father is going to die. Everyone who stands with them will die. When we are done, their existence will never again tarnish this or any other realm. I'm going to give you one chance here—one chance to tell me what I need to know."

"Burn in hell," Gawain sneered.

"Gawain," I said softly. "Lamashtu has gone. She ran away. She left you here."

There was slight concern in his expression.

"I was right when I thought that you'd surrendered because you expected her to save you," I said. "That's good to know. No one is saving you."

"I will remain here until I am needed," Gawain said.

"You will remain here as everything you built burns to ash," I told him.

"I will finish my mission," Gawain said smugly.

"And what mission is that?" I asked. "To be arrested? To be beaten up? Because if they're your mission, you are a fucking superstar."

Gawain stared at me with only hate in his eyes. "I will tell you nothing," he shouted, spitting onto the ground.

"You're a nobody," I said. "You always were."

Gawain darted toward me, but I grabbed his arm and casually backhanded him, sending him back to the bench as several guns were leveled in his direction.

"How do we get to Atlantis?" I asked him.

Gawain laughed. "You can't kill me and take my memories; you can't feed me to your wraith; you can't do a goddamn thing to me. The Horsemen will cometh. They will burn your world to nothing."

"The Horsemen?" I asked. "Arthur is making *new* Horsemen?" That was a concerning idea, considering the only surviving members of the last ones that had been made were Judgement, Mordred, and myself.

Gawain looked dismayed. "Fuck off."

"Atlantis was a destroyed realm. Why go there?"

"A lot of reasons."

"List them," I said, feeling my irritation threaten to bubble over.

"Fuck off."

"Good talk," I said, getting to my feet as Judgement walked into the clearing. "Just so you know, I'm not going to torture you. I'm not going to hurt you to get information. I don't think that would be a good idea."

"And she is?" Gawain asked.

"I'm not sure we've met," Judgement said. "Not properly. I killed Hera. And I hear you might know where my sister Athena is, so I'm going to tear your brain into tiny pieces and let you put them back together again. Remember what you did to Mordred? Well, the runes you placed on him are the same ones on that bench. Want to see how long it takes you to break?"

Gawain glanced at the runes and showed fear for the first time. "You're lying," he stammered.

"Am I?" Judgement asked. "I don't think so."

Gawain looked between me and Judgement.

"You wouldn't," Gawain said.

"I once tore out a man's eyes and made him hold them as I tortured him," I told Gawain. "And of the two of us, I'm pretty sure I'm the nice one."

Judgement smiled.

"Everyone thinks Atlantis is destroyed," Gawain almost shouted. "That it was turned to ruin during the Titan Wars thousands of years ago, and it was. Everyone who lived there was killed. But the realm itself wasn't destroyed, and there's still plenty of places to rebuild."

"Continue," I said.

"Arthur thought that no one would look for us there. No one would think of going to Atlantis. And most importantly, there's only one entrance in and out."

"The realm gate was in Europe," I said. "It was destroyed thousands of years ago."

"There's a second gate. In Avalon."

I'd not been expecting that. "How is that possible?"

"It's under the mountains to the north of Camelot," Gawain said, with an expression that suggested he'd really rather not have said anything.

"You're going to need to expand on that," Judgement said.

"We always knew there was a gate there," Gawain said with a sigh. "My father mentioned it a few times as something he'd heard about. We set off on an expedition. Couldn't do it before our enemies were out of Avalon, and it took a while, but we found it about a year after we thought you were dead."

"What else did you find?"

"The realm gate is one of a dozen. Each gate goes to a different realm belonging to a different pantheon."

"That's how you got to Asgard?"

Gawain nodded.

"Why not use these gates all the time?"

"We couldn't," Gawain said. "They needed to be unlocked. Except Atlantis—that was never locked in the first place."

"Why?" Judgement asked.

"Presumably because no one thought it would ever be used again. Elves locked the others, though."

"They locked them how?" I asked. "And how did you unlock them? Explain."

"Each realm gate was dwarven in nature, but there were elven runes on them. None of them would work."

"But you've found an elf to unlock them?" Judgement asked.

Gawain nodded. "When we first went to Atlantis, all we found was destruction." He chuckled. "And a prison."

"What kind of prison?" I asked, curious as to where this was all going.

"An elven one. Shadow elven, to be exact."

"You found shadow elves inside a prison?" I asked, keeping my anger in check. "Like how Tarron was found? Frozen in suspended animation? How many?"

"Half dozen," Gawain said. "All frozen. We . . . defrosted them. They were not exactly fans of the people who put them there and were keen to help us do what we needed to do."

"They unlocked the realm gates in Avalon?"

"It took us several years and a lot of dead bodies, but they helped us, and eventually, yes, we unlocked them. Our first journey was to Asgard, and you saw how well that went."

"How do we get into Avalon?" I asked.

"Avalon Island," Gawain said.

"We can't get in that way," Judgement said. "No one can. The island is abandoned, and I assume if we send people through the realm gate there a dozen at a time, they're just going to get slaughtered by whatever army you have on the other side. There are two realm gates into Avalon. One on Avalon Island, which is not a good idea. And another behind Kay's home, which we've tried to access from Nidavellir, seeing how that's where it's linked to, and it almost killed the dwarf doing it, so I assume it's booby trapped."

"Obviously," Gawain said with a smirk.

Judgement took a step toward Gawain and removed a knife from her belt. "You don't have any magic right now," she said. "Want to cut out the smug shit?"

"Fine," Gawain snapped. "Only Kay's blood can activate it. And Kay is dead. Oops."

"Is there another realm gate into Avalon?" I asked, trying very hard not to rip Gawain's head off.

"Yes," Gawain said and folded his arms over his chest, followed up with a scream as Judgement drove the blade into his kneecap.

"Care to elaborate?" she asked sweetly.

"It's in Duat," Gawain said.

"You have an army stationed there?" I asked. "How many?"

"No, nothing like that," Gawain said. "You can't go through with many people—the spirits will spot you, and . . . they don't like the living."

"So to get to Avalon, we need to go through Duat, the land of the dead, and into the mountains behind Camelot?" I asked. "That's the only way from the Earth realm into Avalon?"

Gawain nodded. "That I know of, yes. Now either fuck off or kill me."

"One last question," I said. "What are the names of every single shadow elf you found?"

The list wasn't long. When I was done, I stood and looked down at the craven enemy as Judgement walked away to presumably wash her knife.

"You are pathetic," I said sadly. "A parasite of a man who clings to whoever will offer you the most power. The most wealth. The most of whatever you desire. How long did it take you to screw around with Merlin's head to join Arthur's cause?"

"Not long," Gawain said with a smirk. He was happy to be giving this information. Information, I was pretty sure, that Gawain felt hurt me. "Abaddon did most of it. And once he was in our thrall, he had little chance to escape. The day Mordred nearly killed Arthur and required Merlin to tend to him around the clock . . . well, that was the beginning of the end to Merlin's being anything other than Arthur's soldier. *Mordred* did this to our father—*he* turned him into the man he is today."

"Is there any way to save him?"

Gawain laughed.

I turned as Queen Orfeda and a dozen of her soldiers entered the clearing. "We're taking him to a secure facility in the city," she said. "Hades and Persephone will want to question him."

"You can't kill me yet," Gawain said with a laugh.

"Let me know when you can," I said to Orfeda and punched Gawain in the jaw, knocking out a few of his teeth.

Chapter Thirteen

Nate Garrett

City of Solomon, Realm of Shadow Falls

I'd left Washington and headed back to Shadow Falls, where my first port of call was the council room in the palace so I could debrief everyone as to what had happened there. Lamashtu was now considered a high priority, but we had a more immediate way forward, and that was to get into Avalon. I'd finished with the debriefing when Mordred and his team returned, looking remarkably upbeat. The bastards.

"Nanshe and her people are going to help us," Mordred said, dropping a large leather-bound book onto the table. "The Olympians are going to pledge fifty thousand troops to our command. My command. Apparently."

"What's the book for?" I asked.

"This is a present from Nanshe," Mordred said. "It details a realm gate that goes into the mountains in Avalon. It's in—"

"Duat," Hades said.

"Hey," Hel said, looking around. "Do you all know this?"

Everyone nodded.

We spent the next hour sharing information so that everyone was on the same page. Selene sat on one side of me, Zamek on the other. There was an aura of tension over everyone, and even Remy—usually a source of humor even in the darkest of times—was quiet. He caught my eye and winked, making me smile.

"You didn't kill Gawain, then," Remy said.

"I did not," I said.

"Shame," Remy said.

"At least we know Gawain wasn't lying," Judgement said from the corner of the room.

"Small mercies," Mordred said. "I'm sorry I wasn't there."

"It was better you weren't," I said. "Although now that we know Lamashtu is out there, she could be a real problem."

"We'll have people look for her," Persephone said.

"In the meantime, we need to send a small force to Duat and through into Avalon," Olivia said. "They're going to have to get through Avalon to the realm gate and activate it. We're going to send our forces to Avalon Island so that we can get into Avalon once we know it's safe. Unfortunately, not only is the realm gate booby trapped, it's also not big enough to take more than a few dozen at a time."

"I have an idea about that," Zamek said. "I think we can make it bigger."

Everyone turned to look at him.

"How?" Orfeda asked.

"The realm gates can heal themselves," Zamek said. "It should be possible to also make them change shape."

"Should be?" Hades asked.

"We tried it once," Zamek said. "It worked."

"With live people?" Persephone asked.

"With goats," Zamek said. "Lots of goats."

"And they survived?" Mordred asked dubiously.

Zamek nodded. "It's not easy, and it takes a lot of power, but we should be able to change the gate so that it can take thousands in at once, not hundreds."

"That would mean much less time for anyone in Avalon to mount a counterattack," Mordred said.

"Okay, people, get it done," Hades said.

"I'm leading the team into Duat," I said. "This is not open for negotiation. Whatever is inside Avalon is going to need people who can hit hard and fast. Gawain said you can't take a lot of people into the realm, and while I've never been there, I've spoken to Isis. She's coming, too, by the way. She's been to Duat before."

"What did she suggest?" Hel asked.

"That we all get in and run really fast," I said. "Her actual words."

"I wonder," Remy said. "How many people here have been to Atlantis before?"

There was a smattering of people who said that they had.

"Anything we need to know?" Tarron asked.

"When everyone is here," Hades said, "I will give you all the information you need."

I looked up to the end of the table, where Mordred remained silent.

"What are you humming?" I asked him, as everyone else went quiet.

Mordred smiled. "'Still Alive,'" he said. "It's from *Portal*."

"The cake game?" Hel asked. "I thought I recognized it."

"It's not exactly a game about cake . . . ," Mordred said.

"I really wish that Elaine had known about the realm gates in Avalon," someone said, although I didn't catch who.

"No one knew," Mordred said. "And I do literally mean no one. From what this book says, the dwarves built them long before any of us were even sparkles in our parents' eyes."

"Where's the book from?" I asked.

"You remember the fire at the Library of Alexandria?" Mordred asked.

"Not personally," I said.

"Well, a lot of what was there that wasn't destroyed was taken to Olympus. There's enough stuff in there you could spend a lifetime reading and still not be done."

"Unfortunately it's not all good news," Hades said. "Which leads us nicely on to Tarron, who I believe has more bad news to impart."

"Oh, thank fuck for that," Remy said. "I was beginning to think we were on a roll for happiness and was getting concerned for my health."

Tarron stood. "These names that Gawain gave are the names of shadow elves, two of whom I knew before I was frozen. One was a member of a high-ranking elven family, and the other was an officer of the law."

"And they were found in a prison, so guessing not the most well behaved of elven society?" Olivia said.

Tarron nodded. "This one—his name is Estaliar. He was tried and convicted of the murders of one hundred and sixty-two humans and four shadow elves."

"He's a serial killer?" Layla asked.

Tarron sighed. "I don't know why he's in Atlantis. I never realized it was a prison for shadow elves, although it's entirely possible. We did have realms as prisons. Estaliar is dangerous. A trained killer. An elf who will slaughter and continue to do so until he is stopped. He killed the four shadow elves who first tried to apprehend him. He picked humans because . . . well, honestly, because they were like prey to him. This is not someone any realm wants released, and if he's helping Arthur, we have a big problem."

"And the others inside the prison?" I asked.

"Presumably people just like him. This second name—one of the officers of the law, Vusmar—he was one of the investigators of Estaliar's case. I do not know why he was imprisoned; it was after my time."

"And these elves have been released somewhere," Olivia said.

"Yes," Tarron said. "I would be wary. I cannot imagine that Arthur's regime would let people live if they did not match their ideals."

"It never rains, but it pours," Zamek said with a sigh.

"So we need to go to Duat, make it into Avalon, and then possibly fight off shadow elf criminals?" Selene asked.

"We need to get to Camelot and get that gate unlocked," Zamek said. "Otherwise, we're going to be stuck in a city where the vast majority of them would like all of us dead."

"We're going to have to use stealth and a lot of luck," I said. "We move fast, stay low, and try to make sure we move around the outskirts of the city. I lived there for a long time; I think we can do it. Once we're in that realm gate temple, though, you're not going to have long."

"Surely it won't be as easy as that," Selene said.

"Nothing is ever that easy," Hades said. "But for now, let's all try to get ready. Nate, get your team. Whoever you want."

I nodded.

As everyone filed out of the council room, I stopped beside Olivia. "We'll find him," I told her.

"I know," she said. "Atlantis. You think Gawain was telling the truth?"

I nodded. "I'm thinking that Gawain was told to tell us about Atlantis if he got caught."

"You think it's a trap?" Hel asked.

I nodded. "Almost certainly."

"That sounds about right for my father and Arthur," Mordred said.

"How are the Olympian troops getting to Atlantis?" I asked.

"There's a realm gate in Atlantis," he said. "A second one, behind the city; it's been unused for centuries. The dwarves who live in Olympus are going to get it working so when we get to Atlantis, we can link them and bring forward their army."

"We'll send a small team there to work with them," Persephone said. "That way they can create a summoning circle and keep us informed. We'll get to Avalon first and decide the best way from there."

"Sounds like a plan," I said. "How'd you get Nanshe to back us?" I asked Mordred.

"I used Excalibur to make me tell the truth," he said. "And I begged. I may have even groveled . . ."

"It worked?" I asked.

"Eighty-six out of a hundred people voted in favor," Hel said.

Mordred offered me a fist bump, which I took. "Good job, Your Majesty."

"Yeah, that's still weird," Mordred said.

"You got a team in mind?" Hades asked me, clapping me on the shoulder.

"Lucifer, Isis, Selene, and anyone else who wants to come," I said. "I don't think we're going to have time to see Astrid."

"We'll see her soon enough," Selene said.

"No necromancers," Hel said. "Duat is not the place they want to be. You're not a full necromancer, Nate, so you should be fine so long as you don't use your power."

"Thanks for the info," I said. "Okay, well, let's get ready." I walked out of the room with Selene beside me. We made our way through the palace and spotted Kase leaning up against the wall near the palace entrance.

"I'll leave you to talk," Selene said. "I'll see you at the temple in an hour or so."

"Thank you," I said. I went over to Kase. "So," I said casually. "Been a shit day."

Kase nodded. "I'm sorry for what happened in Washington." Her voice was low, barely above a whisper. "I'm angry all the time, Nate. It's like it's just bubbling there and never goes away. The beast wants out, it wants to take control, and it feeds on the anger inside of me."

"Let's go for a walk," I said, and the pair of us walked through the palace to the rear exit.

"This is where your friend died," Kase said.

I nodded. "Galahad died saving my life, and I lost control. I slaughtered hundreds of blood elves out here without a thought. I tortured the man who killed him. I beat him so badly he begged to die. We all lose control sometimes. We all have that need to protect those we love and hurt those who show us that we can't save every-one. You have it harder than most. The beast inside a were wants out; it wants blood and flesh. And so do you."

Kase sat on the steps overlooking the field that led to the dense forest covering a large part of the realm. Just before the tree line was a statue of Galahad. His daughter and pretty much every single member of the council had arranged for it to be built to remember him. It was new and had been done without ceremony, but it was there, and I enjoyed coming to see it.

"I can't stop it," she whispered.

I sat beside her and placed an arm around her shoulder. She rested her head on my own shoulder and began to weep softly.

"How do I make it stop?"

"You can help us find your father," I said. "You can keep it together for when you see him. You cannot let the beast win. If it wins, you will no longer see friend from foe; you will kill and kill and kill until that's all you are. Until no one recognizes you anymore. It was something Tommy was always terrified of. Diana less so—I think she long since made peace with it."

"My dad never really spoke about the beast inside of him," Kase said, rubbing her eyes with the backs of her fingers.

"He had you and your mum," I said. "That's what stopped him. Everyone needs that person they can rely on above all others. I don't mean a boyfriend or wife or whatever but someone they can put their complete trust in. Some people have more than one. I think they're probably the lucky ones."

"Like you?"

I nodded. "Yeah, I guess so. And you, too, Kase. You have your parents, Layla, Chloe, and a dozen others. Even Harry."

"We broke up," Kase said.

"I know," I said. "I saw him drinking away his troubles in the bar in town. He does not handle whiskey well."

Kase laughed but stopped herself and sighed. "It's beginning to feel like everything I do is just a fucking mess."

"That's not true, and I'd like to think that deep inside, you know that. How are you sleeping?"

"I'm not. Not really. I have bad dreams."

"You need sleep," I told her. "Even werewolves need it. Look, if you want to come to one of the realms or go to Avalon Island, I'm okay with it. I'm sure everyone else will be too. We've all done things that we weren't proud of."

"My mum is finding it hard too," Kase said. "I think she's not sleeping. She's upset a lot. She snaps at people."

"Have you spoken to her?" I asked.

Kase shook her head. "I tried, but I was scared that we'd end up arguing. That I'd lose my temper at her. She doesn't need or deserve that."

"Go talk to your mum," I told her.

"She's so damn busy all the time," Kase said.

"Now you're just making excuses," I said. "Go talk to her. Now. She's probably still in the council room. I don't know when any of us are going to get the chance to talk, so if you have something you need to say, do it now. Trust me: leaving things unsaid feels like shit."

"Have you spoken to your mum?" Kase asked me.

"Touché," I said with a smile. "No . . . no, I haven't. She's been off fighting everyone and anyone she can."

"Sounds like someone else I know," Kase said, looking at me with a smile.

"Also, if you can, talk to Harry," I told her. "The man is in love with you, and you are in love with him, and frankly, now more than ever, you both need someone. Now go and try to relax. That's an order."

Kase stood and laughed. "You're not the boss of me," she said. "But I will go and talk to my mum. And if I have time, to Harry, too, but you need to talk to Brynhildr." Kase leaned over and hugged me. "Thank you for listening and understanding and not bouncing my skinny ass over the White House lawn."

I laughed. "You're welcome."

Kase walked toward the palace doors, where she stopped and turned back to me. "Nate, do you think we'll ever be done here?"

I nodded. "I have to think we will. I have to think that your little brother and my daughter will grow up into a better world. We have to stop them, Kase, because anything else will destroy us all. Arthur will turn the realms into his own playthings."

"We'll stop him," Kase said. "We'll stop them all."

I watched her walk away and turned back to the field before me. I walked across the field to the statue of Galahad, where dozens of flowers had been left. Galahad had been beloved by the people who had called him king, and that love hadn't diminished even after his death. I placed a hand on the warm stone and looked up at the statue, at his sword in one hand, his shield in another, ready for battle.

"If I don't make it back, it was a pleasure," I said. "I don't really know what happens to us after we die, but I really hope you're at peace, my friend."

I turned back to the palace. I had no idea how everything to come was going to pan out, but I knew that by the end of it either Arthur or I would be dead. Preferably the former.

Chapter Fourteen

Nate Garrett

Alexandria, Egypt, Earth Realm

After Leonardo and his assistants had changed the destination of the realm gate in Shadow Falls, my team and I stepped through and arrived in Giza. Hades had already arranged transportation in the form of comfortable SUVs for us to get to Alexandria. It had been quite entertaining to exit the Sphinx via a secret door at the rear of the statue, much to the surprise of a group of tourists.

We arrived in Alexandria, and Hades's contact arranged for us to get the horses we needed to ride through Duat, a prospect that Isis had been less than enthused about.

"So the realm gate is where?" Remy asked from beside me as he looked at the horses with distrust. He hadn't taken the news of his having to ride that well.

"Apparently," Isis said, "it's close to the harbor. An old well that leads down to a cavern at the bottom. The realm gate is there. I've been to Duat before, but . . . not this way."

Her tone suggested that this was a conversation that was over.

"I will be able to activate it when we get there," Zamek said. "There are no guardians, and no one has been down there in centuries, so it should be devoid of life."

Apart from Isis, Remy, and Zamek, my team also consisted of Selene, Lucifer, and Tarron.

"How do we get the horses down the well?" Selene asked. "Or did no one think of that?"

"The well has steps and is large enough to march six or seven abreast," Lucifer said. "It's more of a slope than steps. The horses should be fine."

The city of Alexandria was busy, and people gave us a wide berth, although Remy got his fair share of pointing from those we passed. For the most part, he reacted to this with finger guns and winking and, the two times someone said something less than pleasant, his middle fingers and some expletives about their mother.

The seven of us made good time through the city and reached the entrance to the well before nightfall, although it made little difference to the roasting heat that we'd felt since we'd arrived. It didn't help that we were all wearing rune-scribed dark leather armor. Shorts and T-shirts would have been cooler but offered not a lot of protection when going up against swords and bullets, unfortunately.

Zamek placed a hand against the stone wall, and it glowed a faint green color before opening as if it were a sliding glass door. We all stepped inside, and the wall re-formed behind us.

The interior of the well was surprisingly light. There were hundreds of small crystals in the stone walls of the well and more on the path. Runes had been carved all around, and the entire place was plenty large enough for the seven of us and our horses.

"One at a time," Lucifer said. "We don't know what's down there or how safe these paths are."

"I'll go first," Zamek said. "I don't have a horse, so if there are problems with the path, I can hopefully spot them."

I stayed at the back of the group with Tarron, who led his horse silently as we moved slowly down the spiral slope into the hundreds-of-meters-deep well.

"You've been quiet," I commented.

"I thought I was the last of my people," Tarron said. "It is a lot to take in. And it's made worse because those freed may well be criminals. I can only hope that some were imprisoned, like I was, for trying to do the right thing against corrupt regimes."

"Vigilantes?" I asked.

"Yes, that's the word I'd have used to describe my actions, I guess," Tarron said thoughtfully. "Maybe I shouldn't pass judgement on others after my own crimes, but I can't help but be concerned about who was in that mountain."

"I'm sure we'll find out soon enough," I said. "Hopefully there may be more of your people in Atlantis."

"Maybe," Tarron said. "I've all but given up on finding anyone alive. Or at least anyone alive who isn't psychotic."

Shortly after, Zamek found sections of the slope that had degraded, and we had to wait a few minutes for him to fix it before we continued. Occasionally, I could hear the sounds of something splashing far beneath us, but it was a well, so maybe there was still a measure of water.

"Isis," I said. She was in front of me and turned to look back. "Why don't you like Duat?"

"I haven't been back since Osiris, my husband, was murdered," Isis said. "Horus, my son, fled after Avalon was created, shortly after Osiris's murder. He hunted for Osiris's killer, Set. I have heard nothing from Horus since. Duat is a land of the dead, a land of spirits. I am concerned that I will find my son there among those who roam the lands." Isis touched the gold-and-diamond pendant of a falcon she wore around her neck.

"I'm sorry," I said. "I didn't know that. I never should have gotten you involved."

Isis turned back to me and smiled. "It is all right, Nathan," she said softly. "It is something I must confront at some point, and more importantly, this is something that can help save lives. So that no family has to go through what we went through."

As we continued further down the spiral slope, the splashing below became louder and more concentrated. I looked over the edge but saw nothing other than darkness. Still, the feeling of unease remained with me.

Upon reaching the bottom of the well, we found that it opened out into a huge cavern with a deep pool of water between the strip of land we were on and another bank of land fifty feet away, where I could just make out a realm gate partially obscured by rocks.

"How deep do you think that is?" Lucifer asked as he took his horse away from the water's edge and tethered it to one of several large stalagmites. Isis, Selene, and I did the same, but Tarron moved to the water's edge, allowing his mount to get a drink first.

A monstrous crocodile burst from the water with no warning, grabbing hold of the horse by its head and dragging it into the water as two more crocodiles tore chunks from the screaming animal. Tarron dived back from the water's edge.

"That's the biggest fucking croc I've ever seen," Remy said in horror. "Would make some killer boots, though . . ."

He wasn't wrong. It looked like one of those crocs in the cheap films that Mordred liked to watch. It must have been thirty feet long, and the other two were at least twenty feet in length.

"How did they survive down here for so long?" Tarron asked, clearly shaken from being so close to the attack.

"I was sure there were no crocodiles in Alexandria," Lucifer said.

"You want to tell them that?" Remy asked.

"That wasn't natural," Isis said suspiciously.

The gigantic crocodile crawled out of the water onto the bank opposite us, swallowed down what appeared to be a leg of the horse, and began to change shape until it was no longer a crocodile but a man. Crystals lit up all around the cavern, bathing everyone in low levels of warm light. The man was nearly seven feet tall, with dark skin and long dark hair that was braided with jewels. He was muscular and completely naked. He crossed his huge arms over a barrel-like chest and laughed, the sound bouncing around the cavern.

"Isis," the man shouted.

The water between us was clearer in the light, and I could see a half dozen crocodiles swimming around close to the surface.

"You brought me a feast," the man shouted again.

"Sobek," Isis said, not bothering to raise her voice and letting her air magic carry the words across the cavern. "I always wondered what happened to you."

"I have made my home in Alexandria," he said. "It's a beautiful city, and my family and I can live in peace."

"Are all of these crocodiles like you?" I asked.

"No," Sobek said with a shake of his head. "These are normal crocodiles. There is a vast system of caves under here, and we can swim among them freely. Occasionally people use the tunnels to smuggle drugs and weapons, and occasionally they do not make it back out. These caves are dangerous things."

"Because you eat them," Lucifer snapped.

"Yes," Sobek said with a laugh. "I prefer horse, though. It's meatier."

"There's a realm gate behind you," Isis said. "It goes to Duat."

Sobek nodded. "There is. It needs no guardian or dwarf to operate it, but you will not get the chance to use it."

"And why is that?" I asked.

"Because I do not want to let you through," Sobek said matter-of-factly. "I do not work for Avalon; I do not work for Merlin or Arthur; I work for me. Gawain came through here and offered me a snack for allowing him to pass unharmed."

"What do you want, Sobek?" Isis asked.

"Can I assume that *you* are off the table?" he asked with a chuckle.

"I can come over there and tell you face-to-face, if you'd like," Isis said sweetly.

Sobek's smile faded. "No, I think not," he said eventually.

"Who sent you here?" I asked him. "Also, any chance we can do this talk not shouting over a cavern of crocodiles as they eat a horse?"

"As you wish," he said, turning back into the gigantic crocodile and swimming over to us. Then he slowly walked out, his mouth wide, showing huge teeth.

"Grow up, Sobek," Isis snapped.

Sobek turned back into his human form. "You sure do know how to spoil my fun," he said.

"How long have you been here, and who sent you?" I asked.

"I have been here for a few centuries," he said. "Hera told me about this place. She was untrustworthy, but in the long run, I think it worked out better for me than for her."

"Hera's dead," I told him.

"Hence my thinking it worked out better for me," Sobek said with a belly laugh. "I do not care about the realm gate, but I do care about not having to move homes when more of you come here to use it."

"Is there a big number of people clamoring to go to Duat?" Remy asked.

"Maybe," Sobek said thoughtfully. "There have been a lot more deaths recently."

"How many of them were down to you?" Tarron snapped.

"Apart from the smugglers, I only kill those who threaten our way of life," Sobek said, seemingly taking no offense to Tarron's tone. "Also criminals, animals, anything that looks like a good meal. There are half a dozen of us, and we have to remain out of human reach. If we were discovered, the humans would kill us."

"You murder innocent people," I said.

"No," Sobek said with a smile. "I murder those who would murder me. Who would rape and steal from their own kind, who would do harm to children. I bring them down here to be given the punishment they deserve. I hunt them at night through the city."

"You're a vigilante?" Remy asked. "Do you wear a cape? Have a big light pointing into the sky at night?"

"No," Sobek said with a straight face. "Do I need one?"

"So you bring people here to kill; you kill the occasional smuggler; you kill animals," I said. "You want to stay here without anything happening to you and your family. You want peace. You want to be left alone. But we need that realm gate."

"Do you think you can force me?" Sobek asked, a hard edge to his voice for the first time.

"Yes," I said. "If I remember correctly, you're near on immortal. You just resurrect yourself when you die. Your family, I assume, do not."

Sobek's eyes narrowed.

"I do not wish you *or* them harm," I continued before Sobek could take too much offense. "But we both know that a fight between our groups will get some of them killed. You do not want that."

"What do you propose?" he asked grudgingly.

"We use the gate," I said. "We do so on the understanding that we make it known that this gate has then been destroyed. And we also arrange a regular delivery of food. Not people. There are few who deserve to be torn apart by crocodiles."

"Pigs, horses, sheep," Sobek said. "Not cows, though—they are not as pleasant as you humans seem to believe they are."

"Done," Isis said.

"Then we can do business," Sobek said.

"Also," Lucifer said, "you're not going to tell anyone we were here."

Sobek smiled. "Yes, I can keep a secret."

"Who else knows you're here?" Isis asked.

"Some of Avalon's minions who tried to get through and were seen off."

"Who?" Lucifer asked.

"I don't know," Sobek said. "I only recognized one: Megaera."

"The Furies?" Remy asked.

I immediately looked up the tunnel. "You think anyone might have been keeping eyes on this place? We should hurry this up."

"These realm gates are meant to be hidden," Sobek said, ignoring my concern. "Hera knew about this particular one centuries ago, but no one could get it to work, so it was deemed useless. There's writing on the gate that says *Duat*. The writing isn't Egyptian."

"What is it?" Zamek asked.

"Elvish," Sobek said. "Shadow Elvish, to be exact."

Everyone looked at Tarron. "Show me, please."

"If you swim over there with all that blood in the water, my family will attack you," Sobek said. "Without the blood, I could make sure they leave you alone, but with it, they are too caught up in their bloodlust to obey me in such matters."

175

"We can create a bridge of air," Isis said to me. "I think that would ensure we got over in one piece."

There was a small splash in the pool, and I looked over as something else landed in the water. I glanced up at the ceiling of the cavern, expecting to see pieces of it falling down, just as the pool exploded. The water drenched us all, and there were two more splashes, followed by another explosion. I created a shield of air, wrapping it around us, as more water rained down, this time mixed with large amounts of crocodile blood. The head and partial torso of one crocodile dropped onto the sand beside us.

"No," Sobek shouted.

I was about to drop the shield when it was hit by gunfire, forcing all of us back around the corner toward the entrance. Bullets poured down into the water as Sobek screamed in rage and pain.

"You still down there, Sobek?" a voice asked.

"Megaera," Sobek said, his voice barely recognizable as human. "I told you not to come back."

"We need to get across that water," Lucifer said.

"I will give you time," Sobek said. "These interlopers will pay for what they've done."

Before anyone could stop him, Sobek ran toward the entrance to the cavern, changing into his gigantic crocodile form before he reached it. The growl that left his jaws as he ran up the slope toward the attackers was drowned out by the sound of gunfire.

Isis and I created a bridge of air, turning it solid enough that everyone could run across it.

Selene turned into her dragon-kin form and created a wall of ice that separated us from Megaera and her allies. Lucifer and Tarron led two horses each across the bridge as the rest of us followed at a sprint. We all ran around the corner just as the sheet of ice exploded, raining huge shards into the cavern.

"They are *really* keen," Remy said.

We'd all taken cover behind a huge rock formation, close to the realm gate so that Zamek and Tarron could figure out how to get it to work.

"It's not activating," Zamek said. "There's no destination runes that can be changed. I don't understand how this works."

"No Elvish either," Tarron shouted as bullets smashed into the rock close to where we stood.

"Nathaniel Garrett," Megaera shouted.

I risked a look and saw her standing behind a kneeling Sobek, who had multiple wounds all over his very human-looking body.

"You sure he can't die?" Remy said.

"He resurrects," Isis said. "I've seen it happen."

"Keep them talking," Lucifer said as he went over to help Tarron and Zamek figure out how to get the large realm gate to work.

"Good idea," I said.

I stood up, took a deep breath, and stepped out from behind the rock. "Hi, Megaera," I said. "I don't think we've met before."

"I've heard of you," she said. "My sisters have too."

"I've met them before," I told her. "A long time ago."

"My sister died because after you attacked her, she was too injured to protect herself from the next attack," Megaera said. "I will kill you for her death. You can't possibly think you can stop us."

I shrugged. "Thought had crossed my mind," I told her.

"Any last words, Sobek?" Megaera asked, the tip of her knife pressed directly against his throat.

"The blood of my people," he said, looking directly at me. "The blood of my pantheon." He practically screamed the last phrase.

Megaera stared at him. "That's a terrible last line."

"Fu—" Sobek started, before Megaera slit his throat and pushed his body onto the sand.

"I know he'll come back," Megaera shouted. "But I don't think he's going to enjoy where he wakes up."

Two soldiers dragged Sobek's body away.

Isis, her fists clenched, stood beside me, radiating anger. "I'm going to tear her fucking head off," she seethed.

"Isis, we need you," Lucifer said.

Isis walked away, although she clearly didn't want to.

"I'll be seeing you soon, Nathaniel," Megaera said.

"The name is Nate," I told her. "If you're going to try and kill me, you could at least get it right."

She raised her hand, and the six soldiers with her removed grenades from their belts. "This might not kill you, but it'll hurt."

"Right back at you." I opened my hands, and lightning flew from them, smashing into the ground beside Megaera's feet, forcing her to leap back out of its path. A gust of air smashed into two of the soldiers, and one of them dropped their grenade. It exploded before anyone could kick it away.

"Nate, we don't have time," Tarron said.

I darted back around the rock to see that the realm gate was activated.

"Explain later," Zamek said. "We *really* don't have all day."

I watched everyone else go through first. Zamek waited with me, using his alchemy powers to bring down huge amounts of rock, blocking anyone from getting from the cavern to the realm gate without having to clear things out first.

We stepped through the realm gate together into the realm of the dead.

Chapter Fifteen

Nate Garrett

Realm of Duat

The realm of the dead was really quite pleasant after the blood-soaked murder cavern we'd just left.

We ended up on a beach with crystal-clear water lapping the shore. The sun was high overhead, although it wasn't too warm, as there was a pleasant breeze coming off what I assumed was an ocean, considering there was no sign of land out toward the horizon.

"Anyone want to explain what just happened?" Selene asked.

"These realm gates need the blood of their pantheon to open them from the Earth realm," Lucifer said. "Isis opened this one. We can get back through this realm to the Earth realm normally, but the other way is locked out."

"The realm gate to Avalon is to the north, inside the mountain," Isis said.

"What is it with realm gates being inside mountains?" Remy asked.

"Dwarves like mountains," Zamek said, giving a simple answer.

"I'm sorry about Sobek," I said to Isis, who picked up a large stone and threw it into the ocean.

"Megaera will pay for what she did," Isis said calmly.

"So the Erinyes are involved," Lucifer said. "That is not a good thing. Many have tried to kill them over the centuries."

"We will succeed," Isis said, leaving no room to suggest the outcome could be anything else.

I climbed up on my mount, Remy sitting behind me, and Isis, Selene, and Tarron each took a horse. Zamek shared with Lucifer, and we set off at a gentle trot, picking up the pace after we left the soft sand.

"What can we expect inside the mountain?" I asked Isis.

"The spirits roam freely inside," she said. "My Osiris will be among them. It will not be an easy time to see those I have lost."

I pulled up beside Isis. "You going to be okay?"

She shrugged. "I do not know, Nate. I'm sorry."

"No need to apologize," I told her.

"Will they be willing to help us?" Remy asked.

"I do not know," Isis repeated. "Maybe. Maybe not. Spirits are strange like that."

Everyone was silent as we rode through the open plains of the realm. While there were plenty of trees and plants, there were no animals. No birds or insects, no sounds from their calls. The realm of the dead lived up to its name.

It took a few hours of riding, but we eventually reached the entrance to the mountain. It was a giant wound in the side of the massive range that stretched as far as I could see, the caps all covered in snow. The opening in the mountain was bright blue, caused by the crystals that were exposed to the light.

"That's a bit ominous," Tarron said, getting down from the horse.

"Can we take these in there?" I asked.

"It should be fine," Isis said. "We'll have to walk them, though; it's too dangerous to ride."

We all climbed down off our mounts and led them into the mountain, the blue light bathing us all in its glow as I took in the magnificent structure before us.

It looked like dwarven ruins, stretching high up into the interior of the mountain. Statues adorned the pathways, each one depicting a different animal.

"There's no echo," Selene said.

"Who built this?" Zamek asked.

"No idea," Isis said. "It's always been here. It's not dwarven or elven or anything else that we recognize."

"It's magnificent," Zamek said, running his hand over the stone of the path we were on and stopping to admire an archway as we walked under it.

We continued on down the long straight pathway until we came to a crossroads.

"I don't know which path to take." Isis frowned. "The gate I used to come here originally is to the east of here, I think. It's hard to tell. It's a gate close to the Nile. Or was. It was buried in the desert thousands of years ago."

"Good job we went this way, then," Remy said.

"We don't have time to be running around somewhere the size of a small country to find one gate," Selene said. "We need help."

"A spirit?" Lucifer asked. "Isis, do you know where we can find such a thing?"

Isis nodded; her eyes closed. She didn't want to do this, but she would anyway.

Selene placed a hand on Isis's shoulder. "You are not alone here," she whispered. "Our strength is your strength."

Isis nodded slightly, and she pointed toward a set of steps that led down into a blue-tinged mist. "The mist is where they come from," Isis said.

"Do we need to worry about Anubis?" I asked.

"He could be anywhere in this entire realm," she said. "He moves around a lot."

"And Ammit?" Lucifer asked.

"With Anubis, I imagine," Isis said. "Neither are likely to help us, though; they care more for the dead than they do the living."

"Sounds like they've been here too long," Remy said.

"That might be the case," Isis agreed.

I looked down into the blue mist and had a sudden urge to be anywhere but here. "How does this work?" I asked. "Are these random spirits? Will we see people linked to one of us?"

"Could be either," Isis said. "Most likely, the second we step inside the mist, it will call those we knew in life."

"You don't have to do this," I told her. "I can go down and get what I need from whoever turns up."

Isis shook her head. "No, I have to do this. Otherwise, we'll be here for too long. You can come with me, if you like. I'd appreciate the support."

"No problem," I told her.

Isis turned to the others. "Lucifer, you too. Everyone else stay here; keep the horses company."

No one minded not having to go down into the spirit mist.

We descended the steps until the mist was above us, too dense to see our companions standing above.

The mist swirled all around us, causing the hairs on the backs of my arms and neck to stand on end. I had the constant feeling of being watched.

Lucifer and I followed Isis, who walked with the confidence of someone who knew exactly where she was going. Then she suddenly stopped, her eyes closed, the mist swirling quicker and quicker around her.

"Osiris," she whispered.

The mist continued to swirl until it formed a translucent man. He had long hair that fell between his shoulders and wore a simple tunic and sandals. "My love," he said softly.

Isis smiled with tears in her eyes. "I have not been back here for a long time," she said. "I have *missed* you."

"And I you," Osiris said softly. He turned to Lucifer and me. "You brought friends."

"This is Nate Garrett," Isis said. "Son of Brynhildr and Odin."

Osiris bowed his head. "A pleasure." He turned to Lucifer. "You, I already know."

"Old friend," Lucifer said.

"Are you still as troublesome as you were in your youth?" Osiris asked Lucifer with a playful smile.

"I've passed on my troublemaking to this one," Lucifer said, motioning to me.

Osiris laughed, and the mist broke apart, only to be re-formed once again a moment later.

"We're looking for the hidden realm gate to Avalon," Isis said.

"To the west," Osiris said. "An hour's ride. Have you seen our son, Horus?"

Isis shook her head. "Please don't tell me he's here?"

It was Osiris's turn to shake his head. "No. He used to come by and talk to me. To many of us. But he hasn't been here in many years. He hunts Set."

Isis nodded. "He does."

"Set will never be found unless he wants to be," Osiris said. "Horus will search forever."

"That will not put him off," Isis said with a slight smile.

"No, he has both of our stubbornness," Osiris agreed. "Are you happy?"

Isis shrugged. "I got used to being without you, and now that I see you again . . . the pain is as new."

"I ached for you," Osiris said, the mist swirling around Isis. "I *still* ache for you, and one day we will be reunited here. But not today. You must continue on; you must live, Isis. You need to find yourself happiness. Once your fighting is done, what will you do?"

Isis didn't have an answer.

"Go," Osiris said. "Go and do what you came here to do. I miss you, my love, but I do not wish to see you here with me for many years to come."

Isis sighed. "I miss you too, my love. I will not be back for a long time. We are going to stop Arthur from destroying the realms."

"Arthur?" Osiris asked.

"Asmodeus's spirit inside the body of a sorcerer," Lucifer said.

Osiris didn't move, but a feeling of anger radiated off him. "Asmodeus is a name I remember well. He was a monster. If he still lives inside the body of another, you make sure that this Arthur's spirit is destroyed just as much as his body."

"That's the plan," I said. I didn't bother to tell him that we didn't actually have a plan on *how* to achieve that.

"Asmodeus was an evil man," Osiris said. "It took the lives of thousands to stop him when he rode with his devils."

"It's just him this time," Lucifer said. "His devils are dead or gone."

"Good," Osiris said. "Lucifer, you stood against Asmodeus before. You turned your back on your blood brothers and sisters to do what was right. You must do so again." He looked at me. "I can sense the power inside of you," Osiris said to me. "It is difficult to ignore. Your necromancy sings to the spirits."

I looked around me and saw the mass of violently swirling mist.

"While I am here, they cannot harm you," Osiris said. "But when I tell you to go, you must turn and run and never come back down to these parts. Ever. The mist will try to claim you as one of its own."

"I'm only *half*-necromancer," I said.

"I doubt that will matter to some of the more voracious hunters who dwell within this mountain. Necromancy is a beacon of power to these spirits that ignites an insatiable hunger. If you were a full necromancer, I would not be able to hold them back."

I looked behind me.

"Follow the path to the west," Osiris said. "Keep going west; do not deviate. The realm gate was locked the last time I saw it."

"Arthur reopened it in Avalon," Lucifer said.

"Then you must make sure it closes behind you. Duat is too dangerous a place to be used as a shortcut. If the spirits start to gain in hunger, they will leave here and start to hunt above, where the paths are clear. They will take anyone who is with a necromancer. They will not distinguish, except to know you are alive and they are not. I would not dawdle."

I took a step backward.

"I look forward to our reunion," Osiris said to Isis.

"I love you," Isis said sadly.

"I love you too," Osiris said, the mist that made up his body intensifying as it swirled around hers. "Follow the mark of Ra. Now run."

Lucifer and I turned and sprinted toward the steps, with Isis hot on our heels as the swirls of mist almost lunged for us, forcing us to run around them. We reached the steps and didn't stop as the mist gave chase. Isis and Lucifer were first up the stairs, and the mist formed solid matter, tripping my feet. I felt it wrap around my legs, dragging me back down the steps as my friends shouted from above. It wanted power; it *needed* power. Tarron leaped down the stairs, his sword stabbing at mist that vanished and re-formed.

I poured my magic into a sphere and tossed it down the steps; it was completely ignored by the swirls until it detonated. The mist vanished from around me, darting back down to the magic, which tore into the wall at the foot of the stairs, giving me time to get to the top, where everyone was on horses, galloping west.

We followed Isis through a seemingly never-ending maze of pathways, and occasionally the mist spilled out over the sides of the pathway but stopped, as if unsure it could continue further. The deeper we rode, the more the mist encroached upon the path.

"Are we still going west?" Remy asked.

"We're following those," Selene said, pointing to one of the Eyes of Ra that were painted on the stone pillars every few dozen feet. They were all in bright red and difficult to miss.

Eventually, I saw a realm gate in the distance, and we spurred our horses on, but the mist poured out from over the path, snaked across it, and wrapped around my mare's legs, tripping her and throwing Remy and me to the ground.

I used my air magic to steady us both and land safely, and the horse regained her feet. She trotted beside me as the mist continued to hover ominously.

"Nate," Selene called out, bringing her horse to a stop.

I helped Remy get up onto her horse. "Get to the gate," I shouted, making the horse beside me run off after the others. "I'll be right behind you."

"Nate," Selene called out again, her tone hard this time. "You better get there."

I kept my eyes on the mist and gave a thumbs-up. "You're not going to get to them," I said softly.

I threw a small ball of fire to the right of me, and the mist descended upon it. The fire was extinguished by the consumption of the magic, the mist swirling even more violently.

I created a larger ball of flame and threw it into the mist. This time it separated, moving away from the ball for a moment, before springing back into it, devouring it. There was a shriek from the mist. "The magic hurts you," I said. "But you want it anyway."

The mist reared up, moving higher and higher, until it towered forty feet above me. Black, smokelike swirls spilled from my eyes, and I unleashed an explosion of pure magic all around me, destroying the path, tearing through stone as if it were paper. I poured the pure magic out of me and directed it toward the tower of mist, which collapsed over the magic, the shrieks of pain and pleasure from the mass deafening me.

I turned and sprinted away, reaching Isis, who stood by the already-activated realm gate.

"What did you do?" she asked me.

"I gave them all the power they could want," I told her.

The mist that hadn't been hurt by the pure magic continued to spill out over the broken path, heading toward us.

"I never want to come back here," I said and stepped through the realm gate, with Isis behind me a moment later.

The cavern we found ourselves in was large enough to fit a football stadium inside it and still have room. The floor was smooth and tiled, and I spotted Tarron kneeling beside the tiles, an expression of intensity on his face.

"These are dwarven and shadow elf runes," he said as Zamek joined him. "Do you know what this symbolizes?"

No one did.

"The elves and dwarves made this place together," Zamek said. "These realm gates are neither dwarven nor elven but a combination of the two. When we have time, I'd very much like to come back here and spend time deciphering this writing."

I looked around the cavern. There was *a lot* of writing on the walls. I understood a lot of Elvish and Dwarvish, but some of it was even earlier than the ancient dwarves. It appeared to mix words with pictures and dots, and frankly, the whole thing was far beyond my understanding.

"So is this like some kind of communal meeting place?" Selene asked.

"Yes, I think so," Tarron said. "I think it might also be some kind of prison. I think we may need to send some people here to look around, check there's no nasty surprises."

"That's going to have to wait," I said. "Sorry."

"I think it's safe," Tarron said. "I just can't be certain."

"You're the oldest one here," I said to Lucifer. "You ever hear of anything like this?"

"I didn't even know there were realm gates here," he said with a shrug.

"How do we get out of here?" Remy asked. "Because I assume, despite Zamek and Tarron having some kind of brain boner over all this, we do actually need to leave."

"I vote the words *brain boner* are never used again," Zamek said.

"Ever," I said to Remy.

"I calls them like I sees them," Remy said with a grin.

"This is the way out," Tarron said, pointing to an archway at the far end of the cavern. "Each of these archways leads to a different realm gate. I don't know which one goes where, but there must be a hundred caverns here."

We rode up and out of the cavern without a word, continuing until we exited the mountain. It was raining, but stretching far before us was the city of Camelot.

"It's going to be a bit of a ride to get there," Lucifer said. "Do you really think that we can get into the palace and talk to whoever is in charge, getting them to surrender, before we bring everyone down on us?"

"Not really," I said.

I continued to look at Camelot for several seconds. "We know there's no Arthur, no Merlin, no Gawain, no Abaddon, no one powerful enough or stupid enough to wage a war, but we need to know the lay of the land, and we need information. Remy, you worked here—any chance there are people you trust who still live here?"

"Trust?" Remy asked. "No, not really. But there are people here we can get information out of. They work in the palace, last I heard."

"So that's where we go first," Isis said.

I nodded just as part of the city exploded, black smoke and flames billowing out into the dank sky.

My team raced onward toward the city as the sounds of battle echoed all around the plains. It took us some time to reach the outskirts of Camelot, only for us to find a multitude of people wounded or dead on the cobbled streets.

"Help who you can," I said, getting down from my horse as everyone else did the same.

"Go—we'll help," Isis said, rushing over to a large number of people who were trying to keep safe behind a makeshift barricade of stone and wood.

I ran over to a young woman in a dark three-piece suit, who was trying to help up a middle-aged man who'd been badly cut through the legs. "What's going on?"

"The people rebelled," she said as we dropped the man next to two young men, who set about trying to heal his wounds. "The Blade of Avalon . . . they executed a hundred people in the main square. They said that they had betrayed Arthur. Some of them were just kids. That was a few hours ago, and now we're in the shit."

"Where are the BOA?" I asked her.

"Near the palace," she said. "I don't know who you are, but if you go there, they'll kill you."

"We've got a lot of dead and hurt," Remy said, poking his head through the door. "A lot more people angry."

"Remy?" the young woman asked.

"Bethany," Remy said, hugging her. "We worked together for the Shield of Avalon, before, you know, I left and found out that Arthur was psychotic."

"You got out in time," Bethany said. "Most of us were trapped here, forced to work, forced to do their bidding. They have people we care about imprisoned in the palace. If one of us steps out of line . . ."

"So the people executed in the square—they were the loved ones of people they have imprisoned inside the palace?" I asked.

Bethany nodded. "There's a resistance here; we try to figure out ways to thwart Arthur's plans. But we can't leave the realm—we can't even leave the city, not without our loved ones. So we fight in little ways."

"And now you're fighting in big ways," I said. "Remy, I'm going to the palace."

"They'll kill you," Bethany said again.

"Stay safe," I said. "I'll be back soon."

I walked along the road toward the palace square. I'd lived and worked in Avalon for centuries and had considered it, if not my home, then at least a place of safety. A million people had lived in the realm of Avalon. Many had escaped in the early days of Arthur's reign, but many hundreds of thousands of innocent people had been forced to stay. I'd been powerless to help. We all had. That was about to end.

There were two dozen paladins outside the palace, standing guard, their golden shields and armor covered with blood that, judging from the number of dead inside the square, wasn't theirs. People from the city were hiding at the corners of the square, helping those who had been injured to safety. The paladins made no effort to interfere; their job was to keep the place free of enemies.

"Halt," one of the paladins said, stepping forward, lifting his huge gauntlet-covered hand toward me. "Disperse or feel our wrath."

"These were innocent people," I said, my voice little more than a whisper. "Why kill them?"

"They were told to leave," the man said. "They did not."

"So you butchered women, children, innocent people who came to voice their displeasure at having their loved ones killed." My voice got angrier with every word.

The paladin drew his longsword from the sheath on his hip. It gleamed. "Leave, or be next," he said, and the paladins behind him also drew their swords.

I stopped walking and looked beyond the paladin to the palace. It was still just as large as it had been when I'd last been here, but the ominous metal gate and door to the building were new. The gate had spikes on it that I could see were wet with the blood of people who had tried to gain entry.

"The door," I said, ignoring the paladins and pointing beyond them. "Someone is controlling the metal."

"That would be me," the paladin said. "Those who got past us needed to be taught a lesson. This is your last warning."

Thunder rumbled above my head. "You should all start running *now*," I told them. The anger building as fast as the thunderstorm above me.

There was laughter among the dozen paladins. "Who do you think you *are*?"

Lightning streaked from the sky, driving through the paladin and ripping a hole in his chest the size of my fist. He dropped to the ground as smokelike tendrils of magic gathered up around me.

"My name is Nathaniel Garrett Woden," I said, taking a step forward and readying my pure magic. "And you've finally given me a target to release my anger at. You *really* should have run."

I unleashed hell.

Chapter Sixteen

Layla Cassidy

Avalon Island, Earth Realm

Avalon Island was situated off the coast of Wales. It was on no official maps and was outside any shipping lanes. It was, for all intents and purposes, not even there.

Layla and her team had reached the island via boat. One of dozens that had shipped hundreds of rebel soldiers there. If there was one thing that she'd realized during her hours on the freezing-cold island as the rain and sleet beat down, it was that the place was not big enough for hundreds of soldiers to stand around and do nothing.

The team found itself in a room of a large complex that had been built and left vacant for years. The room looked like any normal boxlike office, except the windows had long since broken and large numbers of leaves had deposited themselves inside.

Judgement sat cross-legged, her sword beside her, as Tego lay next to her. Judgement looked to be deep in thought, her eyes closed. Piper and Chloe were sitting together near the entrance, and

Layla was sitting on the other side of where a door had once been. Kase paced up and down the middle of the room.

"You're going to wear a groove into it," Piper said.

Kase stopped walking and looked down at the tiled floor. "I want to get this started," she said. "The wait is agonizing."

"We can't do anything until Nate's team opens the gate," Chloe said.

Layla looked out of the nearby window down at Mordred, Hel, Olivia Carpenter, and two dozen others who had taken up positions close to the realm gate temple on the island. They were to be the first wave. Layla hadn't exactly been surprised that Mordred had told everyone he'd be going first. He wasn't the kind of person to let others fight for him.

"How can you be so calm?" Kase asked Judgement, who opened one eye.

"My father and sister are hotheads," she said with a shrug. "Zeus and Athena, I mean. As strange as it may sound, I was probably the calmest member of my family. If there's one thing I've learned over the years, it's that the best thing to do when you have a chance to relax is relax. Especially before a big battle."

"You think there will be a battle?" Layla asked.

"You don't?" Judgement replied.

"No, I do," Layla said. "I was just hoping someone was more optimistic than I am."

Judgement chuckled. "It might be a *quick* battle."

"That's not really the kind of optimism I was looking for," Layla said with a smile.

Judgement yawned. "Someone comes."

Layla turned and looked out of the doorway down the corridor as Brynhildr walked toward them. She wore full leather armor like everyone else. She entered the room and nodded to Judgement. "It's good to see you again."

Judgement got to her feet and embraced Brynhildr. "I am glad you're well. I guess we'll be fighting side by side again."

"Any word as to what's happening?" Layla asked.

"We're still waiting on the realm gate to open," Brynhildr said. "Honestly, I'm practically tearing my hair out. Orfeda and her dwarves want to get on with it too. They can sense the impending battle."

"So can Judgement, apparently," Chloe said.

"My blood does seem to be very good at that," Judgement said.

"How many are here?" Piper asked.

"Over four thousand," Brynhildr said, looking out of the broken window. "We're running out of space."

Piper stood and joined them at the window. "I can feel the excitement and anticipation of the people down there. Something is happening."

Layla got to her feet beside her. Those below were gesticulating toward the realm gate temple. "I think you're right," she said.

"My son and his team would not have failed," Brynhildr said, pride in her voice as she spoke about Nate. "He's too stubborn."

"Everyone down here in sixty seconds," a man outside the building shouted, his air magic carrying the words to all those around him.

Layla and her team were outside in less than thirty seconds, Brynhildr remaining beside Layla as her team was ushered toward the realm gate temple. Orfeda and her dwarves had changed the realm gate inside the temple so that the entire temple was a gate. It meant large numbers could be taken through at once, but it had to be activated and deactivated to allow everyone into the temple.

It took half an hour for Layla's team to make it into the temple, and a second later there was a flash of light, and they were in Avalon.

"Nice to see you all," Zamek said. "Things are about to get weird."

"Why?" Layla asked.

"Best you go outside and see for yourself," Zamek said.

Layla practically sprinted outside, only to feel quite bemused as she noticed nearly every one of the hundreds of rebellion members who had gone through the gate earlier was sitting down on a nearby grass hill.

"Ummm . . . ," Layla said, looking around. "What's going on?"

"We've walked into a civil war, sort of," a rebellion soldier said, looking up at her. "Best go see those in charge."

Layla followed his directions, and she and her team found Hades, Isis, Persephone, and several others all standing in the middle of a street that had been partially destroyed. The buildings on one side were little more than rubble, while on the other they looked to have been barely touched.

"What is going on?" Layla asked anyone who wanted to tell her.

"We arrived and saw black smoke pouring out of the city," Isis said. "So we ran here and found that a large number of residents who were forced to live and work here had risen up against their oppressors."

"The palace is on fire," Layla said.

"Nate may have lost his temper," Isis said with a shrug.

"Apparently blowing up buildings is now one of his powers," Judgement said.

"Those who rose up are mostly inside the palace," Hades said. "Once Nate tore the front off it and killed a dozen paladins."

"Show-off," Judgement said, coughing into her hand.

"It's a *really* big place," Hades continued. "They're going room to room to check for anyone loyal to Arthur. Unfortunately, there are pockets of resistance inside the palace, some paladins and high-ranking officials, and they're all quite happy to go down fighting."

"And the casualties?" Kase asked.

"The rest are in the hospital and surrounding areas," Persephone said. "Nate's team managed to get here just as the uprising began but too late to stop the execution of a hundred people, which is what started it."

"They executed a hundred people?" Layla asked.

Persephone nodded. "Yes. From what we've been told, people formed an underground rebellion, and they got caught. Someone betrayed them, and it ended with mass executions of their loved ones just outside of the palace."

"That's horrific," Layla said. "How many casualties are we looking at?"

"A lot," Hades said. "We're trying to find places to put them all, considering the hospital is a no-go area for the time being, but these Avalon bastards have put a lot of booby traps around the city."

"And these buildings?" Layla asked.

"The people in charge did this," Hades said. "They wanted to make a point, I assume. There are entire districts that were basically turned into rubble. Thousands of people have died here in Avalon's attempt to control an uprising."

"There were nearly a half million people living in Camelot," Persephone said. "It's going to take a long time to get through the city and find out the true losses."

"Where's the Atlantis realm gate?" Kase asked. Her tone suggested she had interest in only one thing.

"Under the palace," Persephone said. "It's been rigged with about a hundred runes, so we've got Orfeda and her dwarves currently dismantling them."

Kase turned to Layla. "Is it okay if I stay and wait?"

"You don't need to ask," Layla said.

"I know, but . . . I just . . . my head isn't right. I want to find my dad," she said eventually.

Layla hugged Kase, who returned the gesture. "Go eat something and rest," Layla told her. "We'll be fine without you for a few hours. And frankly, you need sleep more than you need another fight."

"I think your mum is around the palace," Persephone said. "Let's go find her."

Kase nodded, and the pair walked away.

"She's exhausted," Piper said. "Even a werewolf can't run on fumes forever."

"We'll take her to Olivia," Hades said. "Hopefully she can get some rest before we have to drug her."

"She's so close to getting to Atlantis and Tommy," Layla said. "I can't imagine what she's going through. My dad was a serial killer and my mom a serial killer's helper and then zombie assassin."

"That makes her sound a lot cooler than she was," Chloe said.

"Is there anything we can do to help?" Layla asked.

"Tarron thinks that the mountains might need to be checked out," Hades said. "We're using the plains between the city and there as a sort of staging area for people we've found prisoners in the palace. There are thousands of them. We need to know who is and isn't friendly, and doing it away from the city seems like a good idea. You could head to the mountains—just make sure we're not about to get a nasty visit from anyone. We sent a small team there after we arrived, but we haven't heard anything yet. Medusa went with them, so I'm sure they're all okay, but it would be good to get an update. I'll send more soldiers that way eventually, but we're a little stretched at the moment."

Layla had to agree that was probably a fair point. "We'll head to the mountains," she said. "You got a way for us to get there that isn't running?"

"Carriages," Hades said. "It'll be an hour or so, but it's the fastest way until we can get the tram system up and running again."

Layla and her team of Piper, Chloe, Tego, and Judgement met up with Tarron and Sky close to the carriages. Tarron gave Layla a hug.

"It's good to see you're still with us," Layla said. "So we're going to check out some mountains."

"We need to make sure no one is going to come through the gates there and attack those people on the plains," Sky said. "I would not put it past them."

Layla looked out of the carriage window at the thousands of people who had been released from the prison and were being tended to in a makeshift city of tents. So many prisoners, so much brutality. If anyone thought that what they were doing wasn't worth it, they only had to look at the toll on life that Avalon took.

On the way, a dozen soldiers joined the group to ride alongside them. They'd come through from Avalon Island, and Layla was glad for the extra firepower. She hoped that the mountain would be free of problems, but she had to admit Sky was right. Avalon would happily attack the injured and sick.

By the time the team had reached the mountains, the rain had started up and dusk had begun to roll in, turning the sky a brilliant purple and orange.

The carriages stopped outside the mountain, and everyone disembarked. "You think there might be some Avalon supporters in here?" one of the soldiers asked Layla.

"I hope not," she said. "But we might as well search for them anyway."

Everyone entered the mountain and continued down the only path until they reached a football-stadium-size chamber.

Layla walked to the middle of the chamber and looked around, stunned by how complex it was. "I've seen *a lot* of things," she said. "But this is incredible."

"The realm gate we came through is down there," Tarron said, pointing to a large hole. "I imagine there are other gates here. A network of realm gates that no one even knew existed."

"We need to find the team sent here," Chloe said. "Although judging from the size of this place and the dozens of corridors, they could well have just gotten lost. I assume no one here has ever seen this place before."

No one had.

Three dwarves walked out of a nearby chamber, raising their hands when everyone turned toward them, weapons at the ready.

"Orfeda sent us," a large male dwarf said. "We got separated from the team we were with, and now we've been turned around and can't find them. We figured we'd come back here and wait, but no one came back."

"Which tunnel did you go down?" Piper asked.

Another dwarf pointed to a tunnel further down the chamber. Light-blue runes glowed on the archway leading in.

"Some have glowing runes, and some don't," Layla said as several of the soldiers with her team ran over to check out the chamber.

"We think they glow as a sort of power-down mode," a dwarf said. "That chamber goes to Duat."

"Why would that one be glowing now?" Judgement asked.

The dwarves all shrugged as one.

Layla's team split into two, with Judgement and Sky taking half a dozen soldiers down one path, while everyone else made their way over to the glowing runes and walked on into the chamber beyond, where several soldiers were already searching the adjoining rooms. Layla moved to an archway next to the realm gate and looked down the dark passageway beyond.

"There's something there," Tarron said from beside her.

Chloe tapped one of the runes on the passage, and it lit up; more and more of them ignited until the entire passage was alight, showing the dozens of entrances to rooms or tunnels beyond. "It's a damn rabbit warren."

Layla turned to a nearby soldier. "Any of you been down this way yet?"

The soldier, a man with a scar that started just above his eyebrow, curved around his eye, and ended on his cheek, shook his head. "No, ma'am," he said.

"We'll take it," Layla told him and took a step into the passageway, almost immediately hearing a crash from one of the rooms beyond.

"Okay, we've got something," Chloe shouted as she stepped behind Layla. Tego stood in the mouth of the passageway, watching intently.

Layla entered the chamber first and touched the runes on the wall, which ignited, bathing the chamber in light-blue light. There were dozens of crates inside the chamber, some piled up to the ten-foot-high ceiling. At the far end of the chamber, lying next to the crates, was a seriously injured woman. Blood poured freely from dozens of cuts on her arms and legs, and she had a nasty cut on her forehead that would probably require stitches.

Layla crouched down in front of the woman. "Hi, what happened?"

"I was a prisoner," she said. "I had a sorcerer's band on. I couldn't do anything. I don't know how long I was down there. I was . . . it was a long time. When the rebellion started, there was a riot by some prisoners. I managed to escape to the plains, but I didn't know where to go. I wanted to fight. I *needed* to fight, but I was hurt."

"Where's your band?" Layla asked. "What's your name?"

"Another prisoner removed it as we escaped, but I've had it on for so long my power hasn't returned yet," she said. "I think it's just maxed out healing me."

"What's your name?" Layla repeated.

"Athena," she said. "My name is Athena."

Chloe and Layla shared a glance. "Judgement's . . . sister, I guess?" Piper asked from the doorway before walking into the room, where she started to examine Athena's wounds.

Athena looked up, suddenly alert. "You know Judgement?" she asked.

"She's here with us," Layla said.

"Here?" Athena asked, animated for the first time.

"Somewhere," Tarron said. "She'll be around soon enough; she's pretty good at turning up when you least expect it."

Athena nodded. "I'm so glad she's okay. I need to see her." She tried to get to her feet but stumbled forward and was caught by Piper.

"Are you okay to walk?" Piper asked.

Athena nodded, looking weaker and more worried than Layla would have expected from someone who was meant to be one of the greatest warriors of all time.

"I'll take her back to the entrance, and we'll hopefully find Judgement on the way," Piper said.

"Take some soldiers with you," Layla said as Piper helped Athena to the door.

Layla watched Athena being escorted out of the mountain by Piper and three soldiers before she turned back to those who were still with her. "Right, let's see if there's anyone else we can find."

Ten minutes later they found a barely conscious Medusa in a room with a large realm gate that didn't appear to have been completed. There were two dead soldiers beside her, both of whom had been decapitated. Layla rushed over and helped Medusa up off the floor, who groaned and sagged against her, barely conscious. Two of the soldiers who had come with Layla's team, along with Tarron, helped move her to an adjacent chamber.

"She's been seriously hurt," Chloe said. "She got stabbed just below the ribs on her left side. It's bleeding badly, and I'm pretty sure the knife was silver. She needs proper medical attention."

"We can make do for now," Tarron said, and he dipped his fingers into Medusa's blood and began to draw a rune around her. "I'm not a dwarf, but this should stabilize her until we can get her to someone who knows how to stop this."

When he'd finished drawing it, red power flowed around it until it completed the entire circle of runes, when it snapped shut. Medusa gasped, her eyes wide open for several seconds.

"What happened?" Layla asked.

"Athena," Medusa said. "Athena did this to me."

"Shit," Chloe said, turning to run after Piper.

"Tarron, make sure Medusa stays in one piece," Layla said before turning to the soldiers. "Both of you with me."

They made it outside the mountain and found several dead soldiers lying on the ground. Several of the horses had been killed, too, and Piper lay up against the wheel of a carriage, her throat slashed, bleeding a considerable amount.

Chloe sat beside her, screaming for help.

A soldier ran back into the mountain to get the rest of the dwarves, who emerged soon after and set to work drawing runes to keep Piper alive. Layla stood back and let people work. The only thing she was able to do was hope as Chloe held her wife's hand and wept.

Chapter Seventeen

MORDRED

Realm of Avalon

"If anyone can tell me just how long all of this is going to take, that'd be great," Mordred said as he leaned up against the wall outside the room in the far reaches of the dungeons beneath the palace.

"We don't know," Jinayca said, looking up from a brightly glowing rune on the floor. "This whole place is like walking through a minefield, blindfolded, while occasionally stopping to perform a dance routine."

"Nice image," Mordred said.

"I have a dozen dwarves in here with me," Jinayca said. "I know how much everyone wants this realm gate to work so we can go to Atlantis and stop Arthur, but the longer I stand here talking to you, the less likely that is."

"You want me to go away?" Mordred asked with mock indignation.

"Yes, piss off and find someone else to bother," Jinayca said with a smile.

Mordred laughed. "Yeah, okay." He walked away. He'd been searching through the palace to ensure that none of the old guard remained in charge, but it seemed that they'd all fled to the hospital in the east, and apparently Nate and those with him had everything well under control. It had left Mordred with very little to do, but he had the feeling that he should be doing *something*.

It took him a while to retrace his steps out of the dungeon, which was a twisty maze of a place. Twice he found himself down a corridor with cells on either side. He looked through the slats in the metal door on the first cell and saw the blood inside, lit by a light-blue crystal in the ceiling. *A lot of people have been killed here.*

He eventually found himself in the throne room. The room was gigantic, with high ceilings and beautiful artwork depicting knights in shining armor, the paladins in their golden armor, and Arthur slaying all before him. In one particularly ostentatious piece, Arthur had slain a dragon and had one foot on the creature's neck, while a woman who at best was barely clothed was draped around his legs like a limpet. Mordred laughed the first time he saw it, as well as the second, and then it stopped being funny. He used his light magic to burn it to ashes and felt better for it.

At one point there had been a large circular table inside the throne room. Unlike in the stories, there were, in fact, three round tables. Merlin had had one placed in the throne room to remind visitors that Camelot's law was always there. Mordred remembered the time he'd returned to Camelot after his mind had been shattered, and he'd buried an ax in one of the tables, although he couldn't remember which one. They all looked the same to him.

The table itself was far too small to fit every single knight, but that wasn't really the point. Despite how the round table was meant to make everyone seated there equal, there was a large black metal chair that was very clearly the head of the table. Arthur still wanting to let everyone know he was in charge at every opportunity.

Mordred sat in the chair and sighed. All this would have to go. All the memories of Arthur, of those who followed him, of those who had murdered and pillaged in his name. Mordred wondered if they could just burn the entire palace down and start again. Maybe this time with something that wasn't so obviously screaming *I'm better than you* to anyone nearby. He felt the same way about the palace in Shadow Falls, but at least that one was home to vast numbers of people who lived in the realm. The palace in Camelot was just a shell of power. An illusion to keep people in check. Even when Elaine had ruled over Avalon, it was never really *her* palace, as Merlin had liked to point out whenever possible.

Mordred closed his eyes and leaned back in the chair. He missed his aunt. She had been a constant level of calm in the rough seas that were Mordred's life. Even when he was trying to kill everyone, even in his darkest, most evil times, she'd been willing to help. She'd tried for centuries to find a cure. "If you could see me now," he said to himself.

"Everyone is looking for you," Hel told him from the doorway.

Mordred nodded. "I went to see Jinayca. We're stuck here for the moment."

"I know," Hel said.

"I am anxious," Mordred said, opening his eyes. "I do not like being anxious. It makes me want to find a dark room to hide in until everything is done. It's not very king-like to hide while everyone else is busy."

"So be busy."

"No one is letting me," Mordred said with a protracted sigh. "Everyone keeps calling me *Your Majesty* and telling me that there are people to do that job. I am getting fed up with being told there are people to do things that I want to do."

"That kind of goes with the territory, I'm afraid," Hel said, taking a seat next to Mordred.

"I came here expecting a fight," Mordred said. "I expected a prelude to the battle in Atlantis. What I got was a lot of dead bad guys, a lot more wanting to surrender, and the rest running away. None of that feels particularly satisfying. We have taken Avalon with a whimper."

"You wanted bloodshed?" Hel asked, fully aware of Mordred's answer.

"No, of course not," Mordred said. "I wanted closure. I wanted to see this fucking table burned to dust. I wanted to see that fucking throne rammed so far up Arthur's arse that he was literally always sat down. I wanted to be able to punch people in the face and laugh at them when they fell down."

"Really?" Hel asked with a raised eyebrow.

"No, not really," Mordred said. "I just wanted . . . *something*. Instead, I've got people telling me it's all in hand, and I should go have a cup of tea or something. That's the other thing—nowhere in this fucking palace is a goddamn kettle. I can't even find tea bags in the kitchen. It's like they were all bloody savages. Who doesn't own any tea bags? What kind of people don't drink bloody tea?"

"You done?" Hel asked with a smirk.

"Probably," Mordred said, throwing his arms in the air and taking a deep breath. "I haven't been here for centuries. The last time I was here, it didn't end well for anyone. I was apprehensive about having to come back, and now that I'm here, I just wanted something to feel like everything is worthwhile, you know?"

Hel nodded. "I do. I don't want you to think that people are coddling you. I think they just want you to relax because they think they're helping."

"They're not," Mordred said.

"I know this, and most people who know you well enough understand that too," Hel said, kissing the back of Mordred's hand. "But people out there now see you as a king. And when the king is walking around asking people if he can help tidy up and if he can help heal anyone injured, it goes over *really* well, but it also makes people nervous."

Mordred chuckled. "I make people nervous." He shook his head with amusement. "I guess that will have to do. Let's go back outside and find out how Nate's doing. There's a fair few people who ran off that way, and I don't want any more clashes between Avalon supporters and those people who'd like to murder Avalon supporters. One side has a lot of grudges, and the other side are just arseholes."

"They executed a lot of people," Hel said. "I think anger from the populace is going to be a serious problem. We need to show them that we're not Arthur and his people. We need to show them that King Mordred is a good king. How about we head over to the district—you can see how Nate is doing, and we can let the people *see* you?"

"I do not enjoy being shown around," Mordred said.

"And I do not enjoy having to hunt you down because you're bored and don't know what to do with yourself, so how about we do my thing so I don't have to put a GPS tag on you?"

"It won't work here," Mordred muttered.

"What was that?" Hel asked, with a smile that Mordred knew well.

"Nothing," he said quickly.

Hel kissed Mordred on the lips. "Thought so."

The pair left the throne room and made their way through the palace to the outside, where they met Persephone and Brynhildr. The former was talking to three soldiers, and the latter was currently dragging a man by his ankle across the ground toward them.

"That's not how you usually move people," Mordred said as he walked to the bottom of the steps outside the palace.

"He threw a punch at me," Brynhildr said. "He's lucky he still has his arms."

Mordred noticed that the man appeared to be semiconscious, and his face was a mangled mess. "Nice work," he said.

Brynhildr dropped the man's leg, and two soldiers immediately ran over from nearby, dragged the man upright, and applied a sorcerer's band to his wrist.

"You seem to be enjoying yourself," Hel said.

"I kind of expected a fight," Brynhildr told her. "My Valkyries came here *for* a fight. We've mostly just been making sure that those who rose up against their oppressors are safe. Occasionally, we run across Avalon employees who think they can take a shot at us. It does not end well for them."

"We're going to the lower quarter," Mordred said. "You want to join us? We'll be seeing how Nate is doing too."

"Well, nothing exploded yet, so I'm going to guess it's either going really well or really badly," Brynhildr said.

"Have you been back to Valhalla?" Hel asked Brynhildr as the three of them started to walk through the city.

"Yes," Brynhildr said sadly. "Briefly. It's a mess there. We've brought pretty much everyone out to live in Shadow Falls for now, but with the combined population of Valhalla, Asgard, and Shadow Falls itself, it's not a long-term solution. Asgard is destroyed; apparently the realm gate won't even accept Asgard as a destination. Valhalla is still somewhere we can live, but a lot needs to be done first."

"You could move to another realm," Mordred said.

"It's something we're going to need to look into once this is all done," Brynhildr said. "For now, we will be satisfied with doing our jobs and trying to help."

"Have you noticed there aren't any Faceless here?" Mordred asked. The Faceless were the masked bodyguards of the most powerful members of Avalon society. They were completely loyal and would do whatever they were commanded to do, which in Mordred's opinion usually involved something unpleasant.

"Now that you mention it, it's pretty weird," Hel said. "We haven't seen any in years. Maybe they got rid of them."

"I hope so," Mordred said.

They hadn't gone far when they heard the shouts of several soldiers as they ordered someone to stop.

"We should check this out," Mordred said and was already making his way toward the group before anyone could tell him otherwise.

A rider had pulled their horse up by half a dozen soldiers and gotten down before Mordred reached them.

"I need to come in," Athena demanded. Blood drenched her arm, where there were several nasty cuts.

"Athena?" Mordred asked, and everyone stopped shouting at once and moved aside. "What are you doing here?"

"Arthur kept me as a prisoner here," Athena stammered. "I escaped, got to the mountain, but there's something there. Something attacked those you sent. Sky sent me back here. I was already hurt; I couldn't keep fighting. Never seen anything like it. It attacked us, killed several guards. They're fighting it off right now, but they need help. Piper was hurt. Badly."

"You need healing," Mordred said, stepping forward.

"No," Athena snapped. "Sorry, you're going to need your power to help those at the mountain. I'll heal soon enough; I've had worse. But they need help. Fast."

"Get people ready to ride," Mordred said to Brynhildr and Hel. "I'll take this horse and head out there now." Mordred climbed up onto the large black stallion. "Athena, please go and rest."

Athena nodded. "These cuts are already healing. The creature there, it did something to the minds of the soldiers, made them attack one another. My sister is there; she needs help."

"You stay," Brynhildr said. "Once you're healed, head back, but right now, you're just going to get yourself more injured."

Athena didn't look happy about the advice, but she nodded solemnly anyway and walked away to take a seat against the wall of the palace.

"Everyone else, get ready to follow," Mordred said.

Mordred was soon on his way, riding the stallion as hard as he dared across the plains toward the mountain—and a threat so dangerous it could make Athena unnerved.

The ride took longer than Mordred would have liked, but he reached the mountain to find pandemonium. Half a dozen guards all brandished weapons at him. There were multiple dead horses on the ground, and several more had seemingly run away and were busy eating the grass in the distance.

"It's me," Mordred said and then remembered he was a king. "Put those fucking things away unless you want me to see how good you are at dodging blades of ice."

"Mordred," Layla shouted from a nearby carriage. "It's Piper. It's bad."

"Athena told me," Mordred said, swinging down from the horse. "She said there was some kind of monster who attacked you all."

"What?" Chloe asked, her head snapping around to Mordred. Her arms were covered in blood, and her eyes were bloodshot and teary. Mordred's gaze settled on Piper, who was pale and looked weak as she lay up against a carriage wheel. She was drenched in blood, and there was a cut on her neck that looked deep and dangerous.

"What the fuck happened?" Mordred asked, his light magic igniting as he knelt beside Piper and placed his hands on her neck.

"*Athena* happened," Chloe said, barely keeping the rage and hate from her voice.

"Wait, what?" Mordred asked, removing his hands from the wound. "What the hell caused this?"

"We don't know," Judgement said. "The runes are keeping her alive, but we're fighting a losing battle. I don't understand why my sister would do this."

"You say that Athena did this?" Mordred asked.

"She attacked me," Medusa said. A cut on her cheek hadn't healed. "We arrived here to ensure no Avalon sympathizers were hiding out here; we found Athena. She looked injured. She wanted to show us something, a creature, she said. Something dangerous. She killed three of the soldiers with me and did this to me."

"I do not believe that my sister could have done this," Judgement said, more to herself.

"Well, fucking believe it," Chloe snapped, before turning to Mordred. "Save her. Please."

Mordred turned back to Chloe. "I'm going to give it my best, but I need to know *what* did this. And I'm guessing it's the same thing that cut open Medusa's cheek."

Medusa nodded. "She has a dagger, white wooden handle."

"I remember it," Mordred said.

"Basilisk-tooth blade," Medusa said.

"Are you sure?" Mordred asked, flashing back to the memory of Elaine's murder with the same type of black-bladed weapon at the hands of Lancelot. "They're one-shot-and-done knives. The blade dissolves after use."

"Only if it kills the victim with the first strike," Medusa said. "The blade needs to enter the body totally for the poison to be injected. Athena only used the edges of the weapon; the poison is weaker there, but obviously opening up her neck with a blade designed to not let her heal will eventually kill her."

"Piper will die if someone doesn't do something," Chloe snapped.

Layla placed a hand on Chloe's shoulder and squeezed.

"Right, well, we know what we're dealing with," Mordred said. He had been unable to save his aunt, the wounds already too grave, the poison inside the blade already injected into her body. He'd held her as she'd died, and there had been nothing he could do about it. He would be damned before he let that happen again.

Mordred picked up a dagger from the ground and passed it over the palm of his hand. He placed his hands together and ignited the blood magic, feeling the swirl of power, of need, that hit him. Blood magic was addictive, and a long time ago Mordred's dependence on it had been one of many reasons that he hadn't been of sound mind. He no longer *needed* blood magic, he no longer *craved* it, but whenever he used it, he still felt that rush of desire.

"This might not feel great," Mordred said. "In fact, this is going to suck."

Piper looked at him and placed a bloody hand on his. She was ready.

"You're braver than I am," Mordred told her and placed his hands against her neck.

Piper's eyes rolled up into her head, and her body began to convulse.

"Mordred," Chloe shouted. "You're killing her."

Mordred ignored her and continued to use his blood magic to pour power into the wound. Layla grabbed hold of Chloe, dragging her away as she screamed at Mordred. Mordred was lost in the maelstrom of sound that reverberated inside his head. He looked down at Piper, who continued to shake as pain racked his hands, traveling up his arms.

Hel arrived with Brynhildr and two dozen soldiers. Mordred wanted to say something, to make this stop, but he couldn't find the words. All he had was pain that traveled up his arms into his chest, his breathing labored and slow, his mind foggy. And like the crack of a whip, he jolted to one side and vomited all over the ground.

"Get out of my fucking way," Chloe snapped. Tego stayed away from the group but watched intently, ready to involve herself should it become necessary.

"Enough!" Mordred's voice boomed around them all, reverberating off every surface as his air magic pushed the words out hard enough that it forced anyone around him to take a step away.

Mordred's light magic ignited, and he placed his hands on a weak Piper, healing the wound in moments. She opened her eyes at Mordred and took his hand in hers.

"Do not try to move," he said. "You are weak, and there is nothing I can do about that."

Mordred got to his feet and looked down at the black vomit that had left him. "The poison is gone, so I could heal the wound. Do you need something similar, Medusa?"

Medusa stared at Mordred for several seconds before shaking her head. "No, I'm not in danger. Venom hurts, but it won't kill me. The wounds have stopped bleeding; they just hurt. Besides, I don't want what you just did. No offense."

"Blood magic doesn't play nice," Mordred said as Hel grabbed hold of him.

"You're swaying," Hel told him.

"That's nice," Mordred said with a smile. "I need a sandwich. With meat. Lots of meat. And beer. I need beer and a meat sandwich."

"We can do that," Hel said with a warm laugh.

Chloe had rushed back to Piper's side and was kneeling beside her. She looked up at Mordred with tears in her eyes. "Thank you. I'm so . . ."

"I know," Mordred said, patting her on the shoulder as he walked past her. "I know."

"I need to get back to the palace," Mordred said.

"You need to sit down," Brynhildr told him.

"Or fall down," Tarron said. "I think it's your choice at this point."

Mordred shook his head, took a deep breath, and let it out slowly. "Athena is in that city, and we have to find out what she's up to."

"Where would she go, and what's she trying to do?" Hel asked.

"I have no idea," Mordred said. "But I want her found, and whatever her plans are, I want them stopped. Someone find Nate. He needs to know what's going on."

"I wish to have words with my sister," Judgement said, her voice iron cold. "Something is wrong here."

Mordred nodded to himself. Something was very wrong.

Chapter Eighteen

NATE GARRETT

Realm of Avalon

"You know, I can think of better ways to do this," I shouted, using my air magic to carry my words to the many windows of the hospital I stood in front of.

Technically, I stood behind a barricade that had been scribed with enough runes to make it almost the safest place I'd ever been, but I was beginning to get fed up with standing and not actually doing anything.

"It's rude to ignore people," Remy said from beside me.

"You want to give it a go?" I asked. "I'll make your words go further with magic."

"Sure," Remy said, nodding. "I'm well known for my negotiation tactics."

I activated my air magic so they could hear him and gave Remy a nod.

"Hey, you hoofwanking bunglecunts, get your fucking dickhead arses out here before we have to come in and start shoving heads into walls." Remy gave me a thumbs-up. "I think that went well."

"That was certainly a unique strategy," Isis said from beside me.

"We still can't just go in there, then?" Remy asked.

"No," Isis said. "There are nearly a hundred people in there who we'd like to keep safe. Unless they start killing hostages, and so far I haven't felt anything of the sort, we stay and negotiate." She paused for a second. "Which is not what you just did."

I sighed and rubbed my eyes. "I know there's nothing anyone can do until we get the runes removed from that room in the palace, but I'm getting really fed up with the waiting around because a bunch of assholes can't just surrender and let everyone get on with their job."

The main doors to the hospital opened, and several men and women left, their hands in the air as they walked down the ramp while soldiers ran to them, swords and axes drawn, magical attacks prepared.

"Did I just end a hostage situation by swearing at them?" Remy asked.

"I think you may have," I said. "I'm not sure this is how these things are meant to end."

No one else said anything for a few minutes, until the last hostage taker left the hospital with the soldiers behind him. They called in a group of medics who had been waiting, and everything suddenly started moving again.

"Well, at least this ended without bloodshed," Isis said.

"Shame," Remy said with a sigh.

"That's a good thing," I whispered to Remy. "How many were inside?" I asked a soldier.

"A few hundred," she said. "No idea how many are wounded; we haven't had a chance to check. Some of the wounds were fresh, though, sir. Some of those people were tortured."

"Thank you, soldier," I said. "Do me a favor—find out who was in charge of that torture and ensure that everyone else thinks they ratted them out."

The soldier's smile was sly. "Will do, sir."

"You're going to get them killed," Remy said. "I really don't have a problem with that."

There were screams nearby, which took my attention, and I saw a bloody woman running toward us. She looked like she'd been in a hell of a fight, and I thought I recognized her but couldn't quite place from where.

"Athena?" Isis asked as several soldiers intercepted the woman, who raised her hands to show she was no threat.

"Athena?" I said, somewhat shocked to hear the name. "What the hell happened to you?" I asked the question after covering the distance between us.

"Mountain," she said, placing a hand on my bare arm to stay upright. "Ran from the mountain. Mordred is there. There was something inside the mountain; it attacked us. Killed many. Several wounded." She collapsed forward, and a soldier rushed to intercept her before helping her to sit on a nearby wooden bench.

"Is Mordred okay?" I asked.

"I don't know," Athena said. "I was told just to run to get help."

"I'm on it," Isis said before I could say anything.

"I'm with her," Remy shouted, running after an already-sprinting Isis.

"Basilisk blade," Athena said. "There was someone there in a mask; they used a basilisk blade."

"The Faceless?" I asked. I'd wondered when the masked bodyguards of high-ranking Avalon members were going to make an appearance. They were usually incredibly powerful and deeply fanatical in their devotion to their masters. Each mask looked different, but all of them wore one, and all of them were dangerous.

Athena cried out in pain. "Mordred told me to wait at the palace, but I heard you were here and had to come find you."

"Let's get you to a hospital," I said.

Athena shook her head. "I'll be fine. I'd rather be somewhere without people. I've been a prisoner here for centuries."

"Centuries?" I asked with a slow realization. "Damn, I didn't know; I'm sorry. Look, you need medical attention."

"There's a cure," Athena said. "Arthur used to brag about it. They used basilisk blades on prisoners."

"Where's the cure?"

"The dungeon of the palace," she said.

I turned to the soldiers. "I'll take her, and you go help Isis and Remy get to everyone at the mountain. Take an army with you if you need to—just get there."

"It's been a bit of a shit day," Athena said.

"You're not kidding," I said as I helped Athena up onto a horse that had belonged to a soldier. I took a second one.

We rode through the city as fast as Athena was able until we reached the palace, where we climbed down and walked up the stairs into the building itself.

I knew where the dungeons were, so Athena followed me through the palace until we'd reached the entrance. There was no one on the first floor underground, as the realm gate was several floors down, and the dungeons themselves had been cleared—if not cleaned—out.

We reached the medical room, and I opened the door for Athena, who walked inside.

"So this is a big room," I said, looking around at the cupboards and desks that stood along one side of the room, while the other had a row of beds. A large number of wooden boxes were stacked up against the adjacent wall. "There's a second medical room upstairs, if we can't find it here, but I think this is where they've brought any supplies."

Athena took a deep breath. "You think you could get me some water? There's no tap or bowl or anything."

"Yeah, I'll be right back," I said, leaving the room. I was standing in the hallway when a rush of power knocked me aside. "What the hell was that?" I asked as I pushed myself away from the wall, feeling a little wobbly.

Jinayca appeared at the end of the hallway before I'd reached it. "Ah, I assume everyone else felt that," she said.

"Yeah, pretty much," I told her. "What was it?"

"We broke the last seal," she said. "On the realm gate—it's operational. You can go to Atlantis."

"We have a problem *here* to fix first." I nodded to the room behind me.

Jinayca crossed her arms over her chest.

I turned to find Athena without any cuts on her arms and face. "Ta-da," she said, showing me a vial with *Basilisk Cure* written on it. "Body is healing now; thanks for the help."

"No problem," I said. "Good thing you found that quickly."

"It was in the second drawer," she said. "Nasty-smelling black stuff too. It was the only vial, though, so I'm guessing that if anyone else gets hurt, we don't have more."

"I don't know," I said thoughtfully. "We could find Lucifer; I think he's at the realm gate temple. We'll ask him. I think we should head to the mountain first, though. I don't want to leave everyone in the lurch."

Athena placed her hand on my arm as if wobbling a little. She nodded. "Good idea. But what if we get there and we need a cure?"

"Valid point," I said. "Okay, we'll make a slight detour to the realm gate temple, and then we'll head to the mountain with more of the cure."

"I'll head to the mountain," Jinayca said with a frown at me. "I can use runes to slow down any poison, but we'll need more of the cure if anyone gets hurt."

"Okay, let's get going," I said and motioned for Athena to go first.

Jinayca took my hand in hers as we walked after Athena and drummed on my wrist in Morse code. *Imposter?*

I nodded once. "Hey, Athena," I said as we reached the outside area of the palace.

"Yes?" Athena asked, turning to me.

"Maybe I should get Judgement to take you to Lucifer; I can go with Jinayca then. Judgement is around somewhere nearby—shouldn't take a second to find her."

"I'd rather not bother her just yet," Athena said. "She'd only worry about me."

"Of course," I said as we descended the steps. "Must be hard work to be apart from your sister for so long. I wonder, Lamashtu, do *you* have a sister?"

Athena stopped walking, continuing to face away from me. "How long have you known?"

"The bullshit about Athena being here for centuries was a big clue. I last saw Athena about fifty years ago. She looked pretty good," I said. "The monster at the mountain was you just wanting people out of the city. You were going to kill me, I assume."

"Yes," Lamashtu said, her eyes blazing red. "Killing you was always in the cards."

"You used a sorcerer's band to get here, but then it all kicked off here, and you escaped with a bunch of fleeing prisoners," I said. "Unfortunately, you tried to get to the mountain, to use the gates there, I presume, and you were discovered by more soldiers, these on our side. Sound about right?"

"Pretty much."

"How were you going to get out of here?" I asked her.

"I'll become someone else and walk out," Lamashtu said. The Athena mask slithered off her face. Her skin was dark, her eyes blazing hot, and a red tongue—long and snakelike—slithered over sharp teeth. She pointed a bony hand at me. "I am Lamashtu," she said, her voice making my skin crawl. "You are my prey."

"You couldn't kill me earlier," I said.

"Too many around."

"And the real Athena?"

Lamashtu shrugged. "Dead. She was Arthur's prisoner for many years. I do not think she died well." Lamashtu laughed as she glanced around at the large number of soldiers who were moving toward us, weapons drawn.

"I assume you won't be coming with us quietly," I said.

"Your mind isn't very receptive to control from others," Lamashtu said. "I tried with Mordred, too, but his brain was having none of it. You weapons are quite powerful little wizards."

"Wizards?" I asked. "Did you just call me a fucking wizard?"

I blasted Lamashtu in the chest with a bolt of lightning, and she flew back across the square, smashing into the side of a building.

I walked over to her as she slowly got back to her feet. "Does it look like I need a fucking wand?" I threw another bolt of lightning, but Lamashtu dived aside, drawing the blade on her belt and throwing it at me. I saw it coming and knew what it was. I sank down into the shadows and came up next to Lamashtu, who threw a punch at me that I blocked. I locked her wrist and pushed back hard enough to take her off her feet and dump her on the ground.

"Basilisk blade," I said. "I wondered when you were going to use it."

"That wasn't the blade," Lamashtu said, striking me in the throat and kicking up. She drew the basilisk blade and tried for my groin, but I dodged back, and two whips of fire trailed from my hands. Lamashtu smiled, turned, and sprinted into the maze of alleyways that made up the center of the city. The guards chased after her before I could say anything. I looked back at Jinayca, who was sitting on the floor, a blade sticking out of her chest.

"Shit! Jinayca . . ." I ran over to help her.

"Well, fuck," she said. "Nate, you need to find her."

"I will," I said. "What the hell happened?"

"She dived into the way," a male soldier said. "She just pushed me aside and took the blade."

"I've always been an idiot," Jinayca said.

I pulled the blade out, and thankfully, it wasn't a basilisk. Just a decoy. "This didn't go into your heart," I told her after examining the damage. "It's just a normal dagger."

"No shit," Jinayca said, removing her leather armor and dropping it on the floor. She had silver chain mail underneath that blazed with red runes. "Good job, too, or that bastard thing would have cut right through me. Now go find that bitch before she kills someone."

I ran after Lamashtu, using my heat vision to track the footsteps of the soldiers chasing her. I found two dead at the end of a long twisty alley and another dead a hundred feet after that. The door to a building had been kicked in, and a man and woman lay dead on the floor. From the positions of their bodies, it appeared the woman's throat had been slashed as Lamashtu had rushed through the door, the man's as he stood in her way of escaping.

I continued after Lamashtu and spotted her heading up the hill toward the temple. When I got there, the soldiers inside were unarmed, and the realm gate was just closing. "That woman," I said. "She used the gate?"

"Yes," a dwarf said, someone who worked with Orfeda.

"Did you need her?" Zamek asked. "Piper was just heading back to Avalon Island."

"Wait, what?" I asked him. "Piper went through the gate?"

Zamek nodded and then looked confused. "Was she not meant to?"

"She's at the mountain," I said. "The woman's name is Lamashtu."

"Open the gate," Zamek said.

Nothing happened.

"What's going on?" I asked.

The dwarf at the gate looked back at us. "There's a problem with the realm gate. I don't think it's working anymore."

"How is that possible?" I asked him.

"It's not," he said, clearly worried.

"Unless the other side has been damaged," Zamek said, heaving a sigh. "I guess that's the work of your fugitive."

I nodded. "Get it working as soon as possible; we need to know just how bad it is on the island." I turned and walked out of the temple, looking back down at Camelot. Lamashtu was a dangerous enemy to have running around. But Arthur was more urgent, so Lamashtu would wait. For now, anyway.

Chapter Nineteen

Nate Garrett

It took a while to sort everything out from the fallout of Lamashtu's attack. One shape-shifting psychopath had done a lot of damage. She'd separated us, hurt us, killed innocent people. And there would be recompense for that.

Jinayca was like a bear with a sore head after the attack, which had left her with a bruised sternum and a bad case of being pissed off.

I found myself sitting on a park bench overlooking a familiar stream, where I'd once fought an evil man.

"The Atlantis realm gate works differently," Lucifer said as he sat beside me.

I nodded. "I'm sure it's fascinating."

"Not really," he said. "It's really dull. But apparently it'll expand to take everyone in the dungeon at once. No need to go through the gate itself."

"Expedient," I said. "So basically it's what Zamek turned the realm gate on Avalon Island into?"

Lucifer nodded. "It seems the Atlantis gate was created by forward thinkers. Zamek and Jinayca have discussed the merits of such a device for all realm gates, and I snuck out. I think Mordred's asleep."

I smiled for the first time in a few hours. "When are we going?"

"A company of dwarves will be first through, along with Tarron, because if anything goes wrong, they can actually get back here. They go through, activate the gate at their end, and we start filtering in. We have several thousand people to send to Atlantis. It's going to take a while, no matter what we do."

I nodded.

"You're angry and anxious, and I get that, but people need to see you," Lucifer said. "You're a damn talisman to some of these people. The boogeyman on their side. You can't come out here and mope."

"I'm not moping," I said, sounding petulant even as the words left my mouth. "Okay, I'm having a momentary mope. Lamashtu escaped, she has a basilisk blade, and we have no idea where she's gone next."

"You don't have any ideas at all?" Lucifer asked.

"She pretended to be the president; she escaped and came here. But there was a rebellion here, too; she escaped, and then we all turned up, and she had to escape again. She's going to go somewhere safe and regroup. If Mordred was the target, she would have tried to kill him, surely. I think I was a target of opportunity. All of this happened because we caught her in DC."

"She's reacting," Lucifer said.

I nodded. "I get she was the president. She was there to make sure that Arthur's agenda was followed. Much easier to use a tame shape-shifter than a human who may not play ball. But what's her plan now?"

Lucifer shrugged.

I had a thought. "Any idea where Chloe and Layla are?"

"Chloe is with Piper in the hospital," Lucifer said. "Piper will be fine. She's hurt but healing quickly."

"Good," I said, relieved that Avalon hadn't taken someone else from us. "Layla?"

"Realm gate temple, I think," Lucifer said. "You're going to send her after Lamashtu?"

I shrugged. "Thinking about it. Chloe will want revenge, and I wonder if Gawain being in Washington might make Lamashtu try to free him. Seems logical."

"We should have killed Gawain," Lucifer said.

"Not disagreeing," I told him.

"Lamashtu would break him out?"

I nodded. "Again, it's what I'd do. Gawain knows too much. You break him out, or you kill him. One way or another, problem solved."

"Lamashtu is old," Lucifer said. "*Really* old. And deadly. I've only ever met her twice, and the first time was because someone hired her to kill me. I literally had to fake my own death to stop her from coming after me."

"And the second time?"

"I caught her butchering a family in Belgium during the First World War. She just about escaped with her life, although I doubt she enjoyed being shot in the face a bunch of times."

"So now she knows you're alive," I said.

"I think she has bigger issues," Lucifer told me.

"She could be anyone," I said.

"She needs to taste the blood of the victim," Lucifer said. "That's her link. So yes, I guess she really could be anyone."

"At any point are you going to try to make me feel better?" I asked.

"No," Lucifer said.

I noticed Zamek making his way toward us.

"We're ready," Zamek said.

"Any traps?" I asked.

"Shitloads of them," Zamek said. "Most of it rune based, and most of it done in the last few decades. Some of it is ancient, though."

"I assume they're all gone," Lucifer said.

"Yes," Zamek said. "The dwarves went through; they activated the gate on their end. There were enemies there, but they've been taken care of. But one of the dwarves said it was weird."

"Define *weird*," I said.

"You'll see. Let's go." Zamek motioned for us both to get up.

"I'm going to the realm gate temple first," I told him. "I need to see Layla."

Zamek nodded. "Sure, don't be long."

I reached the realm gate temple to find Chloe and Layla sitting outside with Piper.

"I thought you were in the hospital," I said.

"I felt better," Piper said.

"You look like shit," I told her, which made her smile.

"Motivational speeches still aren't your thing, are they?" Chloe said.

"I'm heading back to Shadow Falls," Piper said. "Just wanted some air. The hospital needed the room for someone who's *really* hurt."

"I'm sorry," I said.

"She'll get the care and support she needs in Shadow Falls," Chloe said. "And it's safer there."

Tego padded out of the temple and stopped next to me so I could scratch her behind the ear.

"You have a job for us?" Layla asked.

I nodded. "Lamashtu is on the Earth realm," I said. "I'm pretty sure she'll head to Washington, DC."

"To get Gawain?" Chloe asked.

I nodded.

"That's what you'd have done, isn't it?" Chloe asked me.

I nodded again.

"Has anyone ever told you that you're pretty scary?" Piper asked.

"It's come up once or twice," I told her.

"You want me to take a team to DC?" Layla asked.

"Your picks are going to be a bit limited, unfortunately, but I don't think Gawain is done," I said. "He surrendered too easily, and no matter how many people are guarding him, Arthur is going to consider him either a useful ally or a threat. Both reasons give his pet shape-shifter a motivation to get to him."

"Chloe will go with her," Piper said. "She'll argue with me about it when you're gone, but she will."

Chloe looked like she wanted to argue with her about it now.

"Look, just take who you need to," I said. "But go to Shadow Falls first, make sure Piper is okay, and then head to Washington. Roberto should be able to tell you if he's seen anything weird."

"What's her endgame?" Layla asked.

I shrugged. "She tried to kill Piper and me. I can't imagine that she was here to do either, though. Piper was to escape, and me was because she had the opportunity to. Who knows what her endgame is. If you find out, let me know."

"We'll head over," Layla said. "I'll go straight to DC and speak to Roberto; these guys can head over to Shadow Falls and make sure Piper is in good hands."

"I'm sorry you won't have more assistance," I said. "Do *not* engage Lamashtu alone. She's more than a little dangerous."

"I won't," Layla said. "Be careful in Atlantis."

Tego licked my hand.

"I will be," I said and turned to Tego. "Keep her safe."

Tego snorted as if to say, *What else am I going to do?*

I left everyone outside the realm gate and headed back to the palace, walking past dozens of soldiers who were guarding the entrance.

Eventually, I reached the door to the realm gate room. "So what's the plan?" I asked, entering the room.

"We're going to go fight the bad guys," Selene said. "When people stop arguing."

"Why are people arguing?" I asked.

"Because apparently I shouldn't be going," Mordred said.

"Fuck that. Get your ass to Atlantis," I told him with a smile.

"A sentiment I have expressed myself," Mordred told me.

"He is the king," Hades said. "And thus we need to ensure that he's not just running off after Arthur the second we arrive."

"He's got to come with us," my mother, Brynhildr, said. "But we're concerned that his emotions will lead him to make mistakes."

"My *emotions*," Mordred said with a thumbs-up. "I'm a bubbling Crock-Pot of testosterone and vigor."

"I'm pretty sure we're all pregnant now," Lucifer said dryly.

I turned to Jinayca. "Let's argue later. My best friend is in Atlantis, as is the man I need to kill for taking him."

"This is the end, people," Jinayca said. "Come back with your shield or on it."

"Easy," Mordred said, standing beside me. "I never liked shields. Let's go find Tommy and kill a tyrant."

The room went bright purple, and there was a flash, and the next thing we knew, we were standing on a dais in the middle of a large field.

"Can someone tell me what the hell happened here?" I asked, noticing the several hundred people standing all around us.

"That doesn't look good," Mordred said, pointing to the purple sky as we stepped off the dais.

Several dozen people walked off the dais with us. There were a few bodies littering the ground close to where a group of dwarves stood guard.

"You had trouble?" Mordred asked them.

"The little fuckers tried to stop us from keeping the realm gate clear," one of the dwarves said.

The dead wore red-and-black leather armor and had black leather helmets, although they'd been little protection against rune-scribed battle-axes.

"You ever been here before?" I asked Hades as the hundreds of soldiers and personnel began to arrange camps for those arriving through the gate.

He nodded sadly. "Many times. Last I was here, the sky was bright blue; the air smelled of flowers. There was laughter in the city. The buildings as tall as anything you would see in a major city today on the Earth realm. The abilities of the alchemists who lived here were spectacular, and before they'd ever arrived, the ancient dwarves and shadow elves made this place a paradise."

"Until the Titan Wars," I said.

"Until then," Mordred said.

"The city was destroyed," Persephone said. "I came here just after the death and destruction. They caused tens of thousands of people to die horribly here, unleashing a plague and a war upon a peaceful people. All to get to us."

"And now Arthur calls it home," I said. "And I assume that monstrosity is where he lives."

The black citadel was easy to spot even at this distance. It loomed over everything around it; even the tallest of the other buildings couldn't touch it. The citadel was practically touching the clouds above.

"That is not going to be a fun climb," Mordred said.

"My father is in that city," Kase said, her voice low and full of menace. "We need to move."

"I don't disagree," I said. "But we need to make sure we're ready for a full attack." I looked around as more people emerged from the realm gate and Hades, Persephone, and Mordred ordered troops into formation.

I walked over to the edge of the clearing, next to the beginnings of a forest of blackened trees, and watched the horizon. That wasn't a lot of guards for a realm gate, and the nearby city didn't appear to be inhabited. The gates to it were up, and the walls were high enough that I doubted anyone could climb them quickly.

"The dwarves did some scouting," Mordred said, passing me a pair of binoculars. "Part of the city wall is more climbable than the rest. It's through the forest, though, a few miles that way." He pointed behind me. "A small team could get inside, scout out, get that drawbridge open."

"Am I part of that small team?" I asked, looking through the binoculars at the city, taking in the massive citadel, and trying to figure out where the enemy was.

"You could sit here and admire the beauty of all this, if you'd prefer," Mordred said sarcastically.

"Normally, on the eve of battle, you don't send the entire army to camp outside a city without having good knowledge of the city first," I said with a sigh.

"This won't be your typical battle, then," Mordred said. "The second the dwarf scouts came through, Arthur knew about it."

"So why hasn't he attacked?" I asked him.

"That is a question we need an answer to," Mordred said. "Along with where my father is and where Tommy is."

"He's in there somewhere," I said. "Both of them are."

I passed Hades the binoculars as he joined us, and he looked through them. "There's a drawbridge," he said. "It's designed to look the same as the stone around it, but it's there; I can see the gears on either side. Get that down, and we can get into the city in two places. That might be our best shot."

"Mordred, you coming with me?" I asked as Selene and Persephone walked over.

Mordred nodded, taking the binoculars. "Wouldn't miss it. We'll take a team through the forest and into the city, where we'll split up. I'll take half of the team to bring down parts of the wall and drawbridge; you take the other to find out where we're meant to be going. If you can find a map of the city, maybe on a notice-board or just lying in the open, that would be useful."

"I think that's just in video games," I said.

"Shame. That'd come in real handy about now," Mordred said.

"Has anyone else considered that this is all *far* too easy?" Selene asked.

I nodded. "Yeah, there's an air of trap about the whole thing. The realm gate is in the middle of nowhere, and it's not guarded by anything larger than a cursory group. Arthur wants us here."

"It's now or never," Hades said. "We knew this wasn't going to be easy."

"While that's true," I said, "I'd like to know where Arthur and his forces are."

"They're over there," Mordred said, pointing to the city. "See, that was easy."

I narrowed my eyes at him, and he winked.

"You'd best be quick, then," Hades said. "We'll start moving toward the forest here, put some of these trees and hills between us and the city."

While I agreed that we needed to get this done, and the need to get inside the city and find my friend was almost overwhelming,

I couldn't shake the idea that something felt wrong. Arthur might have sent people to stop us using the realm gates on the Earth realm, but he would have had contingencies for our arrival. And abandoning Avalon was . . . odd.

It was a thought I couldn't shake off, even as Mordred, Remy, Zamek, Lucifer, Diana, Irkalla, and I crept through the woods, then stopped at the riverbank before walking across where it was shallowest.

We all crouched down behind a rocky outcrop that led forty feet up over the wall. It was a sheer drop from the overhang to inside the city, but it was the safest way in. And while I was sure Arthur knew we were here, that didn't mean he knew what we were doing. Hopefully the moving army held his attention.

"I'm quite impressed you didn't make any jokes about *Lord of the Rings*," Irkalla said to Mordred as we were scaling the cliff face that looked away from the city, hopefully keeping us hidden for as long as possible.

"I thought it might be too obvious," Mordred said. "I don't want people to think I'm just that guy who's all nerd and nothing else."

"We've always thought that," Remy said.

Mordred and Irkalla reached the top of the cliff first, and Lucifer came last as the rest of us crouched down on the overhang. We all dropped down into the city, Mordred and I using our air magic to help everyone else land safely.

"All of you, head toward the drawbridge," I said. "I'm going up around the side of this cliff."

"No, you're coming with us," Irkalla said.

"Yeah, don't be daft," Diana said.

"Look, we don't have time to search this entire place," I said. "There's a guard post up there. I saw it through the binoculars. That's as good a place to start as any."

Everyone's eyes followed where I was pointing.

"This strikes me as a terrible idea," Lucifer said. "But we're here now, and all of our choices are terrible. It is the least terrible of all our terrible choices."

"I'm coming with you," Irkalla told me. "Don't argue."

I sighed. "Fine, you come with me, and we'll go see what we can find. We'll meet you back here once the drawbridge is down, and we'll collapse this wall. Hopefully by then we'll have an idea of where inside the citadel Tommy is and where Arthur is waiting for us."

"If you're not back here by the time we get that drawbridge down, we're coming to find you," Diana said.

We all went our separate ways into the city. All the buildings were made with the same black stone that I saw in the citadel, and the buildings themselves came in two forms: lanky buildings that stretched high above and low, squat buildings that were single story but three or four times as long as normal houses. I didn't know what the purpose of either building type was, but there didn't appear to be any actual houses.

The streets were set out in straight lines, with alleys between each building. Unfortunately, the gap between them could be several hundred meters, and a lot of the time moving through the city required me to use my shadow magic to conceal us from the dozens of guards who patrolled. Their red-and-gold armor was similar to what the paladins wore.

It took us twenty minutes to get through the city to where I'd seen a squat building that had been built into the hills that sat along one side of the city. We waited in the shadow of a large building and watched as several nonarmored personnel left the guardhouse and walked down the steps to our level before entering another structure nearby.

"I can sense dozens of people in there," Irkalla said. "I'm guessing it's a barracks of some kind."

"What is Arthur doing here?" I asked, almost talking to myself. "These buildings are just weird. And we haven't seen a single person coming or going from them."

Irkalla looked around. "I noticed that. It feels very sterile."

The last of the guards entered the barracks, and Irkalla and I sprinted across the open road and took the steps two at a time. I burst through the door at the top with a blade of flame in one hand, and Irkalla stood beside me with her sword in hand.

"There's no one here," Irkalla said.

The room was completely empty. I looked out of the windows and saw no one coming to find us.

"Why would guards be coming in and out of this place?" Irkalla asked. She walked to the end of the one large room and pushed open the door. "Nate," she called out.

I looked beyond the door, which was built into the cliff, and the tunnel that led down underground.

"Do they all have this?" I asked.

"That would explain why we haven't seen anyone aboveground," Irkalla said. "They're all beneath us."

"This is getting weirder," I said.

The front door burst open, and Mordred, Remy, Diana, and Lucifer ran into the building. "We have a problem," Mordred said, closing the door before looking around. "This is creepy."

"How'd you know where we were?" Irkalla asked.

"I have your scent," Diana said.

"Could you try to not make that sound terrifying?" Mordred asked.

"I thought I was," Diana said with a shrug.

"The problem, Mordred?" I asked.

"The drawbridge is manned by dwarf slaves," Lucifer said.

"They're wearing shock collars and rune-scribed tunics," Zamek said angrily. "There are similar runes on the drawbridge. I think if we blow the drawbridge, the links sever, and the runes on their chests burn through their bodies."

"We'll find another way," Irkalla said.

"Yes, we will," Zamek said, looking down the tunnel.

"You found a hole," Mordred said.

"This whole place is off," Lucifer said.

"I think there are a lot of these," I said, explaining my theory about why we hadn't seen anyone. I walked to one side of the cabin and looked down over the edge of the city wall and the forest beyond. It was a sixty-foot drop from where I stood. A rune came to life on the wall, blazing blue.

"That's bad," Remy said. "I assume, anyway."

"I may have just set off a magical trip wire," I said.

"This is now the most terrible of all our terrible choices," Lucifer said.

"Ummm . . . you should see this," Diana said from beside the door of the cabin.

I looked over at the hundreds of identical red-and-gold-armored soldiers marching toward us, Merlin in front of them.

Chapter Twenty

NATE GARRETT

Realm of Atlantis

"So I'm guessing that Arthur knows exactly where we are," Remy said as Merlin and his forces got closer.

"This building will not be able to sustain huge damage," Irkalla said.

"It would appear our choices are to fight or run down that tunnel," Lucifer said. "Neither is particularly pleasant."

"No," I said. "No, it's not."

"I'll stay and fight them," Mordred said. "Merlin is my father, and maybe I can keep him busy."

"No," several people said at once.

"We take the tunnel," Irkalla said.

Zamek emerged from his exploration of the tunnel. "It's solid, no runes, no explosives—not that I'm sure they'd work here. Basically it seems to be pretty safe. Safer than going out to fight Merlin and whatever those things are."

"Tunnel it is," I said as a blast of something hit the building, dislodging it and tipping it up onto its side, throwing me across the room through the window with a crash. "Run," I shouted to everyone and used my air magic to fling myself back across the gap between the guard post and the top of the rampart. I had to use more air magic to lower myself safely to the rampart just as a second blast of bright-red power smashed into the cabin, destroying it in an explosion of power.

I was on my hands and knees when the doors on either side of the ramparts I'd landed on opened, and a total of six of the red-and-gold-armored soldiers appeared.

I got to my feet and cracked my knuckles. "Let's see what you've got."

I created a sword of lightning and parried the first attack from the closest soldier, which used a sword with a black blade. I avoided a jab from the spear of a second soldier, using my shadows to wrap around the spear, drag it from its hand, and throw it into the soldier opposite. The sword of lightning ended its life a moment later, and a third soldier died after I used it to remove its head.

One of the soldiers smashed its fist into my face, and a second drove a steel boot into my ribs. I rolled away, but they started throwing magic at me, and it was all I could do to wrap myself in a shield of air and then detonate the magic outward to blast them all away.

They were all up on their feet almost instantly.

"Three down, three to go," I said.

One of the three charged toward me, a blade of ice in its hand. I stepped back, grabbed its wrist, and twisted, breaking the bones, but the soldier refused to let go, and suddenly shadows burst out of the ground, wrapping around my legs, trying to trip me. I cut through them with a blade of fire, but it meant letting go of the soldier with the dagger.

The blade of ice passed over my rune-scribed leather armor, and there was a hiss of power as the runes succumbed to the damage inflicted on them.

I rolled across the floor, throwing a ball of fire at the ice-blade wielder while whipping up tendrils of air behind me to stop the two soldiers there from causing me any problems. I charged toward the soldier in front of me, avoided the blade of ice, stepped around the creature, and stabbed it in the head with a blade of fire that was hot enough to melt the armor. I detonated the fire inside the helmet, and the soldier fell forward as steam rose from its head.

"So, just you two," I said. "How do you see properly with those helmets on?"

Both soldiers took a step toward me.

"Fair enough," I said as the soldier closest to me darted forward, its sword striking out to try to get me to move toward its friend.

Shadows leaped from the ground, wrapping around the blade of the sword, dragging the soldier off balance. I stepped around the sword, smashed a sphere of lightning into the soldier's ribs, and detonated it, sending both soldiers flying off the ramparts and into the forest.

I sighed. They had not been an easy fight, although I now had more questions about who they were than I'd had beforehand.

I looked over the ramparts at the remaining hundreds of soldiers, although I didn't spot Merlin, and the soldiers themselves stood there without making any attempt to throw any power my way.

I heard the door open before I turned, and shadows sprang up from the ground, wrapping themselves around me as I dodged an eight-foot version of the soldiers I'd just fought. Its massive metal maul smashed into the stone, obliterating it. Its armor was identical to the other soldiers' except much bigger and covered in spikes. The giant reached out with a barb-covered glove and tried to grab me, but I was already moving back, putting some distance between us, as I felt the change in the air behind me as the door opened.

A shield of air stopped the newly arrived masked soldier from stabbing me in the back with a blade of fire, but it detonated the magical blade, and I had to throw myself aside into the path of a kick from the large soldier. It caught me squarely in the ribs, sending me flying across the ramparts into the wall next to the door.

I dropped to the floor and lashed out with a torrent of lightning, but the smaller of the two soldiers wrapped them both in a shield of lava, which exploded a second later, only my own shield of air stopping me from taking the blast full on.

"What are you?" I asked.

"Horsemen," the smaller soldier said, its voice sounding rough and full of venom, even through the mask.

"You're the Faceless," I said. "You're what Arthur did to the bodyguards of the powerful." It wasn't a question, but there was a chuckle from beneath the mask of the soldier.

I felt sick.

"Not quite," the soldier said with a laugh, drawing a black-bladed dagger from its back.

There was a huge explosion in the distance, and blue and red flames leaped up into the sky. Taking the opportunity while they were distracted, I jumped over the ramparts to the forest below and sprinted through the shallow river into the dense underbrush as the shouts swept over me from Arthur's soldiers. His *Horsemen*. What the hell had he done? What the hell were those things?

My body hurt, but the thought of what was happening to my friends shot to the front of my mind. Some trapped in a tunnel, and others who knew where now. I hoped that everyone there had managed to get through before whatever Arthur's people had done to the realm gate and that those who'd come through were far enough away to be safe. My last thought as I got to my feet was the hope that the realm gate wasn't completely destroyed.

I looked up at the ramparts above me. There was no way I was going back up that way only to fight Merlin, Arthur, and several hundred psychotic superpowered soldiers. I looked behind me at the forest and wondered if I could follow it back around to where Hades and everyone were going to go. At least then I'd have some idea of what our options were.

I ran into the forest and stayed behind a large tree as more of the giant soldiers appeared on top of the ramparts. That way was out. Irritatingly.

As I ran through the heavy woods, the sky darkened, and it began to rain. I took shelter under a large tree with a thick canopy of leaves that meant I was at least moderately dry. I used my fire magic to keep warm and listened to the sounds of the forest. Or rather the lack thereof. There were no birds, no insects—it was just silence, except for the winds as they howled through the night. I ignited my night vision and continued moving, managing a few minutes before there was the howl of a creature.

I stopped dead in my tracks, looking around, trying to pick up anything that might tell me where it was coming from and what it belonged to. It happened again, and then a third time, although it was now from a completely different part of the forest. Or maybe it wasn't; it was hard to tell where sound came from during the night in the woods.

I turned in a complete circle and saw nothing in the distance. No heat print, no movement. Nothing. I had the unnerving feeling I was being watched. There was another howl, further away than before, or at least I hoped it was. Maybe Hades had sent out a pack of werewolves to track for anything useful, or maybe Arthur had sent a pack to start hunting people on the run.

There was movement a few feet in front of me as something darted past my field of vision and disappeared into the thick bushes that were all around me. The howl happened again. The werewolf was massive as it stepped out from behind a tree. It looked at me and roared. There was nothing that had belonged to the human inside of it; it was all animal. The beast set free. It wore a collar around its massive muscular neck, and I could see the little spines on the inside of it as it dug into the fur and flesh of the werewolf.

"Tommy," I said softly. "Oh *God*, Tommy."

Tommy let out an almighty howl, which changed into a low, menacing growl.

Tommy was, without doubt, one of the most powerful werewolves I'd ever met. He was exceptionally dangerous in the best of circumstances, but having to decide whether or not to hurt my best friend before he could hurt me was one of the worst things I'd ever had to do.

"Tommy," I said softly. "Man, come on, you know me; you're my best friend. I've spent the last year trying to get here to get to you. I'm so sorry it took so long."

Tommy, eyes on me, moved slowly toward me. In his werewolf beast form, Tommy was a foot and a bit taller than as a man and weighed maybe a hundred pounds more.

"Naaaaaaaaaaate," Tommy said, as if the word couldn't quite leave his mouth. "Paaaaaaiinnn."

"Tommy," I said softly. "Come on, let me get that collar off you, and then we can go home. You can see Olivia and your children. They've missed you."

"Naaaaaaaaate," Tommy said before snapping his jaws toward me. "Deeaaath."

He dived toward me, all muscle and power, and I blasted him in the chest with air, dropping to the side and rolling away. Tommy fell to the ground and sprang back toward me, forcing me to wrap myself in a dense shield of air or risk being eviscerated by his razor-sharp claws. Even with the shield, he drove me back, forcing me to reapply the magic as he punched and slashed away at it, tearing through my magical shield with no regard for himself. He just wanted me dead. Nothing else mattered.

I turned the shield into a battering ram and smashed it into his chest, throwing him back, away from me. He collided with a tree, but he was soon back on his feet and charged at me once again. I dropped to my knees and smashed a torrent of air into his legs, tripping him and throwing him into the darkness of the forest beyond. He hit something hard and howled in pain.

Tommy was soon back in the clearing, looking at me with hatred.

"Tommy," I said. "Please don't do this. *Please.*"

Tommy roared at me before charging once more. I wrapped tendrils of air around his arms and legs, stopping him in place, but he roared again and charged forward, snapping the air and forcing the feedback up my arms. He was only a few paces from me when shadows leaped out of the ground, dragging Tommy down to a kneeling position.

"I don't want to do this," I said. "I need you to come to your senses. I need to know that whatever they've done to you, you're fighting it. I need to know my best friend is still in there. Please."

Tommy's jaws snapped over and over again as I walked toward him, making sure that the tendrils of shadow were intact, that he wasn't about to break free.

I stood before Tommy, trying to figure out how to snap him out of whatever had been done to him. It had taken Mordred's death to break him free, but I wasn't about to kill Tommy to test out if it would work with him.

"Naaaaaaate," Tommy said. "Kiiiilllll yooooouuuu."

"No," I said. "You're still in there somewhere. I know it."

"Ennnnnnd yoooouuuu," Tommy said. He snapped forward, testing the bonds of shadow.

"You're not going anywhere," I told him.

Tommy roared and took a step back before springing forward, his incredible strength snapping the shadows. He tackled me and threw me back across the clearing. I hit a tree hard and dropped to the ground as Tommy sprinted into the darkness again. I got back to my feet, my head spinning from the smash into the tree, only to be punched in the jaw by Tommy as he ran back into the clearing. I'd only just managed to put a shield up in time, but even so, it was a hard enough punch that it spun me around on the spot, and my shield vanished.

Tommy picked me up by the back of my armor and slammed my head into the tree, over and over again, before he drove his knee into the side of my head and threw me casually into another tree.

I felt blood pouring down my face from an untold number of cuts. I got back to my knees and felt a kick in my ribs that the remaining runes on my armor absorbed, but they flashed once and went dead just before I got a second kick that lifted me off the ground and broke my ribs.

Tommy slammed his fist into the small of my back, picked me up by the scruff of the neck, and broke my arm with one hand. He continued to twist it until I threw a small ball of flame into his face, which forced him to drop me as he scrambled back.

My armor was useless, my vision was fucked from the amount of blood in my eyes, my arm and ribs were broken, and I could barely breathe due to what I suspected was a punctured lung. My magic would heal me, but I didn't know how long it would take.

I activated my blood magic. There had been a time when I was certain that my use of necromancy meant I wouldn't have blood magic anymore, and while I couldn't use it much and it was greatly depowered, I'd been wrong that it was impossible to use. It was nowhere near the level of power that Mordred had, but it was enough to heal my lungs so I could at least take a breath. It took ten seconds for my blood magic to heal my lungs and the cuts on my face and head, but it would take much longer to heal broken bones.

Images of Selene and Astrid came to the forefront of my mind. Astrid. My daughter was *not* going to grow up without a father. She was not going to grow up in a world of tyrants and death, and I was damned if I was going to let my best friend kill me in a shit heap of a realm and thus stop me from making the realms a better place for her.

I wiped my face with my good arm and pushed out a shield of air in front of me, but it was almost immediately destroyed when Tommy ran through it like it wasn't even there, ignoring the pain it must have caused him. He raked his claws across my side as I dodged out of his way, and he kicked me in the knee. I drove a blade of fire into his side and twisted it.

Tommy screamed, grabbing me by the throat as I removed the blade and drove it back in under his armpit. I cut through the collar around his neck and tore it free, half expecting it to explode, but it did nothing. Even so, the moment of split concentration allowed Tommy to lift me off the ground, roaring in pain the whole time. He headbutted me, breaking my nose, and threw me into a tree.

"I'm not playing now," I said, spitting blood out of my mouth, along with several teeth. Thankfully, they'd grow back.

Tommy winced as he took a step toward me, before the wounds I'd given him healed. Even the most powerful of creatures took a little bit longer than a few steps to heal like that.

"Fucking hell," I said.

There was a blur in the forest to my left, and a werewolf sprinted past me, charged into Tommy, lifted him off his feet, and practically threw him away. The werewolf stood between me and Tommy and roared in defiance.

"Tommy," I said softly. "Come on, man."

Tommy turned and sprinted into the forest.

I crashed to the ground and breathed a sigh of relief as Kase changed back into her human form. "After the explosion in the city, I decided to track the forest for familiar scents."

She looked after her father with tears in her eyes. "I don't know how much of my dad was left in that creature," she said. "I want to help him, but we need to get to the others."

I knew it must have been a hard decision, but our friends needed us. We'd come back for Tommy—and no matter what, we'd save him. Even if it meant ending him.

Chapter Twenty-One

MORDRED

Realm of Atlantis

The group had followed the tunnel after the guard post outside had been blasted into splinters, which had in turn collapsed the first dozen feet of the tunnel.

"Do you think this actually goes anywhere?" Zamek asked.

"Personally, I'm hoping for a big pot of gold at the end," Remy said. "I think we all deserve that."

Mordred noted that no one asked if Nate was okay, because the very idea that he'd be killed by what had happened to him was laughable, but even so, Mordred was slightly concerned about Nate having to face off against an army of red-armored whatever they were.

"How long have we been down here?" Diana asked. "I'm beginning to get a little anxious about being underground."

"We went into an actual dwarven city," Remy said. "An underground dwarven city."

"Yes, but the roofs of that city weren't three inches above my head," Diana pointed out. She'd turned into her werebear form almost the instant the cave-in had taken place.

"Not that I want to tell you how to live," Remy said, "but maybe change back?"

"I need to be ready for whatever we're about to face."

"The mole people?" Remy asked.

"Weremoles," Irkalla said. "That would be new. And I'm not sure that moles would be all that frightening. They eat worms."

"Depends on the size of the mole," Mordred said.

"This is not helpful," Diana told everyone, her tone suggesting they immediately shut up.

"My father was out there," Mordred said after a few minutes of silence. "Leading those . . . soldiers."

"I saw," Remy said. "He's still a dick, then, yes?"

Mordred nodded. "I doubt that will ever change."

"It will when he's dead," Irkalla said.

"No, he'll still be a dick in ghost form," Mordred said. "There's no getting away from it."

The group stopped as the tunnel opened out into a large cavern with runes burning on the walls. "What is this?" Lucifer asked. "These runes . . . they look familiar."

"A prison," Zamek said. "This is a prison."

"Where are the cells?" Diana asked.

Zamek walked over to the nearest rune and placed a hand on it. It flashed bright pink and vanished, the wall behind it folding away as if it had never been there.

"Oh shit," Remy said from beside Zamek as they looked through the newly created hole in the wall.

Mordred walked over to join them and saw the prison beyond. It was the size of a football stadium, with a dozen tiers, each littered with large cages. Each cage was separated from its neighbors by a few feet of empty space, and inside the dozens and dozens of cages were thousands of dwarves. The hole in the wall led to a set of steps that would take them down to the top floor of the prison. They would have to follow the floor around and use the steps at the end of each section to get to the lowest floor, a hundred feet below them, where heavily armed guards—all wearing red armor—patrolled.

Diana grabbed Zamek as he took a step forward. "Not yet," she said. "What's behind the other runes? We need to know what we're dealing with."

Zamek grudgingly touched each rune in turn. Two of the six chambers that were revealed opened into long tunnels with more cages, although these had shackles attached to the ground and blood splatter inside them.

"Torture chambers," Diana said with a low growl.

Two more chambers were full of weaponry and torture implements. Mordred wanted to collapse the chambers, but that might give them away, so it would have to wait.

The last rune opened a part of the wall that led to a set of steps heading upward. In the far distance, Mordred made out a small window of light.

"The way out, I presume," Diana said.

"They bring people here to torture or imprison," Irkalla said. "Now can we burn this all to the ground?"

"Why hasn't anyone come after us?" Mordred asked.

Everyone looked back up the tunnel they'd arrived through.

"Zamek," Lucifer said. "I think we should shut that tunnel down as a means of getting to us."

Zamek wordlessly touched the tunnel, collapsing it. "There's forty feet of debris between us and the open tunnel."

"They must know we're here," Lucifer said.

Mordred nodded. "I would imagine so, yes."

"So why haven't they come to get us?" Remy asked.

"Because they know where we are," Diana said. "They can come and get us whenever they like. There's no hurry, because we can either go up and get captured, stay here and stew in our own hate, or go into the prison and fight the guards."

"They know we'll go to the prison," Mordred said, looking back out of the hole in the cavern at the layout of the prison. "But I don't see any guards up here. There should be. There should be guards on every floor. Why take them away? Unless you're so confident you can win that you don't care—or you're trying to make someone believe that all is okay when it isn't. That it's safer than it really is."

Everything began to shake, and for a moment it felt like the entire cavern would collapse as pieces of it fell from the ceiling, but the shaking finished after only a few seconds.

"What was that?" Lucifer asked, looking around.

No one had a good answer.

"I think we really need to decide what we're going to do next," Remy said. "I don't think they're going to just let us stay here."

"My people are in cages and have been for who knows how long." Zamek said. "We will free them."

"And then what?" Mordred asked. "Not to be pragmatic, but we free a bunch of slaves who have lived here for who knows how long, and then what do we do with them? Leave them here while we go kill Arthur? Tell them to head back to the realm gate?"

"They're warriors," Zamek said. "They will fight."

"They might," Irkalla said. "But slaves aren't known for being kept in good conditions at the best of times. If they fight, if they really want to, then fine, but I think you'll find a lot of them aren't up to it no matter how much they want to. We go and free them, we've got to leave them here until we can sort out safe passage out of here."

Zamek nodded, although he clearly didn't like the idea. "We save them; we come back for them."

"Any other way is going to get them killed," Diana said sadly. "Those who can fight, fight, or stay and defend those who can't, but there must be several thousand dwarves in that prison."

"Yes," Mordred agreed. "And we don't know exactly what's waiting for us down there. This isn't going to be a fun time."

"We must do this," Zamek said.

Mordred looked out of the hole at the prison. "Right, so we need help." He looked left and right. "Zamek, Diana, Lucifer, you head to the left. See if you can find anyone who might be able to give us a hand. Stay low—the guards aren't on this floor, but I'm getting the feeling that's not normal."

"And what plan do you have for us?" Remy asked as he stood beside Irkalla.

"We go right and do the same thing," Mordred said.

"I was hoping to cause mayhem," Remy said.

"Mayhem will come," Irkalla said. "It always does."

Remy smiled. "Yeah, that makes me feel a bit better."

Mordred, Irkalla, and Remy moved to the right of the opening. They crept along, stopping every few feet to take a look over the rock formation that doubled as a banister, keeping them from a nasty drop.

"The guards are just milling around," Remy said. "It's like an illusion of patrolling."

"They're waiting for us," Irkalla said.

They continued on until they reached the first cells on the top floor. The cells were fifteen feet square and contained mattresses and two buckets, and that was about it. Three dwarves lay inside the first cage, which Mordred noticed had runes burned into the floor.

"Hey," Mordred said in Dwarvish. "Any chance any of you want to get out of here?"

One of the dwarves sat up. It was impossible to know his age, due to the amount of grime on any part of his face that wasn't a massive beard.

"Get away," he snapped. "Is it not enough that you beat us, make us work night and day? You have to toy with us too?"

"Seriously, take a long hard look at me," Remy said. "I'm half-fox. Do you see a lot of half foxes running around the place?"

The dwarf looked confused.

"My name is Mordred," Mordred said. "This is Remy and Irkalla. We're here to . . . well, rescue you."

"My name is Dethian," the dwarf whispered as the others in his cell stirred. "I have been here a long time. They freeze us, keep us that way for centuries, bringing us out to work for them before putting us back."

"How long have you been out?" Irkalla asked.

"A few years, I think. Some have been out decades, some longer. Most go back under if they don't die first after a few decades."

"How many die first?" Mordred asked, trying his best to keep his temper in check.

"There were thousands of us," Dethian said. "After the blood elves came, many of us fled to Valhalla, but the majority of us—those who had access to the realm gate in the citadel—we came to Atlantis, but it was a trap. We were slaughtered, imprisoned, forced to build and create. Forced to make this realm into Arthur's military base. Many died during those first few centuries, before they started putting us in stasis."

Mordred looked over the top of the low wall they were crouched behind and watched the floor of the prison below. "Something is happening," he said.

Remy and Irkalla looked down, too, at the soldiers, who were moving to the sides of the prison and standing to attention. Merlin strolled into the prison and stood in the middle of the lowest floor with fifty soldiers behind him.

"Mordred," Merlin shouted. "I *know* you're there."

"Bollocks," Mordred said, ducking back down.

"That right there is a massive bucket of fucking dicks," Remy said. "I know he's your dad and all, but he really is a giant sock of wank."

Mordred stared at Remy for a few seconds. "No, that sounds about right," he said eventually.

"Do you have a plan?" Irkalla asked. "Just curious. I'm okay with winging it."

"I'm going to hand myself in," Mordred told them both.

"That's a stupid plan," Remy said.

"Yes, probably," Mordred said. "But it's also the only plan we have at this exact moment, so stupid or not, here we are."

"What about Excalibur?" Irkalla asked.

"It's okay with me," Mordred said. "I don't think Arthur can use it. It's sort of bonded with me. I think I have to let people use its power, otherwise it doesn't work."

"If you don't come out, Mordred," Merlin said, "my Horsemen will happily come find you. And they have no problem killing a few dwarves on the way."

Remy turned to Dethian. Several of the other dwarves in the cell and those surrounding it had woken up and were staring at Mordred, Remy, and Irkalla with a mixture of curiosity and outright fear. "We really are going to save you," Remy said. "It just might take a while."

"I'm not going anywhere," Dethian said. "Thank you for even trying."

"Get everyone out of here," Mordred said, standing. "Hey, Dad. Still a contemptible bellend, I see."

Mordred walked to the staircase and descended slower than he usually might, ensuring that he gave his team time to get back together and get out of the prison before the mass of red-armored soldiers—Mordred refused to call them Horsemen—were sent after them.

"And your friends?" Merlin shouted after there had been silence for several minutes while Mordred made his way down two more floors of cells.

"We were separated," he said when he reached the ground floor, where Merlin had walked over to meet him. "The tunnel collapsed. I was on one side, they on the other. I told them to create a tunnel and go elsewhere. I imagine they're either back in the city or outside of the walls by now."

The look of irritation on Merlin's face made Mordred quite happy.

"Go check," Merlin said to one of the soldiers, who immediately obeyed like a good little lapdog.

"You've made your own set of mindless drones," Mordred said. "Do they sit and do tricks too? Or is it just the murdering?"

"Do you want to know something interesting?" Merlin asked. "*You* helped create them."

"What?" Mordred asked as two of the soldiers grabbed his arms.

Merlin's smile was unpleasant. "You remember when you worked for Hera? You were still under the control of what had been done to you all those years ago, but somewhere in your brain you knew you wanted to kill Hera for the part she played. You remember?"

"Mars Warfare," Mordred said. "Yeah, I remember."

"You remember a doctor who worked there? He tried to re-create the Fates, but you helped him create a method to use children and put them through the Harbinger trials. You remember the trials, yes?"

"Yes," Mordred said, nodding bitterly. "You get put under, and you live in your mind for months while your body goes through changes to make you more powerful, more used to using your abilities. And yes, I remember what I helped the doctor do. We created a lot of monsters, and then Hera sold them to the highest bidder."

"Which was me," Merlin said. "We bought them *all*. We then made some . . . modifications, but they're still the same people you helped create. Your work helped create the Horsemen. This is your doing."

"And you did this to adult humans?" Mordred asked.

"Well, the method has a few issues. We had to burn away their eyes, but as a bonus, they have extra sensory perception. It's quite clever."

"You burned away their eyes?" Mordred almost shouted.

Merlin smiled.

"You turned them into a really shitty version of Daredevil," Mordred said and burst out laughing. "And then you put them in red armor. Holy shit, you're so getting sued if you ever take these to the Earth realm."

One of the soldiers punched Mordred in the stomach, doubling him over, before driving a knee into Mordred's exposed ribs, breaking at least one. Mordred dropped to the ground and tried to remember how to breathe properly as his magic started to mend his broken bone.

"Do you think this is a time to be funny?" Merlin asked. "You are going to see Arthur, and he's going to take that blade from you and use it to murder you. And his Horsemen will destroy everything you love."

"You're the new Horsemen?" Mordred asked the soldiers. "You fucking idiots. And there's no way you can use this sword."

"Because you won't let us?" Merlin asked.

"Because I've *bonded* with it," Mordred said. "Arthur can't use it without my say-so, can he?"

"The sword was never Arthur's," Merlin said. "It was a bone of contention for him. It did not work for him properly, and we were never sure why. Turns out it was meant for you and you alone, and it can only be used by people you've allowed to use it."

"Lucky me," Mordred said, getting back to an upright position. "We done here?"

"I'm pretty sure that if you die, the sword can be used by whoever killed you," Merlin said. "Want to guess where this is going?"

Mordred raised his hand. "You're taking me out for a father-son bonding day. Can we play catch, Pop? And can I have an ice cream as big as my head?"

Merlin's expression darkened. "You were always the buffoon."

"And you were always an asshole," Mordred said, suddenly serious. "You know that your own people rose up against the assholes you left in Avalon."

"Then we'll bathe the realm in their blood," Merlin snapped. "The Earth realm will be Arthur's."

"That's what this is about?" Mordred asked. "Arthur got told no, so now he's throwing a temper tantrum."

Merlin nodded to a Horseman, who punched Mordred in the stomach again. Mordred dropped to his knees.

"Why did you follow him?" Mordred asked through clenched teeth. "Why go against everything you taught me as a child? Everything you taught Nate too? I know there was some mind-control stuff going on, but that's not all of it; you're too powerful for that to happen by itself."

"I wanted the same thing as Arthur," Merlin said. "Peace, an end to war. And he offered it to me if I followed him. I did so gladly. The mind-control thing was a long time ago, to stop me from having issues with the more . . . unpleasant aspects of what needed to be done. By the time you tried to kill Arthur, I was already fully working for him."

"So why did the paladins and Gawain keep playing with your mind?" Mordred asked. "Why let them?"

"Because I needed to let them think they had one over on me so that if the time ever came, they wouldn't know what hit them. If they ever betrayed me, it would be the end of them. Arthur tried to have Abaddon do the same to me, but she knew what I was doing. She was . . . pragmatic about it."

"You were sleeping with Arthur's right-hand woman, weren't you?" Mordred asked, getting back to his feet. "A woman who used to be his lover, when he was Asmodeus."

"I was," Merlin said. "Arthur isn't very good with women. If you let people think they have power over you, it gives you leverage. Playing your hand all the time does you no favors. Like now, Mordred." He blasted Mordred in the chest with enough power that his hastily created shield protected him from harm but couldn't stop him from being thrown against a nearby wall.

"How'd that feel?" Merlin asked as Mordred got back to his feet.

"You do understand that my friends will realize you have me and they'll come to rescue me," Mordred said.

"Let me show you something," Merlin said, and Mordred was marched behind Merlin as he walked through the prison, out of the main entrance, and up to one of half a dozen huge elevators. They waited as the fifty Horsemen took their places on the elevators, and then they all rose up through the left shaft together, until they reached the top and exited to the outside.

"Pretty," Mordred said as they entered a black stone building, leaving the Horsemen outside. "You not worried I'll do something?"

he asked as Merlin shoved his son onto another elevator that took them both up ten stories to the roof.

"This was a guard tower," Merlin said, ignoring his son. "We thought we might need one closest to the prison, but we never actually had a problem with the dwarves. They do as they're told."

"Or you freeze them in stasis?" Mordred asked.

"Yes, that's part of it," Merlin said. "But it turns out when you have thousands of prisoners being forced to work for you and you murder a bunch of them, the rest behave *exceptionally* well."

"Ah, aren't you the lovely boss," Mordred said. "Do they give you cookies at Christmas for being awesome?"

Merlin ignored his son again and pointed across the city.

Mordred squinted to try to see what he was being shown. "I don't get it," Mordred said. "It looks like a smudge on the . . ." Then he realized what he was looking at. The plains were scorched, the realm gate missing from where it had once been. There were bodies littered over the landscape. Even from this distance, Mordred knew that a lot of people had died.

"We sent a group of Horsemen out to attack your people," Merlin explained. "Thousands of them in tunnels underground. They collapsed large parts of the plains and went to work," Merlin said with a smile. "Did you think we didn't realize you'd come? We planned it. Gawain knew what to say. We wanted you here, Mordred. Arthur wanted you here. Wanted to gather you all together and wipe you out in one go. He has other plans, too, but to see you all die—that will be his glory."

"The shaking," Mordred said.

"That was the explosion," Merlin said. "The realm gate itself isn't actually gone. It's still there; you just can't see it because that fog is blanketing everything. The fog kills people. It was poisonous to pretty much everyone, something that Hera also created at Mars Warfare all those years ago. The realm gate was fitted with enough explosives underground that it killed pretty much anyone standing too close. And then that fog was released. Your friends are either dead, wishing they were dead, or scattered to the winds. There's no backup coming through that gate while that fog remains, and the one thing that might be able to remove it is strapped to your back."

Mordred reached for Excalibur.

"Your friends and allies are no more, Mordred," Merlin said with a chuckle.

Mordred turned to look at his father. "You *really* shouldn't have brought me up here."

"Because you're sad?" Merlin asked.

Mordred took a deep breath and slowly let it out. "No, Dad. Because your arrogance will eventually be your undoing, and you've just sealed your fate."

"Are you going to kill me, Mordred?" Merlin asked with a laugh. "Do you know how powerful I am?"

Mordred nodded and looked back over at the distant field. The trees that had kept them hidden were gone, the ground turned over, the fog swirling. He had to find out how many of his friends had survived. He *needed* to find them. To help them.

Mordred turned back to his father. "Where's Arthur?"

Merlin laughed again. "You want to be dead that quickly?"

"You loved me once," Mordred said. "That's what I was always told—that your hatred of me grew as your love of Arthur did. You're going to hand me over to him to kill me; I just thought I'd like to know where I'm going."

"The top of the citadel," Merlin said. "It'll be a long journey. And then the pain that started in that dwarven realm all those centuries ago will feel like a gentle kiss."

"I wish it had been different," Mordred said. "I wish we could have had an actual father-son relationship. I think I would have liked that."

Merlin stared at Mordred for several seconds and then twitched slightly. "I wish I didn't have such a disappointment for a son."

"I know," Mordred said with a sigh. "But tough." Mordred blasted the roof beneath their feet with pure magic, destroying a large portion of it and sending Merlin and Mordred falling the long distance to the ground. Mordred wrapped himself in a shield of air, but when he hit the ground, he immediately started springing through the city to the drawbridge. He would find his father later. He would end all the hate and pain that Merlin had caused, but first, he had to help his people. He was their king, and he was damned if he was going to let them fight and die without being by their side.

Chapter Twenty-Two

Nate Garrett

Realm of Atlantis

Kase and I moved through the forest as fast as we could. My body had mended itself, although I was still sore and would continue to be so for a while. We found the first group of our allies after running almost flat out for ten minutes. There were hundreds of them, all in small groups tending to the wounded.

Hades and Persephone, both looking like they'd been through a war, were busy trying to find out just how many had died in the explosion. Multiple dead Horsemen littered what had once been the plains and were now charred and overturned, as if all life had been taken from them.

"Nate," Persephone said, hugging me. "Where's everyone else?"

I explained what had happened inside the city and how Tommy had met me outside it.

"Where are Selene and the others?" I asked.

"We were on opposite sides of the explosion," Hades said. "The entire earth erupted, and this fog was cast over it. It killed people before we could do anything to stop it, so we ran. The fog seems to be concentrated around the realm gate, though—there's no movement away. It's kept there somehow. When we thought we were safe, then these red-and-gold-armored *things* burst from the ground and attacked."

"I'll go look," I told him.

"Whoa," Persephone said. "Sorcerers died there too, Nate. I'm not sure how your magic will cope with this."

I nodded. "I understand. Still going to take a look. Mordred and the others are in the city. I imagine Merlin is going after them. If those . . . Horsemen of his find them, it's not going to be a fun fight. We need to get to the city and help. We need that fog gone, or at least to know what it is."

"Horsemen?" Hades asked.

"That's what these things are," I said. "What one of them called itself. They're monsters. Barely alive but full of power."

"Arthur's new Horsemen," Hades said with a sigh. "His evil never truly ends."

"I'm coming with you," my mother said, getting to her feet.

"Me too," Olivia told me.

"I assume you will be with me too, Kase," I said.

Kase nodded.

"Tarron," I shouted. "You up for a wander?"

Tarron picked up his dual swords and stood, stretching. "Sure, why not?"

The five of us ran through the forest and stopped at the edge of the clearing after several miles of terrain to watch the fog as it swirled around the realm gate. There were hundreds of bodies littered around the gate, most of them either our soldiers or wearing the armor of the Horsemen.

"Goddamn it," I snapped.

"The gate appears to have fixed itself," Tarron said. "I doubt even Arthur thought that it would have done so as quickly as this, but anyone coming through there is going to be dead in seconds."

"And the fog could go into other realms," Brynhildr said.

"And Nanshe will be bringing her people through from Olympus soon," I said. "They'll walk straight out into *that* . . ."

"I've never seen anything like it," Kase said.

"I have," Olivia said, her tone like steel.

"Me too," I agreed. "Hera was making something like it back in Mars Warfare. It was a shitty substance that I'd hoped I'd never see again."

At the tree line on the other side of the massive clearing were a dozen allies, including Selene. I waved, and she waved back, and my heart fluttered a little bit. She was fine. Hopefully she'd stay that way.

I pushed out my air magic, trying to move the fog down toward the city or up into the air, but it just stayed where it was. "It's like trying to grab something covered in oil," I said. "It's not behaving like normal fog. Which I know it isn't, but still, I'd have liked it to behave like it was."

"When you saw it last time, how was the fog used?" Brynhildr asked.

"It was pumped into rooms," I told her. "I assume it was kept in canisters or something along those lines, but that could be affected by my magic. Apparently, they improved upon its use."

"How do we get over there and find out how to remove it?" Brynhildr asked.

"It looks like the fog is being kept in place with runes," Tarron said.

"So your plan is?" my mum asked.

"Nate," Tarron said, placing a hand on my shoulder. "The plan is Nate."

"And what am I going to do?" I asked him.

"Throw a fireball at it," he said.

I did as he asked, and the fireball hit the gas and ignited it, the blue-and-red flame shooting up into the sky.

"The gas caused the explosion I saw," I said. "Someone threw fire at it."

Tarron nodded. "Yes. One of the sorcerers there did it. I think your air magic won't work, but fire might. Unfortunately, the amount of power you'll have to keep pouring into the fog to burn it away depends on how much of it is stored under the ground there."

"Just once, I'd like it to be easy," I said with a slight sigh.

I looked across at Selene and spotted Judgement standing beside her. "Judgement," I said, letting my air magic carry my words. "You think you can give me a hand with this one? We need a constant stream of flame."

Judgement smiled. "Sure thing."

Judgement wrapped me in a shield of dense water as I poured flame into the fog. It immediately ignited, causing a massive explosion of power that forced me back, the water shield vanishing in an instant. We tried again, bracing for the explosion this time, and began to walk toward the realm gate. The closer we got, the less fog we saw as the flames managed to ignite it the second they touched.

Eventually, we were both twenty feet from either side of the realm gate, and the earth was a scorched mess. The fog, however, was still coming up, albeit slowly.

"We need the earth lifted up," Tarron shouted.

"Is he taking the piss?" Judgement asked.

"Apparently not, no," I said with the sigh of someone who had been having several exceptionally long days in a row.

"You got this?" Judgement asked me. "You keep burning; I'll do the lift thing."

I nodded, using all my concentration to keep the flames focused on the fog, almost crushing it, while at the same time using the flame to shield the explosions from hitting both Judgement and me. It was hard work, and sweat poured down my face through sheer exertion of power as Judgement slammed her hands onto the ground and the water tore the earth apart, revealing half a dozen large metal barrels, each one with runes on it that allowed the gas to escape through a hole in the top.

"That's not dwarven," Judgement shouted.

Tarron was next to us in an instant, looking over the barrels, while I forced the flame to change into six different streams and stuffed them over the barrels to try to stop the fog. Each barrel was the size of a large bathtub, so after a few seconds of this, I was already on my knees, my entire body telling me I *really* needed to stop.

"Stop," Tarron shouted after he'd spent several seconds writing over the runes that were on the barrels.

I shut off my magic, collapsing back onto the dirt.

Judgement's smiling face appeared above me. "That sucked, eh?"

I nodded. "Let's not do it again."

"Is it safe?" Judgement asked Tarron as I accepted her hand and got to my feet.

"There's still gas in here, and they need moving, but I've disabled the runes," Tarron said. "These are elven."

Selene walked over to us all and gave me a brief kiss. "How is it you're always wherever it's most dangerous?" she asked.

"Luck or I'm cursed," I said. "You pick."

I told her what had happened in the city.

"So Mordred is still in there?" Judgement asked. "I'm going to go find him, then."

"I'll join you," I said. "Tommy ran off, too, and I have no idea where he is, but I don't know if my friend is still in there. I don't know how I can break whatever was done to him."

"Excalibur," Selene said. "That might work."

I nodded. "It's worth a shot."

Once the barrels were moved and the area was declared safe, the two groups remained apart, but a third was created further away from the realm gate so that they couldn't all be seen from the city. We'd lost 106 people. Their bodies had been destroyed in the initial explosion or melted by the fog. Hera's legacy of creating horror continued.

Arthur had lost nearly a hundred Horsemen, but I got the feeling they were acceptable casualties to him.

I remained by the realm gate with Judgement, Selene, Hel, and Loki.

I looked down toward the city. It was a fair distance away, but there was a blast of something that caught my eye, and I was pretty sure that the large plume of smoke that was thrown up into the air had something to do with it.

"More trouble?" Loki asked me.

I shrugged. "I'm not sure yet, but probably, yes."

"Nothing is happen—" Loki said just as the drawbridge to the city evaporated in an explosion of light so big it also took out a large chunk of the wall on either side. Pieces of debris rained down into the river, and a bridge of ice appeared through the smog and dust that were thrown up. Mordred walked across it.

"I knew it," Hel and I said in unison.

We all walked out from the trees, and I threw a ball of flame into the air, letting Mordred know where we were. He saw us and started running. It was a long run, and it took him a few minutes, but he reached us, dirty, exhausted, and looking less than happy.

"Where's everyone else?" Judgement asked.

"Long story," Mordred said and proceeded to explain what had happened since we'd last seen him.

"So everyone else is still in the city?" Loki asked.

Mordred nodded. "I think so. I'm going to go back and find out. I just wanted to make sure we had a way in."

"Yes, it was very subtle of you," Hel said with a smile.

"That's me," Mordred said, looking back as hundreds of soldiers, their red armor standing out against the black stone walls, stood amid the remains of the drawbridge.

"I think we might have to fight our way back in," Loki said.

"Good," I said. "They know we're here; we know they're here. Tommy is no longer a factor in that he's not a prisoner, so they can't use him as leverage. I say we go give them a fight."

"There are thousands of dwarven prisoners in there," Mordred said. "If we can set them free, we can hopefully make sure these assholes have two fronts to fight. I'm not sure how prepared centuries of imprisonment is going to make these dwarves, but we need everyone we can get."

"They're dwarves," Tarron said. "They'll keep fighting."

"We have people in the city," I said. "We do whatever it takes."

The realm gate hummed and activated, and Orfeda, her dwarves, and several others started to move through it. By the time they were done, there were thousands of very angry-looking people who had come through the realm gate and were standing beside it. Nanshe stood at the front, saw me, and raised her sword and shield in greeting. I nodded a hello and turned back to the oncoming army.

"Hades, get everyone ready to fight," I shouted as the Horsemen continued to march slowly toward us, more and more of them flooding out of the city until there were thousands of them, although I was pretty sure our numbers were greater.

Hades looked my way and gave me a thumbs-up.

Hades, Olivia, Persephone, Loki, and my mother quickly arranged the thousands of troops into platoons, each one a set distance away from the others. The dwarves were at the front; their ability to use alchemy was going to be necessary once we were inside the city. The sorcerers were at the back with the elementals and anyone else who could throw magic around at distance. Griffons flew above our heads, as well as several dozen Valkyries on any of the flying horses that had still been alive after the battle in Asgard.

"We go in and end this," I said.

"How are you all getting in?" Hades asked.

"We're going to get in the same way I got out," I said. "But this time, I'm not too concerned about making noise."

"Good luck, my friend," Hades said, and we grasped forearms.

"I will see you inside," I said.

My team set off at a run through the forest. It was still dark, and it was a fair distance, but it was going to take the army we'd brought together some time to make their way down toward the partially ruined front wall.

"I never did say well done on the drawbridge," I told Mordred.

"Yeah, I may have lost my temper a bit," he said. "I saw my dad. I sort of dropped him off a building."

"Is he dead?" Orfeda asked.

"I doubt it," Judgement, Mordred, and I said at the same time.

"You three are weird," Tarron said. "Not bad weird, just . . . odd."

"That's fair," Mordred said.

"So you know where this prison is?" Orfeda asked Mordred.

"Under the city," he said. "There's a lift that takes you down there. Not sure where the stasis part is, but I assume the dwarves know."

There were several huge explosions of power from the city, and we all stopped for a second as the sky was momentarily filled with jets of fire.

"It's begun," Mordred said. "I was never sure we were going to make it this far."

"Whatever happens now, we'll make sure Arthur remembers it," Tarron said.

"No," Judgement said. "He won't remember anything. It's hard to remember something when your head is no longer attached to the rest of you."

The dwarves banged their axes and swords against their shields in agreement, and we continued on toward the ramparts I'd fallen from. To bring war to Arthur. To end his tyranny. Once and for all.

Chapter Twenty-Three

NATE GARRETT

Mordred, Judgement, and I destroyed the wall that I'd jumped off instead of fighting an entire battalion of Horsemen by myself. We stepped into the city as the sounds of battle could be heard from where our allies had engaged with the enemy.

"Mordred, lead the way," I said.

The first group of Horsemen we ran into attacked without pause. There were a few dozen of them, and Judgement was the first to dive into the fray, her blades of light cutting through anyone stupid or unlucky enough to be in her way.

I dodged the swing of a huge maul from a mutant Faceless that had become one of the massive Horsemen, and I drove a blade of lightning into its groin, lifted it up to its heart, and detonated the blade, ripping the Horseman in half.

The dwarves, including their queen, and Tarron did their bit, but mostly they just let the three of us take point and defended rearguard. We fought wordlessly, our magic rending flesh, killing, and maiming, until all the Horsemen before us were dead.

I dropped an ax onto the ground next to the headless Horseman who'd used it, and we moved on without a word.

"Mordred, you okay?" I asked.

Mordred nodded.

"You sure?" I asked. "That guy was a headless Horseman, and you said nothing."

Mordred forced a smile. "I'm saving up my quips for when I face my father."

"You got any good ones?" Judgement asked.

"I thought *Die, motherfucker* would be my go-to," Mordred said before we ran across a street. I spotted several more Horsemen running toward the battle at the city entrance.

"Catchy," Orfeda said from behind me.

We reached the top of the lift shaft without incident and descended into the prison. I felt on edge, like Arthur was going to do something bad. There was no chance he didn't have a contingency in case the city started to fall.

Freeing the dwarves would be one thing, but actually getting them out of the city. . . well, that was going to be a whole different ball game.

We reached the bottom of the lift shaft and exited the elevator into darkness. I ignited a ball of flame, and Mordred and Judgement both did the same with their light magic, which was considerably brighter.

"Show-offs," I said, extinguishing the ball of flame in my hand and changing my vision to thermal imaging. If something was waiting for us in the darkness, I wanted to know about it before any light touched it.

We walked through the tunnels, Mordred leading the way, and stopped as we entered a massive cavern, where my thermal imaging lit up like a Christmas tree. There were hundreds and hundreds of dwarves just on the few levels I could see. In the middle of the room was a pile of Horsemen corpses. I walked over, and Mordred threw several large globes of light up into the air, illuminating everything and revealing that the corpses had mostly been decapitated or ripped to pieces.

"What happened here?" Tarron asked, looking around.

"That would be us . . . *we* happened," said a familiar voice.

"Remy?" I asked, looking up.

"Hey," Remy said. "We got bored waiting, so we started without you."

Diana's werebear head appeared over the top floor, and I took a step back so I wasn't craning my neck to look at them both.

"We came back," Irkalla said. "I think we've got pretty much everyone free at the moment; we couldn't do much until you'd left with Merlin, but once he was gone, the other soldiers here weren't much of a problem."

"Where are Lucifer and Zamek?" Mordred asked.

"Zamek is busy trying to remove a lot of runes," Irkalla said. "Now that Queen Orfeda has arrived, I assume you can all help with that."

"Yes, we can," Queen Orfeda said, ordering her guard to do exactly that.

They ran off to either side of the prison and set about working to remove the runes on the cells as several of the dwarves let out cries of relief.

"You need to hear what Dethian has to say," Irkalla said, introducing a hunched-over dwarf.

"I'm Nate," I said.

"It's a pleasure," Dethian said, his hands almost forming claws. Whatever happened to those responsible for this, however brutal and painful, it wasn't going to be enough.

"Tell him what you told us," Irkalla said.

"They had humans," Dethian said. "Tens of thousands of humans. We'd see them brought through the realm gate and marched through the city. Most were screaming as they entered the buildings all around the city. Then there was silence. I don't think they're human anymore. I think Arthur and his people did something to them. I had to work up on the surface for a few moon cycles, and I made buildings that were empty except for runes all over them. Elven runes. I don't know what they did; I wasn't allowed to study them."

"Humans locked up and experimented on," I said. "And elven runes in empty buildings."

Dethian nodded. "I don't know what they have planned, but I know it's a kind of evil that most people can't comprehend."

"Tens of thousands of humans," I said, mostly to myself. "Nothing good comes from that. Thank you for telling us."

Dethian nodded. "And bracelets," he said.

"What?" I asked.

"We were forced to make a lot of things—buildings, roads, weapons—but we also made bracelets. They're made from the same black stone as the buildings. I don't know what was done with them."

"Sorcerer's bands?" Irkalla asked.

"I don't know," I said, concerned that there was a lot more going on in Atlantis than I'd first considered.

"Thank you, Dethian," I said. "Go rest; we'll get you all out of here as soon as we can."

Dethian turned to walk away but paused. "If you see Arthur, kill him. He shouldn't be."

"You'll get no argument from me," I said, and Dethian slowly made his way to the side of the cavern.

"And Lucifer?" Judgement asked.

"There's a tunnel back there," Irkalla said. "There were more dwarves in there in stasis. Elves too."

Tarron set off at a sprint that caught me by surprise, and I found myself running after him. I stopped as the entire place shook.

"What the hell was that?" I called back to Irkalla.

"No idea," she shouted back. "It did it a while ago."

I turned and continued on after Tarron, adding the shaking foundations of an underground prison to the list of problems I needed to go deal with.

I stopped when I entered a room with a deep blue-and-purple glow. There were thousands and thousands of hatches on the ground, and Tarron stopped by one of them, dropping to his knees and rubbing away the frost on the glass window. He gasped and began to weep.

"Tarron," I said, my voice echoing around the chamber.

"My people," he said softly. "My *people*."

I placed a hand on his shoulder. "We'll get them out."

"Yes, we will," Lucifer told me. "I just don't know how."

"These are a mixture of dwarven and elven runes," Tarron said. "They're a modified version of what was used to keep me in stasis. I'm staying here to help deal with this."

I nodded. "Get these people out of here," I said. "I'm not leaving the realm without them."

Tarron looked back down at the hatch, stood, and walked to another, then another, until he was hundreds of feet away from me.

"How many?" I asked Lucifer.

"Each hatch is atop a cell that is several dozen feet deep," he said. "I think there are about a quarter of a million people here. There's a second and third chamber to the end, both with a similar number of hatches as this one. They kept their slave labor on ice until they needed it."

I turned and marched out of the chamber just as Remy ran toward me. "Mordred and Judgement left," he said.

"Wait, what?" I asked.

"The shaky thing," Remy said. "Apparently, it might be Merlin trying to bring the prison down on top of everyone in it."

"Of course it is," I said and started to run back toward the main prison. "Where'd they go?" I asked.

"Back to the lift," Irkalla said.

"Stay here; help get everyone out and back to the realm gate," I said. "Tarron and Lucifer found a lot more down there. No one gets left behind."

"And what are you going to do?" Diana asked me.

"I'm going to go find Arthur and kill him," I said. "And then I may have a bucketful of whiskey."

"I could go for a whiskey," Remy said. "Or just pure ethanol at this point. With a little umbrella."

I turned and looked at him.

"Because I'm classy," Remy said with a smile, and I turned to leave.

I was halfway up the lift shaft when the tunnel above my head started to collapse, large pieces of rock striking the top of the lift and disengaging it, flinging it forward into the abyss a hundred feet above the ground. I was launched out of the front of the lift and used my air magic to latch on to the side of the shaft before swinging myself across to one of the metal columns that kept the lifts in place.

More rock fell down onto where I'd been standing only moments ago, and the lift itself was ripped apart and sent plummeting down the shaft. I held on to the column, my air magic keeping me in place in the darkness, and looked up to see three faces above me looking down. I activated my fire magic, using night vision to look up at them. They were only forty feet above my head, and I made out their faces easily. Two of the three belonged to the Furies—Alecto and Megaera—and the third was a shadow elf, his face longer than Tarron's, with a missing ear and horrific scarring over one side of his face, as if someone had held it to a white-hot plate and burned it away.

"You think he's dead?" one of them asked.

"Probably," another one said as I moved across the metal beam that connected the columns to the wall of the lift shaft. A light came down from above, and one of them called out my name as I sank into my shadow realm.

I immediately spotted the light I needed to move toward and headed in that direction as the wraith flittered around inside the darkness. I could feel its need—its need to eat and grow powerful.

"Will protect you," it said in the darkness.

I exited the shadow realm behind the two Furies and the shadow elf, all three of whom were still looking over the edge of the tunnel.

I drove a blade of lightning into the back of Alecto and removed her head as she fell forward into the shaft.

The shadow elf turned toward me first, a hatchet in one hand and sword in the other. I hit him with a sphere of air that threw him a few dozen feet back, where he connected with a wall and slid down it, motionless. Shadows leaped out around him, dragging him under to be devoured by the wraith.

"You bastard," Megaera screamed and leaped at me. I moved aside and blocked her attack, kicking out the back of her knee and dropping a ball of flame onto her. She rolled aside, almost falling over the edge of the tunnel, and got back to her feet as the ball of flame detonated and spread flames out toward her.

Megaera dived over the flames toward me, her clothes catching fire in the process, and cut me across the cheek with a silver dagger that caused me to gasp in pain.

"I'm going to have your eyes," Megaera screamed and lunged again.

I stepped aside, created my battle-ax soul weapon, and drove it into her chest. She gasped and blinked at me as I removed the soul weapon, leaving no mark, and swung it up over my head to bury it in her skull.

She pitched forward onto the dirt, and I reached out with my necromancy, sensing for any traps that might have been laid for anyone trying such a thing but finding none, and I claimed her soul.

I immediately dropped to my knees as Megaera's entire life flashed through my mind. Every cruel, awful, evil act relived as if it were me carrying it out. I didn't like to take the souls of those who had carried out evil acts, as it did little but hurt my psyche, but I needed information, and I needed it a lot quicker than I could get it through any other means.

When the visions subsided and the death toll of Megaera's life had ended, I saw the bodies left in the wake of the Furies. Erebus had died at their hand inside the citadel. Erebus, who had given part of his soul to be placed inside of me and bond with my magic—who had helped me, taught me, and been someone I'd called a friend. Erebus's spirit had vanished once my true power had unlocked on Mount Hood what felt like a lifetime ago, but I'd always hoped I'd be able to find the man and say thank you. Now that wouldn't be possible. For that, I wished I'd taken longer to end their lives.

I blinked and found myself on my hands and knees, sucking in air. I coughed and sputtered and spat a nasty taste out of my mouth. Necromancy was never the most fun thing to do when dealing with the recently dead, and the more powerful my victim, the worse it was for me.

Megaera and the other Furies had been involved in the torture and corruption of Tommy's mind and the murder of hundreds of dwarves and elves who were slaves in the realm and dozens more prisoners inside the citadel. Arthur's throne room was near the top of the citadel. I stood, and the image of Demeter came to me. She was working with Arthur and, from a few of the memories, doing a lot more than just working.

"Now I need some bleach for my brain," I said.

Images of Demeter and Arthur caught in a compromising position notwithstanding, Megaera was a wealth of intel. Athena had been chained to the roof of the citadel to be attacked by harpies over and over again, until finally she'd been unable to heal. She'd died up there, alone and angry.

The last thing that I saw was Lamashtu, Megaera, and the elves being told to go to Washington, DC. To punish those who were there while we were here in Atlantis. Arthur's plan. To get us in one place and then murder everyone we'd left behind on the Earth realm. To leave no one standing. No one to stop him.

I turned toward the front gate, wanting to sprint there and tell everyone about the imminent attack on Washington, DC, if it wasn't already happening, but a Horseman ran toward me, lance in hand, ready to run me through. Tendrils of shadows leaped out of the ground, taking hold of the lance and pulling it down to the ground, forcing the Horseman to let go or be catapulted.

"I really don't have time for this," I told it through clenched teeth.

It ignored me, which I'd pretty much known it would, but before I could do anything, a large werewolf barreled into it, taking it off its feet, ripping its head off, and tossing it aside in one movement.

"We can't keep doing this, Tommy," I said. "You turn up, try to kill me; I hurt you; you run away, only to jump out like some crazed eighties slasher killer. It's going to get old fast."

Tommy roared at me and leaped the distance between us, but a blast of ice from beside me drove him away. I turned, expecting to see Kase again, but Mordred stood several feet back and drew Excalibur.

"People need to stop saving your life," Mordred said to me as he stood beside me.

"I can't kill him," I said. "I just . . . can't. I can't go through what I went through with you. Again."

Mordred laid a hand on my shoulder. "I know," he said and took a step toward Tommy, Excalibur held before him.

Tommy got back to his feet and rolled his shoulders before running at Mordred, who raised Excalibur above his head and activated the power it held.

Tommy stopped dead in his tracks. He blinked twice and let out a scream of pain. He clawed at his head, drawing blood, then turned and fled into the city.

"Let him go," Mordred said to me as I moved to chase him. "There's no telling what Excalibur can do to someone under the kind of curse I was under. If he returns, we'll make sure to try again."

"I saw a memory of Lamashtu," I said, explaining the vision about Washington.

"Oh God," Mordred said. He turned to several allies who were running up behind him and gave orders to get people back to DC.

The idea of Lamashtu's attack in DC, where so many people were recovering, sent a shiver up my spine. And Layla was out there somewhere . . .

The soldiers ran off toward the realm gate.

"Nate, they'll get the message to people who can help," Mordred said, placing a hand on my shoulder.

I nodded, but a cold pit of fear sat in my stomach as we ran through the deserted streets of the city.

"I think Judgement went this way," Mordred said.

One of the floors high above us exploded with magical power, and three soldiers fell the several hundred feet to the ground and hit with an unpleasant sound.

"Right, well, I think we found her," I said.

We took a step toward the front of the citadel as Merlin stepped out of the doors. More and more Horsemen flooded out until they almost surrounded him. "I think you'll find this a lot harder than you were expecting," he said as energy crackled all around him.

Chapter Twenty-Four

LAYLA CASSIDY

Realm of Shadow Falls

Layla, Chloe, Tego, and Piper arrived in Shadow Falls, where Leonardo immediately shouted for medical aid, which arrived quickly and whisked Piper away to be checked over. Chloe followed behind, and while Layla knew that Piper was going to be fine, she was still concerned for her friend's well-being.

"We need to head over to the palace and speak to whoever's in charge," Layla told Leonardo and Antonio.

"We expecting trouble?" Antonio asked.

"Lamashtu," Layla said. "Shape-shifter, murderer, and generally just an all-around bitch. She hurt Piper. She almost killed her. Tried to kill a bunch of other people too. Maybe Athena."

"Athena's dead?" Leonardo asked. "I never thought that was going to happen."

"We're not sure, but maybe," Layla said sadly. She'd never met Athena, but anyone who'd died at the hands of Arthur and his minions had died at the hands of awful people. Layla didn't wish that on too many people.

"So what do you need?" Antonio asked.

"There's a possibility that Lamashtu is heading to Washington, DC, to break out Gawain," Layla said. "I don't have long before I need to head there and check with Roberto."

"I can change the destination," Leonardo said, and he turned to the realm gate.

Chloe walked into the temple. "So we going or what?" she asked. "If Lamashtu is in Washington, I plan on turning her into the world's largest pincushion."

"How graphic," Leonardo said as the realm gate came to life. "Good luck, you three."

Tego bumped into Leonardo, who sighed and scratched the huge cat behind the ear, before she followed Chloe and Layla into the realm gate.

Once in Washington, DC, they were soon out of the Lincoln Memorial and running toward where all the humans were. They reached the edge of the cordon at Lafayette Square, and Roberto spotted them and waved them over.

"And what can we do for you both?" he asked.

Layla and Chloe told him about what had happened since they'd left the Earth realm.

"Lamashtu might come back here?" Roberto asked, looking around, suddenly concerned.

"She could be anyone," Layla said.

"Gawain is in a safe house," Roberto said. "It's guarded by enough dwarven runes to be a serious problem for anyone, no matter their power. Lamashtu can't get in there as someone else—her shape-shifting wouldn't work."

"Okay, how about blowing it up?" Chloe asked.

"She'd need a nuke," Roberto said.

Layla looked around. "Could she get a nuke?"

"No," Roberto said, putting an end to that fear.

"Okay, so Gawain isn't the target," Layla said. "Maybe she doesn't come here. Maybe she goes elsewhere. I do feel a little better for having checked, though."

"I'm still uneasy," Chloe said.

"I can take you both to the safe house," Roberto said. "It's not far from here."

"Would that be okay?" Layla asked.

"Let me go check on a few things, and I'll be right back," Roberto said and walked off toward one of the large tents.

Chloe entered a nearby tent, which was full of people in army fatigues or suits, looking over large amounts of paper spread over a table.

Layla joined her, and several of the people in the tent stopped what they were doing.

"Can we help?" a middle-aged woman with short dark hair asked.

"What's that?" Layla asked, pointing to the blown-up photos on the table.

"We're with the rebellion," Chloe said. "We might be able to help."

The lady looked beyond Layla and Chloe to Tego, who took up a large portion of the tent entrance.

"Is that tame?" she asked.

"Tego is a her," Layla said. "And not even slightly tame, but she's friendly so long as you don't call her a 'that.'"

Tego yawned, revealing the razor-sharp teeth.

"We found this mark in sixteen different spots around the White House North and South Lawns, Pershing Park, the President's Park, and all the way down to the Washington Monument," the woman said. "Same mark. Hundreds of times."

"Have you had any dwarves read it?" Chloe asked, picking up one photo and staring at it.

"None of them can translate it," a young man in army fatigues said. "It's elven, apparently."

"Tarron could read this," Layla said. "If he wasn't in a different realm."

"So someone is writing Elvish all over Washington?" Chloe said.

Roberto arrived before anyone could say anything else. "Hey, you're in here. We've been given clearance."

"These marks—any ideas?" Layla said, holding up a photo to Roberto.

Roberto shook his head. "We've been trying to get Gawain to tell us, but he's essentially turned into the Joker at this point. Mocking and laughter. That's all we've gotten from him."

"Have you tortured him yet?" Chloe asked.

The room fell silent.

"We don't do that," Roberto said.

"Do we need to find someone who does?" Chloe asked.

"Let's go see Gawain," Roberto said hurriedly, ushering Chloe and Layla out of the tent, with Tego following behind.

It was a short walk to the safe house, which was in an otherwise innocuous building on the other side of Freedom Plaza.

Roberto opened the door and motioned for everyone to go into the foyer beyond, where twenty heavily armed individuals stood next to a set of elevator doors.

"Tego, you stay here," Layla said. "Just in case."

Tego curled up on the floor next to the elevator, and Layla stroked her head before getting in and heading up to the top floor. The doors opened, revealing another dozen heavily armed personnel.

"They're at least taking Gawain seriously," Chloe said as Roberto led them down a corridor and used a key card to get inside a room with cameras and a one-way mirror, which looked into a much smaller room that contained a chair, table, and mattress. Runes adorned every surface inside the cell.

There were three people inside the room with Layla, Chloe, and Roberto: President Lopez, a Secret Service agent, and a general who Layla was pretty sure was called Blake. Gawain was sitting down on the mattress, staring at the one-way mirror. Occasionally, he waved.

"He's not bleeding a lot," Layla said. "That's unexpected."

"He's not doing anything," President Lopez said. "He occasionally swears at us."

"You want to try?" General Blake asked Layla and Chloe.

"No," Chloe said. "I'm really not the person you want in there with him."

Layla sighed. "I can try—not sure it'll do any good. I'm thinking Mordred or Nate would be better suited to getting him to talk."

The Secret Service agent opened the door, and Layla stepped into the cell.

"Layla, isn't it?" Gawain asked.

Layla nodded.

"You going to take this off me?" Gawain asked, showing the sorcerer's band.

"No," Layla said.

"No, I suppose that's too much to hope for," Gawain said.

"The runes all over the city—what are they for?" Layla asked.

"Graffiti is a terrible crime," Gawain said smugly. "But some people just need an artistic outlet. They're art."

"They're elven," Layla said.

"Elven art," Gawain told her with a smile.

"Where is Lamashtu?" Layla asked, trying to think of anything to say that might get Gawain to cooperate.

Gawain shrugged. "Mars?"

"Bye, Gawain," Layla said. "They're going to throw you in a deep dark hole, and you're going to die horribly."

"Ladies first," Gawain said, staring through Layla with a gaze that made her shiver.

The door burst open, and General Blake walked in. "You vile little shit," he shouted, waggling a finger at Gawain. "You think you can sit there and smile. You attacked our country; you murdered our president. You're going to be tried as a war criminal for this, you're going to be executed, and if I have my way, it'll be a slow, long death."

Gawain looked over at Blake, who was three feet away and flushed with rage. "I guess he's a lady," Gawain said, and he sprang up from his bed toward Blake and tore out his throat with his teeth. Layla dived into Gawain and dragged him away as Roberto and Chloe entered the room; the latter smashed the butt of a fire extinguisher into Gawain's face.

Layla pushed the semiconscious sorcerer to the floor, and he started to laugh, his broken nose making the sound even more unnerving.

Paramedics dragged the general out, but he'd stopped breathing, and as everyone else cleared out of the room, Layla heard one of them say that he'd died.

"Where's President Lopez?" Layla asked.

"She's been taken out of the building," Roberto said. "Back stairs, to an underground system of tunnels. She's safe."

Layla glanced back at Gawain, who was sitting upright again.

Roberto's radio went off, and he left the room, leaving Chloe and Layla alone.

"You think we should just kill him?" Chloe said. "It would be doing the world a favor."

Layla stared at her friend for a second. "You okay, Chloe?"

Chloe shook her head. "I can't stop wanting to wash my hands. I've scrubbed them a dozen times, and I still keep thinking Piper's blood is on them. I keep smelling it."

"You want to go back to Shadow Falls?" Layla asked. "I can hold the fort here, try and figure out if Lamashtu is actually turning up and, if not, try and figure out where she's gone."

Chloe shook her head. "No, I want to stay here."

Layla took her friend's hand in hers. "I'm glad," she said.

Roberto reentered the room. "We've got a situation," he said. "There's a really angry dwarf lady over at the square yelling at people."

"How angry?" Layla asked.

"She threatened to tear the head off a soldier and stuff it up the ass of another one," Roberto said.

"Jinayca," Layla and Chloe said in unison.

The trip back to Lafayette Square was done at a jog, and Jinayca's voice could be heard well before any of the three reached her. As they turned the corner and reached the edge of Lafayette Square, it was apparent that Jinayca was not alone. There were two dozen dwarven soldiers and Selene with her.

Selene spotted the three first and ran over to meet them.

"What's going on?" Chloe asked.

"Lamashtu is here," Selene said. "Nate took the memories of a Fury, and he saw the plan they hatched. She's here with those elves."

"There's Elvish written all around this part of the city," Layla said.

"What does it say?" Jinayca asked, having finally been convinced to stop berating the soldiers.

Layla, Roberto, and Chloe took everyone to the tent, while Tego milled around outside. Jinayca took one look at the writing and almost gasped. The human members inside all turned to watch the newcomers with a mixture of concern and interest.

288

"That's a realm gate destination rune," Jinayca said. "They're trying to turn a part of Washington, DC, into a giant realm gate."

"Can't we just erase some of the runes?" Roberto asked.

"I'd need time to figure out the way to do it without them exploding or doing something worse," Jinayca said. "And I'm not sure we have that time."

"They're going to bring an army through into here," Layla said, horror dawning on her.

"We need to find them now," Selene said. She looked up at the humans in the tent. "Get everyone you can ready; we're going hunting."

Chapter Twenty-Five

NATE GARRETT

Realm of Atlantis

The ground beneath my feet tore apart and threw me back, my shield of air keeping me from any serious damage as I smashed into the wall of a nearby building. I tore my way through the rubble that fell onto me and saw that the building was completely empty inside. I noticed the elven runes that Dethian had mentioned but didn't have time to investigate anything further, and I sprinted back into the fray, wrapping dense lightning and air around my fist and driving it into the helmeted face of the closest Horseman, sending it flying back into its brethren.

Mordred had a few cuts on his arms as he avoided a spear by grabbing the shaft, stepping into the attacker's space, and driving a blade of ice up into the Horseman's throat. He twisted his hand, and a second later a dozen spikes shot out of the inside of the Horseman's helmet, killing it, and he stepped over the body to face the next one.

I avoided a blast of fire from one of the Horsemen, and the shadows leaped up from the ground, wrapping around him, and dragged him down into the shadows.

Merlin stood back, watching with his arms folded over his chest as Mordred and I carved through his Horsemen. We were bloody and bruised, and more than once we were punched down to the ground, but we kept getting back up, kept fighting. I was damned if I was going to let anyone stop me from what I needed to do.

After an unknown amount of time, Mordred and I regrouped. Both of us were breathing hard, sweat and blood on our faces.

"This is not how I wanted to spend my afternoon," I said, spitting blood onto the ground.

Mordred drew Excalibur, and I saw the look of amusement on Merlin's exceptionally punchable face.

Dark smoke circled my hands, and I thought I heard Mordred shout "No!" just as I poured my pure magic out in a stream of power that smashed into the Horsemen and Merlin with no stopping it. The power engulfed them, tearing into the citadel's lowest floor behind them and ripping through it.

I took a step back as my pure magic died down, and I saw that the Horsemen and Merlin, who should both have been turned into hunks of molten goo, were standing exactly where they'd been only a moment ago. A shield of purple matter magic lifted up off the ground, controlled by the Horsemen, and Merlin brushed off the tops of his shoulders, as if removing some dust from them.

"I'm going to take a guess that pure magic doesn't work on the Horsemen or Merlin," I said with a sigh.

"Do you feel stupid yet?" Merlin asked. "You can't win here."

"I beg to differ," I said.

"Kill them all," Merlin commanded.

I picked up from the ground a longsword that had belonged to one of the Horsemen. It would have to do for now.

The attacks came fast and unrelenting as I dodged and parried weapon attacks while throwing magic at those close enough. Fighting against a never-tiring mass of armored psychopaths was not a fun experience.

The bodies of the Horsemen littered the ground, but for every one Mordred and I killed, two more arrived to fill the void, leaving us both constantly on the back foot.

I parried an ax attack, but a Horseman appeared out of the shadows beside me and drove its fist into my jaw before I could stop it. The axman twisted the sword out of my grip and kicked me in the chest hard enough to send me back a dozen feet. I crashed to the ground near Mordred, who removed the hand of one Horseman who was reaching for me.

"This sucks," I said, getting back to my feet. I'd been taking Horsemen into my shadow realm when possible to continue to feed my power, but it wasn't going to be a long-term solution to fighting dozens of well-trained, heavily armed monsters.

"When it happens, catch it," Mordred said, swinging Excalibur down into the neck of the closest Horseman. Dodging the next attack, he drove the sword up into the Horseman's chest before blasting it away with his air magic.

Mordred spun and tossed Excalibur toward me, and I used my air magic to guide it to me before catching it in one hand and driving it up into the head of my closest attacker. I swapped hands, pulled the sword free, parried another strike, and stabbed the Horseman in the heart. A whip of lightning in one hand and Excalibur in the other, I killed two more Horsemen before I threw the sword back to Mordred, who caught it without looking and impaled a Horseman by his side before spinning under a second attack and removing the leg of the assailant.

We carried on like that for a while, each killing several Horsemen with Excalibur before bouncing it over to the other one and repeating the process. Excalibur didn't dull; it didn't get stuck—it drove home true, and nothing stopped it. Every time I held the sword, I felt my power increase, I felt the overwhelming need to use that power to destroy, and giving it up was incredibly difficult, but I did it nonetheless.

We'd killed a few dozen before the Horsemen stopped coming, and Mordred and I stood back to back, exhausted.

"These assholes just don't know when to quit," Mordred said.

"Are you both done?" Merlin asked.

I took a deep breath. "Nah, just getting a second wind," I said.

Merlin laughed. "I would have enjoyed working with you, Nate. It's a shame things didn't work out."

"You murdered people," I said.

"Yeah, that's less 'not working out' and more down to you being a psychopath," Mordred said.

While Merlin was engaged with Mordred, my shadows crept around the dead Horsemen, stretching out until they were under the feet of everyone standing before us.

"You done?" I asked.

Mordred nodded.

The shadows leaped up off the ground, engulfing everyone within reach. They had dragged half a dozen down into the shadow realm before they were stopped, and while the pain of having my shadows severed or burned was less than pleasant, the power that those dead Horsemen gave me more than made up for it.

"You play video games?" Mordred asked.

Merlin's expression was the picture of rage. "Of course not. I'm a grown man."

"Well, this will be new to you, then," Mordred said.

Lightning tore out of my hands, smashed into the first Horseman, and exploded. It bounced from Horseman to Horseman, exploding with every new one it touched. Charring armor, breaking inside, and obliterating the living being.

One of the explosions bounced to Merlin, who wrapped himself in fire as the lightning detonated, throwing him twenty feet back across the face of the citadel. He impacted with a nearby building and vanished from view.

Mordred raised his hands high above his head and created a huge sphere of light magic.

The lightning died down, and I took a step back as Mordred unleashed the light magic. It turned into hundreds of daggers of light, which smashed into the remaining Horsemen with frightening speed and power.

"Chain lightning, bitch," Mordred shouted to his father, who still hadn't emerged from the hole he'd created in the wall of the building.

"There a name for the light-dagger thing?" I asked as the remains of most of the Horsemen steamed on the ground.

"Light-death-dagger thing," Mordred said. "I'm thinking of copyrighting it."

I offered Mordred a fist, which he bumped while smiling.

"You guys want to run away or what?" I asked the remaining few dozen Horsemen, who all had pieces of their brethren on them.

The building beside us was torn apart, the stone thrown at us with such incredible force that I only just managed to create a shield of lightning to stop it. A shield of air wouldn't have been enough, and even the lightning shield faltered. I was thrown back several feet, landed on my knees, and rolled back to my feet.

"You mock me," Merlin said as he hovered out of the building. "You *dare* mock me."

I spotted Mordred a few feet away from me, his ice shield almost completely destroyed.

Merlin continued to hover toward us until he stopped by the remaining Horsemen. "Go; do what you need to do."

The Horsemen ran off into the city without pause, leaving an exceptionally pissed-off Merlin to face Mordred and me.

Merlin didn't pause and started throwing huge chunks of rock at Mordred, who managed to dodge most of them. Two of the head-size rocks hit his shield, the first one obliterating it and the second catching him in the chest, which, judging from the sound, broke his ribs and/or sternum. He went down hard, and Merlin threw another rock at his kneeling son, but I blasted it away with air magic and walked over to Mordred, keeping my eyes on his father.

"You okay?" I asked.

"Broken. Hard. Breathing," Mordred managed. "Be okay."

"It's so touching that you came to his aid," Merlin said, rocks spinning around his hand like moons around a planet.

"He's your son," I snapped.

"So?" Merlin asked. "He never had the guts to do what needs to be done here. He was never going to be the one to stand up against everything that needed to be stopped. He didn't have the backbone to do it."

"You loved him," I said.

"I did," Merlin said. "That was my mistake. One of many."

"Another being that you aided a genocidal maniac?" I kept Mordred behind me and walked steadily toward Merlin, hoping that the time spent keeping him talking would let Mordred heal up.

"One man's genocidal maniac is another man's hero . . ." Merlin threw a tendril of air at me, but I sank into my shadow realm and came out behind him, a blade of lightning in my hand.

Without Merlin even turning around, spikes of rock broke out from the ground, and I had to throw myself aside to keep from being impaled.

"Why are you holding back?" Merlin asked me. "You can't hope to kill me like this. Is it because you care what Mordred thinks of you? Is it because you hope I'll see the devastation wrought by Arthur's desires and suddenly change my mind? This is not a fairy tale, Nathaniel. This is not one of those ridiculous films about good versus evil. You make decisions and deal with the consequences. I made my decisions, and I made my peace with what had to happen because of them. I am not going to suddenly believe that you're right. I am not going to suddenly think that Arthur should be killed.

"You think of me as a villain, but you're shortsighted. I am not a villain; I am a visionary. I know what needs to be done to keep the Earth realm and all those connected to it safe. I know the power it requires. If only you'd seen that instead of thinking in such black-and-white terms. If only you'd considered that maybe you were wrong here. That Arthur as king is what's best for everyone. No war. No need for anyone to die of famine, disease; no need for pain and suffering. We would have made it a paradise."

"And all it takes is the murder of everyone who wants free will," I said.

"It's a small price to pay," Merlin told me. "An infinitesimal price. Millions die so billions can live in peace."

"That's not peace," I said fiercely. "That's slavery! I saw in America when you sent me there, all those years ago, how damaging that was."

Merlin laughed. "I honestly thought that when you went to America after your wife's death and started butchering people who deserved it, you'd finally realized what needed to be done. I sent you away to remove that moral code you were so goddamn fond of, and instead you met people who just helped you make it stronger."

The realization that Merlin had been against me and everything I thought he'd stood for was like a punch to the gut.

"I was wrong about you," I said. "I thought you were a good person who was dragged into something he'd wanted no part of, made to be the villain in a story that wasn't even his. I was wrong. You were always the villain; I just didn't want to see it."

"Grow up, Nathaniel," Merlin snapped.

"Yes," I said. "I think I should."

I created a sphere of magical lightning in one hand and sprinted toward Merlin, who reached out with his matter magic to shield himself from the blast.

I drove the sphere into the ground a few feet in front of Merlin and detonated the magic. It flung him up into the air, where he was met by a sphere of light magic that Mordred had thrown.

Merlin couldn't move the shield he'd created in time to stop the sphere of light from hitting him in the side. Mordred snapped his fingers, and for a moment I was blinded as the sphere detonated.

I blinked several times but couldn't find either Mordred or Merlin. The building where Merlin had been was collapsing, and then I saw a blast of light from further away as Merlin and Mordred continued to fight.

I paused, not wanting to leave my friend.

"He's got it," Zamek told me as he joined me, pointing to several figures in the distance sprinting over to help Mordred.

I nodded as part of the citadel exploded high above us, raining down huge chunks of stone between where we were standing and the battle being waged between Mordred and his father.

"Judgement isn't the only one up there in the citadel fighting Arthur," Zamek said. "One of the soldiers saw your mother and Lucifer head in after her. They need help more than Mordred."

I didn't disagree. I sprinted into the citadel. I tried the lifts, but the doors were completely destroyed, so I made my way up the first few flights of stairs, using my air magic to make me faster and more agile, jumping the stairs three or four at a time as I bounded up toward whatever I was going to find above.

There were dozens of bodies that had, judging from the mess they were in, met Judgement on her way up, and I hoped that when I reached them, Arthur would already be dead. Job done.

I kept running until I reached the tenth floor. I stopped momentarily by a large window at the end of the floor and looked out over the city as the buildings crumpled all around, as if they were being flattened by some invisible hand.

"What the hell is going on now?" I wondered aloud.

I continued up the stairs at a lightning pace, just in time to reach a hole in the wall, beyond which I saw Arthur drive a blade of fire into my mother's stomach. Lucifer was on the floor, bleeding from a wound, and Judgement was barely moving in the corner.

A whip of fire trailed from Arthur's hand, and he was two feet away from the wall when I vaporized it with my magic, throwing Arthur across the far end of what appeared to be his throne room.

I stepped inside, magical power crackling all around me, lightning moving up over my hands and arms. I cracked my knuckles. "My turn, motherfucker."

Chapter Twenty-Six

MORDRED

Realm of Atlantis

Mordred had become separated from Nate when part of the citadel had fallen, and Merlin had tried to use it as a distraction to escape. Mordred had spotted the attempt and given chase, which he had to admit might not have been the smartest idea he'd ever had.

He caught up with his father next to two large buildings, both of which were at least fifty feet high. Mordred noticed that there were no windows on either building. They were basically fifty-foot-high bricks.

"You like?" Merlin asked.

"What are you doing here?" Mordred asked him.

"We're going to finish what we started," Merlin said. "I can't stop now."

"You could have always stopped."

Merlin laughed. "The evil I've done for the cause, the methods I've used to put us where we are today—there's no coming back from that. I sent you to your death. I didn't know you were going to be tortured for a hundred years at the time, but I knew they were going to try and bring you over to our side."

"Your side?" Mordred asked. "I was turned into a weapon to murder everyone I cared about. You and your friends did that to me."

"I wasn't kept informed of the methods," Merlin said. "I wanted you beside us. Arthur was scared that you'd want to be king, which you were meant to be, but I convinced him that you could be brought around."

"Why create me?" Mordred asked. "Why bother?"

"I didn't know that Arthur was alive until after you were born," Merlin said. "He was more powerful; it was simple mathematics."

"I was tortured for simple mathematics?" Mordred asked and started to laugh. "That's both the most ridiculous and most evil thing I've ever heard."

"I did what needed to be done. Can you say the same?" Merlin snapped.

Mordred drew Excalibur. "Yes," he said softly. "I can. You want to know something? If you'd have just left me alone, I never would have been tortured, never would have come back and put Arthur in a coma. If you'd have just left me alone, you'd have probably achieved all of your goals centuries ago against a vastly underpow-ered me and Nate. We'd have been killed off or brought into the fold. You'd be in charge right now. All of this, all of the death and destruction on your doorstep—you brought this on yourself. You are responsible for your own demise. Good job, dumbass."

Merlin stepped forward, and the ground beneath Mordred's feet burst open. The rock snaked up, trying to grab hold of him, but Mordred had thrown himself aside, using ice to create a divide between him and the stone.

Mordred made his way toward Merlin, who continuously tore the ground apart, vines of stone trying to grab hold of Mordred and pull him underground. Mordred cut through those that got too close with Excalibur, and when there were too many to avoid, he activated the sword's power, and they collapsed as if their strings had been cut.

Merlin snarled as his magic was made ineffective and used his matter magic as a magical force, blasting it toward Mordred, who again activated the sword's power. The blast moved around him.

Merlin smiled.

Mordred knew that was probably a bad thing and sprinted to the side as huge chunks of the building behind him fell away, smashing into where he'd been standing only moments earlier. Unfortunately, that meant Mordred was no longer concentrating on Excalibur, and the power it held deactivated, leaving Mordred open for Merlin to close the gap between them and punch him with a matter-magic-enhanced fist.

Mordred spun in the air as he impacted with the partially crumbling building, Excalibur slipping through his fingers as more rubble fell around him. Mordred ignored the sword and kept moving, staying away from the pieces of stone that were now seemingly aiming themselves at him.

A shield of air stopped a large stone from crushing him, and another obliterated it. Mordred gathered up the tiny pieces of stone, spinning them faster and faster in a vortex of air and ice, and threw them back at Merlin, who quickly wrapped himself in his own shield of stone.

Mordred sprinted toward his father as the barrage of rock, air, and ice he'd created hit Merlin's shield and obliterated it. It left Merlin open for Mordred to drive a sphere of light right into his father's chest and detonate the magic immediately.

Merlin's matter magic activated once again, protecting him from the worst of the power Mordred had unleashed, but he was still thrown back several feet, his leather armor all but destroyed despite the runes that had been placed on it.

Merlin and Mordred stood apart, staring at one another, each of them breathing hard.

"You've grown as powerful as I'd heard," Merlin said.

"Go fuck yourself," Mordred said.

Merlin smiled. "You can still join us," he said.

"You know what, Darth, I'm good," Mordred said, rolling his shoulders.

Merlin sighed.

Mordred was readying himself for another fight when he was hit in the back by a bolt of lightning that took him off his feet and dropped him on the ground, leaving him gasping for breath.

He turned to fight the newcomer and managed to block a blade of lightning to the back of his head, then drove a blade of ice up into the chest of the red-armored Horseman and twisted it. He removed the blade, only to have the ground open up beneath his feet and smash around him as he fell forward.

Mordred wrapped himself in air and ice, pushing it out as the earth continued to crush him, pulling him down until his legs and lower torso were completely buried. He felt his legs break from the pressure and cried out in pain as he tried to force the earth back with his own magic, light breaking through the cracks in the ground.

The earth was torn apart and thrown up all around him as his light magic exploded outward. Mordred created a shield of air as he lay in the ditch he'd created, and he stopped the hundreds of shards of earth that Merlin had conjured out of the cloud of earth and thrown at Mordred.

Mordred's legs began to heal, but he was now at a serious disadvantage. He activated his blood magic, letting its power wash over him so he could heal, but Merlin kicked him in the legs, causing him to momentarily lose concentration.

Merlin stood above Mordred and tutted. "You always were a disappointment," he said, a blade of ice in his hand.

Necromantic power smashed into Merlin, who hadn't been anticipating an attack. "Get away from him, you son of a bitch," Hel said as she stood beside the injured Horseman and reached out, taking control of its spirit and tearing it out of its body. Hel's eyes rolled up into her head, and her necromancy swirled around her before being launched at a recovering Merlin, driving him into the building behind him, which partially collapsed from the impact.

Hel was beside Mordred a second later. She placed Excalibur beside him. "I think you dropped this. You okay?"

"Blood magic is healing me," he said. "I really wish I didn't have to use it, though."

Hel knew of Mordred's past with addiction to the power of blood magic, and despite the concern on her face, Mordred knew that she wouldn't judge him for its use.

Hel cut across her arm with a dagger from her belt and forced Mordred's hand over the wound. Her power crashed into him, making him gasp as he tried to steady himself. His legs healed, his body coursing with newly found energy. Hel sat on the ground and took a deep breath as Mordred released her arm.

"That was dangerous," Mordred said.

"So is fighting Merlin alone," Hel said. "Dumbass."

Mordred smiled as he got back to his feet and noticed that Hel's wound had already healed. He rolled his neck.

The building that Merlin had been thrown inside was torn apart as he exited. "You are not going to throw me into any more fucking buildings!" Merlin screamed at the top of his lungs.

"He seems mad," Hel said.

Mordred put up a shield of air that stopped the car-size boulder from pulverizing Hel and himself. "Yeah, a bit," Mordred agreed.

"I'm going to stay here and make sure no more of those assholes interrupt you," Hel said and immediately sighed when she saw several Horsemen advancing toward them. "Quit playing with him and *finish* it."

Mordred and Hel ran in separate directions, Mordred blocking and deflecting everything that his father threw at him. The look of concern on Merlin's face was compounded when he detonated a sphere of shadow magic that shot tendrils of darkness out like Cthulhu was trying to get into the realm and Mordred created a shield of light magic and started to hum the theme tune to *The Legend of Zelda*.

The shadows recoiled as they touched the light, and Mordred increased the intensity and power of the shield as he walked slowly toward his father. Occasionally, a tendril of shadow would devour part of the shield, but Mordred simply replaced it, never taking his eyes off his father.

"Stop with that infernal song," Merlin shouted.

"It calms me," Mordred said softly. "It makes me smile."

Mordred was five feet in front of his father, who had stopped the shadows and stood before his son, his mouth open in shock.

"I'm stronger than you," Mordred said. "Much, *much* stronger. We could be here all day trading power, but you created me to have your power *and* my mother's power. So we both know I'm stronger than you."

Merlin swallowed and suddenly looked nervous.

"Funny thing is, I don't want to kill you," Mordred continued. "I know I should. I know you're nothing but an utter bastard, but I still don't want to."

"Because you're weak," Merlin spat.

Mordred detonated the shield, forcing all the power directly in front of him. Merlin couldn't get his shield up fast enough, and the power smashed into him completely undefended, blinding him, burning his skin and hair. His cries of pain were lost in the maelstrom that Mordred had created, combining his light and air magic into a whirlwind of magical fury that Merlin had no answer to.

The amount of power that Mordred had used left him drained, and when the magic subsided, he had serious issues remaining upright and decided to just drop down to one knee instead of collapsing in the scorch-mark-stricken street.

Merlin lay prone before him, his skin red and raw, his hair all but gone. Changing his light magic to create heat was something that Mordred found to be difficult but effective. Unfortunately, it was also hard to control, so he'd had to wait until there were no bystanders around before using it.

"How?" Merlin asked, his voice raspy.

Mordred forced himself back to a standing position. "I told you, Dad. I am better than you. You made me better than you. That was the whole bloody point."

Merlin nodded. "You and Nate were what Arthur feared," Merlin said, his magic already working overtime to heal his voice.

"I know," Mordred said. "I think that was partially because you made sure of it." Mordred crouched beside his father and drew Excalibur. He activated its power to remove magic and lies and placed the blade of it against Merlin's chest.

Merlin smiled. "I joined him because I thought I could control him. Because I thought he was right, and I figured that with me by his side, I could point him in the right direction. I said that I'd never cross a line. And then that line moved. Slowly, over time, it moved further and further away. It takes a strong person to say no and not move with the line. I was not a strong man. I was a cruel, vindictive man. I did evil because I thought it was for the greater good, and then it was too late to go back.

"When I thought that Arthur was in a coma, I wanted to save him, to make him realize that his way was misguided. I'd invested so much in him as our savior; I refused to see him as anything else."

"I know," Mordred said.

"You know that without my magic, I will die?" Merlin asked.

Mordred nodded. "I don't want to kill you, but I also know you *need* to die."

Merlin smiled again. "Killing me by removing my power and just letting me die. I always thought I'd live forever."

"No one lives forever," Mordred said. "Not even Arthur."

"He wants his enemies crushed," Merlin said. "I can't lie, can I?"

Mordred shook his head. "For the first time in millennia, you can't hide behind tricks and lies. You can't convince yourself of anything that isn't true. What's Arthur's plan?"

"These buildings—they have hundreds of monsters in them," Merlin said. "Actually, it's probably thousands of monsters. Magically resilient monsters. They used to be human. They were taken and experimented on. Some were forced to learn the dwarven runes. They made bracelets. You've seen them before."

"I have," Mordred said. "Where do they go?"

"Shadow Falls," Merlin said and chuckled. "Damn you for making me say all of this."

A cold pit of fear started inside of Mordred. "Thousands of monsters are being sent to Shadow Falls to kill everyone there."

Merlin nodded weakly. "Not just Shadow Falls. They're going to Washington, DC, too; Gawain was meant to make sure the entire area around the White House was turned into a realm gate, but he got caught. So I sent Lamashtu and the elves there to get it finished. Once Arthur knew that Poseidon was no longer an option, he sent word to your brother to stay in Washington and allow himself to be captured. He said not to make it look too easy, though. I promised Gawain we'd get him out when the invasion started.

"Arthur wanted you all here. Once you're here, you're trapped; you'll never get back to Shadow Falls in time to stop the massacre there."

"When does it start?" Mordred asked, stopping himself from running off to warn everyone.

"There's a signal."

"What is it?"

"The collapse of these buildings," Merlin said. "Each one has tunnels under it that lead to chambers, much like the one that was under the realm gate, except everyone in these has bracelets on that take them to Shadow Falls or Washington. The power needed to make them work will destroy the buildings above them. You can't kill Arthur before he gives the signal. You should run, Mordred. Take everyone you love and run as far and as fast as you can. It's the only way you can survive what's coming."

Mordred stared at the windowless buildings, wondering how close he was to a mass of monstrous chaos right then. "We'll stop Arthur before he does anything."

"No, you won't," Merlin said.

"I'm sorry you were too weak to stop Arthur," Mordred said, getting to his feet. He looked over at Hel, who had been joined by Orfeda and several others. They were engaged in kicking the shit out of anything that was stupid enough to come and fight them.

"Your Horsemen weren't that strong," Mordred said mockingly.

"They're fodder," Merlin said. "They needed years more to be what we needed them to be. You forced our hand. You forced us to destroy Asgard, and you killed so many of our forces we didn't have a choice. They're fine for what we need."

"How do I remove the curse from Tommy?"

Merlin chuckled. "Same way as you."

"I'm not a werewolf," Mordred said. "Tommy doesn't have a one-up waiting for him to pop him back to life. He dies, he stays dead."

Merlin tried to shrug and started to cough up blood. "You'll have to figure that out, I guess."

"Still a dickhead to the end," Mordred said with a shake of the head.

"I am what I am, son," Merlin said.

"You might have been my father, but I'm not your son," Mordred told him, his voice cold.

"You really think they're going to accept you as king?" Merlin asked with a smirk. "After all the horrors you inflicted on the world?"

Mordred stared at his father for a few seconds, and instead of a powerful man to be feared, he saw a sad, pitiful man who was going to die having never achieved the thing he wanted the most: Arthur in complete control.

"It's taken me a long time to realize it," Mordred said wistfully. "But I am their king. I might not be great at it, I might make a lot of errors along the way, but I will try my damnedest to be a good king. A good man. I want future generations to know that we did something important and that we stood up for what was right. And I'm going to make sure that no one like Arthur or you or Hera or any of those pieces of crap you surrounded yourself with will ever be able to push their agendas on people again. Partly because they're all going to die."

"You really want me dead?" Merlin asked, blood trickling out of the corner of his mouth.

Mordred nodded. "I really do; I just didn't think it would be me doing it. My only sadness is that you ruined so many lives before you died."

"You're not man enough to just put me out of my misery."

"You misunderstand me," Mordred said softly. "You're going to die a human. You're going to die powerless, pathetic, alone, with nothing and no one to mourn you. You're an evil fuck, and you don't get to go out in a blaze of glory, Merlin. You get to die on a field of mud and stone, while the plans that you put so much of yourself into are burned away. Your name won't matter to those in the future, because you never did anything that might last long enough to have an impact on their lives. You wasted your potential, you wasted your life, and you wasted my goddamn time. You don't deserve anything else."

"Maybe you're more like me than I thought," Merlin said, his eyelids fluttering.

Mordred kept the sword on Merlin's chest and bent forward to whisper into his ear. "I'm nothing like you, Merlin. I never was; I never will be. If there's one thing you've achieved in life, it's to show me how not to behave like, in the words of my good friend Remy, a hoofwanking cockwomble."

Merlin kept his eyes open for another second, and then he died.

Mordred stood above him, looking down, just to make sure, and then he created a sphere of light magic and poured every bit of magic he could inside it, heating it to a level he'd never tried before. The sphere was six feet long by the time he dropped it over his father's body, which was incinerated.

Mordred staggered back and found himself sitting on the ground again. He was exhausted, but he couldn't have left his father's body. Not for Merlin's supporters, who might use it as a sort of shrine, or for those who would defile it just to let out their anger. It needed to be removed from the equation.

Mordred sat there for some time as a large group of his allies appeared not too far from the citadel, all of them giving him the space he needed.

"You okay?" Hel said from behind him.

"I'm okay," Mordred said. "Weak. Took a lot to do what I just did."

"Emotionally or physically?" Hel said, sitting beside Mordred and taking his hand in hers.

"Both," Mordred said. "We need to get to Shadow Falls or kill Arthur, whichever one comes first."

Mordred stood, and with Hel beside him, he walked over to the increasingly large group. He told Hades and Persephone everything that Merlin had divulged.

Hades turned to Zamek. "Get that realm gate working to go back to Shadow Falls as soon as possible."

"On it," Zamek said. He stopped by a large group of dwarves. "All of you—with me."

The nearly forty dwarves set off at a run through the city.

"Anything else?" Persephone asked.

Mordred looked around. "Where's Nate?"

"He took off up there," Irkalla said.

Mordred took a step toward the citadel, and there was a rumble beneath his feet as the ground shook violently. Before anyone had time to react, building after building collapsed all across the city, the plumes of smoke and dust threatening to cover everyone.

"Anyone with air magic, get to it," Mordred commanded and started to push out the dust coming toward the group of nearly a hundred people.

The soldiers with air magic capabilities encircled everyone else, Mordred shouting commands as needed.

When the buildings were all down and the earth stopped rumbling, Mordred looked around the ruined city.

"What just happened?" Irkalla asked.

"The monsters are all gone," Mordred said, the fear in his voice something he couldn't hide. "We need to get to Shadow Falls, *now*."

Chapter Twenty-Seven

LAYLA CASSIDY

Washington, DC, Earth Realm

The soldiers in Lafayette Square moved aside to let Chloe, Layla, Selene, Tego, and Jinayca through toward the tent where President Lopez had originally been. It was now full of various high-ranking officials who were trying to decide how to deal with the continued Avalon-centric problems facing the city.

All the soldiers were battle hardened and had seen combat against Avalon forces in the years since Arthur's return. They were dependable and would do their jobs tirelessly to the very best of their abilities. But Jinayca had an expression that suggested that she might fuck someone up for getting in her way, and even Selene would be cautious of that.

The group was stopped by a guard, and Jinayca pushed past him wordlessly. The guard was about to open his mouth to shout something when Layla stopped beside him and whispered, "I would just let her talk to who we need to. Have you seen any shadow elves?"

"Shadow what?" the soldier asked and looked at Tego before swallowing. Jinayca hurried into the tent and started asking questions in a raised voice. Layla had never seen Jinayca so angry, so determined to hunt someone.

Layla described the shadow elves and Lamashtu, both in her own form and in Piper's.

"Yeah, they went over toward New York Avenue," he said. "There's an abandoned building there; we sent some of the Avalon human prisoners there for interrogation."

"Thanks," Layla said as Jinayca exited the tent. "You're going to want to tell everyone in charge that it wasn't Piper but Lamashtu, the same person who masqueraded as the president."

"They've posted guards at each of the elven runes but haven't destroyed them for fear of some kind of booby trap." Jinayca said. "We need to go, now . . ." She was already at a full run toward two SUVs that Roberto had requisitioned from the Secret Service members there, and everyone got in. The agents drove as fast as possible toward New York Avenue.

The abandoned building was five stories high, with a revolving door at the front of the gray, drab building. It was far enough away from the mess at the White House that people were still walking around. It was daytime, and the curfew didn't come into force until nightfall.

"Clear the streets," Roberto said to one of his people, who took three other agents and set about doing as they were told.

"Let's try to do this without demolishing any buildings," Roberto continued, talking to everyone else.

Chloe walked up to one of the large plate glass windows and punched it, activating her ability to absorb and redirect kinetic energy. The window shattered, and she stepped into the building.

"That wasn't subtle," Layla said, stepping over the glass as she followed Chloe inside.

"Worked, though," Chloe said.

"That revolving door will take too long," Jinayca said, a battle-ax in her hands.

"This isn't going to be quiet, is it?" Roberto asked. Layla had spotted several newly arrived FBI agents looking slightly concerned about what they'd gotten themselves into.

"Nope," Layla said.

"Where are the prisoners kept?" Jinayca asked.

"Top floor," Roberto said. "Everything above the third floor is rune scribed. No powers. No way of activating them. Zamek himself did it."

"So we're powerless?" Selene asked.

"Inside the building, yes," Roberto said.

"You got any weapons left in here?" Chloe asked.

"No, of course not," Roberto said, motioning to four FBI agents, who were bringing up the rear, each one carrying a crate of guns into the building. "But we brought some with us; I assume these will do."

The guns were mostly a combination of MP5s, Sig Sauer nine millimeters, and Glock 17s, although there were a few that didn't fall into those camps. Layla took a Glock 17 and a handful of magazines. She still had a sword that hung from her hip and a few daggers at her back, but if she was going to lose her power, that meant losing her arm too. That was not something she was going to be able to do much about.

"Tego, you stay here," Layla said. "If any enemies come down, kill them."

Tego snorted and sat down.

When everyone was geared up, the large group separated, each going to one of two stairwells. Roberto took his team, along with Jinayca, Layla, and two Secret Service agents, while everyone else went with the soldiers.

The stair climb was tense, and no one spoke, Layla and Jinayca taking point the whole way up. Jinayca carried a Remington 870 twelve-gauge shotgun, and Layla was a hundred percent certain she knew how to use it. Everyone took a radio, and Layla put the earpiece in place and activated it.

When they reached the fourth floor, Layla's metal forearm and hand melted away. She sighed.

They reached the fifth floor soon after and found the door to be almost bent in half. "Sure about the no-powers thing?" Layla asked, looking back at Roberto.

"Not now," Roberto said with a shake of his head.

Layla pushed the door open and stepped inside the corridor beyond. It was oddly quiet, and she knew that the other half of the team would be moving through an identical door, into an identical corridor, on the other side of the floor.

There were seven dead in the corridor, slumped up against walls. All of them wore tactical gear and still had their weapons in their hands. Blood spray covered large parts of the wall. There were bullet holes in the floor and ceiling, too, but no bodies of their attackers. That didn't bode well for just how dangerous a foe Layla and her team were about to encounter.

"Lamashtu and her elves," Jinayca said. "I'm guessing we found them."

They all moved slowly along the corridor, the FBI agents in their tactical gear checking the various rooms along the way.

They reached the end of the corridor, and the FBI and Roberto took point.

"Can we take out the runes?" Layla asked, looking at the bright purple-and-blue marks all over the walls.

"No," Jinayca said. "I checked them. You cut through them, this whole place explodes. You try to remove them without the proper work-around, they explode. I could do it if I had maybe an hour. I doubt even Zamek could do it in less, and he put them here."

The FBI agents crouched behind the door and placed a camera under it to check for explosives or people who might be waiting to shoot anyone coming through. They turned around and nodded to Roberto.

"It's clear," he said.

The agents opened the door and crept into the room beyond. Layla and Jinayca took up the rear, and as they reached the door, they could already see the FBI agents and soldiers from the other team moving around the edges of the room to converge before the stairwell.

Layla knew that the stairwell leading from the floor they were on to the offices above would be a death trap. She looked out of the large windows that faced the street below. More runes were drawn on them. Zamek was nothing if not thorough. She continued to stare for several seconds; something was off about them.

And then it hit her.

They weren't dwarven.

"Everyone down," Layla shouted as the windows exploded inward toward everyone in the lower part of the office, showering them in glass.

The FBI agents closest were already hunkered behind several overturned tables and chairs that had been piled around the lower level, but the soldiers that had come with Layla from Avalon found themselves bombarded with the blast and the glass it created, which cut through several of them as they dived aside.

Bullets rained down from above, and Layla saw two soldiers die from the gunfire as they retreated back toward the corridor. One of the FBI agents, a young man with short hair, took a bullet to the head and crumpled to the floor as Layla grabbed a second injured agent and dragged him back into the corridor.

"How do we get up there?" Roberto shouted over the sounds of bullets tearing into the furniture, floor, and walls of the main office. Everyone moved away from the wall that joined to the main office and ran into a smaller office that gave more protection from any gunfire.

"We've got wounded here," Selene said through Layla's earpiece.

"Here too," Layla said as another wounded agent was dragged into the room, leaving a trail of blood.

"We've four down here," Selene said.

"Three here," Jinayca said.

"And we have no idea how many enemies are up there," Chloe said.

"I have an idea," Jinayca said. "There are runes all around this place. They used elven runes on those windows. They're less powerful than dwarven, but as you can see, they're still quite potent."

"And the plan is?" Chloe asked.

"We go up and come down on top of them," Jinayca said.

Layla looked over to Roberto. "Is that possible?"

"You'd have to go through several feet of concrete and metal," Roberto said. "But there are runes up there too."

"That's fine; I can change the direction of the blast," Jinayca said. "Where's the door to the roof?"

"Other end of the corridor," Roberto said.

"Selene," Layla said. "You think you guys can keep our trigger-happy friends occupied?"

"Yeah, I think we can do that."

"When I give the signal, the ceiling above the balcony is going to collapse," Jinayca said. "I would advise you not to be under it."

Jinayca, Roberto, and Layla left the FBI agents to tend to the wounded and help keep Lamashtu and her people occupied. It was easy enough to get to the roof, and there was no one up there to bother them as they ran across it, until Roberto pointed to a spot just above the stairwell to the balcony.

Jinayca did some quick measurements in her head and strolled around the roof until she stopped. "We're above where the enemy is," she said.

"What if they've put more runes on the ceiling of the office?" Roberto asked.

Jinayca pointed at him as if to say that was a good point and found a second site a few feet to the side.

Layla and Roberto stood guard while Jinayca went to work, the sounds of gunfire easy to hear from below. Sirens could be heard in the distance, and Layla hoped that none of the police would try to involve themselves. She was all for humans standing up and doing what was right, but human police weren't in a position to help with what they were fighting against. If it weren't for the residential area, she might have just asked Roberto if he could arrange a drone strike, although she wasn't exactly sure how that would go down on the news channels, some of which were still spouting Avalon propaganda.

"I'm done," Jinayca said. "We're going to want to move back."

Everyone did as they were told, crouching down behind a huge air-conditioning unit on the other side of the roof.

Jinayca placed a hand on the floor, where she'd drawn another rune. "Good luck," she said, and the roof imploded.

Layla was already up and running around, her weapon in hand, as the gaping hole in the top of the roof got larger and larger.

Roberto and Jinayca were the first two to jump into the hole, with Layla not too far behind them. All three of them took advantage of the stunned shadow elves that were inside the office they'd landed in.

The fight was brutal and short, and even without Layla's hand once again, the half dozen enemies were no real match for them.

Layla spotted Lamashtu in the office at the far end of the floor. She raised the Glock in her hand and fired twice through the open door of the office she was in. The bullets impacted on the thickened glass that surrounded them. The elf was busy finishing up a drawing on the wall beside him, while Lamashtu bared her teeth and howled with laughter as she raised her hand, showing a detonator in it. She pushed the plunger, and the windows along one side of the floor were blown out. She waved at Layla and pushed the elf out of the window before jumping down after him a moment later.

Chloe and Selene, who had both been in the middle of the floor below just after the roof had caved in, gave chase. Selene turned into dragon-kin form and picked Chloe up, and the pair flew out of the building.

Layla dodged a sword attack from a shadow elf and shot him in the head twice before running past with Roberto and Jinayca behind her.

Layla was at full sprint when she reached the edge of the window and leaped out, dragging as much metal as she could with her, wrapping it around herself and forming spiderlike legs. She turned and caught Jinayca in a web of metal. Together they ran down the side of the building, Layla's new spider legs cracking concrete and glass with every step.

They both reached the bottom of the building and were in a flat-out run a moment later, Layla's arm re-forming as they chased after Selene and Chloe, who were easily spotted in the sky. Tego crashed through one of the windows of the lobby to join them, and Layla and Jinayca climbed up on her back.

"Lamashtu and the elf are on foot," Layla said as they raced through the city toward the White House.

A black SUV pulled up beside them, Roberto winding the window down. "Get in," he shouted.

"This is faster," Layla said, and Tego snorted, increasing her speed.

They followed Selene and Chloe through Washington until Roberto stopped the SUV next to the camp outside the White House.

"What's going on?" Layla asked.

"Lamashtu jumped the gate," he said.

"What's inside there that she might want?" Jinayca asked.

Everyone exited the vehicle, and Selene landed beside Layla.

"The bitch got away," Chloe said.

"And the elf?" Layla asked.

"Not sure," Selene said. "Didn't see him, but possibly."

"Let's go get her, then," Chloe said.

Layla spotted Roberto having a deep conversation with several people, some of whom were in military uniform. He walked over to them.

"Lamashtu killed three of ours when she entered the White House," Roberto said. "We have permission to go reclaim her."

"But?" Chloe asked.

"The White House was damaged last time; try not to do it again," Roberto said. "Please."

Chloe walked over to the partially destroyed gate, everyone else following after.

"Where'd she go?" Jinayca asked.

"West Wing," Roberto said.

There were several dozen armed agents outside the West Wing, all looking very nervous as Layla and her team arrived.

"We'll make sure she doesn't try to leave through the back," Selene said and took to the skies with Chloe.

They'd vanished from view when the remains of the West Wing exploded, showering pieces of brick and stone, killing several of the agents, and knocking everyone else to the ground.

Layla had been hit in the head by a large piece of rock and was dazed when she saw Lamashtu, still wearing Piper's face, walk toward them from the ruin of the West Wing. Jinayca and Roberto ran toward her, the former brandishing her battle-ax and the latter firing his gun. Two bullets hit Jinayca's black leather armor in the chest, causing the runes to spark, but she wasn't harmed. Lamashtu threw her knife at Roberto, who dodged just as Jinayca swung her ax at Lamashtu's head.

Layla got back to her feet in time to see Lamashtu evade the ax swing and spin back toward Roberto, driving her sword into his heart.

Layla avoided a blade thrown at her as Jinayca's and Lamashtu's blades connected time and time again. One would gain the upper hand for a moment, then need to retreat from an attack from their opponent. More than once, Jinayca's ax came close to cutting through Lamashtu's body.

Jinayca continued the offensive until her ax cut through the runes on Lamashtu's armor, and even with the distance between them, Layla saw that Lamashtu's expression of joy melted into desperation and rage. She parried Jinayca's attack and drove her sword into the side of Jinayca's head, twisted it, and pulled it free as Layla screamed in rage.

Lamashtu left Jinayca's body where it fell and strode over to remove Roberto's head.

Layla reached out with every bit of power she had, and Lamashtu stopped walking. Layla sprinted toward her opponent at high speed.

Lamashtu regained the use of her body and threw a plume of fire at Layla, who easily dodged it, just as Tego crashed into Lamashtu, taking her off her feet and using her massive claws to tear through the remains of the now-useless armor.

Lamashtu yelled in pain and created a block of ice around Tego's head, kicking the saber-tooth panther away.

Layla reached out and used the metal in Tego's armor to smash through the ice.

"You can't kill *me*," Lamashtu said, getting back to her feet and brushing herself down. "Two of your friends are already dead. You're just adding to the tally at this point."

Tego's growl was low and menacing as Lamashtu stalked toward her, a sword in her hand. As Layla charged toward her, manipulating the sword to try to bind Lamashtu's hands, the shape-shifter turned and punched her in the face, sending her flying backward.

Layla smashed into the remains of what had once been an FBI car and was now little more than a heap of scrap, but she was too slow to stop Lamashtu closing the space between them and punching her again in the stomach.

Layla took control of the metal in Lamashtu again, but she laughed as she kicked Layla away.

"That won't work twice, girl," Lamashtu said. "I have too many tricks, too many ways to alter my body."

Layla caught Lamashtu's kick, broke her knee, and pushed the shape-shifter away, who healed her body almost instantly. "I can't die," Lamashtu said mockingly. "You hurt me, I just heal and change my body. You can't win here."

Layla swung her hand toward Lamashtu, changing the metal into a whip in an instant. It cut through Lamashtu's face, the silver causing the shape-shifter to scream and turn to flee. Layla used the same whip to trip her, and Lamashtu fell onto the ground next to Tego, who slashed across Lamashtu's already-injured face, and what had been an unpleasant wound was now almost half of her face gone.

Lamashtu punched Tego in the jaw, and Layla tackled her to the ground before Lamashtu could drive her dagger into the feline.

Layla broke Lamashtu's elbow, which began to heal once again, but the face remained a raw, bloody mess, one eye all but gone.

Lamashtu grabbed Layla by the throat and threw her over toward the front of the White House. She gave chase and punched Layla in the side of the head.

"I'm going to tear your face off," Lamashtu said, her words coming out all wrong as the side of her face that was relatively untouched continued to change shape. She grabbed Layla by the throat again and slammed her up against one of the columns leading to the White House entrance.

"You won't win," Lamashtu said. "I was just the decoy."

"And you're not that smart," Layla managed.

Lamashtu turned in time to see Tego launch herself at her. Lamashtu's blade came up, but it was too late—the massive feline clamped her powerful jaws around Lamashtu's arm, dragging her to the ground, where she grabbed her around the back of the head. Tego crushed Lamashtu's skull like a grape.

Layla walked over to Jinayca and crouched beside her friend. "Damn it," she said softly, the tears welling up. They'd been through so much, and to lose her like this . . .

Selene landed beside them, and Chloe threw herself over to Layla, hugging her. Selene gathered Jinayca in her arms and keened.

Layla looked over at Roberto. "He was a good man," she said softly.

"The elf isn't here," Layla said. "Lamashtu said she was a decoy."

"A decoy for what?" Selene asked, looking up from Jinayca's body.

A crisscross of light-blue power filled the grounds of the White House, and Layla looked beyond the gates and saw that the magic was the same everywhere as far as she could see. The ground began to shake, and screams sounded out from somewhere in the distance.

"We're not done yet," Layla said.

Chapter Twenty-Eight

Nate Garrett

Realm of Atlantis

I had never been angrier. Arthur had helped murder my friends, my dad, people I cared about, people I loved. He'd taken Mordred's eye, turned Tommy into a walking homicidal monster, left Judgement for dead on the floor, along with a seriously injured Lucifer, and hurt my mum. I was going to fuck. Him. Up.

I sprinted across the throne room, jumped over the ruined throne, and blasted Arthur in the chest with enough lightning to kill an elephant. Arthur, smoke rising off his body, dropped to one knee but was back on his feet just in time for me to grab him by the face and smash the back of his head into the wall behind him.

I created a sphere of lightning in my free hand and drove it into his chest; the resulting explosion of power took him through the wall into the room beyond. I stepped over the ruined wall to continue the assault. I wanted to check that everyone was okay, but if I gave Arthur even a second to recover, we were all in trouble.

Arthur had rolled along the ground and got back to his feet as I poured more lightning into him. A shield of blood magic wrapped itself around him as I noticed that we appeared to be in a bedroom. The remains of the huge four-poster bed were littered all across the floor, and feathers floated around the room.

Arthur pulled himself up out of the remains of the bed and launched himself at me. Shadows leaped out of the ground, smashed into his chest, and threw him aside, and he collided with the window at the far end of the room, the glass spiderwebbing from the impact.

I crossed the room and drove a blade of fire down at where Arthur's head was, but snakes of blood magic shot up at me, wrapping around my arms and causing me to yell out in pain as I tried to pull away. I felt the magic move up my arms, the agony almost all I could think of. I ignited my fire magic, spreading it up over my hands and arms, covering my upper body and forcing the blood magic to leave.

I pulled away the second I could, putting distance between myself and Arthur as he got to his feet. "Did you think it would be easy?" he asked.

I tried to get back to my feet, but branches had covered my legs, pinning me in place. I tried to burn them away but couldn't both remove them and defend myself from a kick from Arthur that would have probably knocked me out without a shield of fire protecting me.

The branches snapped from the heat, and I grabbed Arthur's foot as he tried a second kick, wrapping my arms around his leg and lifting him up and over my head, then dumping him on the ground behind me with a crunch.

I was punched in the head before I could move further, then kicked in the chest with enough force to cause me to fly back across the room into the one remaining wooden bedpost, which exploded. The pieces appeared to move apart before they slammed back into me at high speed, causing the air to leave my body. I fell to the ground and saw Demeter walk into the room.

She wore red-and-green leather armor and was barefoot, her long hair flowing freely over her shoulders as she moved her hands. The wood from the broken bed launched at me while magical vines wrapped around my neck.

"Nate," Demeter said, in the same tone one would use to call someone a shitbag, twisting the vines around my throat further.

Fire ignited over my hands, and I grabbed hold of the vines, incinerated them, and dropped to the floor. A moment too late I noticed that Arthur had gone, and I was hit in the side by a blast of air magic that threw me across the room. Arthur was on me in an instant, throwing punch after punch at me that I couldn't block or deflect, driving me down into the floor. He stomped on my chest, and I felt something give.

"Damn you," Arthur shouted at me, kicking me in the ribs. "You are a continuous thorn in my side. But at least I'll get to kill you and Lucifer now."

He looked over at Demeter, who passed him something while I placed my hand under his armored trouser leg and unleashed a bolt of lightning directly into his skin.

Arthur screamed in pain but kept his mind enough to stomp on my head, breaking my nose in the process.

More vines covered my body, and I felt them tightening as Demeter reached down and grabbed my arm, keeping it out of the vines. I used my blood magic to start healing my chest and nose, but it stopped almost as soon as it started, and I looked up at Arthur, who pointed to the sorcerer's band on my wrist.

Arthur picked me up by my throat and held me against the wall, my feet dangling above the floor. "This is a special band I had made *just* for you," he said with a smile. "Of all the bands in the world, this one is unique. No key. I'm going to make you watch as I kill everyone you care about. You were made to kill me, Nate, to hurt me. But still, I was benevolent. I gave you the chance to stand beside me, and you spat in my face."

I spat in his face in response.

He punched me in the stomach, and I gasped in pain, unable to breathe properly.

"You sicken me," Arthur said. "So because you were always that great hope, you're going to get to watch as everyone and everything else burns. Only then will I kill you—only when you've realized that I am better than you." He dropped me to the floor.

Demeter kicked me in the ribs. "That was because you always were a little shit," she said.

Demeter passed Arthur his spear and a second band, and he put the latter on his wrist while she put one on hers.

"You want to know what those buildings were?" Arthur asked. "They were the destruction of Shadow Falls. Have fun watching it die."

Arthur and Demeter placed their hands over their bracelets, and the two vanished; the bracelets clattered to the floor a second later.

I picked one up. It was almost identical in appearance to a batch of similarly used bracelets that Chloe's mum had been making for Merlin several years earlier. These were better quality, and Chloe's mum was very dead at this point, so it couldn't be her. But it could be any human who knew dwarven runes.

I pocketed the two bracelets and staggered to the hole in the wall just as the building moved. It was like an earthquake that never ended, and after several seconds I'd made it to the destroyed throne and found my mum and Judgement, both seriously hurt but healing, and a critically wounded Lucifer, who looked pale and needed urgent attention.

"Okay, let's get out of here," I said. "No magic for me, so try not to get me to do anything stupid."

"Define *stupid*," Lucifer said as I helped him up, blood drenching his torso, his arm draped over my shoulder.

The four of us made it out of the throne room as the building began to make the noise of metal being twisted.

"Stairwell—now," Judgement said.

She helped me carry Lucifer down the corridor as an almighty crash from above became a constant stream of noise; the roof above us was caving in. We'd only just reached the stairwell door when the entire ceiling collapsed, and the stairwell began to fold in on itself.

Judgement and my mum shoved me and Lucifer to the ground and dived on top of us, keeping shields of necromancy and magical light above us as the entire citadel caved in.

All the air rushed from my body as we free-fell for an untold number of feet while the shield around us stopped the worst of the debris from smashing into us and more than likely killing us.

Lucifer wrapped his arms around me and held me close, twisting us both in the air so I was on top when we smashed into the ground at high speed. The breath was taken from my body in one rush of pain. The shield of light took a lot of the impact, but the onslaught of rubble eventually caused it to collapse, while Brynhildr's shield of necromantic power forced her to her knees as she strained to keep us from being crushed.

The sounds of the citadel's destruction rang in my ears, and I blinked, noticing that Lucifer had wrapped me in magical power to ensure that I wasn't killed in the fall.

I rolled off Lucifer and lay there beside him, my breathing shallow, despite all the help I'd been given to survive. I eventually rolled onto my side and saw the blood pooling under Lucifer's head.

"What happened?" I asked.

"Skull fracture," Lucifer said. "I think. Don't have enough power to heal at the moment; the spear hurt like all hell."

"He got hit in the chest," my mum said, exhausted. She'd managed, with Judgement's help, to push aside the majority of the rubble above us. "It's lucky we weren't further down the citadel, or we'd all most likely be turned into goo."

My mum knelt beside Lucifer and examined his wounds. She looked at me and shook her head.

"I'm dying, right?" he asked.

"I think you took more of an impact than is survivable," my mum said. "Arthur's spear may have pierced your heart."

"It's Arthur's blood magic," Lucifer said. "It infested my heart. I can feel it making its way around my body, killing pretty much everything. The silver in the spear means my magic isn't as powerful as it should be."

"Arthur compromised Lucifer's immune system, and then Arthur poured his own blood into him," Judgement said. "I doubt even Mordred could heal him."

I shook my head. "No, you can't die here, Lucifer."

"I can die somewhere out there if you'd like to carry me out," Lucifer said with a smile. "But I am dying. I'm sorry."

My mum and I hoisted Lucifer up, and with Judgement's help, despite her being seriously wounded, too, we all managed to drag him up onto the pile of rubble that had once been the citadel.

I was about halfway up when my legs went, and I found myself unable to move further.

"Nate?" my mum asked, sitting beside me.

I raised my wrist. "This damn thing. I can't use my magic."

"There's no lock," Judgement said. "I've never seen a sorcerer's band without a lock."

I removed one of the other bands that Demeter and Arthur had been wearing and passed it to Judgement as Lucifer was placed beside me.

"This is a realm gate band," Judgement said. "I didn't think these existed."

"I've seen them before," I said.

When used, the realm gate bands were left behind, so at least we had a clue as to where they might have gone.

I was wheezing and coughing, and it hurt.

"Son?" Brynhildr said.

"Arthur broke my ribs, sternum, nose, probably something else," I said. "I was midheal when he slapped this thing on me. I think the adrenaline has worn off, and with our magical free fall now over, I think my body is starting to protest."

The wheezing was getting worse, and I coughed dark blood onto the ground.

"You've got some internal injuries," Lucifer said from beside me. "I can sense them in you."

"You can *sense* them?" I asked.

"I might be a doctor now," Lucifer said, "but I'm still a sorcerer. My matter magic means I can see injuries. It took me a long time to learn, but it's come in handy."

"You could have mentioned it earlier," I said with a half-baked chuckle.

"People find it weird when I can literally see into their heart," Lucifer said. He'd become pale and looked weaker than I'd ever seen him.

"I'm going to go see if I can get help," Judgement said. She looked back at Lucifer. "You saved my life. Thank you for that."

Lucifer forced a smile. "Couldn't let you get yourself killed before Arthur was dead. Didn't expect this, though."

Judgement nodded slowly but didn't say anything, and instead she turned and started to climb out.

"I'm okay here," I told my mum. "She's hurt; go check she doesn't do anything stupider than what we just did."

My mum opened her mouth to argue and nodded instead, climbing up after Judgement.

"After all this time, he finally killed me," Lucifer told me. "Honestly, it's a miracle that I'm still alive at all."

"You don't sound sad."

"I'm not," he said. "I'm about ten thousand years old, I think. I've seen everything you can imagine and things you probably can't. I wish I could see how this plays out, but I can't. Make sure you win. Anything else would be bad for everyone."

I raised the bracelet. "I need to get this off before I can do anything."

"Just rip it off," he said.

"And be incinerated?" I asked.

"You know, I've never known anyone to actually try," Lucifer said.

"You think it's bogus?" I started coughing again, the wheezing causing me to try to control my breathing. It hurt.

Lucifer shook his head. "No. I think the runes there do act like magical napalm. I just wonder if it's powerful enough to kill you. There has to be a second's delay before it ignites. If you can use your magic in that second."

"That's a big if," I said.

"Last-ditch plan," Lucifer said. "Please don't try it otherwise. I don't want to die for nothing."

"Look, stop saying that," I said and felt like my chest was about to burst into flames.

Lucifer placed his hand on mine. "Nate, I wish I could do more." He removed a knife from his belt and passed it to me. "A gift."

I took it and looked at the intricate carvings that appeared to flow from the handle to the blade itself, which was at least partly silver. Lucifer took hold of the blade and snapped his hand up across it in one motion, the blood dripping onto my own hand.

I tried to open my mouth to stop him, but Lucifer clamped his hands around mine in a show of strength I hadn't even known he had. I let out a cry as his power flowed through my body, healing my injuries. I felt my ribs popping back into place, the fluid leaving my lungs, my sternum finishing the job of fixing itself. Every bit of it hurt. Blood magic gave no shits when it came to your own pain.

When it was done, I lay there on the cold black stone of what had once been the citadel, and I tried to remember how to talk. The memory of the pain that had racked my body was fading but still felt like it could come back at any moment.

"It's a shame you can't heal yourself with that," I said, sitting up.

Lucifer's eyes were closed.

"Lucifer?" I said, already aware of what had happened. "Goddamn it," I whispered with a lump in my throat.

There was no way I was going to leave his body there, and when my mum's head appeared over the hole above us, she dropped down to the ledge of rubble where I was and helped me carry Lucifer's body up out of the mess. When we were out, I saw the devastation that had happened to Atlantis.

"Anyone else hurt?" I asked my mum as Lucifer's body was carried away by the dwarves.

"A lot," she said.

A hand was placed on my shoulder, and I turned to find Hades. We embraced, grieving over the loss of so many of those we had loved like family.

I removed the bracelet from my pocket and passed it to him, but Orfeda snatched it out of his hand. "This is where they went?" she asked, clearly concerned.

I nodded. "They both wore one. Judgement has the other. You know the destination?"

"It's the same runes that were inside all of these buildings, or at least the buildings I'd seen inside of before they collapsed. It goes to Shadow Falls."

"There were monsters in there," Judgement said. "Arthur told me. Tens of thousands of monsters that had once been human. Hera's experiments. All to go to Shadow Falls and destroy it."

My memory flashed back to what I'd fought in Kilnhurst. "We need to get to Shadow Falls, *now*," I said. "My *daughter* is there."

"We're already working to get the realm gate destination changed to get to Shadow Falls," Hades said. "We have to hope that the humans and those we left in Washington can help deal with Arthur and his cronies. Once we're done in Shadow Falls, we can go to the Earth realm. Everyone is waiting at the realm gate for the second it opens; we'll stop whatever Arthur has planned."

"Selene is in Washington," Orfeda said as Hades walked away. "Layla and Jinayca too."

I closed my eyes and sighed. "We don't have time for all of us to go to both places." I spotted a bloody and battered Tarron as he walked down the remains of the street toward us. There were two shadow elves beside him; both looked unsteady on their feet. I called him over and told him everything that had happened.

"You want me to make an elven realm gate?" Tarron asked me. "There are a lot of us; it will take time. It will take time to get so many of us to move to one place. It would have to be done in batches. And then it would take time to get from the mountain down to Solomon to help with whatever is happening there."

"How many dwarves are working on the realm gate?" I asked Orfeda.

"Zamek and a few hundred more."

"How many are in that prison?" Hades asked.

"My people were imprisoned, beaten, tortured, starved; they're in no shape to do anything to help."

"If we don't get that gate open, Shadow Falls will die," I said. "And everyone in it. I've fought these things, and they will not go easy."

"I'll see what I can do," Orfeda said.

I turned to Tarron. "Any chance you can work with some of the dwarves and elves we found here to make this realm gate much, much quicker? Maybe boost its power or something?"

"We can try," Tarron said.

Orfeda paused and stared at the sorcerer's band on my wrist. "Nate, you're human?"

I nodded. "And a fun time was had by all."

She lifted my hand to look at the bracelet. "There's no lock on this. You can just remove it."

I stared at the band. "Seriously?"

"Yes, haven't you studied it?" she asked.

"A building literally collapsed with me inside," I said. "Not a lot of time for reading."

Orfeda lifted my arm and looked closer at the band, reading the runes. "This says that if you remove it, everything around you dies."

"Yeah, we got that bit," I said.

"Nate, this isn't like a normal band," Orfeda said. "Normal bands, the magical power inside them goes inward, toward the victim. This goes inward and out. This is a serious scorched-earth-policy kind of band."

"So Arthur put a band on me I can remove at any time so long as I'm willing to kill myself and anyone near me," I said.

Orfeda nodded.

"Well, shit," I said with a sigh.

"We'll find a way," Orfeda said. "Have faith."

"Tarron," I said as the dwarves ran off. "Get that realm gate done. We're going to have to send people through both parts for as long as we can."

"I assume we can't make more bracelets?" he asked.

"They take too long to make, and we don't have any humans who know runes that could do it," Hades said. "Oh, you should know. Merlin's dead."

That was a surprise. "How's Mordred?" I asked.

"Good, considering," Hades said. "Or as good as Mordred ever pretends to be. He killed his own father."

"I'll go find him when I get a moment," I said.

Everyone set about their jobs. Then suddenly I spotted Tommy at the far end of the road. He was alone, in human form, his clothes tattered and bloodstained. I walked toward him cautiously and noticed that a lot of armed guards had appeared close by, their weapons ready.

"Tommy, that's close enough," I said. "Don't really want to have to fight you again."

"I saw the citadel collapse," he said.

"Lucifer died; Arthur escaped; I'm human," I said. "It's been a *shit* day."

There was a growl to the side of me, and Kase, in full were-beast form, crouched low and moved toward us, her mum, Olivia, behind her.

"Hey, honey," Tommy said.

"Dad?" Kase asked.

Tommy nodded. She took a step forward, and Tommy moved back. "I . . . I can't. I can't turn into a wolf, or I lose control again. It's everything just to stay human. That sword of Mordred's really did a number on my brain. It cleared it long enough for me to turn back into my human form, but I'm not sure for how long."

"We can fix it," Olivia said. "We can try."

"We will," Tommy said. "I just . . . I need to be shackled. I need to be restrained. I can't be trusted."

"We can arrange that," I said.

"I want to kill you, Nate," he said, tears in his eyes. "I want nothing more than to tear you in half, and it's breaking me to fight it. I don't know how to stop it. I want to kill all of you. I want to hurt my wife, my daughter, my son, everyone. The bloodlust is all-consuming. The need to taste death almost too much."

A soldier ran over, and I stopped her from getting too close. She tossed a set of shackles and a sorcerer's band to Tommy, who put them on eagerly. He sighed when it was done and sank to his knees, openly weeping as Olivia and a now-human Kase, both still wearing leather battle armor, ran to him. They, too, dropped to their knees as they were reunited.

"We're going to Shadow Falls," I said. "There's an army of monsters there."

Tommy looked up. "My son," he said.

I nodded. "And Astrid. It's not like Shadow Falls is defenseless," I said. "But we need to get there as soon as we can."

"And we're both essentially human?" Tommy asked me.

"I never said it would be easy," I said, offering him my hand, which he took, and he got to his feet and hugged me. "Glad you're back."

"I'm not, Nate," he said. "I can't risk turning into a werewolf. I can't fight like this."

"We'll figure it out," I told him. "In the meantime, go find some clothes—we've got a lot to do and not a lot of time to do it all in."

Tommy and Olivia walked off together, leaving me with Kase.

"My dad's not exactly back, is he?" she said.

"While he stays in human form, he's good," I said, hoping I was right. "I think your dad shouldn't be left alone with anyone right now. We need to make sure he's clear of Arthur's influence even while in human form. Persephone is over by the realm gate; go see if she can give you some people to ask. There are a few psychics and empaths, I think."

"Mum and I are heading to Shadow Falls to help stop Arthur's attack. My dad has to stay here; keep him safe."

Kase ran off, and I looked down at the bracelet on my wrist. Arthur had made sure I couldn't fight him again. But I'd find a way. Even if I had to grab hold of him, tear the damn bracelet off, and let the magical napalm incinerate us both.

Chapter Twenty-Nine

MORDRED

Realm of Shadow Falls

Shadow Falls burned.

Mordred had been one of the first through the realm gate in Atlantis once it was ready to be activated. It had taken less than an hour, and in that time, Mordred had wanted nothing more than to tell people to hurry up. It wouldn't have helped.

Mordred ran out of the temple with hundreds of people behind him, right into the fray with a horde of snarling creatures, their jaws snapping over and over as they tried to get to him. He used light magic to drive them back, but even in Shadow Falls—where magic was wild and unpredictable, much more powerful than in any other realm—the creatures continued to come.

Mordred cut through them with Excalibur and was relieved to discover that even if magic wasn't as potent against them as he'd like, at least a sharp sword still did the trick.

Hades, Persephone, and dozens of others helped Mordred and those who had come with him to push the creatures back down the hill toward the city, killing many of them with swords, axes—any weapons that they could get their hands on—only to have them replaced with more. A seemingly never-ending line of death.

Mordred stabbed one creature in the chest and activated Excalibur's power, and the creature bucked and screamed.

"There's got to be a better way than this," Mordred said, using Excalibur to decapitate another creature as Hel used her necromancy to tear another apart, then threw a dagger that caught a second in the throat. It died clawing at its own neck in an effort to try to get the blade out.

"They don't like silver," Hel said. "And they don't like necromancy."

"Both are useful to know," Mordred said, and soon anyone with necromancy powers was flinging them around at the enemy with aplomb.

"At least they stay dead," Diana said, in full werebear beast form, as she threw the head of one creature at an incoming second. The head bounced off its face, leaving a bloody mark, but otherwise did little to slow it down. Diana dived at the creature, ripping it apart with her massive claws.

"They die, but they just keep coming," Mordred said and spotted the flash of red armor belonging to the Horsemen as they moved toward the palace.

Hel placed a hand on his arm. "What did you see?" she asked.

"Arthur's Horsemen are going for the palace," Mordred said. "He wants to bury this realm. It stood against him last time—it's always been a beacon of anti-Avalon life, but it's also the one place he's never come close to conquering. Galahad lost his life to stop them the last time Arthur was here; I'm not going to let my friend have died in vain."

Diana turned back to them both. "I'm coming with you," she said, ignoring the dagger that whirled past her head into the eye of a creature. Medusa calmly walked over and removed it, crushing the skull of another creature beneath her boot.

"We going to kill them all, yes?" Medusa asked.

Diana nodded. "That's the plan, yes," she said.

"Good, let's go," Medusa said.

Twelve soldiers joined Mordred, Hel, Medusa, and Diana as they carved their way through the city of Solomon. They were soon joined by Olivia, who fought alongside Diana and Medusa at the front of the group, killing everything that came toward them.

Mordred had always thought that Olivia was an accomplished fighter, but seeing her there, now, was something else. She was rage given form, seemingly unstoppable as she let out her anger and frustration on anything stupid enough to get in her way.

The streets of Solomon were drenched in blood by the time they'd gotten even halfway through, and more than one contained the remains of those civilians who had lived here in peace. Mordred caught a glimpse of Harry and Kase, back to back, fighting off a large troll-like creature, and Olivia flew into a rage, racing over toward them both and helping them kill the giant beast.

They reached the stairs to the palace, killing their way through dozens of creatures on the way, only to find a hundred Horsemen standing at the top of the stairs, looking down on Mordred and his allies.

"You got a plan?" Hel asked.

"Hoped you would," he said. Mordred looked up at the griffins that were flying over the city, dive-bombing the enemy to tear off heads and limbs with their huge talons before taking to the skies again.

A few of them flew close to the palace, and the Horsemen readied themselves as Mordred and his allies began the run up the stairs.

It was a longer run than would be considered a good idea if intending to fight people who had the high ground, but the griffins distracted the Horsemen, diving at them and dragging their talons across the red armor.

By the time Mordred's team reached them, the Horsemen were already engaged and had killed two of the griffins by dragging them to the ground and ripping off their wings.

Mordred carved through two of the Horsemen with Excalibur, drove the tip of the sword into the helmet of one enemy, and left it there as the dead Horseman toppled back, leaving Mordred to use his magic. Ice exploded all across the top of the stairs, impaling several of the Horsemen and encasing two in ice.

Hel threw one Horseman down the steps, and Olivia froze it in place before Hel tossed a small amount of pure necromancy at it, ripping it in half.

The battle was short and bloody, and more than one of Mordred's soldiers succumbed to wounds, but when it was over and the ground ran slick with the blood of the Horsemen, Mordred and his people were victorious.

Mordred pushed a dead Horseman down the stairs and looked out across the burning city. His city. There were still tens of thousands of the creatures down there, and he'd seen more of his people dead than he ever wanted to see again, but they would continue to fight until their last breath, and even from the distance between them, Mordred saw the steady stream of new people coming through the mouth of the realm gate temple.

Mordred looked away and headed into the palace. Something felt wrong. He couldn't quite put his finger on it, but he'd expected more of the creatures and Horsemen than he'd actually seen. Certainly more of the Horsemen. But apart from those who were dead on the floor, there'd been little in the way of actual resistance from them.

"You okay?" Hel asked.

Mordred nodded, and while he wanted to give voice to his concerns, he needed to be ready for Arthur. He had Excalibur; he was ready. Or as ready as he'd ever be.

Before they reached the throne room, a large part of the doorway and corridor beyond it was torn apart in a blast of light. A Horseman was thrown into the hallway as everyone readied their weapons, and Judgement walked out, brushing herself down.

"It's empty," she said, looking back into the room. "Well, it's a bit of a mess."

"How'd you get here so fast?" Hel asked.

"Griffin dropped me on the roof," Judgement said. "There are no way near enough creatures here to destroy Shadow Falls."

"We've been set up," Hel said. "Arthur lied. He never sent half of his forces here, but he knew we'd divide our forces if we thought that he had, just to stop those we care about from being killed."

Mordred ran back through the palace to the front entrance and looked out over the battle of Shadow Falls. "We need to get to Washington, DC. Now."

"Hey," Hel said, coming to stand beside Mordred as the realm gate temple exploded in a ball of flame.

There were screams throughout the city, and Mordred ran toward the sound of the explosion just as a second one rang out. Mordred looked across the city to see the realm gate temple collapsing down the hill as thousands of the creatures ascended it, all of them standing between the destroyed temple and the city.

"What the fuck?" Judgement shouted.

"He wanted to keep us here," Mordred said. "That's why he wanted us to come. If trapping us in Atlantis failed, then he'd trap us here. He told my dad that he was sending people here, but he didn't tell him everything. Arthur doesn't trust anyone. I should have known that."

Diana, Medusa, and the soldiers all ran past, down into the fighting in the city. Olivia arrived. "I need to help," she said.

"We need to get the temples open and operating," Mordred said. "We need to get to DC now."

"He can't possibly think that this is a long-term way to stop us," Hel said.

"It's not," Mordred said. "But it's a short-term way for him to get to Earth and get however many Avalon people are there to rise up and kill those opposing them. By the time we get to the Earth realm, a lot of humans will be dead. He knows there's going to be a bigger battle—a lot of them; he just wants a head start."

No one else said anything, and Mordred took off at a sprint, running through the streets that had been crawling with enemies not long ago and now contained only their bodies and the bodies of those who had died fighting them.

Hel and Olivia joined Mordred, and the three of them reached the bottom of the stairs that led to the realm gate temple, which was now nothing more than rubble. The forces of Shadow Falls had already begun the assault on the creatures, who numbered in the thousands. Every time one was killed, two took its place.

Mordred and the others dived into the fight, killing anything that moved, but it was like fighting against the inevitable. The stairs were slick with blood and bodies of the fallen, and soon the number of dead Horsemen made it harder and harder for the defenders of the city to get to the realm gate.

Magic burned and froze Horsemen in equal turn; the earth ripped apart beneath the feet of the seemingly endless creatures. Lightning smashed into them, and huge stone golems tore through their ranks, and still they kept coming.

They were joined by the magically resistant creatures, who cut through anyone too close to them, and after what felt to Mordred

342

like a lifetime, there were still hundreds more to kill before they got to the realm gate.

Mordred shouted to get back, using his air magic to carry his words as far as he could along his line. People stepped back, but the creatures didn't follow; they were there to stop the ascent, not hunt those who moved away.

A faint white glow appeared around Mordred's hands, moving over his body as the enemy before him snarled. Any hint of their once being human was long gone. They were abominations now, closer in Mordred's mind to ghouls and blood elves than anything with humanity in it.

Mordred unleashed the pure magic he'd built up, aiming it directly at the baying mob of Horsemen in front of him. It obliterated everything between him and the realm gate. Hundreds of Horsemen died, only to be replaced by more as they willingly walked into the beam of pure magic, with seemingly no interest in their own preservation.

Mordred moved the pure magic in an arc in front of him until he was completely spent and dropped to one knee as his allies roared and charged forward into the remaining creatures.

The battle was easier, but it still took some time to clear out the monsters that were there. The Horsemen had been all but obliterated, and any remaining eventually died too. Mordred got involved in the fight again and killed two himself before running into the remains of the temple.

The bodies of a dozen rebellion soldiers littered the remains of the temple. The realm gate was seriously damaged, and though it was healing itself, it would be out of use for some time. At the far end of the temple, part of the rock crumbled away, revealing Leonardo, Antonio, and three soldiers, all of whom were badly injured but alive.

"Those things killed themselves," Leonardo said, his voice hoarse. "Blew themselves up to destroy the temple."

"They've done the same to the other dwarven gate," Mordred said. "The elven gate too."

"We are trapped here," Antonio said. "For now, at least."

"It's never ending, isn't it?" Mordred said with a shake of his head as Hel helped the rebellion soldiers out of the realm gate.

"So what do we do?" Hel asked.

"We finish clearing out these bastards," Mordred said. "We get these gates working, and we try to figure out how we get to Washington and find Arthur. We're going to end this, and there's no way Arthur is going to get away."

"Can we somehow get word to Nate and Tommy?" Judgement asked.

"There are still a lot of people in Atlantis who aren't here," Hel said. "They need to be told."

Mordred considered it for a moment. "Find me Orfeda," he said. "We're going to see if we can make a summoning circle."

Mordred glanced back up at the realm gate temple, the hill before it littered with the bodies of enemies and his allies.

"You okay?" Hel whispered.

Mordred shook his head. "I wanted this to be the big fight. Good versus evil. Me finally getting to put Arthur down. He took so much from me, including my eye the last time we fought; I wanted to be able to say I stopped him. I know that's a bit selfish, and it's not about me, but I almost needed to have another shot. And he's played us all. And no one knows where he is or what he's doing, but whatever it is, he wanted us out of the way for it."

"You might still get your chance," Hel said. "He still needs to be stopped."

Mordred nodded. "I know. I just hope we can stop him before he gets whatever he's after."

Chapter Thirty

Nate Garrett

Realm of Atlantis

I'd been watching more and more people heading into Shadow Falls when the realm gate had simply stopped working. Despite Zamek and the other dwarves trying to fix their realm gate, nothing was working. Whatever was happening in Shadow Falls, we were going to take no part in it. To suggest that I was frustrated was an understatement. To suggest that I was more frustrated at being reduced to a human again was probably something only Remy could find the right amount of swearing for.

As it had become quickly apparent that the realm gate wasn't going to be working anytime soon, the dwarves had taken Tommy away to try to figure out exactly how they were meant to stop him from trying to kill me once he took werewolf form.

In the meantime, I discovered a patch of rubble that had once been a building housing untold numbers of monsters and searched for more of the bracelets in the hope that I'd find one that wasn't used. I gave up after a few minutes of finding exactly nothing to help.

It was the end of the war, and I couldn't even get to the right realm to help. So I went to assist in defrosting the shadow elves and helping the dwarves out of their prison. I'd been there at most half an hour when Zamek shouted to me from across the prison, my name echoing all around the chamber.

"Mordred," Zamek said, out of breath.

"What about him?" I asked.

"Summoning circle," he said. "They've turned the realm gate into a summoning circle."

"You can do that?"

"Apparently," Zamek said. "The attack on Shadow Falls was to keep everyone busy. They destroyed the realm gates, all of them, and cost thousands of lives doing it, but the dwarven gates are fixing themselves, and they used the power inherent in the gate to turn it into a summoning circle. Frankly, it's quite astonishing; I've never considered using the power—"

"Zamek," I said softly. "Maybe not the time."

Zamek nodded as if his brain was finally catching up with his enthusiasm. "Right, well, Mordred wanted to let you know."

"Okay, so how's the elven realm gate working?" I asked, looking around to find Tarron.

"He's working on it," Zamek said.

We found Tarron nearby, along with two dozen shadow elves and more than a few dwarves. They were all staring at the floor.

"So it's going well, then," I said.

Tarron looked over at me.

"We have a problem," he said. "We can get the realm gate to work; we've got enough blood and runes, but . . . well, it won't work for long."

"Define *long*," I said.

"We're not sure—probably seconds, if that. The number of runes that were destroyed in the city to collapse those buildings has caused unpleasant things to happen to the soil in the city," Dethian the dwarf said. "It's going to take time to create runes that will bypass the problem, or anyone who uses the gate and isn't human is going to fry their power stepping through it."

"That's convenient," I said.

"Well," Dethian said, "it was probably a by-product of their plan. We can't use any realms; we can't make more. We're sat here until we figure something out."

"Okay, I'll go," I said. "Can you link it to the realm gate under the Lincoln Memorial?"

Zamek nodded. "I can. Easily. But I shouldn't, because it's insane. You're human."

I looked at my friend and nodded. "I know. But we know where Arthur is, and we know that we have people in Washington who are going up against an army. They need help. I can at least pick up a gun or something. I'm not helpless. Once I'm through, you need to get that realm gate fixed and get through too. We're going to need backup. A lot of it."

Zamek sighed and passed me his battle-ax, which hummed with power. "You're going to need it. It should help keep you in one piece."

"Thank you," I said.

"We'll be there when we can," Zamek said as the runes on the earth burned brightly. "They're working as fast as they can to get the dwarven realm gate operational. Normally, it's minutes, but the blast from Shadow Falls really did a number on the gate here too. We're not exactly at our finest hour here."

"One human against Arthur, probably the most powerful being who ever lived. This should be interesting."

Zamek offered me his hand. "Good luck with that."

I laughed and shook his hand. "It's been an honor," I told him.

"Yes, it has," Zamek said. "At least try not to die. Selene will not be happy."

"If I don't come back, tell her I love her," I said.

"I will," Zamek promised. "Astrid will know the kind of man her father was too. I swear on it."

I stepped into the humming mass on the ground, and everything went dark; my entire body felt like it was being turned inside out. As quickly as it had started, I found myself on my knees next to the realm gate in Washington.

I tightened my grip on the battle-ax and made my way up the stairs to the outside, the sounds of baying and cheering easy to hear well before I reached the exit at the side of the memorial.

The Lincoln Memorial was packed with people. Thousands of them, moving along the reflecting pool, all looking toward the Washington Monument. In the distance plumes of smoke took to the skies. It was daylight, but there was a light rain, although no one seemed to mind.

I moved slowly around the monument and grabbed the first person I saw who wasn't going to raise an alarm, pulling them back around to a group of shrubs and placing the tip of the battle-ax against their throat.

"I'd start talking," I said.

"Arthur arrived with these creatures," he said. "He killed anyone in his way. Everyone. The White House is burning. We are about to start a new world order."

"You're KOA?" I asked.

"Proud of it," he said.

I removed the dagger from his hip and drove it into his skull. "Good for you," I said, retrieving a Glock from his holster. Silver bullets. At least in death, he'd be able to do more than he had in life.

I took his hoodie, too, which thankfully was still blood-free, and ran to the side of the reflecting pool. I kept my head down as

I made my way through the park, past the Constitution Gardens and World War II Memorial.

The crowds were thicker after that, and I spotted Arthur standing atop a set of steps that had been constructed around the monument and appeared to consist of mud and vines. Seeing how Demeter was standing beside Arthur, wearing an elegant green gown and a cruel smile on her face, I assumed that she was responsible for the decor.

People around me cheered and shouted as Arthur stepped toward the edge of the podium. He stood there and soaked in the applause, nodding along with it, while his KOA shouted his name as the sounds of battle could be heard in the distance. The humans were fighting back. I really hoped they were winning.

I'd seen this sort of thing many times during my life. One man telling a group of angry people that it wasn't their fault that their lives were shit; it was the fault of whichever group they wanted people to hate instead. In this instance, it was the rebellion, the humans who stood against Arthur's plans, the nonhumans who fought him. They were the enemy. They were who needed to be exterminated.

I looked around at the crowd, and most carried weapons: swords, staves, the occasional spear. My ax didn't look so out of place, then. More had guns, though, and I spotted a large number of Horsemen over to the side of the memorial, all of them standing to attention.

I moved away to the other side of the memorial and saw the creatures next to it. They were all penned together in the field.

There were hundreds of creatures, and all of them were sitting down, doing nothing. I wondered exactly what Arthur was going to do with them.

I spotted dozens of media trucks that had been parked in the field during the battle at the White House. Microphones covered the front of where Arthur stood, the world's media allowing the people to take in their new dictator. It didn't matter where they lived; Arthur was going to make sure that he was the only person in charge.

"My people," Arthur said, "I am your *savior.*"

The cheering made me feel nauseous.

"Your leaders have betrayed you," Arthur continued as I moved through the crowd. "Those you trusted to keep you safe have done nothing of the sort. The rich get richer and do nothing for the poor. You are the forgotten. I will change that."

More cheering.

"I will eliminate poverty. I will eliminate war. I will eliminate disease. I will take this world and ensure that it becomes what it was always destined to be. The rebellion stopped me from helping you once, but they are not here. They will not stop me again. They will not stop what we can achieve. Right now, throughout this country, throughout all countries, our allies are burning away everything that opposes us. In this very city, my Horsemen are destroying those who stand against us. We will soon join them in battle; we will soon be victorious. And once this land has come under my rule, no one will *ever* take it from us."

The cheering grew louder, and I took the opportunity to move through more of the crowd, the noise increasing as I went, until I reached the metal barrier at the edge. Armed guards stood beyond it, and one motioned for me to move back. I did as I was told. I needed another plan.

I stopped listening to Arthur's incessant ramblings and threaded through the crowd. I tightened my grip on my ax and removed the gun from my hoodie pocket, holding it down by my side.

"I am your salvation," Arthur shouted, raising his spear high into the air.

The roar of the crowd was deafening, and I aimed the gun and fired twice. The first bullet hit an invisible shield that had been created at the front of the platform; the second struck the same spot and fractured it. I tried to fire again but was tackled from the side, and the gun skidded out of my grasp. Two dozen KOAs set about kicking and punching me as I curled up and tried not to get killed.

"Bring him to me," Arthur demanded, his voice full of rage.

I was hauled to my feet and dragged to the front of the crowd, though we stopped every few feet so that someone else could punch or kick me.

"Nathan Garrett," Arthur seethed. "Will you ever cease plaguing me?"

"Sure. When you're dead," I told him.

There was an audible gasp from the sycophants in the crowd, followed by a chant of "Make him pay."

Vines wrapped around me, and I was picked up off the floor and carried over to the platform. I remained there, hanging ten feet in the air as Demeter walked toward me.

"I should have torn you apart long ago," she said and threw me behind her. I smashed into a stone wall and dropped to the ground.

Arthur kicked me in the ribs to the cheering of his supporters. He turned back to the microphones. "This . . . worm has been sent to end me. He has been sent to stop my destiny. Your destiny. He will be dealt with. Let it be known that those who dare stand against me will be met with similar levels of fury and retribution."

Arthur picked me up by the back of my collar and dragged me to the front of the stage. He kneed me in the face, and blood poured from a freshly broken nose. I reached for the bracelet on my wrist. If I was going to die, he was coming with me. He kneed me again and stomped down on the hand without the bracelet, breaking the bones in my fingers. He crouched beside me. "You can't remove it with a broken hand."

"I'll use my damn teeth if need be," I snapped and got a punch in the jaw for my trouble.

"Take him to the pit," Arthur said. Vines wrapped around me again, pinning my arms back to my sides, and I was dragged off-stage to the cheering of a crowd baying for blood.

"You should have just killed me," I shouted to Arthur.

"You are right," Demeter said. "And now you will die. And you will feed the creatures who you failed to save so many times. Your rebellion is over. Shadow Falls is either eradicated or neutralized; we will control this world. All of those countries you thought had fought us off are discovering what happens when we return. Cities who stood against us are burning, their people dying. You cannot hope to stop us all. You are nothing."

"Arthur doesn't care about any of you," I said.

Demeter stopped dragging me. "I know that, you idiot. But I will get to kill Hades for taking my daughter from me all those years ago. And that is all I ever wanted."

"Your hate has twisted you."

"It gave me purpose," she snapped as we continued on.

I was thrown over the six-foot-high fence into the pen with the creatures, none of whom moved. They simply all turned to look at me.

"Your screams will give me sweet dreams," Demeter said, and she walked away chuckling to herself.

The creatures were beginning to realize that they had some food in their midst. There were growls. One of them rushed toward me, and I punched it in its face, knocking it to the ground. The rest moved around, watching me, as I tried to get myself toward a fence simply so I could have something against my back.

Several of the creatures screamed and charged. I put the sorcerer's band in my mouth and ripped it free.

Shadows sprang from the ground, wrapping around me as the hands of the wraith shot up out of them. The shadows encased my body the moment the sorcerer's band exploded. The heat was incredible, and I was dragged down into the shadows as it tore the shadow magic apart. I screamed in pain as my arms and face were badly burned, my armor doing nothing to stop it. I continued to scream until there was nothing but the shadow realm.

I lay on the ground, panting, my entire body hurting, my magic only now kicking in to heal me. The wraith was devastated. Its body was a mass of burned shadows, and whatever passed for skin was covered in burns.

It stepped into the light, its hood almost burned down to nothing, revealing a face that looked identical to my own.

"Are you okay?" I asked, wincing as I got to my feet.

"I will survive," the wraith said. "I protected you."

"You did," I said. "Thank you."

"I am part of you," it said, placing its ruined hand against my chest. "We are one."

I gasped and felt the kick of power as my magic flooded my body.

"Erebus was part of you," the wraith said. "Erebus was darkness. He was your magic. I am darkness."

"You're Erebus?" I asked, confused.

The wraith shook its head. "No. I am *you*. Part of you that was always there. The darkness. The power. You were made to kill gods. And devils. Your father and mother knew that. Erebus knew that. Erebus ensured that you could do what you needed to."

The skin on its body was healing, and at the same time its powers of speech were improving. I looked down at the pink skin on my arms, which had been charred and blistered a moment earlier.

A ball of pure magic appeared in its hand, the smoky tendrils billowing out around me. I took it.

"I don't understand," I said.

"You are not pure magic," the wraith said. "You are darkness personified. Death personified. It is why they gave you that name. Arthur fears you because you can beat him. I will always protect you. I am your wraith. But you are Death. It is time you showed Arthur just what he has come up against."

I looked down at the pure magic sphere as my wraith placed its cold hands on mine and pushed it into my chest.

"Your magic," the wraith said. "Arthur removed your magic. But I was still here. Cut off from you, but with access to your power. I have gathered it. I have nurtured it. This is your power given to you all at once. Burn them all."

I stepped into another pool of light and arrived back in the pen, the inferno from the sorcery band still ongoing. I'd been gone mere fractions of a second. The screams of the creatures as the inferno tore through them were horrific, and shadows leaped out of the ground, taking dozens at once as the inferno covered me.

I let the heat bathe me, comfort me. I allowed it to swirl around me, and I breathed in, my own fire magic touching that from the sorcerer's band, and as the inferno vanished, all that was left was me standing in the destroyed pen as Arthur and his crowd cheered, before it slowly dawned on them all exactly what they were seeing.

I breathed out the fire, a huge plume of dragon-like breath high into the sky above me.

"Arthur," I roared, my air magic carrying the words to all around us. "Time to face your destiny."

Chapter Thirty-One

Nate Garrett

The Washington Monument was not created to withstand a blast of pure magical power. Even so, I threw enough to hopefully force Arthur back and put distance between him and his crowd.

Instead, Arthur dragged Demeter into the blast, disintegrating her upper torso. The magic still smashed into Arthur, lifting him off his feet and throwing him back into the monument.

He unleashed his own magic a second later, and the monument began to crumble from the impact of vast amounts of magic.

Shadows continued to leap out of the ground, pulling down the remaining creatures who got too close. Their deaths kept my magic at full power while I calmly strolled toward the monument as it toppled forward.

The crowd of KOA realized they were in deep shit about ten seconds before it hit them. Over five hundred feet of monument crashed down onto the watching masses, most of whom had tried to flee only to find themselves trapped by their own people. Huge amounts of dust and mud were thrown into the air, covering those closest to the impact.

I ignored the screams, the pleas for help. They'd murdered and destroyed with impunity. I figured a monument falling on them was probably about as close to karma as I was ever going to see. Besides, I wasn't feeling particularly charitable at that exact moment.

To compound their misery, the creatures had managed to get free and were—to put it mildly—freaking out. The fight-or-flight instinct had kicked in, and most had run into the park, but quite a few had chosen the direction where the remains of the KOA audience stood. Which meant fresh meat and blood, driving those who went that way into a frenzy.

I ignored the sudden and inevitable betrayal of animalistic monsters and continued on toward Arthur.

Part of the monument had fallen onto him, and I'd reached the earth steps when it exploded, raining pieces of stone and metal all around. A shield of air kept me from being injured in any serious way, but the same couldn't be said for the KOA. It really was turning into a bad day to be a follower of Arthur.

"Why do you insist on *ruining* everything?" Arthur shouted as I walked up the stairs toward him. He was covered in blood, although whether it was his or Demeter's was hard to tell.

"Bet you wish you'd worn armor," I said. "But you just had to be a show-off. Just had to be sure that everyone knew how powerful you are."

I charged the last few feet, dodging a punch from Arthur, and drove my left elbow into his ribs. He gasped, taking a step back, as I created a sphere of lightning in the palm of my right hand, which I slammed into his chest and detonated.

The platform of earth we both stood on was decimated as the power from the sphere tore it apart, and Arthur was thrown back off the platform, collided with the side of the Washington Monument, and remained there as I picked up a small microphone from the floor, attached it to my lapel, and leaped across the gap, using my air magic to make the jump possible.

Arthur spat blood onto the ground and got to his feet. "You want to complete what you were made for," he said and spat again.

"Your people are dying," I told him as some of them cried to Arthur for help.

"I don't care," he said.

"They can hear you," I said, pointing to the microphone.

"Let them," Arthur sneered. "I don't *need* them. I don't *need* anyone. I was born to rule all. I will not let some *experiment* stop me."

I flicked down a whip of fire toward Arthur, who caught it in one air-wrapped hand, smiling the whole time. "You will have to do better than that."

I removed the fire whip and rolled my shoulders. I created a blade of lightning in each hand and closed the distance between Arthur and me. He rushed to intercept me. I drove one of the blades toward his face, and he blocked it with a shield of blood magic, the tendrils leaping out to wrap themselves around my hand. Pain lanced through me, but instead of trying to pull free, I detonated the magic in the hand that was covered.

Arthur screamed in pain as the lightning tore the blood magic apart, leaving him open for me to drive the second blade into his chest and immediately explode the magic. Arthur headbutted me and drove his own blade of fire into my side, twisting it as I noticed that the clothes he'd been wearing had taken the brunt of the impact from my magic. So he hadn't come quite as unprepared as I'd expected.

I grabbed the arm that had driven the blade just under my ribs and wrapped tendrils of air around it, crushing the limb and trying to block the agony as I moved. Arthur removed his hand and tried to twist away, but I snaked the air around his arm, crushing the limb further before unleashing an electric shock as I activated my lightning magic.

Arthur stepped back again, and I raised my hand to the sky. Lightning streaked down, hit my hand, traveled through me, mixing with the magic inside, and exited through my other hand directly into Arthur.

I kept hold of Arthur as the lightning magic tore into him as if it were a hungry predator. His roars of pain were lost in the maelstrom of noise from the power I threw at him. I didn't see until too late that Arthur had created a sphere of pure magic and detonated it between us.

I was thrown back fifty feet, bouncing along the monument—I hit the ground hard. The pure magic hadn't hurt me; I was as immune to its devastation as Arthur.

I rolled onto my front and got back to my feet. The KOA had all but scattered now, leaving only a few, and they had bigger problems than me.

My hand was a ruined mess but was healing itself quickly enough. Most of the Washington Monument lay on its side along the ground. I started after Arthur, whom I'd last seen running along the remains. I climbed the monument, using air magic to punch holes in the side of it until I'd reached the top. Arthur was gone.

I sprinted toward where I'd last seen him and spotted him running back toward the Lincoln Memorial. I sank into the shadows and darted from light to light, hitting four before I dragged myself back up into the daylight above. I hadn't seen the wraith, but I knew it was there and would always be there when I needed it.

I was thirty feet behind a fast-moving Arthur when the shadows tripped him and he fell to the ground. He saw me running toward him and activated his matter magic, the purple glyphs burning across the backs of his hands as he got to his feet. I activated my own matter magic and slowed to a walk.

"Where's your spear?" I asked him, having only just remembered that he'd had hold of it earlier. "Did you drop it?"

Arthur got to his feet, brushing the grass and dirt off his trousers. "I don't need it to kill you, whelp."

I laughed. "Whelp?" I asked. "That's it? All of these years of hating me, and that's the best you can come up with, you contemptible piece of weasel shit?"

Arthur's eyes narrowed.

"I know—I can do better," I admitted. "And Remy has a whole dictionary of words for you."

I was only a few feet from him now, and if I started throwing around magic, there was no telling what his matter magic would let him do with it. All I knew was that while he had it activated, he couldn't use his blood magic. That was enough.

He threw a punch, which I avoided, and I hit him in the jaw with one of my own, causing him to stagger back. Instead of staying back, he immediately sprang forward, and I couldn't avoid the knee to the chest, which picked me up off my feet and threw me back. I landed in front of a tree and rolled aside as Arthur sprinted toward me and tried to drive a knee into my face. He missed and hit the tree, which was all but vaporized from the power, showering me with thousands of tiny blades of wood.

Arthur didn't stop, and I was forced to block or dodge punch after punch and, when he got close enough, kicks and knees. He kicked out at my knee and the outside of my thigh, trying to cause me to slow, to give him a chance to close the gap between us, but I continued to block. My matter magic ensured that I was stronger, but occasionally a blow got through and caused me to retreat. Unfortunately, it quickly became apparent that Arthur was not about to tire, and I spotted a number of KOA agents who were holding back and watching the fight with interest.

I sidestepped Arthur's punch and drove my fist into his jaw, snapping his head aside, and followed up with a knee to his ribs, where I pushed out my matter magic into a physical force. Arthur's ribs snapped like kindling, and I followed it up with a punch that he blocked, wrapping his arms around mine and snapping my elbow before kicking me away.

We stood there as the rain began, both of us hurt, neither of us giving up. I activated my blood magic, and it set about healing me, the magic fading the longer it lasted.

A KOA agent ran over to Arthur to check on him, and Arthur tore out his throat with his teeth, drank the blood down, and pushed the body away. "One of the benefits of being a vampire," he said, wiping his mouth with the back of his hand and leaving a smear of red on his face.

"Not sure your KOA fans will enjoy that," I said.

"Fuck them all," Arthur said. "They'll enjoy what I tell them to enjoy. If I want them to give me their blood, they'll willingly do so. This isn't a democracy. They get no vote, no say."

I moved my neck from side to side as my arm reset itself. "Wow, we're onto the hard sell of your shitopia, are we?"

"We can do this all night," Arthur said. "But you don't have all night, do you?"

"Why's that?" I asked.

"The creatures have run off into the city. They will tear it apart in search of sustenance." Arthur laughed. "And there are still thousands of angry KOA over there. Watching us. Waiting. If you succeed, you die. If you lose, you die. You cannot win here, Nathaniel."

"I don't know," I said with a sigh. "I think killing you would be winning enough for me."

"You'll never see your loved ones again," Arthur said, pushing himself off the tree he'd been leaning against. "Let me tell you something, Nate. When you're dead, I am going to murder everyone you love."

"You keep saying that," I told him. "You've had chances to kill me, and yet here we are. You either want my approval, or you just suck at killing me. What is it? Do you still think I'm going to join you? Do you still think I'm going to stand by and watch? You put a sorcerer's band on me, and I survived it. You made sure that the only way to get that off was to kill myself. No key needed. And I survived it. You can't kill me, can you?"

My arm was fixed, and I tested it, hearing the joint crack. My blood magic faded to nothing a moment later. At least it had gone out with one last use. "You ready to go again?"

"I will stand alone," Arthur said. "Against you all. I will stand alone."

I shook my head sadly. "Come die, you little cretin."

Arthur unleashed a torrent of fire and air at me, tendrils of blood magic slithering through it all, while I wrapped myself in air and shadows and stood, bracing myself against the power. And then it stopped, the trees around me reduced to ash, the ground now a charred mess.

I removed my magic as one of the KOA presented Arthur's spear to him. *Oh shit.*

Arthur's smile was cruel, and I spotted a sword on the ground that had belonged to a now-dead Horseman and picked it up. It

361

was a wicked, dark-bladed weapon with a slight curve. It was less than ideal quality-wise, but I wasn't about to complain. Arthur had the gall to laugh before he launched his spear at me.

The spear moved faster than I'd have thought possible, and I had to throw myself aside to avoid being skewered. Arthur strolled casually toward the spear, and I charged him, hoping to reach him before he could get his weapon back. But blood magic snaked to the spear and pulled it back to Arthur just as I launched my attack, and he blocked the sword swipe to the neck. The side of my sword hit the shaft of the spear, and the sword broke from the impact. He twisted the spear and drove it up toward my chest; I had to dart back and swipe it away.

"I always loved this weapon," he said smugly. "It increases my power; it removes your power. It's frankly wonderful."

I ignited a ball of flame in my hand. "Your spear is broken," I said and pointed to the fact that I'd hit the spear so hard that the sword had cut into it, removing one of the runes there.

Arthur was incensed. "How dare you," he snapped.

"I can't believe no one ever did that before," I said with a shrug, picking up another sword from the ground.

I closed the gap between us, driving my one-handed sword toward Arthur's face. He snapped the spear up, knocking the sword tip aside, and brought the spear down on the back of my hand. I couldn't move in time to stop him from cutting through it.

I let out a yell of pain but moved back. The silver in the blade burned, and it wouldn't heal as well as it might have otherwise, but it wasn't a killing cut. I was beginning to wonder exactly what I needed to do to kill Arthur, who looked no worse for wear.

We'd reached the steps to the Lincoln Memorial, and I walked up them backward, keeping an advancing Arthur in my sights. His KOA were in the distance, moving closer with every moment. There were still hundreds of them. How was I meant to stop them all and stop Arthur? I needed to find a way to neutralize his ability to use blood magic so quickly and to stop him from using his magic, which was as potent as my own. And now he had a weapon that made him even stronger. The runes were cut, which meant he couldn't stop my magic, but that didn't make much of a difference. Where was a sorcerer's band when I needed it?

"You can't do this forever," Arthur said. "Whether you have your magic or not, while I hold this spear, I'm more powerful than you can possibly imagine. We might have been tied without it, but with it, you will die at my hands."

I'd reached the top of the steps and was happier to be on the same level again. I still had no plan. All the talk about power and being Death—sure, it was designed to make me go fight, but in reality, once you'd thrown everything you had at someone and they were still there, it didn't really matter what you could and couldn't do. You couldn't beat them.

I took a deep breath and created a sphere of lightning in my hand, spinning it faster and faster as I poured more and more magic into it. Shadows leaped out of the ground, joining the sphere, as Arthur continued to stalk toward me.

"You think that will beat me?" he asked.

I kept quiet, concentrating on the sphere, making it grow until it was a meter in diameter. I sprinted toward Arthur, who looked surprised that I'd chosen to attack. He readied his spear and jabbed it toward me, trying to catch me off balance, but I knocked the blade of the spear aside with my sword, which opened up Arthur's side. He tried to step to the side, but shadows leaped out of the ground, forcing him to step back. A shield of blood magic appeared between us, and I detonated the sphere, sank into the shadows, and appeared directly behind Arthur, instantly creating a second sphere and pouring everything I had into it.

Arthur turned to me the second I plunged the sphere into his side.

The crater I created took out most of the promenade in front of the Lincoln Memorial. The blast was big enough that Arthur's top half was now raw and looked painful as he dislodged himself from the stone he'd impacted with. His jacket and shirt were gone, his trousers now a tattered mess. He held the spear in one hand, but the shaft had broken in half, the second half lying on the ground at his feet.

I slumped to my knees as pieces of stone continued to fall all around the stairs.

"That it?" Arthur asked, looking unsteady on his feet.

I'd used the amount of magic that had killed War back in Asgard. And Arthur just stood there. Goddamn him.

"That it?" Arthur asked again, his body already repairing itself at an alarming rate.

I let out a long breath and raised a shield of air beside me as my magic felt something close by. The bullet struck the shield, followed by a second and a third, taking my attention off Arthur. He punched me in the jaw, knocking me to the ground, as his blood magic tendrils began to wrap around my body.

"I took your friend's eye," Arthur said as I tried not to scream from the pain. "Maybe I'll take your tongue first."

I tried to sink into the shadows, but Arthur dragged me away, his fire magic burning the shadows and causing me more pain.

Darkness had reached the edge of my vision when a massive werewolf charged into Arthur, picked him up, and threw him away. The magic around me stopped, and the werewolf looked back at me.

"Tommy?" I asked.

Tommy nodded. "Brought friends," he said as dwarves charged over the crater, dropping down and running toward

Arthur, who was back on his feet and killing anyone who got close enough.

Hundreds and hundreds of dwarves charged down the steps toward the KOA as I got to my feet and saw Zamek and Tarron.

"We had to help," Tarron said. "My people needed to help."

The shadow elves were at the rear of the charge and moved considerably more slowly than the dwarves, but they still wanted to help stop the people who had used them for centuries.

"Thank you," I said. "The creatures ran off into the city; they need to be hunted."

"On it," Tommy said and ran off with dozens of shadow elves and dwarves following him.

"How?" I asked before I could stop myself.

"A conversation for later," Zamek said and ran off.

Tarron ran into the fray and helped several dwarves and elves who were keeping Arthur busy.

My body felt weak, and I needed a moment to catch my breath, but in that time Arthur killed three dwarves and plunged the broken spear through Tarron's throat. The elf staggered back, and Arthur drove the spear up into his heart, killing him instantly.

"You keep getting your friends killed," Arthur shouted, pushing Tarron's body aside as he walked toward me.

Thunder rumbled overhead.

"I'd suggest that you could end this now," Arthur said, parrying the strike from an elf and killing her where she stood before moving on as if nothing had happened, "but you can't. You will all die."

Arthur was only a few feet away from me when a sword struck the ground in front of me. Excalibur. I looked up to see Mordred standing above me. "Kill *him*," Mordred said.

I gritted my teeth, took hold of the hilt, and raised the sword as I got to my feet, and Arthur charged me. I felt power flow through me, and lightning left my fingers, smashing into Arthur and throwing him across the crater.

I ran after him and activated Excalibur's ability to remove the power in another. Arthur, realizing what had happened, threw the broken spear at me, but I moved aside and kept on coming. He turned to run, and I reached him and drove the sword through his back, pinning him to the stone.

"You always wanted this," I whispered in his ear as I kept hold of the hilt. "You always wanted Excalibur. Well, congratulations—you got your wish."

I twisted the sword, and Arthur let out a cry.

"No power, no magic, no army, no nothing," I said. "I just want you to see how much you've lost."

Arthur turned his head toward me. "I always hated you," he said as blood flowed freely out of his mouth.

"Feared," I said softly. "You always feared me." I pulled Excalibur out, and Arthur crashed to his knees. "And you were right to do so."

I swung the sword down, cleaving his head from his neck. Magic exploded out of him, throwing me back across the crater. Excalibur was still in my hand as I landed next to Mordred's feet.

"I would have tried to fight him on his terms," Mordred said, taking Excalibur from me. "I would have tried to beat him fairly. I knew you wouldn't. You'd just win."

"How'd you get here?" I asked.

"We got one of the realm gates working. It's not everyone, but it's enough."

"Tarron is dead," I said.

Mordred nodded and offered me his hand to help me to my feet, which I accepted. "So are Jinayca, Roberto, and thousands of others."

Hearing Jinayca's name among them hit hard.

"Arthur is dead," Mordred shouted at the top of his voice as hundreds of others began to run past: Diana, Irkalla, Hades, Layla, Loki, Hyperion, and so many other friends and allies.

"We still have a lot to do," I said.

"Yes, my friend," Mordred agreed. "Yes, we do."

Chapter Thirty-Two

Nate Garrett

The KOA who had come to cheer Arthur on folded like a bad hand of cards. Turned out that when you got a few hundred exceptionally pissed-off dwarves running at you, you tended to reevaluate where you'd gone wrong in life.

Arthur's body was taken by Hades, Loki, and Persephone back to Shadow Falls. It would be destroyed. No trace left for people to try to track down or turn into a martyr. He'd died hard, and he'd deserved every single second of the pain he'd suffered. If I'd had my way, his ashes would have been shot into space.

Washington was a mess, which pretty much summed up most of the world at this point. The KOA had attacked cities all over the globe, and there were millions of dead. The human race had a long way to go before it would heal from the wounds that had been caused, and probably an even longer way before they'd trust anyone who wasn't human. We'd stood shoulder to shoulder with many of them, and I hoped that would help.

Arthur hadn't wanted to just rule over the realms; he'd wanted to punish all of those who had stood against him in the past. That had been his downfall: his arrogance and hatred of having people say no to him.

I found myself sitting up against the gate of the White House, which was pretty much a charred ruin by this point.

Layla sat beside me. We'd both lost people we cared about; we'd both had to fight for our lives. And judging from the expression on her face, neither of us had any idea what we were going to do next.

"Are we actually done?" she asked me.

I nodded. "I think so," I said. "I hope so."

"I'm not even twenty-five, and now I have to figure out what I'm going to do with my life now that the war is done."

"You want some advice?" I asked.

She nodded and smiled. "I really do."

"Take a break. Go find yourself. Go backpacking through the realms. Whatever you need to do. There's no hurry."

"Backpacking through the realms?" Layla asked with a chuckle.

"Ah, it was that or get high as fuck and try to figure out the mysteries of life."

"Why not both?" she asked.

I laughed, and she hugged me.

"What are you going to do?" she asked.

"I have no idea," I admitted. "Raise my daughter. Be with Selene. I don't really have any enemies to lay waste to anymore. Maybe build a house somewhere quiet."

"There's still a lot to do," Layla said.

"I know," I agreed. "But that won't take forever. We've chopped the head off the snake—the rest will crumble. The KOA will be hunted down. Arthur's allies will be hunted down. Shadow Falls will be fixed; hopefully Asgard can one day be fixed." I watched as Kase and Harry walked along the street in front of us, hand in hand.

"Both are happier," Layla said. "Kase was pushing everyone away in her anger."

"I know something about that," I said. "Still not sure what they did to Tommy."

"Ask," Layla said, pointing to Zamek, who was walking toward us.

"My friend," I said, getting to my feet and hugging him. "I'm glad you're okay. Thank you for the timely assist."

"My pleasure," he said, taking a seat on the ground.

I sat beside him. "Worked out for the best. A few minutes later, and I'd have really been in trouble."

"We like to do these things," Zamek said. "It's more poetic. The early save isn't nearly as romanticized."

"I'm sorry about Jinayca," Layla said. "I will miss her very much."

"Me too," Zamek said. "She was a force of nature like no other."

"You seen Mordred?" I asked.

"He's helping to round up the KOA and creatures," Zamek said.

"And Tommy?" Layla asked.

"Tommy has blood magic curse marks on him. Marks we can't remove without killing him," Zamek said. "So we altered them."

"Meaning what?" I asked, apprehensive.

"The blood curse marks were put there to make him want to kill everyone he loved. Starting with you. Thankfully, unlike Mordred's marks, or your marks for that matter, Tommy's were placed on there in considerably less time, so they were still in a sort of flux. We changed the marks so that instead of wanting to kill them all, he wants to kill the person who put the marks there. Merlin. Who is now dead."

"So his marks are redundant?" I asked.

Zamek nodded. "We can try and remove them normally, and I can't say that Tommy is going to have a fun time of it, but he's safe from going after people he cares about."

I got to my feet. "Good. I'm going to go find out just how badly things are going everywhere else, and then I'm going to try to find Selene and Astrid."

"I'm sure they're okay," Layla said. "Selene and the rest of us were out in DC fighting those damn creatures and Horsemen when Arthur appeared. We hunted down the shadow elves that were helping Merlin and Arthur. We killed them all."

"I'm sorry about Tarron," I said. "He was a good man."

Layla nodded. "Yeah, he was. His people are safe at least in part because of him. As for Selene, she's probably having a really big glass of vodka somewhere."

"I know they're fine," I told her. "I'm pretty sure Astrid was the safest person in Shadow Falls. I just want to see her."

"Go be a dad," Zamek said. "I'm going to sit here with my friend until someone tells me where the nearest open bar is. Then I will get very, very drunk."

"I like his plan," Layla said.

I left them both there and found Selene over by the remains of the Washington Monument. She hugged me and kissed me on the lips. "Everyone keeps telling me that Astrid is fine," she said. "Eros and Brynhildr have her. They literally stood between her and the Horsemen and killed everything that came within fifty feet."

"That was a lot of information," I said, happy that everyone was okay.

Selene smiled. "Sorry, I've been waiting to say it all since I got here. We lost a lot of good people, and I'm trying to stay positive."

I held Selene against me, and for a brief moment the rest of the world could have gone to hell. Or further toward it.

"There's something I want to talk to you about," I said eventually, cursing myself for ruining the moment.

"Sounds important," she said.

"It is," I told her. "But later, when we're not all covered in blood and gore. I just . . . remind me, okay?"

She nodded. "Have you seen Mordred?"

"He ran off just after Arthur died," I said. "He had things to do. He's now the face of those of us who aren't human. Which might actually be the most amazing thing I've ever heard."

"He's with Judgement," Selene told me. "She killed hundreds in Shadow Falls. The rage inside her was . . . it reminded me of you and Mordred."

"We're kin," I said, as if that explained it in any way. "Sort of, anyway."

"Go find Mordred so we can sort out whatever needs to be done, and then we can go home and sleep." Selene paused for a second. "Or rather, we can go home and watch our baby sleep and never move from there. Ever."

"I love you," I said.

"You're a soppy fucker, Mr. Garrett," Selene said with a beaming smile. "And I love you too."

I found Mordred talking to a large crowd near the Lincoln Memorial, which had become some sort of gathering place for the media and anyone who just wanted to know what the hell was going on.

I stayed far enough back from the crowd to ensure I was ignored, as Mordred, carrying no weapons, explained that Arthur was dead, that his tyranny was over, and that the people of the world had nothing to fear from those who had stood against him. It was a good speech; he was becoming better and better at it the more he gave them.

I was proud of him. Proud of the king he'd become, proud of the man he'd become. I was glad that, if nothing else, he'd been able to turn his life around and fight against the evil that had captured him for so long. Okay, he'd had to die and come back to do it, but it made me happy to know he'd done it.

The impromptu press conference finished, and Mordred thanked everyone for coming. He turned, spotted me, and walked over as several large guards stopped the press from running after him, shooting questions the whole time.

"I'd better get used to that, I guess," he said.

I nodded.

"You got any ideas what you want to do after this?" Mordred asked me.

"Retire?" I suggested.

Mordred laughed. "I was going to offer you a job. Head of . . . well, what *was* the Law of Avalon and will no longer be called that. Can't really keep something that was used to subjugate."

"You keeping Avalon?" I asked him.

Mordred nodded. "I think so." He looked at the massive number of allies who were helping, tending to the injured, and talking to humans who had come over to help too.

"This might just work," I said. "That's what you're thinking, isn't it?"

Mordred smiled and nodded. "I really bloody well hope so."

"Where's the sword?"

"Hel has it. I thought it best not to wander around with it on. I won't be wearing a crown, either, despite several people telling me I should. A democratically elected king. I'm not sure that's how it's meant to work, but it's bloody well how it's working."

I placed my hand on Mordred's shoulder. "You did good."

"You killed him."

"Yeah, but all of this is because of you, not me. You motivated; you gave them something to look up to. I hit people really hard."

"And you're good at it," Mordred said. "I assume you won't be taking the job."

"I don't know," I said honestly. "I need to talk to Selene. I need to figure out what's best for all of us."

I spotted Judgement across the reflecting pool, sitting with several workers, all enjoying a beer and, judging from the occasional amber glow, a little smoke of something else.

"We need to bury our friends first," I said. "Help clean up. Help make sure that humans and us don't try to kill one another again. Hunt down the KOA. Hunt down Arthur's friends. And basically save the world and make it a better place for everyone."

"You want to hold hands and sing a song too?" Mordred asked me.

"Maybe later," I said, and we both laughed.

"We did a good thing today, Nate. Not just today but every day since Arthur appeared. I just wish we could have done it without all the death and destruction. The new president survived Arthur's attack; she's hurt but okay, so that's something." He paused. "You think the humans will forgive us?"

I shrugged. "I hope so. We can only try, Mordred. We can only be the best we can be. We saved a lot of human lives, but there will always be some who don't see it that way. You can't please everyone all the time, so don't bother trying. Just do the best you can and hope it's enough."

Mordred stared at me for several seconds. "I'm glad you killed me, Nathan Garrett. Thank you for that."

"Anytime," I said with a chuckle.

I clapped him on the back as people spotted him and began to make their way over to us. "Go be the king, Mordred."

I watched him walk off to do his duty and knew with a hundred percent certainty that the world was a better place because people like Mordred were in it.

Epilogue

Nate Garrett

I sat on top of the roof of a building in downtown Manhattan and looked over it to the street below. I'd been hunting my prey for two months now and had bribed, threatened, or promised an awful lot to more people than I'd expected.

The prey had become a hard man to find. He'd moved around a lot. He'd wanted to stay hidden, but he was a man of refined tastes, and refined tastes meant he could only stay away from the finer things in life for so long.

"So how's Nidavellir?" Tommy asked. He was sitting beside me; he wore a *Star Wars* T-shirt with a picture of Princess Leia on it that Kase had given him. He was pretty much back to normal at this point, although the knowledge that the blood curse marks on him couldn't be removed was something he'd have to learn to live with.

"Cold," I said. "It's winter."

"We'll have to come visit," he said.

"I've been telling you to," I told him.

"I know, but we're all so damn busy at the moment. Kase is working with Layla, as is Harry. Chloe and Piper are, too, although the latter is having some counseling to help her get over what happened to her. Olivia is now working for Mordred, and I'm teaching Daniel the ways of the Force."

I looked over at him and raised an eyebrow.

"We watch a lot of *Star Wars*," he said.

"You not working yourself?" I asked him.

"I want to be sure that the marks can't change back," he said. "Zamek's mum is a doctor, or whatever the dwarven-rune equivalent is. She's told me to leave it another six months and I should be fine."

One of the few good things to come out of what had happened in Atlantis was that Zamek had found his parents. Both had been hurt, but they were alive. I'd been told that his dad had not dealt well with being told he wasn't going back to being king, but that was just tough. Orfeda was in charge, and the elders who had been gone for so long could either deal with it or leave. Most dealt with it.

I moved the Accuracy International Arctic Warfare AWC rifle and looked through the scope again. No sign yet.

"So how's your new settlement?" Tommy asked.

"It's going well," I said. "The houses are now made and the old ones clear of anything that wants to eat people. The community is thriving. More people are coming through from Shadow Falls and Avalon. Quite a few humans from the Earth realm too. We're hoping to get a second settlement going closer to the mountains."

"Cool, cool," Tommy said.

"Right, what is it?" I asked, turning to him.

"I just . . . I miss working," he said. "I love my kids, but my God, I want to do something else. I thought that maybe I could bring Daniel to Nidavellir and show him around."

"Do it," I said. "Spend a few weeks there; bring Olivia. If she can't get away, I'm sure she'll be fine with you coming alone. There are a bunch of kids there Daniel's age; he'll be fine. Not a lot of TV time, though. So I hope he likes reading and walking around a lot."

"I could show him how to track and hunt," Tommy said, enthusiasm in his voice. "Not kill—he's too young for that, even as a werewolf—but to know how to deal with nature, how to behave around it. It would be nice."

"And we have mead," I said. "Turns out it's dwarven tradition to bring mead to anyone moving into a new settlement, and they had a lot. Remy and Diana turned up, and I don't think I've ever seen them both as happy as the moment they saw several hundred barrels of mead."

I looked through the scope again and held up a finger to quiet Tommy as I got comfortable. The door to the town house far below opened, and two large men walked out; both wore suits. One walked to a newly arrived BMW and opened the rear passenger door.

I moved my trigger finger a fraction of an inch and breathed out slowly.

There were runes drawn on the side of the BMW and similar ones on the door of the town house. I'd walked past myself. I had a very short window of opportunity.

Gawain stepped out of the town house and looked around. He wore an expensive gray suit that I'd discovered had been made by a tailor in Italy who had been instructed how to put runes inside it to make it bulletproof.

He'd managed to escape during the battle in Washington, DC, and with the help of several KOA, he'd been able to remove his sorcerer's band. From there, he'd stayed off the radar and created a fake identity. It wasn't going to save him.

I breathed out again and counted to five. There were twelve steps from the door to the pavement. Twelve moments where I could have pulled the trigger. Gawain reached the pavement and looked around him. He'd done this every day for a week. I'd been tempted to kill him on day one, but I'd needed more intel about him, about the runes he'd used. I needed to make sure he did not get away.

He stood behind the armored, rune-scribed BMW door and looked like a man who had nothing to fear.

I pulled the trigger.

The bullet hit the door in its center and tore through it like it was made of paper. Zamek had put his own runes on the bullets. There was nothing Gawain could do that would stop it. Gawain fell toward the pavement, and I pulled the trigger again, catching him in the chest as he fell.

One in the groin, one in the chest. Gawain looked up toward me.

"Fuck you," I said, and I put one more through his eye.

I dismantled the rifle, put it away in the bag, and passed it to Tommy. "I'll see you soon," he said. "Take care."

"I look forward to it," I told him. "And you too."

Tommy took off at a run across the rooftops, jumping between them like he was playing a video game, while I made my way to the street and got into a British-racing-green Jaguar F-Type and drove away.

I stopped the car a few hours later, when I'd reached Maine, where I made my way to the realm gate underneath what had once been a bar but had become a restaurant after the bar had been destroyed a few years earlier.

I grabbed a thick winter coat and boots and stepped through into what many would consider a winter wonderland. The snow was thick, the air full of the smells of winter. It was a short walk from the realm gate temple there to the settlement, which still needed a name. Remy had suggested Remytopia, which, shocking no one, had been ignored.

I found my mother sitting on the porch of our three-bedroom, one-story wood-and-brick house. It was a little away from the rest of the settlement, and our nearest neighbor was a few minutes' walk, which I didn't have a problem with.

Astrid was playing in the snow by the front of the house with Frigg. Frigg had all but been declared honorary grandmother almost instantly by Astrid, and no one had suggested otherwise.

My mother came over and hugged me. We were still two strangers in many respects and now had to figure out how we worked as mother and son outside a war.

Astrid jumped into my arms. "Daddy," she yelled. "I made a snow troll."

She led me over to the frankly gigantic snow troll, which Frigg was almost prouder of than Astrid.

"Mummy's inside," Astrid said, jumping up and down.

I kissed Astrid on the head and walked into the house, shaking off the snow and finding Eos, Hyperion, and Selene all inside. The former two left soon after, and Selene kissed me softly.

"It's done," I said.

"Mordred will be glad he didn't have to do it," Selene said.

"I am too," I told her. "No more war, no more killing—I just want to live here with all of you."

Selene led me out onto the porch, and we sat down on the comfortable chair, her head on my shoulder.

"The start of something new," I said. "Something good."

Selene squeezed my hand as we watched our family play together in the snow. Astrid was throwing tiny snowballs at Hyperion, who pretended he'd been hit by gunfire.

"Yes," she said softly. "And if anything threatens what we have here, I'll happily wipe them from the face of every realm. When you said you needed to talk to me, I hadn't imagined you'd considered setting up all of this. It was a good idea, Nate."

I kissed the top of her head. I'd been created to be a weapon. To kill those who had been deemed unkillable. I was power and death personified, and I was finally in a place where I felt happy. Where I felt at peace. And if anyone like Arthur emerged from the darkness to try to take everything we'd fought for, then I would be ready for them. And by the time I was done, they would regret the day they'd been born.

As night fell, Mordred, Hel, and many others arrived. We built a large bonfire in the middle of the settlement, and as the children ran and played, I sat next to Mordred.

"This is nice," he said. "There's been a lot of talking to humans and trying to figure out where to go next. A lot of prisoners to deal with too."

I knew that Mordred was saddened that he wasn't working alongside me and the rest of us who had come to Nidavellir, but I also knew he understood why we'd moved here. Nidavellir needed to be prosperous again, and with the dwarves back here, and with the knowledge of the realms now firmly enshrined in human memory, it wouldn't be long before someone started letting humans go to the other realms. Making them safe was a good start.

"Remy is trying to get everyone to play Dungeons & Dragons," Selene said to me as the night got rowdier. Once the kids had been taken to bed, the drink flowed freely.

"The last time we did, Remy wanted to be a half troll, half badger who was in love with his sword," Hel said from beside Mordred.

"Remy is odd," Mordred said slowly. I watched as he reached into his pocket and retrieved a ring before placing it on the arm of the chair next to Hel.

Hel looked at the ring. "That's a lava diamond," she said.

Mordred nodded. "I had it made in Helheim. It took a lot of being really sneaky to get it done, and turns out it's a giant—"

"Stop talking," Hel said, not taking her eyes off the ring. She picked it up and stared at it.

"Marry me," Mordred said. "I have never loved anyone like I love you. I have never felt this way. I have never been so terrified and enraptured by a woman. Marry me."

"Terrified and enraptured?" Hel asked.

"Every single day," Mordred said. "Hopefully for the rest of my exceptionally long life."

Hel looked up at Mordred, her eyes wet. "Yes," she said softly. "I love you."

Mordred and Hel kissed, Hel slipped the ring on her finger, and everyone cheered, raising a toast to them both.

An hour later I found myself next to Mordred again, watching everyone enjoying themselves. "You were always the best of us, Mordred," I said. "And look around—you've proved it."

I offered him my hand, and he ignored it, hugging me tightly instead. When he pulled away, he wiped tears from his eyes. "Goddamn you," he said with a sniff.

"You're a good man," I said. "And you'll make a great king. You'll be a so-so husband, though."

"Just don't make me cry again," he said with a smile.

Hel spotted him as she danced with several others, and she motioned for him to join them.

"I have never been prouder to call you my friend," I whispered as he took a step toward them.

I looked into his tear-filled eyes, and he smiled and said, "You son of a bitch."

I winked and walked off, feeling my own eyes tear up.

ACKNOWLEDGMENTS

After spending so long with all these characters in my head, I have to say that it's a strange feeling to be finishing Nate's story. Or at least finishing Nate's story where Arthur is concerned. Hopefully, one day I can return to this world and write more about everyone—and there are stories to tell—but for now, it's time to let them rest.

Thirteen books and something like 1.5 million words to tell one huge story. It's been a joy and a privilege to work with so many amazing people over the years, but before I get to everyone who helped get these books into your hands, I'd like to say thank you to every single person who reads my books. Everyone who loves the characters, who emails me with passion and desire to see what happens next, who tells me that they see themselves in my characters, who laughs out loud in public because Remy swore. Again. You're all awesome, and I would not be here right now, writing this final chapter, without your support. Thank you.

As per usual, though, no book is created by just me, and there are a lot of people to thank.

My wife, first and foremost, mostly for just being awesome but also for being a fan of my work and being the most supportive and loving person I could hope to be married to.

My kids, for just being them, for being my inspiration to write, for making me want to make them proud. You're all giant pains in my backside, and I love you dearly.

To my friends and family, you all rock. Your unwavering support over the years has helped me get here, and I'm not sure I can ever thank you enough for that.

To Paul Lucas, my wonderful agent. You, sir, are a gentleman and a scholar, and I'm proud to have you as my agent and friend.

To Julie Crisp, my incredible editor, who read my garbled word salad and helped turn it into something approaching an actual book. Thank you—it has been a genuine joy and pleasure to work with you on the Rebellion Chronicles, and I hope to have the opportunity to work with you again in the future.

My publisher, 47North—you've stood beside me, you've promoted me, and frankly you've let me write some of the most batshit-crazy stuff I could think of, and you've always been okay with it. You've been a partner I've enjoyed working with since *Crimes Against Magic*, and each and every one of you needs to be thanked. A special shout-out to David Pomerico, Alex Carr, Sana Chebaro, Emilie Marneur, and Jack Butler. You might not all work at 47North anymore, but you all helped and championed my books, and for that I will forever be grateful.

Writing books isn't all that hard, but writing books that don't suck is. I've been lucky to work with and be supported by some of the best people I could have hoped for. And while the story of Nate is finishing, here's to what comes next. Because I'm not close to being done.

ABOUT THE AUTHOR

Photo © 2013 Sally Beard

Steve McHugh is the author of the bestselling Hellequin and Avalon Chronicles. He lives in Southampton, on the south coast of England, with his wife and three young daughters. When not writing or spending time with his kids, he enjoys watching movies, reading books and comics, and playing video games.